The Beast

The Beast

Faye Kellerman

An Imprint of HarperCollins*Publishers*

THE BEAST. Copyright © 2013 by Plot Line, Inc. All rights reserved. Printed in the United States of America. No part of this book may be used or reproduced in any manner whatsoever without written permission except in the case of brief quotations embodied in critical articles and reviews. For information address HarperCollins Publishers, 10 East 53rd Street, New York, NY 10022.

HarperCollins books may be purchased for educational, business, or sales promotional use. For information, please e-mail the Special Markets Department at SPsales@harpercollins.com.

FIRST HARPERLUXE EDITION

HarperLuxe™ is a trademark of HarperCollins Publishers

Library of Congress Cataloging-in-Publication Data is available upon request.

ISBN: 978-0-06-225361-3

13 14 ID/RRD 10 9 8 7 6 5 4 3 2 1

To Jonathan, as always
To my editor, Carrie Feron
And to my fans who have supported me
for the last twenty-five years!

The Beast

Chapter One

It was the stuff of nightmares, starting with the slow walk down the courtroom aisle: as if his stall tactics had the power to stop the inevitable. Seven hours of testimony, but it wasn't the length of time that was horrific. When practicing the piano, Gabe had done marathon sessions twice as long as that. But he had always used his music to zone out, and that was impossible to do when being grilled on the witness stand. It had required concentrating on things he was trying so hard to forget: how *that* day had started out so normal and within minutes had turned into something almost deadly.

By four in the afternoon, the trial had finally recessed and the prosecution was essentially done, although Gabe knew the lawyers would have more questions on redirect. He walked out of the courtroom with his foster mother, Rina Decker, on one side and his foster dad, the lieutenant, on the other. They guided him into a waiting car. Sergeant Marge Dunn was behind the wheel.

She maneuvered the silent group through the streets of the San Fernando Valley—a suburb of L.A.—until they reached the driveway of the Decker house. Once inside, Gabe collapsed on the living room couch, took off his glasses, and closed his eyes.

Rina took off her tam, liberating a sheet of black, shoulder-length hair, and regarded the boy. He was nearly bald—courtesy of an indie film he had starred in—and his complexion was pale and pasty. Little red bumps covered his forehead.

She said, "I'm going to change and get dinner ready." At the sound of her voice, Gabe opened his eyes. "You must be starving."

"Actually I feel queasy." He rubbed his green orbs and put his specs back on. "Once I start eating, I'm sure I'll be okay."

Decker and Marge came in a moment later, chatting about business. The lieutenant loosened his tie, and then took a seat next to the boy. The poor kid was constantly jockeying back and forth between the teen and adult worlds. For the last year, his foster son had been at Juilliard, finishing almost two years in one. Decker threw his arm around the kid's shoulder and kissed the top of his peach fuzz head. Gabe wasn't totally bald, but what was growing in was blondish.

Gabe asked, "How'd I do?"

"Phenomenal," Decker said. "I wish every witness I had was half as good as you."

Marge sat opposite the boys. "You were a dream for the prosecution: completely credible, plainspoken, and damn cute." When Gabe smiled, she said, "Plus being a movie star doesn't hurt."

"Oh jeez. It was barely above a student film on a shoestring budget. It'll never go anywhere."

Decker smiled. "You never know."

"Believe me, I know. Did I ever tell you about my breakdown scene? I'm running down this long hallway of the sanitarium buck naked with my hair flying in back as attendants in white coats try to catch me. When they catch me, they start to shave my head and I'm screaming, 'Not my hair, not my hair.' I haven't seen the movie, so I'll have to take the director's word that it was a great scene."

"You haven't watched your own movie?" Marge asked.

"No. Too embarrassed. Not at me being naked, but I'm pretty sure I'm a dreadful actor."

Marge smiled, stood up, and picked a piece of pilled wool off of her beige sweater. "Well, gentlemen, I've got to go back to the station house. I left a pile of paperwork on my desk."

"Not to mention everything that I dropped in your lap," Decker said. "Thanks for picking up the slack."

Rina walked in. She had donned a long-sleeved black T-shirt, a jean skirt, and slippers. "You're not staying for dinner, Marge?"

"Can't. Too much work to do."

Decker looked at his watch. "I'll come join you in about an hour if you're still around. I'll bring you a care package from tonight's dinner."

"In that case, I'll make sure I'm around." Marge waved and left.

Decker said to his wife, "You need any help?"

"I'm fine. It's been a long day and a little quiet is okay with me." She disappeared into the kitchen.

Gabe said, "I should shower. I smell pretty bad. I was sweating a lot."

"Normal."

"I suppose this is only a warm-up for tomorrow. Defense is going to have a field day with me."

"You'll be fine. Just stick to who you are and tell the truth."

"That I'm the son of a hit man?"

"Gabe—"

"I mean who are we kidding? You know they're gonna bring him up."

"Probably. And if they do, your lawyer will object, because Christopher Donatti is irrelevant."

"He's a criminal."

"He is, but you aren't."

"He runs whorehouses."

"Whorehouses are legal in Nevada."

"He cut up Dylan Lashay and turned him into a mass of jelly."

"Now you're speculating." Decker looked at the boy. "Okay. I'm the defense and cross direct, okay." He cleared his throat and tried to act like a lawyer. "Have you ever participated in anything criminal? And be careful what you answer."

Gabe thought a moment. "I smoked weed."

"Ever take pills?"

"Prescription medication."

"Such as."

"Paxil, Xanax, Zoloft, Prozac . . . a cornucopia of pharmaceuticals. My doctors rotate around to see what's affective. And the answer to that is—nothing."

"It is sufficient to just list the medications, Gabriel."

"I *know.*"

"Are you anxious now?"

"I'm very anxious."

"Good answer," Decker said. "Who wouldn't be anxious during this process? The prosecution has presented you today as a gifted teen that has gone through a very traumatic experience. On cross, defense will try to trip you up. They'll ask you about your dad, they'll ask you about me. Always pause before you answer to give the prosecution time to object. And whatever you do, don't speculate. On redirect, the lawyers will make sure that the jury knows that you are *not* your father's son."

Gabe said, "I don't really care about myself. I'm worried about Yasmine. It kills me to picture her being hammered at by some jerk lawyer."

"She's sixteen, sheltered, an A student, and physically, she's small and delicate. She'll probably cry. Everyone will go lightly on her. What they'll do is ask her to repeat verbatim what Dylan and the others said to her and argue about the meaning of their statements. I'm sure the defense will say something like they were just kidding around. Bad taste, but no serious intent."

"Dylan was going to rape her."

"He might have even killed her if you didn't step in." Decker paused. "It could be she won't make it to the witness-box. After your testimony, they may try again for a plea bargain."

"Dylan's physically messed up. Why didn't they plea bargain in the first place?"

"The Lashays wouldn't agree to jail time. We offered them a prison hospital, but the parents wouldn't take it, claiming the prison hospital doesn't have the wherewithal to care for Dylan in his current state."

"Surely someone can wipe his drool," Gabe muttered. "I hope he dies a terrible death."

"He probably will," Decker said. "In the meantime, he's living a terrible life."

Riding with the windows down, Decker enjoyed the air after being locked away in a stuffy and tense courtroom. He wasn't anticipating anything more than a mountain of paperwork to deal with, but then his cell went off just as he was parking in the station house's lot. Bluetooth told him Marge Dunn was on the line. "Yo, Sergeant, I'm right outside."

"Stay there. I'm coming down."

The phone disconnected. A few minutes later, she came out of the building and jogged over to the car. Sliding onto the passenger seat, she closed the door. The night was cool, and she wrapped her hands in the sleeves of her knitted hoodie. She gave him the address, which was fifteen minutes away. There was a tense look on her face. "We have an issue."

"Yeah, I ascertained that."

"Do you remember an eccentric millionaire named Hobart Penny?"

"Some kind of engineer-inventor. Made his money in aerospace I want to say?"

"That was Howard Hughes. But you're not too far off. He holds about fifty different patents for high-heat polymers including glues and plastics used in aerospace. The consensus on the Internet says he's worth around a half-billion dollars."

"Sizable chunk of change."

"Exactly. And like Hughes, he became a recluse. He's now either eighty-eight or eighty-nine, depending on what site you're at. Did you know he lived in our district?"

"Lived?"

"Or maybe it's still the present tense, but I don't think so. He rents an apartment in the Glencove district and has resided there for the past twenty-five years."

"I had no idea."

"Neither did most of the people in the area. We got a call about a half hour ago from a unit adjacent to his. Something stinks inside Penny's apartment."

"That's not good."

"Not good but not unusual, considering his age. Okay. So he's been dead for a couple of days. We can deal with that. But here's the problem. The complainant has been hearing strange sounds coming from his apartment."

"Like?"

"Clicking, scratching, and an unmistakable roaring."

"Roaring? As in a *lion* roaring?"

"Or it could be some other big cat. The complainant had gathered up some of his fellow apartment dwellers along with the building's manager, whose name is George Paxton. I talked to the manager, told him I was sending some people down to get everyone out of the apartment building—as in immediately."

"God yes! We need a total evacuation of the structure."

"If you want the apartment buildings adjacent to be evacuated for good measure, I'll radio for more units."

"Yeah, go ahead. Better to be safe, right. You've called animal control?"

"Of course. I've requested people with experience working with big cats. That might take awhile."

Decker shook his head. "This is crazy."

"It's a first for me."

Silence.

Decker said, "How did you end up with the call?"

"Someone in-house transferred the call to homicide. Not a bad decision, considering we've got an old recluse, a rotten smell, and a roaring animal. I'd say the chance for finding a dead body is very high."

The area was largely residential: a mix of apartments, condos, and single-family homes, but there was a small strip mall of businesses located across the street from the address. The black night mixed with floodlights and with blinking lights from the bars on the cruisers. Several ambulances had been called and were standing by, just in case. After double parking, Decker and Marge got out, flashed their badges, and were allowed entry into the activity. About fifty yards up was a huddle of animal control agents in tan uniforms. He and Marge fast walked over to the circle and displayed their badges. At that specific moment, something bestial let out a ferocious bellow. Decker jumped back. The roar was especially eerie because it was a foggy and moonless night. He held up his hands in a helpless gesture. "What the hey?"

A sandy-haired, muscular man in his thirties stuck out his hand, first to Marge, then to Decker. Introductions were made all around—three men and a woman roughly ranging in age from midtwenties to midforties. "Ryan Wilner."

Decker said, "I thought it was going to take a while for you guys to get here."

"Me and Hathaway were in GLAZA, teaching a seminar on big cats. Zoo is a straight shot to here if there's no traffic."

Hathaway was tall and bald. His first name was Paul. He said, "We're usually the big cat guys, but we do everything."

Marge said, "How often do you deal with wild animals?"

"Wild animals all the time—raccoons, skunks, possum . . . even bears coming in from Angeles Crest. Exotics are another bag of tricks. We deal with a big cat maybe once a year, mostly lions or tigers, but I've done jaguars and leopards. Couple times I've been asked to help out with wolf-hybrid packs that had turned on their owner."

Wilner said, "I just did a chimp about a month ago."

"Lots of reptiles." The woman who spoke had close-cropped blond hair and gray eyes and stood about six feet. Her name tag said ANDREA JULLIUS. "Local poisonous snakes like California rattlers or sidewinders. But like Ryan said, we get the exotics. Just recently, me and Jake pulled out a Gaboon viper and a monitor lizard from a trailer in Saugus."

Jake was Jake Richey. He was in his twenties with yellow hair. He looked like a surfer dude. "I've done lots of snake captures, but that was my first Gaboon viper."

Andrea said, "You wouldn't believe the things people keep as pets, including crocs and alligators."

"What about that grizzly about a year ago?" Hathaway said. "That was a trick."

Wilner said, "And how about that female Asian elephant two years ago? In the same month, we captured a runaway male bison that was the family pet until it went into puberty and nearly took down the entire house."

But Decker was concentrating on the problem at hand. "How on earth do you get a big cat into Los Angeles?"

"Mail order. You acquire some land and a license and say you're going to set up a breeding program or a for-profit zoo or circus."

"That is crazy!" Marge said.

"Not as crazy as the people who keep them as pets," Andrea Jullius said.

Wilner said, "People are delusional; always think that they have magical powers over the beast. Inevitably a wild animal lives up to its name. That's where we come in. If everything works out well, the animal winds up in a sanctuary. It's no fun putting down an animal that isn't doing anything wrong except living out its DNA."

Another fierce roar pierced the miasma. Decker and Marge exchanged glances. She said, "That animal sounds pissed."

"It's very pissed," Wilner said. "We're going over our next step."

"Which is?" Decker said.

"Drill some peepholes and see what we're dealing with."

"My bet's on a Bengal female tiger," Hathaway said.

"I agree," Wilner said. "A male lion would be five times as loud. When the area is cleared out, we'll put on some protective gear and drill some holes. Once we see what we're working with, we figure out how to tranquilize it and get it out of here before we have a major problem."

Another howl echoed through the dripping fog. It was engulfing, as if being swallowed alive. Decker spoke to Marge. "We should assign some agents to the apartment doorway, just in case our friend feels like busting loose."

"One step ahead of you. It's already done," Wilner said. "I got one with a tranquilizing gun, one with a hunting gun. We aren't taking any chances." He turned to Agent Andrea Jullius. "What's going on with the equipment from the zoo?"

"Twenty more minutes."

Wilner tossed keys to Hathaway. "You wanna go get the protective gear?"

"Sure," Hathaway said.

"Do you have a vest for me?" Decker said. "I want to take a look through the peepholes. Homicide was called because the apartment was rented to an old man."

"Our policy is no civilians," Wilner told him. "And what are the chances that the old man inside is still alive?"

Decker said, "This is my community, and I feel responsible for everything that goes on here. I want to see the layout of the apartment so I know what I'm dealing with."

"It's gonna be grisly."

"I've done grisly before. Once I saw a dead guy being gnawed on by a wild mountain lion. It bothered me, but that's okay. When things stop bothering me, I'll know it's time to quit."

Chapter Two

With his pillow vibrating underneath his head, Gabe awoke with a start. It was eleven in the evening and he'd been out for an hour, falling asleep with his glasses on, his book landing on the floor. He groped around and pulled out the cell. "Hello?"

"How was it?" Her voice was a whisper.

Instantly Gabe was up and alert. He and Yasmine weren't supposed to be talking to each other, especially once the trial started, which was perfectly fine with Yasmine's mother. Sohala Nourmand was the typical Persian Jewish mama who wanted her daughter to date solely within the tribe. Not only was Gabe the wrong ethnicity, he was also the wrong religion. So over the past year, Sohala had forbidden contact between them. He and Yasmine hadn't exchanged phone calls, IMs, e-mails, texts, or Facebook posts. He knew that Sohala had checked Yasmine's electronics on a regular basis.

But nothing was foolproof. They had kept in touch the old-fashioned way—snail mail. When Yasmine first wrote to him by hand, he couldn't answer her back, a source of frustration. Finally, she got a POB. It was strange, writing real letters instead of e-mails, but after a while he really enjoyed the personality that came through her handwriting. His stamp output was one of his main expenses.

He hadn't heard her voice in almost a year. It was simply thrilling. He sat up, curling his knees to his chest. "Where are you?"

"In bed with the covers pulled over my head. I borrowed my friend's phone to call you. How was it today?"

"Really tiring."

"What'd they ask you?"

"It was Nurit Luke—the state's lawyer. She just led me through *that* day."

"Was it horrible?"

"It was . . . it took up a lot of time, but at least she was on our side. Tomorrow I have the cross with Dylan's lawyers. That'll probably be horrible, especially because of my background."

"I'm so sorry." There was a catch in Yasmine's voice. "Gabriel, I miss you so much."

"I miss you, too, cuckoo bird." He felt his eyes water. "We'll get through this. The good news is you don't have to worry about Dylan. The guy is major league messed up physically. You don't ever have to be afraid again."

"I hope you're right." But her voice was cracked.

"When you see him, you'll know I'm right. It breaks my heart to hear you so anxious."

"I'm okay." But she wasn't.

"The lieutenant thinks that there's even a chance for a plea bargain. If that's the case, you won't even have to testify."

"That would be fantastic!" A long pause. "Too much to hope for."

"One step at a time, Yasmine. It's the only way to stay sane. How are you otherwise?"

"Most of the time, it's like I'm on autopilot. Just kinda numb."

"Are you talking to anyone?"

"You mean like a therapist? I already went down that road. It didn't work. It's better for me to just throw myself into school work." A pause. "So afterward . . . like you're going back to New York?"

"Probably. Why? What do you need?"

"Nothing."

"What's on your mind? Tell me."

"I was just hoping that you could wait until *I'm* done testifying before you go back. But that's just being selfish."

"I don't have to do anything specific. I'm caught up, and my next performance is six weeks from now. If you need me, I'm here. End of story."

"What are you playing?"

"A Schubert four-hand piece with a guy I know from Germany and a sonata by a contemporary composer named Jettley who lectures part-time at Juilliard. I'm also doing Beethoven's fourteenth sonata—Moonlight."

"Oh . . . that's not so bad. Even I can play that . . . not like you of course."

Gabe smiled. "The first two movements are all emotion and finesse. The third movement's a little trickier. You can hear it on YouTube. Glen Gould. If you want to see the fingering, look at Valentina Lisitsa."

"Okay. I'll do that right after we hang up."

"If you want, sure. The point is I can practice in Los Angeles as easily as in New York. If you need me, I'm here for you."

"I just thought that maybe we could see each other after it was over."

"I'm in." Gabe's heart started thumping. "Tell me when and where."

"It can't be until after I'm done testifying. Can you wait that long?"

"I'd do anything for you. Like I said, when and where?"

"I was thinking about next Sunday. I've already told my mom that I'm going to the library to study. I don't think she fully believes me, but maybe by the time she finds out, you'll be back in New York."

"Perfect. Where should I pick you up?"

"You don't have to pick me up, Gabe. I drive now, remember."

"Yeah, that's right." A pause. "Wow. Where did the year go? So Sunday is great. Where do you want to meet?"

"Somewhere private." Yasmine's voice started to crack again. "It's been so long and I've been so miserable. And I'm sure after they shred me to bits, I'll be even more miserable. No one except you can understand. I just want a couple of hours to be alone with you, Gabriel."

"I feel the same way, Yasmini. You know how much I love you."

"Do you still?"

"One hundred percent."

"It's just we're so far apart and I never get to talk to you. And I'm sure you have a zillion girls around you all the time, now that you're a movie star."

"You're joking, right?" No response. Gabe said, "Yasmine, I'm bald, broken out, and I lost the weight that I gained because I've been so nervous. I look like Supergeek. I've got nothing in my life except a piano. I work all the time. I haven't had a moment to be bad, even if I had wanted to. I *pine* for you like a pathetic old dog. Just tell me where you want to meet and I'll be there."

She didn't speak for a long time, so long that Gabe thought she had disconnected. "Hello?"

"I'm still here." Another pause. "There's a motel not far from my school." She gave him the name and the street. "Can you do something with that?"

His heart was beating so fast, he felt faint. "Yeah, definitely." A long pause. "Are you sure? I don't want to get you in serious trouble."

"So what if my mom found out. What could she do? Ground me again?"

"She'd ship you off to Israel."

"She can't keep us apart forever. Let me worry about my mom. You take care of the arrangements, okay?"

Gabe's mouth was dry. "Okay."

"And bring something to eat. I'll meet you there at three, so I might be a little hungry. And be outside in the parking lot, so I don't have to go up to the desk or anything. That would be real embarrassing."

"I'll be outside in the parking lot at three with food, waiting for you. Be on time—for a change."

"I swear I will." Then Yasmine said, "You know what happens when we get together, Gabe. It's like instant chemistry."

"I know. I can't help it."

"I can't, either." A pause. "I'm not saying yes or anything, but you should bring something . . . just in case. You know what I mean?"

"Yeah." His voice was hoarse and his heart was galloping in his chest. "I know exactly what you mean."

"We've got a Bengal female." Wilner stepped aside and allowed Decker to look through the peephole. The space had been demolished—overturned furniture streaked with blood and feces. There were deep, clawed grooves on walls and floors. Flies buzzed everywhere. A wretched odor of a decayed carcass wafted through the hallway.

The animal, however, was magnificent, even as it paced amid the wreckage. Her fur gleamed amber and black, and she had reflective gold eyes, massive sharp claws, and ivory-colored fangs. Decker had never seen a tiger that close, nor had he actually heard an animal's roar at such a high decibel level. It sent shock waves coursing through his body. He stood aside from the viewing spot and gave Marge a chance to see. She peered inside and then backed away with a single shake of her head. "She's dragging a chain around."

"I noticed," Decker said. "It's attached to a collar around her neck."

Wilner said, "She probably broke it off from her mooring. We'll saw it off when she's out." The animal agent was looking over his carefully devised schedule. He had a checklist of supplies, and an animal gurney along with a steel enclosure had been placed outside the apartment's front door. Wilner had also acquired the key to the service elevator, since the passenger one was too narrow for the cage.

"This is the plan." He was still reading off his list. "Jake'll get a clean shot off. After she's tranquilized, we'll bust in and take her out on a gurney, load her into the pen, and take her down in our truck." Wilner looked up. "After Jake fires the shot, no one moves a muscle until I give the all-clear signal." He demonstrated the sign to his fellow officers: a hand in the air swooping down.

Decker asked, "What if the tiger busts out before she's tranquilized?"

"We've got big game guns, Lieutenant. As much as I hate putting an animal down, we know where our priorities are."

"I want to stick around," Decker said. "This is my community."

"Me, too," Marge said. When Wilner looked skeptical, she said, "Cross my heart I won't get in your way."

Paul Hathaway threw them a pair of protective vests. "Stay way down the hallway behind the barriers we erected. If something goes wrong, we'll take care of it. Don't try to help out."

"That's a Roger Wilco with me," Marge said.

Jake Richey was looking through the hole. "Ideally, we could enlarge this area so I could see and aim through the same hole. But I'm worried if I make the hole too big, she can get a purchase and stick a claw through." He was still assessing the situation. "How about I drill right about . . . here?" He marked a spot eye level with the first hole but about two inches to the left. "Just big enough so I can stick the bore through it. I think that'll work."

Wilner handed Richey the drill. As soon as the noise came on, the animal began to scratch furiously at the door. When it bellowed, Decker's heart took a jump.

The sound enveloped him in a 360-degree cage of anger and muscle.

Richey was unperturbed. A minute later, he stopped and placed the bore through the new aperture. "I think I'm okay. Let's give it a whirl."

Hathaway ordered Decker and Marge behind the makeshift barrier. The protection wasn't much more than wood beams temporarily nailed across the hallway. Decker took out his gun, and Marge did the same. She gave him a smile, but she was nervous. That made two of them. The scene suddenly became devoid of human voice, the aural vacuum disturbed only by the fierce grunts and clawing that came from behind a wall.

Richey lifted the gun and positioned the tip of the bore inside the hole. Then he peered inside the sight hole with his left eye. If he was tense, there was nothing about him on the exterior that registered anxiety.

Waiting.

The seconds ticking by.

Waiting again.

More time.

Richey squeezed the trigger and then immediately took several giant steps backward. Amid a pop, a howl, and a roar, the animal crashed against a wall. The building shook on its foundation, a quick jolt underfoot as a razor-sharp claw suddenly splintered through the upper section of the door. Wilner kept his hand in the air, indicating that no one should move as the tiger mauled the door in a feral rage.

It was one of the longest thirty seconds of Decker's life.

Eventually the ferocious howls dwindled to half-hearted growling, then mewling until the claw fell back into the apartment and all was quiet inside. Wilner nodded to Richey, who looked inside. "She's down."

Wilner gave the signal, and like horses out of the gates, the control officers went to work. Within a matter of minutes, the front door was down, the agents were in, and the tiger was loaded onto the gurney. The poor girl was sacked out, her mouth agape with her tongue hanging out. As if the animal didn't weigh enough already, a steel collar encircled her neck, and that was attached to six feet of chain.

Using brut muscle strength and extreme caution, they transferred her from the gurney into the enclosure, which lifted up on pneumatic wheels. Before they shut the steel door, Wilner gave her another shot of dope. "A quiet ride is always a happy ride."

"Did you see a body inside?" Decker asked.

Wilner shrugged. "I didn't see anything like that, but I wasn't searching for one. That's your bailiwick. Wear a mask. It stinks inside."

The service elevator doors opened, and the tiger along with her keepers were gone.

They had left the door to the apartment wide open. The hot air inside the hallway had become foul . . . gag inducing. Decker's heart was still racing as he and Marge emerged from behind the barrier.

"Quite a show." He put his gun back in his shoulder harness. "Now our real work begins."

Chapter Three

M arge began to suit up in earnest: a paper cover for her hair, paper shoe covers, a face mask, and double latex gloves. Even with all that protection, her stomach roiled. The fetid odor was overwhelming. "We're walking into a biological hazard as far as I'm concerned. There must be twenty generations of bacteria growing inside by now."

Decker said, "Wait out here and I'll go look for a body. If there isn't one, why should both of us be grossed out?"

"Thanks, but I'm coming with you. Suppose there are a bunch of tiger cubs hidden in the bedroom or something. Or maybe he kept other exotic pets like a Gaboon viper or a monitor lizard. Someone has to call 911 if you get bit."

Decker smiled as he put on his face mask. "Your loyalty is admirable. C'mon, Dunn. Let's get this over with."

The living room was a hurricane with putrid waves gassing up from the steamy floors. Deep claw marks striated the walls, and the furniture was torn to tatters. There were enormous piles of feces flecked white with maggots and bread crumbed with flies and beetles. Insects hummed everywhere. The refrigerator had been knocked over, food spilling out onto the wood floors turning them as sticky as tar. Butcher paper had been shredded to confetti. Most of the meat from the fridge had been consumed, but what hadn't been eaten was gray and oozing brown liquid. It took a steady foot and good balance to avoid stepping in something toxic.

Marge felt light-headed, but she soldiered on, following Decker into the bedroom.

That scene was made even more appalling by the presence of a distorted, bloated body. The corpse had partially liquefied, vital fluids and tissue soaking into the sheets and dripping on the floor below. Blood and guts were everywhere, sprayed on the walls and splashed onto the furniture.

Marge said, "I'll call the coroner's office."

Decker nodded.

"Mind if I make the call from the hallway? Even with the mask it's still stinky."

"Sure. Then we'll figure out a to-do list."

Marge fished out a pencil and her notebook. "Tell me what you need."

Decker said, "After you call up the Crypt, call . . . let me think who's on tonight." A pause. "Tell Scott Oliver and Wanda Bontemps to come down here. We need to relocate the residents for a day or two. The apartment building is off-limits as a biological hazard. Nobody comes back until this mess is cleaned up. If you need another detective, call up Drew Messing." Decker was still staring at the body. "Do we even know if this is Hobart Penny?"

Marge just shook her head.

Decker continued. "No one comes inside here except those with official business."

"The tenants might want to go back and grab some clothes or a phone or a computer. What do I tell them?"

"We can probably escort them in and out. It'll take awhile, but it'll keep them less pissed off. I'll also need a couple of uniforms at the door to secure the scene."

"Anything else?"

"That's it for now."

Marge talked through her face mask. "You're going to stick around inside?"

"I am. I'm still not sure what I'm looking at."

Marge held off making the phone call to the Crypt. "You know . . . if I ignore all the disgusting mess—and the fact that a tiger lived in the apartment—this looks more like a homicide than a natural death . . . all that splatter on the walls?"

"That spray was definitely the result of ruptured arteries pumping out fresh blood." His eyes scanned the room. "This splotch over here looks like blow-back from a blunt force trauma injury. You wouldn't get these kinds of droplets and blood mist from simply dying and then having a tiger eat you."

"If the tiger mauled you or bit you when you were still alive, you'd very well have this kind of spray."

"That's why I'm looking for signs of mauling and/or bite marks. It's hard to tell because the body is so distorted."

Marge continued to study the scene: nauseating to look at and even more sickening to smell. Still she began to think like a professional homicide detective. "The face . . . such as it is . . . looks elderly. The stubble is white."

"I agree. It's an *older* man. How old is Penny again?"

"Eighty-eight or eighty-nine."

"The body could be that old. To me, it looks like a thin, elderly man that has bloated up with gas postmortem."

"The corpse is decomposing by the minute. The organs are leaking out and the body's framework has lost a lot of its integrity, but . . ." She pointed a latex-gloved finger. "I can make out some scratches on the skin's surface over here . . . over here as well."

"Good eye." Decker stared at the spot. "The scratches don't seem all that deep."

"Agreed. Less like a mauling and more like the tiger was pawing him, maybe?"

"Trying to get a reaction from a corpse."

"Yeah, that could be." Marge studied the body. "It's hard to see skin surface detail with all the discoloration. The scratches could actually be deeper, but because the body is so bloated, they appear more superficial."

Decker nodded. "Do you see any bite marks."

"Not so far. Wish we could turn him over."

"That'll happen soon enough." Neither he nor Marge could touch the body, which officially belonged to the coroner's office. But they still could make observations. "His forehead is misshapen. The cranium could have caved in from his brains liquefying. Most likely, someone took a whack at his forehead."

Marge nodded. "Looks like a stellate pattern. With that and all the blowback, we should be hunting around for a weapon: something hard with a round end."

"A weapon would be good. I'd also like to find some ID. It'd be nice to have the victim identified. Makes for a neater case file."

The coroner's assistant was someone Decker had worked with on other cases. A Hispanic in her forties, Gloria was perfect for the job because she was competent, cordial, and efficient. Wearing the official black jacket with yellow lettering, she was sweating profusely in the bedroom, now christened the "sauna from hell." Carefully, she rolled the body onto its side and scrutinized the back, the skin currently colored eggplant purple thanks to lividity—the pooling of blood to the lowest gravitational spot. The skin was beginning to slough off from the musculature underneath. "Okay. Here we go."

She lay the body back down and moved over to the other side. She rolled it ever so gently and pointed to a hole.

"Looks like a bullet wound." She lay the body back down and studied the front of the decaying corpse. "Can't see any exit hole. The body is very swollen, so a hole may not be apparent. Did you find any bullet or bullet casings inside the apartment?"

"Not yet," Marge said. "But now that we know a firearm might be involved, we'll look for something. Would the wound have been fatal?"

"Impossible to tell until you open him up." She stood up and regarded the bloated corpse. "There was definitely blunt force trauma to the forehead." She pointed to the lower eye sockets. "This caved-in part is caused by the eyeballs dropping down inside the head—a natural phenomenon. But over here . . ." She pointed to the upper brown section of the skull. "Someone hit the victim with something hard."

"We noticed that," Marge said. "Homicide?"

"I'm not the medical examiner, so I don't make the determination," Gloria said. "But don't go on vacation anytime soon."

Marge smiled. "I'll call up SID."

"Thanks, Gloria." Decker picked up a paper evidence bag, and the two of them walked into what once was Hobart Penny's living room. "What I want to know is how the killer got past the tiger?"

Marge said, "There was around six feet of chain on her. If she was originally chained up, she'd have a little room to move about. But possibly you could sidestep the animal. Or maybe the victim escorted the killer around the tiger."

"If the killer was escorted by Penny coming in, how did the killer get around the tiger coming out of the apartment once Penny was dead?"

Marge shrugged. "Maybe the guy threw the animal meat laced with a sedative. There's a lot of rotting meat . . . along with piles of shit, diarrhea, and vomit. Maybe the animal was poisoned."

Decker thought about the theory. "So the perp killed the victim with the gun and a possible whack on the head but didn't shoot the tiger. Instead, he gave the tiger poisoned meat?"

"Maybe he ran out of bullets. Maybe he did shoot the tiger, but unless the shot was perfect, it would probably take more than a shot from a pistol to bring it down."

"Do we even know if the tiger was shot?" Decker asked. "It wasn't walking like it was injured."

"It sounded pretty pissed off."

Decker conceded the point. "So you're figuring that the victim knew the perpetrator and escorted him by the animal to get in. Then the perp shot the victim and gave poisonous meat to the tiger?"

"I have no idea," Marge said. "Maybe the perp knew the victim and his habits well enough to know how to get around the animal."

Decker shrugged. "Possibly. Let's go outside."

They went into the hallway—hot and humid and stinky. Two uniformed officers were on either side of the door, both of them wearing pained expressions. Detective Scott Oliver looked up from a sheet of paper. He had come down to the scene, dressed in a black suit and a pink shirt. He waved his hand in front of his nose. "I was just about to go out and help Wanda and Drew with interviewing the tenants. We really need to canvass the apartment building."

"The apartments do need to be canvassed but not by you," Decker said. "I'm giving Marge and you the vaunted assignment to look for evidence."

Oliver's shoulder's sagged. "Lucky me."

"Luckier than the victim."

"What evidence are we talking about?"

Marge said, "The CI found a bullet hole in the body. A dent in his forehead also looks like blunt force trauma. We're looking for shell casings possibly and a weapon that fits the depression."

"Have we made an ID for the vic?"

Marge said, "We found a wallet on a dresser with an old ID card belonging to Hobart Penny. It's hard to tell if the body is him from a small picture."

"Any driver's license?"

"Not in the wallet," Decker said. "I've bagged a brush, a toothbrush, and a dirty mug of coffee for DNA evidence." He turned to Marge. "I know the man was a recluse, but what about relatives? A guy that rich . . . there must be people we could contact."

Marge said, "From what I read, he's twice divorced. The last time he was married was twenty-five years ago. There are two kids from the first wife, whom he divorced thirty-five years ago. The first wife died ten years ago. From what I read, he's also estranged from his kids because of papa's odd behavior."

"Odd is an understatement. What kind of person keeps a tiger as a pet?" When no one offered any psychological insight, Decker said, "How old are his children?"

Marge checked her notes. "The son—Darius—is around fifty-five, wealthy in his own right. He's a lawyer and some kind of capital venture person. The daughter—Graciela—is fifty-eight. She's a New York society woman married to a count or a baron."

"What about the second wife?" Oliver asked. "What happened to her?"

"She"—a flipping of the pages of her notepad—"is still alive . . . Sabrina Talbot, fifty-eight. The marriage lasted five years."

"So she was twenty-eight when they married?" Oliver asked.

"Yeah . . . he was fifty-nine. He gave her a generous settlement, and I read something about his adult children not being happy about it." Marge looked up. "But this all happened twenty-five years ago. Who holds a grudge for that long?"

"Someone was pissed enough to bash in his head and shoot him," Oliver said.

Decker said, "I'll research the family history from the station house. I have access to a computer and it smells a lot better." He took in Oliver's sartorial splendor. "You might want to leave your jacket in the car and roll up your pants. Marge has shoe covers for you."

"Ugh," Oliver said. "It's going to be one of those nights."

"Scotty, it's already been one of those nights," Decker answered. "You just arrived fashionably late."

Chapter Four

M arge could *almost* remember a time when one in the morning meant being asleep. For the last twenty years as a homicide cop, one in the morning meant a phone call directing her to a crime scene, some of them more grisly than others but all of them horrendous. At present, she and Oliver were gathering forensic evidence. Amid the mess and the outrage, there were a few directional arrows that pointed to what went down. When she spotted something shiny winking from a pile of feces, she had a good idea what it was. But that didn't make the task any more pleasant.

"I don't really have to do this, do I?" Marge's question to Oliver was not rhetorical. "I outrank you."

"But you also love me," Oliver said.

"Not that much."

Silence. "Flip a coin?" Oliver suggested.

Marge pulled a quarter from her purse, tossed it in the air, and caught it. "Call."

"Heads."

She slapped the coin on the underside of her arm and took away her hand. George Washington was staring up at her. "I'm going to cry now."

Oliver pretended not to hear, making busy by trying to find a weapon that matched the depression in the victim's head. Since the coroner's office had removed the body, he was left with only photographs of the wound. It seemed to be more round than ovoid, about an inch to an inch and a half in diameter. Oliver's first choice was a hammer. He was attempting to locate a toolbox or a tool drawer.

Cursing her luck, Marge bent down. The smell was atrocious. She wrinkled her nose, and then stuck two gloved fingers into a squishy mound of tiger poop. Extracting the metal, she regarded the slime-coated hunk of steel. "A twenty-two. At least I found something valuable to offset the gross factor. Can you give me a bag, please?"

"Just because you said please." He handed her an evidence bag. "I guess the logical question was how did a bullet get inside the mound of shit? It doesn't seem like something an animal would normally eat."

"Yeah, Decker and I were wondering about why the victim was shot but not the tiger. At least, I don't think the tiger was shot. We were also thinking about how someone got around the tiger to get to the victim."

"What'd you come up with?"

"The tiger was drugged by a piece of tainted meat. The tiger knew the perpetrator and didn't view him— or her—as a threat. The tiger was chained up, so the perp could move in and out without being attacked. Or the tiger was shot, and in all the commotion, no one saw a bullet hole. Let me know if you can think of anything else. I'll call Agent Wilner in the morning and find out the status of the big girl."

"Where does one take a stray tiger? Last I heard there was no pound for big cats."

"There are a few sanctuaries for wild animals. I seem to recall some kind of nonprofit wild animal shelter when I worked in Foothill—around two decades ago, so I don't even know if it still exists." Marge dropped the bullet in the bag. "We've got a problem."

"Talk to me."

"If we already found one bullet in poop, is there other important evidence in poop that we're choosing to overlook?"

Oliver glared at Marge. He said, "Why don't we just bag it all and give it to SID?"

"Why don't I take these two massive piles and you take that one and that one?"

"You can't assign a rookie to this one?"

"My X-ray eyes are scanning the room as we speak." Marge turned her head to the left and to the right. "Only you and me, bud."

"I don't see why I have to do this."

Marge said, "In case you didn't get it the first time. I take these, you take those."

"How about if I canvass the neighborhood and Wanda gets her hands dirty."

"How about we get this over with ASAP? This is reality, not a reality show, and I don't have all night. Actually, I do have all night, but I don't want to use up all night."

Reluctantly Oliver bent down in front of the first pile of feces. "What I don't do to earn a paycheck."

"At least you've got a job."

"This is disgusting."

"True, but irrelevant. Just go for it. Today is the first day of the rest of your life, blah, blah, blah."

He plunged his hand into the pile and groaned. "Frankly, Dunn, I prefer the past to present. I was younger, I had dark hair, and I had yet to pay a cent of alimony."

Rina was an early riser, but Gabe must have gotten up with the sun. "How are you feeling?"

"Okay." He ran his hand over his downy scalp. His hair was beginning to grow in. It was a few days away from looking like a buzz cut. "Want some coffee? Machine's all set, but I didn't want to turn on the pot until you were up. Stale coffee sucks."

"That's considerate of you. I'd love some coffee. How long have you been up?"

"About an hour."

"Couldn't sleep?"

"I slept a little. I'm all right."

"Nervous?"

"Yeah, a little."

"You did terrific yesterday."

"No one was hammering away at me. I'm sure today will be different. It's okay. Whatever happens . . . I mean what can I do about it?"

Rina took down two mugs. "You're a pretty cool character, Gabe. You'll be fine."

He played with the knot on his tie. "Where's the lieutenant?"

"He's still at work. It was an all-night."

"Wow. What's the case?"

"This one is for the books." Rina smiled. "Last night, he and animal control extracted a tiger out of an apartment."

"A *tiger?*"

"Yes, a tiger that was living in an apartment."

"Wow." A pause. "Cool."

Rina poured the coffee and handed him a mug. "More like, wow . . . dangerous."

Gabe smiled and sipped. "How'd they get the tiger out?"

"Someone from animal control shot it with a tranquilizing dart. Once it was down, they went inside and took it out in a cage."

"Whoa." He sat back in the chair and was silent for a moment. "I hear a composition in this. Like double bass for the growl, and tuba for the lumbering animal, and a high-pitched staccato from the violins every time it scratches and then this like almost trumpet clarion blare for the animal control, then several measures of rest followed by an earsplitting pop as the dart goes into the body and this shimmering but electrifying strings as it loses consciousness . . . and deep bass as it's dragged out . . ." Gabe stared at nothing in particular. "I can hear it like . . . perfectly."

All Rina heard was noise from the refrigerator. "Kind of like *Peter and the Wolf* on crack."

Gabe laughed. "Exactly." He put down his coffee and rubbed his eyes under his glasses. "And this extraction took up the entire night?"

"No," Rina said. "Once animal control got the tiger out, they found a dead body inside the apartment."

"So the tiger killed the guy inside?"

"From what Peter told me, the body was the result of a homicide. The tiger was incidental and had nothing to do with the man's death."

"That's really weird."

"As a lieutenant, Peter only works on the weird cases. Because he was up all night, he may not show up to the trial until much later."

"That's okay. Life goes on." He looked at Rina. "But you'll be there, right?"

"Of course I'll be there." She put down her coffee cup and kissed his nearly naked head. "Don't worry. It should all be over soon—"

The phone rang. It was a quarter to seven in the morning. Usually when that happened, it was one of the kids calling from back east. They never paid attention to the three-hour difference.

Rina said, "Excuse me. It's probably Hannah either wishing you luck or she's in crisis."

"Either way, tell her hi for me."

Rina lifted the receiver. "Hello?"

"Hi, it's me," Decker said.

"Are you all right?"

"Just tired, but that's not why I'm calling. Last night while I was dealing with wild animals, Dylan Lashay had a stroke. He's in the hospital in critical condition. Nurit Luke talked to his lawyers. Everyone agreed to postpone the trial indefinitely."

"Oh my!" A pause. "How does Wendy Hesse feel about that?"

At the mention of Wendy Hesse's name, Gabe picked up his head. "What's going on?"

Rina held up her hand to Gabe. "Could you repeat that? I couldn't hear."

"I said that Wendy's not happy, of course. Her son is dead and she wants justice, but with these new circumstances, even she isn't in favor of dragging it out any longer. The entire case should be pled out in a couple of hours, and that, my dear, is the end. Tell Gabe, it's over."

"I'm sure he'll appreciate getting the monkey off his back."

"What monkey off my back?" Gabe asked.

Decker said, "I'll be home in an hour or so. Maybe we'll all go out for breakfast before I drop off to sleep."

Rina smiled. "That would be great. Love you."

"Love you, too." Decker disconnected the line.

"What monkey are you talking about?" Gabe was exasperated.

"Dylan Lashay suffered a stroke. He's in critical condition. The trial is indefinitely postponed and will probably be pled out. To quote the Loo, 'Tell Gabe it's over.' "

"Wow! That's great!" Gabe sat back. "That's really *good* news. I won't have to go to court anymore. And Yasmine won't have to testify, either. That's great, great news!"

"A big relief to you and to her, no doubt." Rina paused. "When was the last time you spoke to her?"

Gabe looked up. It was always better to tell the truth.

But maybe not the whole truth.

"Rina, I haven't called her in over a year. I haven't e-mailed her or texted her or talked to her on Skype or anything. But that doesn't mean I can't be happy for her."

"Of course you can be happy for her. And I suppose your personal life isn't any of my business."

"It's okay. I know you mean well."

"I do. Should I change your flight to leave tomorrow?"

"Actually, I already changed it. I decided to stay through the weekend, if that's okay with you guys."

"Of course, it's okay." A pause. "Can I ask you why?"

Gabe was prepared for the question. "I'm all caught up at school. I felt that I could use the extra few days to unwind before I go into fully operational mode. I'm much more relaxed here than at school."

"That's really nice. I want you to feel like this is your home, too." Rina finished her coffee. "The Loo wants to go out for breakfast. You're invited."

"I'd love to come. Can I change first?"

"Although you look adorable in a suit, I'm sure jeans and a T-shirt would be much more comfortable."

The smile on his face was wide and bright. Gabe headed off to his room, not feeling the least bit guilty about stretching the truth. He loved Rina for what she had done for him, but certainly she didn't have to know everything about his personal business.

It was his life to live

It was his life to love.

It was his life to crash and burn.

Chapter Five

Revived by calories, caffeine, and several hours of sleep, Decker read about the night's activities on the front page of the *Daily News,* a picture of the cage being carted out of the apartment building. When he was done, he started sorting through the pile of pink phone slips that had amassed during his three-hour absence. He had finished the majority of the callbacks when Marge and Oliver knocked on his open office door. The clock read one in the afternoon.

"That was just about the worst crime scene I've ever been to from a forensics' point of view," Oliver groused. "It was so contaminated by animal blood and shit that it was impossible to tell what I was looking at."

Marge said, "The good news is we found another twenty-two bullet and a couple of casings . . . I won't tell you where. Okay, I will tell you where." When she did, Decker made a face.

Oliver said, "I also bagged a couple of tools that *might* have made the depression in the skull, but I'm not loving any of them."

"Like what?" Decker asked.

"A broom handle, a soup ladle, the back of a cleaver." A pause. "I'm thinking what's an old guy doing with a cleaver? Then I'm thinking that someone had to cut up the meat for kitty."

Marge was paging through her notes. "Okay, from the canvassing, we didn't get too much. Hardly anyone remembers seeing the old man."

"What about noises coming from his apartment?"

"Yeah, we got a few of 'I might have heard something' or 'I thought I heard something.' The people I spoke to didn't call it in. He did get a lot of deliveries. Not unusual for a shut-in."

"Meat for the cat?" Decker asked.

"Deliveries from the local Albertsons and Ralphs. I'll find out the specifics," Marge said. "As far as phone records, he had a landline but no cell phone. That's pretty much in keeping for a recluse and a guy his age. Did you by any chance receive a phone call from Ryan Wilner?"

"Regarding?"

"I wanted to find out where they took the tiger and if she was shot. It might make a difference in how we approach the case if she was harmed. If she wasn't, maybe the perpetrator knew the beast."

"I'll call him," Decker said. "But who uses a twenty-two to take out a tiger."

"Not on her skull, but soft tissue is soft tissue."

Decker acknowledged the point.

Marge said, "What about Penny's kin?"

"The rich ones are always protected, but using charm, the Internet, and a phone book, I did get some numbers." Decker flipped his phone messages. "Here's a contact for the daughter: Baroness Graciela Johannesbourgh. When you call up, ask for Hollie Hanson. I believe she is the executive secretary of the baroness's foundation." He handed Marge a piece of paper with the information.

"Foundation for what?"

"Cervical dystonia," Decker said. "I looked it up. It's when your head rotates to the side of your neck and freezes in that position. The medical name is tor-ticollis. It's treated with botulinum toxin to relax the muscles. It can be genetic. I have no idea if the foundation is a personal thing or just the goodness of her heart."

Decker rifled through more papers.

THE BEAST · 51

"Here we go. This is a contact number for Darius Penny at Klineman, Barrows, Purchas and Penny. Darius's secretary is named Kevin." That pink slip with the information went to Oliver.

"Did you tell them what it was about?" Scott asked.

"Just that it concerned Hobart Penny," Decker said. "No details. I'm sure they both assume that it has to do with his death—the man was old—but I told them nothing about the murder. Both numbers are two-one-two area code: Manhattan. Whatever you do, be cautious. These types lawyer up when you ask them about the weather."

"What do you know about their respective financial situations?" Oliver asked.

"Nothing."

"Okay. I'll do some digging."

Marge said, "What about the ex-wife?"

Decker said, "Sabrina Talbot lives in Montecito in Santa Barbara County. I Google-mapped the residence and plot. The house is one of those huge Mediterranean things set on lots of acreage. I suppose that you wouldn't mind driving up to talk to her."

"I can handle that." Marge smiled. "Might you want me to call Will or anyone in SBPD who knows anything about her?"

"Now there's a fine idea," Decker said. "What's your schedule like tomorrow?"

"I can leave around eleven."

"I'm free," Oliver said. "I'll come with you."

"Will you now?"

"I'm good on a road trip."

"Oliver, haven't you heard the old saying about two people versus three."

"That is the old saying. The new one goes, two is company, three's a party."

"I'm taking this from a guy who thinks Facebook is a collection of mug shots."

"True, I'm old-fashioned when it comes to social networking," Oliver said. "But when it comes to just plain social, I'm always game."

The call came in a few hours later. "This is Lieutenant Decker."

"Ryan Wilner."

"Hello, Agent Wilner, how's our baby doing?"

"It was a long night for her. She's disoriented, but Vignette told me she's starting to feed, which is a very good sign."

"Vignette?"

"She's the director of the sanctuary. She wants to talk to you."

"Okay." A momentary pause. "Do you know what it's about?"

"Just that she was upset about the old man's death. Apparently he was a big supporter of the sanctuary, so she knew him well."

Decker's ears perked up. "I'll give her a call. Do you have her number?"

Wilner read the digits over the phone. "You should visit the place. She and her staff do a great job."

"I just might do that." He hung up and immediately punched in Vignette's numbers. It rang twice before it was picked up. There was a lot of static on the line.

"Global Earth Sanctuary." The voice was female.

"Yes, this is Lieutenant Decker from Los Angeles Police. May I please talk to Vignette?"

"This is Vignette. Thanks for calling me, Lieutenant." The voice was youthful.

"No problem," Decker said. "I'm getting terrible reception."

"It's awful out here. Most of the time, my cell doesn't even connect. We may get cut off."

"Okay. So we'll take what we have. How can I help you?"

"It's about Mr. Penny. I can't believe he's gone."

"He was eighty-nine."

"But so vital."

Vital, Decker thought. The man sounded like a shut-in, but maybe he had another life that only she knew about. "Did he visit the sanctuary often?"

"Not often. He didn't like leaving Tiki alone. I'm sure you understand why."

"It would be a problem if the tiger got out."

"That wasn't the issue. Mostly it was because she was so attached to him. She didn't like it when he was gone."

"Did you know the tiger well?"

"Tiki and I had a healthy respect for each other."

"So may I assume that you visited Mr. Penny and Tiki in his apartment?"

"Of course. Someone had to give Tiki her shots."

"You gave a tiger shots?"

"After she was sedated of course."

"Vignette, I'm sure you know this. But it's illegal to keep a wild animal like a tiger in a suburban area."

"Of course I know that. That's why Mr. Penny didn't come here all that often. All he wanted was to live out his life with Tiki." A sigh over the line. "I guess he got his wish."

Decker tried to be patient. "Vignette, if you are aware of other wild animals living in residential areas, you should report them to the police. You've got to know that the chance for a disaster is high."

"No other tigers as far as I know. It's all I can do to take care of what animals I have here. And I have a license to do that, in case you're wondering."

She not only sounded youthful, but she was also acting like a petulant kid. Decker said, "That's good to know."

"Look, Lieutenant, I begged Mr. Penny to give her up, but he wouldn't. So what should I do? Snitch on the biggest supporter we have?"

Rather than confront her, it was best to keep things civil. "When was the last time you were at the apartment?"

"I was just there maybe three, four days ago. And Mr. Penny seemed just fine. Was it a heart attack?"

She seemed blithely unaware. Or she was a good actress. Decker sidestepped the question. "Do you know where he got the tiger?"

"Not offhand. You can get cubs through mail order. Sometimes you can get animals from smaller defunct zoos or circuses or animal acts. But I don't know about Tiki."

Perfect segue, Decker thought. "You know, I'd really like to come down to your place and see your sanctuary. That way we can talk in person, which is much better than over the phone."

"What's there to talk about?"

"Just wrapping things up," Decker lied.

"What things?" A pause. "Why are the police involved?"

"We were called in to take care of the body."

"Oh . . . okay."

"But I still have a few questions about Mr. Penny. Maybe you can help me."

She said, "I'll answer your questions if you'll answer mine."

"What are your questions, Vignette?"

"I know this is going to sound like I'm a vulture . . . do you know if there was a will or anything like that?"

Decker said, "I don't know."

"It's not for me personally," Vignette said. "It's totally for the animals. Mr. Penny was a great supporter. I don't know how long the sanctuary can last without him."

You mean without his money. Decker said, "Could we meet tomorrow and talk a little more?"

"Sure. Come down. I'll show you what we do, so you won't think that I'm just about greed."

But it was always about greed. "What time works for you?"

"Around eleven would be perfect."

"I'll see you then, Vignette. I'm sorry; I didn't catch a last name."

"Garrison."

"What's your official title?"

"Acting director of the sanctuary. We had a permanent director . . . he was a vet actually, but he moved to Alaska to study the mating habits of the Kodiaks."

"Not for the fainthearted."

"It's really just a matter of gaining trust, Lieutenant. When the trust is there, it doesn't matter how fierce the animal is. You can have grizzlies that behave like puppy dogs and puppy dogs that behave like grizzlies."

"That's true," Decker said. It wouldn't serve his purposes to argue. In his mind, he'd much rather face a snapping puppy than a happy grizzly. "I'll see you tomorrow at eleven."

"Great!" Vignette chirped. "I'll give you the grand tour. And maybe you can find out about a will?"

"I'll see what I can do." Decker hung up.

Did the word *grasping* mean anything to her?

Yet, she had a point. Surely the man had a will.

And where there's a will, there's a lawyer.

Chapter Six

The Web site for the Cervical Dystonia Center was founded twenty-five years ago by Baroness Graciela Johannesbourgh. The pictures of gala events in the recent past showed a tight-faced, tight-lipped, stick-thin blonde in her fifties wearing a multitude of gowns on a multitude of occasions. In the earlier archival pictures, Marge had noticed the baroness's pronounced cant of the head to the right side. As the years passed, the twisting had lessened until her posture seemed completely normal. It used to be that cervical dystonia was a problem without many solutions, but now the condition was treated quite successfully with Botox.

Two in the afternoon, PST, meant five in the afternoon, EST. The foundation was probably closed, but she called anyway. The phone was picked up by a smoky voice.

"Cervical Dystonia Center."

"Yes, this is Sergeant Marge Dunn from the Los Angeles Police Department. Is Hollie Hanson available?"

"This is Hollie." A pause. "What can I help you with, Sergeant?"

"I'm trying to get hold of Graciela Johannesbourgh. I was told that you could connect me to her."

"What is this in regards to?"

"Hobart Penny."

"Is he all right?"

"It's a personal matter."

"I see." A pause. "If you give me your name and number, I can pass the information forward to the baroness."

Marge reiterated her name and gave Hollie the cell phone number. "If she could call me back, I'd appreciate it."

"You know, Sergeant, I am aware of Mr. Penny's age. And I also know that a call from the police isn't typical unless there's something wrong."

Marge said, "Please have Ms. Johannesbourgh call me back."

"I'll give the baroness your message."

"Thank you very—" But Marge was talking to a dead line. Next was Darius Penny. With any luck, he'd still be in the office. The line connected, she was transferred, and transferred, and transferred until she actually reached Darius Penny.

"It's about my father?"

"Yes, sir."

"He passed?"

"Yes, sir, he did."

"When?"

Marge hesitated. "Probably two days ago."

"Probably . . ." Silence. "It took a while to discover the body."

"Something like that."

"No surprise there. My father was a hermit. Where's the body now?"

"With the county coroner."

"Do you have a contact number? I'll call right away and have someone transfer the body to a funeral home."

"Sir, the body is being autopsied."

"Autopsied? My father was eighty-nine. What on earth merits an autopsy?"

The man sounded annoyed. Since there was no easy way to break the news, Marge decided to be forthright. "I'm sorry to say this, Mr. Penny, but your father was found murdered."

"*Murdered?* Oh my God! What . . . what happened?"

At last some genuine emotion. She said, "I can't say for certain. That's why the coroner is doing an autopsy."

"Was it bad? Oh my God, it must have been bad. Was it a robbery? Not that my father kept anything of value in that cruddy apartment. But sometimes he had cash. This is just crazy. *Was* it a robbery?"

"We're still investigating."

"Are you part of the investigation or is it your job to call people up and drop bombshells?"

"I'm sorry for your loss, Mr. Penny. And yes, it is a bombshell."

"Do you have a suspect?"

"The investigation just started, Mr. Penny. All this just happened last night."

The lawyer paused. "Do you want to know where I was last night?"

She was taken aback. "Sure."

"I worked until around midnight, then came home, grabbed six hours of sleep, and was back at my desk by seven. That has been my routine—day in and day out—for the last twenty years except for vacations. The last time I took time off was six months ago. My wife and I went to our island in Greece. Any other questions I can answer for you?"

"I do have a few. Are you coming to L.A. to deal with the burial?"

"I suppose I have to. I've barely had time to process what you've told . . . murdered?"

"We think so. Would you have any ideas about what happened?"

"Not really. I know my father made many enemies, but he's been out of commission for years. Why would anyone harm him now, especially with death looming at his door?"

"Do you have names of some of those enemies?"

"No one specific comes to mind. My father was very abrasive. He had half of the Dale Carnegie method right. He influenced people. The friend part . . . not so much."

"Okay. Does your father have a lawyer that we could talk to?"

"Dad has a slew of lawyers. He generally used McCray, Aaronson and Greig as his firm. Why?"

"I assume your dad had a will. Sometimes a will points us in the right direction."

"I've been in charge of Dad's estate planning for the last twenty-five years. He definitely has a will and he's changed it a number of times, depending on who has curried his favor. Dad was mercurial."

"What kind of changes did your father make?"

"I'm not at liberty to discuss the particulars. Let's just say his changes had to do with who was flattering him. When you are worth over half a billion dollars, you deal with a lot of sycophants."

"Did you invest his money personally?"

"No, no, no. I am the president of his foundation. But Dad used our firm for his estate planning, so I am well aware of what he's worth. But as far as control over his fortune, I had nothing to do with how the money was invested or spent. But I do know that Dad has his assets spread out among a dozen different brokerage houses. Sometimes, I'd write checks at his behest."

"What kind of checks?"

"Charity. As I told you, I'm president of his foundation."

"So you were in regular contact with your father?"

"My father was a recluse. I haven't seen him since he married Sabrina. And even after the divorce, we rarely spoke. Whenever he wanted something specific, he'd notify me via phone call but mostly written word. Then I'd execute the order."

"So you two must have had some kind of relationship if he gave you that power."

"I think I was the least of many evils. We don't really have a relationship, but my father recognized that I was honest."

Don't have a relationship. Still using present tense. "What kind of charities did your father support?"

"They'd vary, depending on his mood. And let me tell you, the man was very, very temperamental. He was my father and he supported his family, but he's not likable. He was a womanizer and a louse when he drank. Is this interview going to take a while? If it is, could I call you back in a bit?"

Marge said, "Just a couple more questions. Are you coming to L.A. to make arrangements for the body?"

"My dad had made prior arrangements to be buried somewhere in L.A. I'll come in for the burial. I can't talk for my sister— Oh dear. Did you call her? My sister?"

"I left a message with Hollie Hanson to have her call me."

"So you haven't spoken to her?"

"Not yet."

"I'll call and tell her the news. What else do you want to know?"

"If your firm did your father's estate planning, you must know the contents of your father's will."

"That's not a question, Sergeant, that's a statement."

Marge was quiet.

Penny said, "This is not a discussion to be had over the phone. Let's just say there is plenty to go around.

No reason for any of the principals to be covetous. I'm wealthy and my sister is even wealthier. We both were aware that it was only a matter of time before my father passed on."

"A matter of time? Was your father in poor health?"

"Not that I know of, but he was old." A long pause. "The fact that someone hurried his death along is troublesome. I'm wondering if a phony will isn't about to make an appearance. Anyway that's not your concern. Or maybe it will be your concern. I should hang up now. I have to call my sister. This is just terrible—the murder. No one deserves to have their life cut down."

"Could I call you later?"

"How about if I have time, I'll call you later."

"When do you think you'll be coming into L.A.?"

"When are you done with the autopsy?"

"Probably by tomorrow."

"Please call me when you're done so I can transfer the body to a funeral home. I'll try to schedule the funeral on Monday or Tuesday."

"Do you think your sister will come out?"

"I honestly don't know. Graciela had even less tolerance for Dad than I do."

"When you come out to L.A., I'd like to talk to you a little more at length."

"No problem. I really do have to go now, Sergeant Dunn."

"One more thing. Were you aware that your father kept a tiger in his apartment?"

"A *tiger?*" A pause. "Are you *serious?*"

"An adult female tiger. We had to extract the tiger before we could even enter the apartment."

"Oh my God! Did the tiger attack . . . no, that wouldn't be a police matter. Is my father's body even recognizable?"

"As far as we could tell, the tiger didn't lay a paw on your dad."

"That's good to know. I knew my father was giving that crazy organization some money, but I had no idea he had become so personally involved in wild animal rescue. To keep a tiger in his apartment is beyond ludicrous."

"What wild animal organization did he support?"

"Global Earth Sanctuary. It's in San Bernardino. I know because I sent out the checks."

"Was he giving them a lot of money?"

"Pocket change for what he was worth: a hundred thousand a year. If you have further questions, you'd be better off calling them. I really must hang up now."

"Thank you for your time. Be sure to call us when you're in Los Angeles."

"Yes, I will. Bye."

Marge hung up the phone. The man was professional and straightforward when answering questions. For the time being, Marge put him at the bottom of the list.

I have an appointment to tour the sanctuary tomorrow at eleven," Decker told Marge. He was at his desk with his feet propped up; she was sitting on a chair and paging through her notes. "You can come if you'd like."

"I'd love to come with you, but Sabrina Talbot called back. Oliver and I are meeting her in Santa Barbara tomorrow at eleven in the morning."

"That's fine. If I get a weird feeling about the place, we'll do a return visit."

"Have you looked up the organization yet?"

"Just the Web site. It began with a woman named Fern Robeson, who bought some acreage in the San Bernardino Mountains in 1975. According to the bio, she started taking in wild animals because there was no other refuge for them. One thing led to another, and now her place is a way station for all sorts of wild animals."

"What kind of animals?"

"Anything—lions, tigers, bears, snakes, apes, chimps, crocs. She has her own private zoo."

"Is she licensed to do that?"

"Now she is. The place was almost shut down thirty years ago. Fern persevered, went on a massive fund-raising campaign, and received over a million dollars for the cause. Eventually she managed to secure a license to house wild animals. Fern died three years ago at seventy-two. There is some money in her foundation to care for the animals, but it is quickly running out. When I talked to the acting director—a woman named Vignette Garrison—she wasn't sure that Global Earth would last more than a year without Penny's support. I don't know how much he gave, but it must be sizable. Exotic animals are expensive to feed."

"Penny's son said the old man was giving about a hundred gees a year."

"Well, that is sizable."

"You know, you just can't put all those animals together," Marge said. "They live in different environments. The place must be large."

"I'll find out tomorrow."

"Know anything about Vignette Garrison?"

"She's thirty-seven, unmarried, and has devoted her life to saving wild animals. She worked as an assistant in a vet's office before becoming involved with Global Earth. She's been there for fifteen years."

"Do you have a picture of her?"

"Not on me. I can pull up the Web site."

"Let me guess," Marge said. "She's tall and stick thin with stringy blond hair and no makeup."

"I don't know how tall she is, but she looks very thin." Decker pushed a button and printed out her picture from the sanctuary's Web site. He gave it to Marge. "She was Fern Robeson's protégée. She asked me about Penny's will when I spoke to her."

"Really," Marge said. "That's not only crass, but it also says to me that she has something to gain by his death."

"Penny was giving her money while he was alive," Decker said. "Unless she expects a windfall once he dies, why knock him off? And that brings up another question. Penny was old. Why kill him at all? Makes more sense to just wait it out and let nature take its course."

Marge said, "Darius Penny said his old man was mercurial. If the old guy was about to change his will and leave you nothing, you might want him dead before he has a chance to make the change."

"How would Vignette Garrison know if he was about to change his will?"

"Maybe she pissed him off," Marge said. "Maybe he told her."

"Why would he tell her?"

"To manipulate her or maybe just to be mean," Marge said. "Darius said his father had made a lot of enemies. He was a mean guy, especially when he drank." She thought a moment. "I don't remember seeing alcohol bottles around. I'll ask Scott about that."

Decker ran his fingers through gray hairs streaked with youthful red. "If Darius Penny's firm handled the estate, he would know if his dad was changing the will."

"He doesn't seem like a good prospect for the murder. He's rich in his own right. Plus for the last two months, Darius has been at work from seven in the morning to midnight."

"And you've verified that?"

"Not yet, but something like that would be easily verifiable. He works in a skyscraper near the Battery. Those buildings have video cameras everywhere." Marge gave him a smile. "If you want to send me to New York for verification, I'm willing."

"I bet you are." Decker laughed. "Look, sister, I've put in for meals and gas money for your upcoming trip to Santa Barbara. Don't look a gift horse in the mouth. All you'll find there is bad breath."

Chapter Seven

Arriving home by seven in the evening, Decker was surprised to find the house dimly lit with no aromas wafting from the kitchen. He flipped on additional living room lamps and called out Rina's name, but received no answer. It was unlike his wife to be a no-show without explanation. Maybe it was time to check his phone message. Then Gabe came out of his room.

Decker said, "Any idea where my wife is?"

"Your wife had a school meeting. She said she'd be home around nine."

"Fabulous."

"There are some leftover cold cuts and potato salad in the fridge."

"Sounds real yummy."

Gabe smiled. "Wanna go out? I wouldn't mind a steak. I'll even pay. My bank account is flush."

"Steak is fine with me, and I'm not yet destitute."

"Want me to drive?"

Decker held up a finger as he listened to his phone message, then stowed his phone in his pocket. "Uh, how about we take the Porsche?"

"That's fine. I can drive a stick."

"You can, but you won't." Decker went over to a desk drawer and fished out the ignition key. "I'll get the car and meet you out front. Put on the alarm."

Five minutes later, Gabe hopped into the passenger seat of Decker's silver 911 Targa. He was wearing a black T-shirt and a pair of jeans two sizes too big. He wasn't making a fashion statement with his pants. Of late the kid hadn't eaten enough to maintain his weight. "Thanks for rescuing me from starvation."

"I was working all day. What is your excuse for not eating?"

"I dunno. It took me a long time to settle down."

"From the news about Dylan Lashay."

"Yeah. Wow, what a relief! I've been a basket case this last month just thinking about testifying. God, I'm glad it's over! Maybe I can finally move forward."

"Maybe you can put on a couple of pounds. I've heard that Manhattan has one or two good restaurants.

Take my daughter out and the check is on me. When are you going back?"

"Tuesday."

Decker was taken aback. "You're staying through the weekend?"

"Yeah, like I explained to Rina, I just want to unwind a little bit."

Decker threw him a look, and Gabe blushed. "So when are you meeting her?"

"What?"

"Don't snow me, kid. You're a terrible liar." Gabe was silent. Decker said, "Don't do it, Gabriel. It'll set you back. Just as important, it'll set her back. And from a selfish point of view, I don't want to have to deal with her parents again."

"They won't find out."

"That's what you said the last time. And stop clenching your teeth."

Gabe tried to relax. "Are you going to rat me out?"

"I should, but I won't." The boy had curled into in a ball. "Gabe, you need to think of her welfare."

"Peter, I swear we're not gonna do anything." A lie: Decker wasn't buying it. "I barely had contact with her the past couple of years." Another lie that didn't wash. Finally Gabe threw up his hands. "What's the big deal?"

"Gabriel, if her parents find out, she's got a lot more to lose than you do."

He ran his hand over his head. "For the record, she called me."

"That's irrelevant. You're the one who has to say no."

"I don't want to say no. Why should I?"

"Because she's smitten with you and can't think straight."

"I'm smitten with her."

"I don't doubt that, but guys function differently. You're both way too young for commitment. Surely there are girls in New York that come with a lot less baggage."

"Surely there are, but I'm not interested, okay?"

Decker smiled. "Must be true love."

"Can we change the subject? How's the tiger doing?"

"Funny you should ask. I'm going to visit her tomorrow at a wild animal sanctuary."

"Cool. Can I come with you?"

Decker looked at him. "You want to come with me?"

"Sure. It sounds interesting. I love what I do, but occasionally it might be fun to venture outside."

"Uh, it's official business."

"Okay. I understand."

Decker shrugged. "I suppose you can tour around while I conduct my interviews."

"That would be great! Who are you interviewing?"

"Can't say. It's part of an ongoing murder investigation."

"Can I help?"

Decker held back a smile. "Uh, I think I've got it covered."

"I'm sure you do." Gabe laughed. "Thanks for letting me come. I promise I won't get mauled by a lion."

"Maybe you'd rather face a lion than face Yasmine's father?"

"We're back there again?"

"All I'm saying is we both could use a good steak dinner and everyone's entitled to a last meal."

"Nothing is going to happen!" Gabe said.

"Yeah, yeah, famous last words." Decker parked the car in front of a kosher steak house. "Let's go, Romeo."

The two of them got out of the car. Gabe said, "Thanks for taking me out to dinner."

"My pleasure."

"And thanks also for being a cool guy."

"I'm a cool guy?"

"Peter, you are the essence of coolness. If everyone was as cool as you are, we'd never have to worry about global warming."

Sliding up the on-ramp of the 210, Decker followed the Foothill freeway for forty-plus miles until it hit Highway 15, a dividing line between Angeles Crest and the San Bernardino Mountains. The range, going north and south, cleaved Southern California into Pacific Ocean to the west and the Mojave Desert on the east, the lowest place in the United States at 282 feet below sea level.

The road climbed upward until the elevations were measured in thousands instead of hundreds. In the late fall, the dogwoods, maples, and oaks had lost their leaves, standing dormant and skeletal. But there was still plenty of green provided by the plethora of pines and cedars. The air was cold and crisp, the sky was overcast, and as the car scaled the heights, the road twisted and curled. A sprinkling of snow attempted to cover brown detritus of rotting leaves, pine needles, and animal scat.

It was slow going. Then the road forked into two unpaved lanes. The navigation system became unglued and Decker had to rely on directions and a two-year-old hiking map. The car bumped along a rutted strip at about ten per hour. After twenty minutes, he saw the weathered post topped by a makeshift sign: GLOBAL EARTH SANCTUARY 3MI. An arrow pointed the way.

The temperature had dipped to the low forties, and Decker cranked up the heat. Assuming they'd be outside most of time, he had packed scarves and gloves and had given Gabe one of his bomber jackets. The length was okay, but being that he outweighed the kid by eighty pounds, the girth was way off.

Gabe had been listening to his iPhone most of the way. As they passed the sign to the sanctuary, he took out the earbuds and stared outside, rubbing his arms. "This is Southern California?"

"It's a big state. You can get just about any climate you want except glaciers."

"Sometimes . . . when I see unspoiled terrain like this . . . I just want to jump out and lose myself in nature. The problem is with my body weight and mountain man skills, I'd probably last about a day."

"Did you ever go camping with your family?"

Gabe laughed. "Are you kidding me? Chris Donatti camping?"

"The man knows how to shoot."

"Only two-legged prey. No, I grew up suburban, urban. How far is this place?"

"According to the directions, it's three miles from the sign."

"Thanks for taking me. Sorry if I've been bad company."

Decker smiled. "You're exactly the type of company I like. The quiet helps me think."

"Yeah, you don't even turn on the radio or anything. I couldn't last more than ten minutes without something filling up my ears."

"When it's silent, your brain fills in the music," Decker told him. "After all these years, I think I've finally learned how to listen."

They rode the rest of the way in silence.

The lane finally dead-ended in a dirt lot that had been cleared for parking. There were several vehicles—a white van, a four-wheel drive, a Honda, and a golf cart that sat underneath a naked sycamore. The property held three trailers along with miles of chain-link fencing crisscrossing the trails. He and Gabe got out, the boy sticking his hands in his pockets. Decker adjusted his scarf. A bald, stoop-shouldered man came out of one of the trailers and walked over to a white chest refrigerator. He opened the lid and began to stuff plastic bags of meat in a leather pouch.

"Excuse me," Decker said in a loud voice.

The man looked up. "Can I help you?"

Decker walked toward him so he wouldn't have to shout. "I'm looking for Vignette Garrison."

The man pointed at the trailer in the middle. "Her office is there, but I think she's out with the animals."

THE BEAST · 79

"Okay if we wait inside her office? Little chilly out here."

"Fine with me, but you won't find it too much warmer inside. All we have are floor heaters." Despite the slumped posture, the man was tall with cornflower blue eyes and white stubble.

Decker said, "Do you work here full-time?"

"Volunteer. I make my money as an accountant. Used to be at this time of the year, I'd never see daylight. A heart attack later, I found myself thinking about things other than quarterly estimates. Too bad shoveling shit doesn't pay as much as manipulating numbers." He closed the flap on the pouch. "Mealtime for the kitty cats. Wanna come see what we have here?"

At that moment, Decker saw a woman with long hair in the distance walking toward them. She wore a knitted cap, a thick jacket, tight jeans, and hiking boots. "Is that Vignette Garrison?"

"Yep."

"We have an appointment. Thanks for the invitation though."

The accountant gave Decker a wave. "I'm off."

Gabe said, "I'll come with you. I've never seen lions and tigers up close."

"Well, come along and enjoy the experience." The man stuck out his hand. "Everett James."

"Gabe Whitman." He took hold of the man's right wrist with both hands and gave him the musician's handshake. "Thanks a lot, Mr. James."

"You can call me Everett." The man took out a set of keys. "This way."

James opened the gate to go in just as Vignette was about to go out. They spoke for a few seconds, and when it was over, Vignette came jogging over.

Up close, she looked younger—late twenties or early thirties. Her hair was light brown streaked with blond and hung past her shoulders. Her complexion, even in the winter, was bronze in tone. Vignette's eyes were round and dark, her nose was thin, and her lips were full and chapped. She rubbed her gloved hands.

She stuck out a hand. "Vignette Garrison."

"How are you?" Decker took her hand. "Lieutenant Decker."

"Golly, it's cold. I'm wearing thermal socks and my feet still feel like two chunks of ice."

"If you want to go inside, I won't object," Decker said.

"Not that it's all that warm inside. But at least my feet can thaw out."

He followed her up the three steps that led into the middle trailer. Inside, Decker saw a bank of metal file cabinets, four desks, and about a half dozen chairs. There was also a small kitchen with a refrigerator, a microwave, several hot plates, three space heaters, and a standing fan.

"Have a seat." She pulled out a chair. Then she bent down and turned a knob on the space heater, then rolled it toward Decker. "This will help a little."

"Is this battery operated?"

"Kerosene. We do have a generator out back. It runs the fridge." She took off her gloves and hat. "Most of the animals are cold tolerant, but we always have backup heating just in case we have prolonged cold snaps. We also have our hot days. For the animals, we can control the heat by dumping ice in the water pools. We have a variety of animals that live in a variety of climates. What's comfortable for savannah lions isn't necessarily good for jungle tigers."

"I'm sure it takes a lot of work to get it right."

"You can say that again. People don't realize that you just can't dump animals in a single environment and expect them to get along let alone survive." She sat down. "I'm glad you came to visit in the cold rather than the heat. You'll see the cats at their best. The fur is magnificent. Is that your son who went off with Everett?"

"My foster son."

She wrinkled her nose. "He looks a little old to be in foster care."

"He's been with us for a while. By now, we consider him a member of the family."

"We're not so different, then."

"How's that?"

"I adopt strays, you adopt strays. It shows a giving spirit . . . to take in something and nurture it back to health. I often think of Global Earth as one big foster home."

"Well, I hope it runs more efficiently than county care."

"Oh it does." The joke was lost on her. She pulled off her boots and then placed her sock-covered feet atop the space heater. "Did you find out anything about the will?"

"I found out there is a will."

"Great. Do you know when it's going to be read?"

"Uh, I don't know if it's like the movies where everyone sits in a lawyer's office and hears all the allocations read aloud."

"So how does it work?"

"I'm not positive, but if I were to guess, I'd say his lawyers along with the executor go over the provisions one by one. Then they are supposed to carry out the wishes of the deceased."

THE BEAST · 83

"What happens if they don't carry out the wishes?"

"If you think that someone deliberately took assets that were allocated to you, you can sue, I suppose."

"Sounds very messy."

"It probably is."

She took out a tube of ChapStick and coated her lips. "So how will I know if I get any money?"

"Are you expecting money from Penny's will?"

"No, not me personally. Mr. Penny did say he intended to support Global Earth after he died."

Decker took out a notebook. "He said those specific words to you?" She was staring at the notebook. "Do you mind? Memory isn't what it used to be."

"No, sure, go ahead."

"Did he say how he intended to support the sanctuary?"

She shook her head no. "I didn't ask him. I thought it was greedy and ghoulish to get into specifics. It's not about me, Lieutenant. I live in a one-bedroom apartment that's as spare as the trailer. But I do care about the animals. Ever since Fern died, I've been trying single-handedly to carry on the legacy." A tear rolled down her cheek. "I miss Fern. She was an incredible woman. No one could possibly do what she did."

"She died a while back, didn't she?"

She swiped her cheek with her sleeve. "Three years ago. She was the backbone of this place. If Mr. Penny hadn't come along, we might have folded."

"How'd you meet Mr. Penny?"

"He found us." She rubbed her toes. "Now that you're here in person, I'll tell you what I knew about Mr. Penny and the tiger. He had inherited the cub from an exotic animal importer who wound up in jail. I never got the whole story. What I do know is that he was going to donate the cub to us. That didn't happen right away, and I guess after a while, he grew attached to her. I kept telling him that a tiger wasn't always going to be a cub. I tried to let him know that she was going to grow up to be a very large and dangerous animal. And he kept on saying that he knew that and he'd eventually give her up. One day, he called up and asked me to come to his apartment. I thought that this meant he was ready to let her go."

She shrugged.

"Instead we talked for a long time with the tiger in the room. At the conclusion of our conversation, he whipped out his checkbook and gave us fifty thousand dollars. I should have reported him, but I was stunned by his generosity. And . . . we really needed the money."

"I see."

"I'm sure you're making assumptions, but it wasn't just about money. Tiki is an unusually calm cat. She's gentle once you gain her trust. And she really did seem bonded to the old guy."

"I'm sure she was."

Vignette swallowed hard. "Did she hurt him in any way after he died?"

"Actually, no she didn't."

The woman was visibly relieved. "See? That's Tiki. The two of them were exceptionally close. I know it was stupid to let it slide. But it came from a deep love between Hobart and Tiki and a firm commitment to this place."

"What would happen to the animals if the place closed down?"

"I don't want to think about that." She set her boots atop the heater. "Are you warm enough? Would you like some coffee? It's only instant, but it might warm you up."

"Sure, I'll take a cup."

Padding around in her socks, she took down two mugs and filled them with hot water. Then she added a heaping tablespoon of instant coffee and doused it with milk before Decker could tell her that he drank his java black. "Thanks."

"You're welcome." She sat down. "So you don't know anything about the will?"

"No, I really don't." The woman looked dispirited. Decker pressed on. "I'd like to know what would happen to the animals if the place closed down."

She shook her head. "I'd like to think that a zoo or a circus would pick them up. But the truth is that some of these animals are so inbred that zoos wouldn't have any use for them. Zoos need wild stock to prevent inherited diseases. Lots of these animals were bred by for-profit dealers. The majority of the animals are too unpredictable for circuses and zoos, but they've lost their instincts to exist in the wilds."

Decker nodded, and she continued.

"If we couldn't find another sanctuary, the majority of the animals here would have to be put down."

"Sad."

"That's why Mr. Penny was so important to us. When he saw what we were doing, he became a major supporter."

"He visited here?"

"Yes, he did."

"He was very reclusive. How'd you manage to get him out here?"

"It took a lot of cajoling, but I got him here several years ago. I wanted him to know what his fifty thousand dollars was doing. He seemed pleased. Then, a month later, I got a check for six figures. I nearly fell off my chair. We have other supporters, but he was the biggest contributor. His money gave us slack so we didn't have to constantly fund-raise."

"Do you have a professional fund-raiser?"

"Good God, no. Most of our help are volunteers. Like Everett James, the gentleman that you met. On top of helping with the animals, he helps us with our accounting. We can't afford a big staff like a zoo or anything."

"How many paid employees does Global Earth actually have?"

"Full-time, it's only me. The costs come from feeding and maintaining the animals, state licenses, vet services, all that kind of stuff. I started off volunteering. Then, after Fern died and they offered me a junior position, I jumped at it. Allan was made president. Then after he left for Alaska, they were going to close the place down. I couldn't let that happen without a fight. So I took over with a salary of twenty thousand a year—barely enough to pay for my car, food, and rent. A short time later, I got the call from Mr. Penny. It was like manna from heaven."

The walkie-talkie on her belt suddenly belched out static. "Excuse me." She took out the squawk box. "Hi, Vern, what's up?" Static over the line. Vignette said, "I'll be right there." She signed off, slipped on her hiking boots, and began lacing them up. "One of our grizzlies isn't eating. Want to come with me and see what we do?"

"That would be . . . interesting."

Vignette slipped some supplies into the pockets of her jacket. "Never met a grizzly before?"

"Nope." Decker managed a weak smile. "An encounter with a grizzly never made it to my bucket list."

Chapter Eight

No matter how many times Marge made the ride, she always felt that spark of excitement when that blue expanse peeked from the horizon and then came into full view. In the sun, the Pacific was all sparkles and diamonds, frothing at the break line, the front yard of miles of luxury real estate. Lately she and Will had been talking about the next step. It made her anxious to think about it, but life was about change.

Her mood was light, and Oliver seemed at peace. He didn't grouse, he didn't carp, and he didn't bellyache. He ate his tuna sandwich and potato chips while looking out the window, licking his fingers like a fourth grader at lunch. He said, "Tell me again why we're working in L.A.?"

"Because our lungs have become adept at filtering smog." A quick glance at her surroundings. "And despite the plunge in home prices, I do believe that neither you nor I make enough to afford one of these puppies."

"How does your boyfriend do it?"

"His bungalow is a one bedroom and it's inland. No view of the ocean, but he does have a huge sycamore in his tiny backyard, and the place is within walking distance to the hiking trails." She inhaled and let it out. "You know we're thinking about taking it to the next level."

"Which is?"

"Getting a ring."

Oliver's eyes widened. "Nice." A pause. "I hope not too soon."

Marge's smile was genuine. "Not immediately, no."

"That's good." Oliver bit his lip. "I mean . . . it's good to take your time."

"We've been working together for years, Oliver. Say it out loud. You'd miss me."

"I would miss you." He meant it. "I hope you're not contemplating a move to Santa Barbara?"

"Not at the moment."

"He's moving to L.A.?"

Marge said, "That would be a no as well. Right now we're okay with the arrangement."

"Good deal from where I'm sitting." He was visibly relieved.

"Aw . . . you care."

He squirmed and changed the subject. "What kind of ring?"

"He's resizing his late mother's old diamond—three-carat emerald cut."

"That's the real deal."

"Yes it is."

"Good for you, Marge. I'm happy for you."

"Thank you, Scott. I'm happy, too. I've got a good guy. I know that the ring's only a symbol, but it's still nice. Not only will it look pretty on my finger, but jewelry is always a good investment in times of economic uncertainty."

Sabrina Talbot lived behind gates in a multi-million-dollar estate house on multiple acres with multimillionaires and a few billionaires as neighbors. The structure wasn't visible from the road. It was masked behind a forest of trees and iron fencing. The metal pickets had been forged into seven-foot-high helmeted men sporting pikes. Directly behind the fencing were rosebushes, sprouting thorns on each branch. Every ten feet or so were brick pilasters topped with decorative lights and security cameras. The guard house bisected the driveway to the house. Marge stopped in front of the gate and rolled down the driver's window. The sentry pulled back a door revealing a very big man: around six feet three with at least 275 pounds of fat and muscle. His bluish black skin tone spoke of Africa, so Marge wasn't surprised when he spoke with an accent.

"How can I help you?"

"I'm Sergeant Marge Dunn and this is my partner, Detective Scott Oliver. We're from LAPD, and we're here to see Sabrina Talbot. Her secretary set up an appointment today at eleven."

"One moment." The door slid shut. It took several minutes. The guard stayed ensconced in his protective chamber, but the gates parted majestically. Directly in front was a golf cart with a sign on the back that read: FOLLOW ME.

They rode an asphalt trail that cut through acres of greenery—silvery olive trees, California oak, bare sycamores, and varieties of menthol-exhaling euca-lyptus, all of the trees underplanted with thick foliage and bushes. Eventually the specimen trees gave way to acres of avocado groves: evergreens with dark green polished leaves and gnarled trunks. A pale blue sky held filmy clouds. The air was mild and perfumed.

It was taking a very long time to reach the house, but that could have been the fault of the golf cart, which was ascending at a particularly slow rate. Finally there was a clearing of newly sod lawn and surgical landscaping, hedges trimmed to a precise ninety-degree edge, and symmetrical flower beds of deep jewel hues of pansies and primroses.

Every queen has her castle, and Sabrina's three-story stone Tudor estate came complete with mullioned windows and a turret. The cart stopped, and two uniformed valets came rushing over to open the car doors.

Marge and Oliver stepped out of the car. She said, "Do I need a ticket?"

The valet stared at her. Another giant of a man answered in the valet's stead. "No, you don't need a ticket. I'll escort you inside." He held out a hand. "Leo Delacroix."

"Like the artist?" Marge asked.

"Same spelling. No relation." His touch for a big man was surprisingly light. "This way. You're right on time. Ms. Talbot is a stickler for punctuality."

"Then we have a lot in common." Marge looked around as they walked to a two-story iron front door. "Although we probably have a lot more *not* in common."

Delacroix's face remained stony. He pressed a button, and the full chorus of Beethoven's "Ode to Joy" resonated through speakers. The doors split and a third guard took over. He was young, white, and muscular with a thick neck and a military buzz cut for hair. He introduced himself as Thor Weillsohn, leading them down a marble hallway into a reception room, modest in size but not in ornamentation. The furniture was all-white curlicue legs and backs, upholstered in jacquard blue silk. Persian rugs lay over a parquet walnut floor, and tapestries hung from white paneled walls. Angels and cherubs hovered above in a sky filled with puffy clouds.

"Ms. Talbot will be with you in a minute," Thor told them. He left, closing two white paneled doors behind him. Both of them remained standing, neither wanting to park a butt on something that was breakable and/or priceless. Oliver let out a low whistle.

Marge said, "I guess Hobart gave her a decent settlement."

"How old is this woman?"

"In her fifties. She was in her twenties when she married him."

"She did well."

Another minute passed, and then the doors opened. This time it was a uniformed maid carrying a tea and coffee service, three cups and saucers, and a plate of cookies. "Please have a seat on the divan."

Marge and Oliver looked at each other and sat down simultaneously on what they thought was the divan. It wasn't padded much and was ramrod stiff on the back.

The housekeeper said, "May I pour for you?"

"Thank you," Marge said. "That would be lovely."

"Tea or coffee?"

"Coffee. Just milk."

"Same for me," Oliver said. "Thank you."

She set the service down on a table and poured in silence. Then she passed around the cookie tray. They each took one out of politeness and placed it on the saucer. The maid put the cookie plate and napkins on a coffee table, and then she left.

"This is all good stuff," Oliver said. "Do you think if I turned on enough charm, Ms. Talbot might give me a roll in the hay?"

"No."

"Don't be too vague, Dunn. Tell me what you really think."

"I like this lemon bar. If I didn't think I was being watched, I'd sneak a few up in a paper napkin and hide them in my purse."

Oliver laughed. Five more minutes passed and then a rush of wind burst through the doors. The detectives stood up.

The woman was a presence: over six feet with broad shoulders, slim hips, and a mane of blond hair. She had blue eyes, high cheekbones, and pale skin. There was spiderwebbing at the corners of the eyes and mouth, but none of that shiny stretched skin common to plastic surgery. She was dressed in a dirty shirt and gardening pants, a floppy hat on her head. She tossed the chapeau on the French furniture.

"Gawd, I'm a mess." She checked her hands then offered them to Marge and Oliver. "Sabrina Talbot. Sorry about the dirty fingernails. Even with gloves, I lunched my French manicure. Nails and gardening don't mix." She brushed off her pants, bits of dirt falling on the Persian rug, and then sat down on a chair. "Sit, sit. And don't worry if you spill. I reupholster the furniture every two years. It's about that time. I'm thinking of going deco. I was in my 'ice' phase when I did this room. Now it reminds me of an igloo. Sit, sit."

The detectives sat, introduced themselves with each of them giving her a card.

"I know that you're here about Hobart." A single tear down the cheek. "Who would want to harm an eccentric old man?"

"So you know he was murdered," Marge said.

"Gracie phoned me last night. It was a brief conversation, and she was also short on the details. I'm hoping you can fill me in on what happened."

"Gracie is Graciela Johannesbourgh?" Marge asked.

"Yes."

"So you're still in contact with Mr. Penny's daughter."

"Gracie and I have become friends—mostly out of our concern for Hobart's mental health. Over the years, he'd become increasingly odd. Now I'm not immune to eccentricity. My entire maternal half lives in a series of tiny English villages, each one more quirky than the next. But with Hobart, it had crossed the line from different to problematic."

Marge had taken out her notebook. "How's that?"

"We met when I was young. I was immediately taken with him. He was a very vital man. He reminded me of my father, so I understood men like Hobart very well."

"What do you mean 'men like Hobart'?"

"You know, these hypermacho males always trying to prove to themselves that they're Ernest Hemingway's successor—running with the bulls at Pamplona, mountain climbing in Nepal, navigating an uncharted river in the Amazon. Men like that are well understood in my circles."

"What are your circles?" Oliver asked.

"You mean you didn't *Google* me?" She stared at him with mock offense.

"I looked you up," Marge said. "All it mentioned was that you were the former wife of Hobart Penny."

"Then I've done my job well," Sabrina said. "My parents believed that you should be in the news for birth, marriage, and death. I suppose divorce now is acceptable, but that's it. Let me give you a little family history. My great-great-grandfather was Jacob Remington—as in Remington aircraft. My mother was a Remington. My father was an Eldinger on his mother's side. If you look up the families, you'll see that I come from old, old money. We're the old-fashioned snooty WASPs. My parents were thrilled when I married Hobart . . . that someone wasn't going to fleece me. Not that they needed to worry." She pointed to her head. "I know where every dollar goes. Meticulous is my guideline. Hobart liked that about me. That I wasn't just arm candy. Even with my pedigree and my looks and my brains, it took Hobart five years to propose. It probably had to do with his divorce from his first wife and my age. We met when I was nineteen."

"Was Hobart's divorce a messy one?" Marge asked.

"Not terribly messy, but there was no love lost. I was not the cause of the breakup. Hobart always had other women. And he was always odd, the stereotypic mad inventor. Not the most socially adroit. I think number one wife had had enough of him."

Oliver flipped over a notebook page. "How did you two meet?"

"At a boring old fund-raiser for some disadvantaged something. We locked eyes, and that was it for me, although his roving eye was apparent even when we were dating. I thought that being wed to me would cure him, silly goose that I was."

"Can you clarify what you mean by a little odd?" Marge asked.

"Although Hobart exuded animal sexuality, he really didn't give a shit about people—except for beautiful women, which he more or less objectified." She draped a leg over the armrest. "He'd always had a fascination with wild animals—a TR kind of thing, you know."

"TR?" Oliver asked.

"Teddy Roosevelt. The man who shot lions and rowed down the Amazon when he wasn't being president. Now I loved a good safari just like the next person. But I like safaris the way that I do safaris—first-class accommodations and armed guards in the open jeep. Maybe a hike or two as long as someone else is carrying the backpack. Hobart wanted to camp out in the wilds of Africa. I mean *camp* for goodness sakes. As in pitch a tent and eat out of tins and make our own fire and gather up the water from a stream two miles away. Now I ask you. Do I look like the sleeping bag type?"

"Not to my eye," Oliver said.

Sabrina sighed. "Something cracked in Hobart as time passed. He went from being rich and odd to being a very odd, rich man. What really scared me were the delusions."

"What kind of delusions?"

"This is going to sound ridiculous, but he started to believe that he was a wild animal trapped in a human body much the way that people think that they're vampires or witches or werewolves. In his case, he was certain that he was really some kind of a big cat. Sometimes it was a lion, sometimes it was a tiger. It wasn't as if he lost his grip on reality. He could tell you every single stock on the NYSE. He was completely oriented. And he knew that he wasn't *really* a big cat. He just felt that inside his human body was the soul of a tiger. He began to grow a wild beard. He also grew out his nails. He scratched the hell out of me every time we made love. Then he started to bite. Nibbles at first, but it progressed until several times, he broke skin. That was when I said to him, 'Hobart, you need help.'"

"And?" Marge asked.

"He went into treatment. The psychiatrist told me that underneath the delusions was a severely depressed and schizoid man. So they medicated him and gave him mood elevators. He didn't like the drugs. He claimed they interfered with his sexual function. That part wasn't a delusion. But instead of going back for a different medication, he just dropped out. Once he was off the medication, he reverted back to his former ways. He got weirder and weirder. I'd finally had enough when he started marking the furniture."

"Yikes," Oliver said.

"I begged him to get help, but he flatly refused. He might have gotten help eventually if he hadn't gotten involved with all those . . . clubs."

Marge's ears went on high alert. "What clubs?"

"Private clubs that did God only knows what as well as the crazy animal rights organizations that fed his delusions. He gave them money in exchange for their tolerance."

Marge said, "Can you be more specific about the private clubs. It might give us a lead in his murder."

"Sadomasochistic. This was years ago. I'm sure the ones he used have all folded and newer ones have popped up." Sabrina sighed. "Hobart used to travel all over the country to ferret out the ones he liked. He found women who would dress up in cat suits and masks and have sex with him."

"He told you this?" Oliver asked.

The woman's face went red. "He confessed, but only after I found pictures of him humping young girls wearing tiger masks. I also found pictures of him with . . . animals. It was nauseating."

Marge and Oliver nodded sympathetically.

"He said it wasn't personal, that a tiger had to do what a tiger had to do." She waved her hand in the air. "I mean, do I look like an idiot? I tried to reason with him . . . I held on as long as I could . . . but I knew it was over."

Silence. Oliver said, "Ms. Talbot, if you could remember any of the names of the clubs—even if they've folded—it might help."

"He never told me." Sabrina examined her nails. "He moved out about a year after I found the pictures. The divorce was amicable. He gave me a very large settlement. His children were not happy about it. I couldn't blame them. Hobart was not in his right mind. Being noble, being rich myself, and not wanting to get involved in lawsuits, I put two-thirds of the money into trusts for Hobart's grandchildren. The other third was my combat pay. My generosity with the grandchildren did not go unappreciated. Gracie and I became friends. Darius called to thank me. The one thing the three of us did do was to convince Hobart—in one of his more lucid moments—to put his estate planning in the care of Darius's law firm."

"And he agreed?" Marge asked.

"Yes. Darius was smart about it. He funded whatever Hobart asked him to fund. Every so often, the two of them would go over his assets and how Hobart wanted to structure his will and what charities to give money to. So far as I know, there was never any impropriety on Darius's part."

She crossed her arms over her dirty shirt. "After we divorced, he slowly sank into the life of a recluse. He took that tiny wretched apartment. Eventually he just became a shut-in. Never went anywhere except to that sanctuary that he supported."

"Global Earth Sanctuary?"

"Beats me." A pause. "Talking about this has given me a big headache."

"I'm sorry, Ms. Talbot, but the conversation has been helpful," Marge said. "I am curious about those sadomasochistic clubs. You asked who might have killed an eccentric old man, and now I have an idea. What if your ex-husband had been giving money to someone in the sex trade and suddenly stopped? These people are not only sleazy, they're also dangerous. Maybe someone got angry."

Sabrina said, "He hasn't been going to those kinds of clubs for decades."

"Are you sure?"

"Not positive but . . ." She shrugged.

"What about hiring out?" Oliver said. "Lots of escort services make house calls."

"Maybe . . . if she could get past Tiki."

Marge turned and faced Sabrina. "So you knew about the tiger?"

"Oh my word, she nearly bit my head off when I came to visit him that one time. I never went back."

Oliver said, "Ms. Talbot, if you knew he kept a tiger, why didn't you report it to authorities?"

She rubbed her temples. "Look, Detective, I should have. But at the time, I didn't want to crush the only living thing that the man cared about. And I knew that Hobart would just mail away for another animal. Since Tiki seemed to be bonded to Hobart, I thought the known was better than the unknown."

Sabrina checked her watch.

"I really do need to end this. I can't say that this has been fun, but it's been . . . therapeutic in a sense. I haven't really thought about Hobart in years. I do hope you'll catch the person who did this to him."

Marge stood up. "Ms. Talbot, did you keep anything personal that belonged to your husband after he moved out?"

"Personal? Like diaries?"

"Diaries, letters, old photographs or old papers."

"There might be a box or two of his possessions in the storage wing."

"Do you think we might have a look at them?"

"Sure, but I don't know exactly where they are or if I even have them anymore."

"We don't mind hunting around if it's okay with you." Oliver sneaked another cookie.

Sabrina said, "Would you like a box of cookies? I have a freezer full of them. Eleanor bakes them all the time." Before he could answer, she pressed a button and the maid came back. "Could you give these nice people a box of your delicious cookies?"

"Yes, Madame. Of course, Madame."

"Thank you."

The maid left, and a moment later, Thor reappeared: a staff that ran like a well-oiled machine. "How can I help you?"

"Thor, could you take them to the storage wing for me? They want to see if I have anything left from my ex-husband."

"They can stay here, Ms. Talbot. I can look around to see if you've retained anything from Mr. Penny."

She looked at Oliver, who said, "We always find it helpful to hunt around ourselves."

Marge said, "We understand if you don't want two strangers looking around your belongings. He can come with us if that would make you feel better."

"Yes, that would be a grand idea. I suppose it would be rather reckless of me to have you snoop around without supervision. Thor, go with the detectives. If they have any questions, feel free to answer them. But don't get in their way."

"Certainly, Ms. Talbot."

"Take care." She waved. "And don't forget the cookies, Detective Oliver."

"Thank you."

"You can always come back for more." She smiled. "Bye."

When she left, Thor said, "This way."

"Thank you," Marge told him.

Thor walked six paces ahead down the marble hallway. Oliver whispered to Marge, "Was it my self-deluded ego or was she actually flirting with me?"

Marge shrugged. "The proper word is *toying*."

"Sure wouldn't mind being her plaything." A big grin.

"Don't be fooled by the charm. She could eat you for a prelude to a midnight snack."

"Yum, yum."

Marge laughed. "You know, Oliver, you're lucky that I've got your back." A beat. "I not only have your back, I've got it protected by a loaded gun. And let me tell you, brother, there's nothing sexier in this world than a woman with a dead aim."

Chapter Nine

The Global Earth Sanctuary sat on acreage that was dissected by multiple sinuous trails hugging numerous enclosures of chain-link and barbed wire fencing. The air was filled with animal sounds: roars, growls, grunts, hoots, hollers, huffs, yips and yaps, and other things that go bump in the night. It smelled ripe, and the odor would have been stronger had it been warmer. Vignette was walking at a good clip, so Decker didn't have a lot of time to look around. But on the occasions when he did turn his head, his eyes took in blurry and shadowed shapes walking on all fours. His own feet were feeling the chill even through his socks as he hiked up the narrow pathways of mud and pebbles. Eventually a man of about sixty years came into view. He was dressed in a work shirt, vest, jeans, and boots. He gave them a wave.

"Hi there, Vern. I'm going to check out Cody now."

"I'll go with you."

"Might be a good idea." The three of them kept walking until they neared a cage containing an upright mass of fur that was limping and pacing at the same time. The animal wasn't just roaring. It was an ear-shattering bellow. It was only machismo that prevented Decker from covering his ears.

Vignette looked around the cage and shook her head. "He didn't touch his lunch." She pointed to a pile of fruit, leaves, and other undecipherable blobs. "Cody's normally a good eater. He's agitated about something."

Y'think? Decker said, "How strong are those pens?"

"Cody's not going anywhere." She turned to Vern. "Well, I suppose I'd better have a look. Do you have the rifle?"

"It's down at the trailer."

"S'right. It'll be okay."

"Are you sure about that, Vignette?" Vern was concerned.

"I'll be fine." Without hesitation, she approached the beast, stopping at the wire fencing. She held a bag of raw fish and a spear. To the grizzly, she said, "What's going on, Cody?"

At the sound of her voice, the animal lumbered over to the fence, dropped to all fours, and groaned.

She said, "Grizzlies don't see well, but their smell and hearing are excellent."

Decker just kept staring, his heart beating faster than usual. He hoped he wasn't about to witness something gruesome. Penny's crime scene was still fresh in his brain.

She said, "What's the matter, little guy?"

Little guy?

She took a whistle from her pocket and blew it once. Cody's verbal protests had reduced to whimpering. The animal stood upright and pressed his right paw against the fence. The claws were thick and long and very sharp. She examined the paw carefully, and then fed him a hunk of raw fish impaled on the tip of the spear. "He'll do anything for salmon."

She blew the whistle again. This time the left paw was offered for examination. Afterward, he was rewarded with more salmon. "No problem so far." A third blow of the whistle.

The bear sat on his rump and showed Vignette his right foot. "Oh my. That looks nasty, Cody. I'd be pissed, too, if I were you."

Decker was five feet behind her. "What's wrong?"

Vignette gave the bear a chunk of pink flesh on the spear. "He cut his foot pad on something sharp. I'm going to have to treat it before it gets infected." She took out a small chub of salmon and put a capsule in the dead fish's mouth. "Okay, guy, let's see what I can do for you." She fed Cody the laced flesh—using the spear as his eating implement—and then looked at her watch. Five minutes later, the bear rolled over and started to snore. She threw Vern the keys. "You know the rules. Lock me in. Keep an eye on him. And if I get caught, do NOT open the door under any circumstance."

"You're going in there?" Decker was aghast.

"I got about fifteen minutes to work." Vignette winked at him. "Wish me luck."

Decker was speechless. Vern unlocked the cage door, and Vignette went inside. She worked swiftly and professionally. First she disinfected the cut, washing it out with a squeeze bottle of salt water. Then she followed with a medicinal salve or ointment. Lastly, she sealed the wound as best she could with liquid bandage material.

Decker was constantly checking his watch. With each passing minute, he became more nervous. Vern said, "He's startin' to move, Vignette."

"I'm almost done. I just want to make sure . . ." Her words trailed off.

It was Decker who now began to pace. "Please get out of there."

Vingette got up. "I'm fine. Main thing is he's fine."

"No, the main thing is that you get out of there alive and whole."

She smiled and dusted her pants off. Vern opened the gate and closed it quickly, rapping the solid chain around the gate and securing it with a padlock. As soon as the bear was upright, he teetered over to Vignette and moaned. She offered him more fish, and even though the animal was woozy, he took the bait.

"That's a good boy," she cooed. "You feel better?"

The bear grumbled then walked away, limping of course, but it was less marked.

The three of them watched in silence as the bear tried to restore his balance. Every few minutes, he hobbled over to Vignette, who fed him salmon in progressively tinier pieces until she told him, no more. Fifteen minutes later, his nose twitched and he trudged over to his lunch. He started with an appetizer of raspberries on the branch.

"Good job," Vern told Vignette.

"Just glad he's better."

"Wow." Decker was daunted. "I can see why Mr. Penny was a supporter."

Vignette's smile was in full wattage. "Now you understand why I care so much. It's for Cody and Tiki and all the animals here. They can't talk, so I talk for them."

"You seem to be a good interpreter," Decker said.

Vignette smiled. "How about a tour, now that Cody's been taken care of."

"Sure."

She turned to Vern. "Keep an eye on our fellah. If he becomes agitated again, we'll do it officially and call in the vet."

"I'll do just that, Vignette."

"This way," she told Decker. They walked a few moments in silence. "So you really don't know anything more about Mr. Penny's will?"

"I told you all I know."

"I know I seem greedy, but running a nonprofit is like the jungle. Only the strong survive. If you're timid, you either die of starvation or you're eaten alive."

As they continued to stroll, Vignette pointed out the different cages and enclosures, giving Decker a personal story of each animal: how it was obtained, how the environment was maximized for survival, how the diets were individualized, and finally the cost of maintaining the animal. "We barely manage on a shoestring budget. We depend on people like Mr. Penny for support."

"How much support did he supply?"

"A lot of our operating costs came from his generosity." She stopped in front of a tiger pen. "Tiki's in the back of the enclosure, protected in her own cage. It's going to take a while before she'll be allowed to roam in the enclosure. We have to make sure that Juno and Bigfoot will accept her."

"You've got a male and a female tiger?"

Vignette nodded.

"How is Tiki doing?"

"All I can tell you is that she's been eating. That's good."

"Have you had a chance to examine her?"

"The vet comes this Friday."

"So you don't know if she's hurt or anything?"

"No." Vignette turned to Decker. "Why would she be hurt?"

"She was left alone in the apartment for a while. There were all sorts of broken glass and sharp objects on the floor."

"Oh, I see what you're getting at. So far as I can tell, she's fine. But I have no idea what she ingested and what she looks like internally." They stared at the two tigers in the enclosures. "Gorgeous animals."

"Where did these two come from?"

"A for-profit zoo that went under and another mail-order fiasco. We're lucky that these two get along."

"Are you going to breed them?"

"Not a chance. Like I said, we don't know the genetics, and the last thing we want are unstable and unhealthy lines. All the males have been neutered and the girls have been spayed."

They moved on. Decker said, "I know from my reading that Global Earth Sanctuary originally started out in the Santa Clarita Valley area. Why'd you move?"

"This place is like twenty times bigger than the old one in Santa Clarita. Fern was quite the visionary. Man, that was crazy when we moved! It took forever to transport all the animals. We had to do it at night for safety reasons."

"So does Global Earth own the land here?"

"Yep."

"Outright, or is it mortgaged?"

Vignette stopped walking. "Why?"

"Just trying to get an idea of costs. If it's just paying to maintain all the animals, that's bad enough. But if you have a mortgage, wow, that's really hard."

"Tell me about it. Seen enough?"

"Whatever you want."

"I'm a little cold. Let's go back." The woman reversed directions, and the two of them started down the trails.

Decker said, "I'm just wondering how Fern got the money to pay for all of this."

"I don't know." Vignette bit her lip. "But I do know you're asking questions out of more than just plain curiosity."

"Did Penny help Global Earth buy the land?"

"The first time I ever talked to Penny was when he called up and asked about tiger cubs. If he had contact with the organization before that, I don't know about it. Like I told you, after Fern died, Allan Gray worked as the acting head of Global Earth."

"The vet who took off for Alaska to study grizzlies."

"Yes. He left behind a real mess. Records were incomplete and indecipherable. I could have reached him and asked questions. But it was easier to just start from scratch. I took this job out of love for the animals, not because I was particularly good at leading organizations."

Decker nodded. "So you don't have any old records or . . ."

Again, Vignette stopped. "Why are you asking me all these questions?"

"There's no good way to tell you this, Vignette." A pause. "Hobart Penny didn't die a natural death. He was murdered."

The eyes widened and the color drained from her cheeks, which had been red because of the cold. *"Murdered?"*

"Yes. That's why the police are involved. It's not just because of an errant tiger."

"Oh my God!" She brought her gloves to her cheeks in a silent scream. "What *happened?*"

"Investigation is ongoing. That's why I'm talking to you. Mr. Penny seemed to have been a recluse the last twenty-five years. You've had recent contact with him. Anything you can tell me about him would be very helpful."

"Oh my God!" She stared at Decker. "And here I am talking about a will. You must be looking at me as a suspect!"

"Right now all I'm just trying to do is get some facts."

"I had absolutely nothing to do with his murder! I just want you to know that."

Decker nodded. "Would you mind answering a few more questions?"

"Not at all."

"You said the last time you saw Penny was three or four days ago, when you gave Tiki her shots?"

"Yeah, that's— How was he murdered?"

Decker rubbed his hands and ignored the question. "My homicide detectives and I have had a lot of discussion about the crime. One question keeps coming up. How could anyone get past a loose tiger?"

"Tiki wasn't chained up?"

"Oh . . . so when you came over to visit, Penny chained her up?" Decker asked.

"At first, she was chained up . . . for sure." Vignette thought a moment. "Slowly we started to trust each other until we both felt comfortable being around each other. Tiki's a very gentle soul. Not much of the wild in her."

"So she got used to your presence?"

"Yeah, pretty quickly, too. We used to knock her out before I gave her the shots so she wouldn't realize that someone was hurting her. You always take a chance when you knock a big animal out. Even if they remain healthy, when an animal comes out of anesthesia, it's always unpredictable." Again Vignette seemed lost in thought. "Hobart had a collapsible cage in the closet. Maybe Tiki was caged when the murderer came in."

"We didn't find a cage in the apartment. She did have about a six-foot-long chain around her neck."

"The chain makes sense." A pause. "Maybe Penny got rid of the cage. Initially we used it so I could give Tiki her shots. Then she got wise to us—that the cage meant shots and she wouldn't go in. That's when we started to knock her out with drugs." Vignette sighed. "She never held it against me. She's just a real nice tiger."

"But she's still a tiger."

"Yes, of course. But even among wild animals, there are different dispositions." She hesitated. "Was it a robbery? He didn't keep a lot of stuff in his apartment."

"From our observations, I would agree with you."

"Who on earth would want to hurt an old man?"

"I don't know that, either."

"Talk about wild animals." The woman shook her head with woe. "I'll take my beasts over your beasts any day of the year."

Chapter Ten

The decent seemed faster than the ascent: standard in travel as well as in life. Decker hardly remembered driving down the mountain, each twist of the wheel on autopilot as his brain fired one idea after another, none of which would explain why Global Earth Sanctuary had anything to do with Hobart Penny's death. As soon as the car hit the bottom of the foothills, his Bluetooth sprang to life.

Marge's voice. "I've been trying to reach you for the last half hour. Where were you?"

"Out of cellular reach," Decker told her. "What's up?"

"Hobart had an interesting past, more than the usual sex, drugs, and rock and roll. It seems our guy liked to go to sex clubs all over the country, dressed up like a tiger and screw women from behind."

Oliver added, "Sometimes it was a lion or a leopard . . . just for variety's sake."

Decker glanced at Gabe. The boy had his head tilted back with his eyes closed. He appeared to be lost in his music. "Who told you this?"

"The ex," Oliver said.

"And you believe her?"

Marge said, "We found the snapshots in a few left-over boxes in the storage wing of Sabrina Talbot's house."

"Storage wing?"

"Yep. Her house is big enough for an entire storage wing. The bigger question is why she kept the pictures. She certainly didn't need them for blackmail. Sabrina Talbot is filthy rich."

"Filthy, filthy rich," Oliver added.

Marge said, "Sabrina told us that in the recesses of Hobart's mind, he actually thought he was a tiger in a man's body. Sabrina said it got to the point that when they screwed, he used to claw and bite her on the neck."

Oliver said, "Then she came across pictures of Hobart fucking young girls, all of them in tiger masks. Even with that, it still took her a year to make the divorce final."

Decker shot a quick look at Gabe. The teen still had his eyes closed but was doing something to the volume of his iPhone. Decker said, "Turn that thing up."

"What thing?" Marge asked.

"I'm not talking to you, I'm talking to Gabe."

Gabe opened his eyes, a slow smile spread on his face. "Excuse me?"

"What's *Gabe* doing with you?" Marge asked.

"I'll explain later." To the boy, Decker said, "Stop eavesdropping."

"You're talking very loud."

Decker said, "Let me call you back."

Marge said, "When will you be back at the station house?"

"About an hour."

"Okay. We'll see you then."

Decker was about to sign off. Then he said, "How old were the pictures?"

"Penny looked to be in his fifties. The pictures were Polaroids. 'Memba them?"

"I do. I'll talk to you later."

"You never told me what Gabe is doing there with you."

"Sorry you're breaking up." Decker cut the connection.

Gabe took out his earbuds. "What're Polaroids?"

"Not important."

"I can look it up on my iPhone."

Decker said, "Way back in the Pleistocene era, before mankind as we know it went digital, you took pictures with film."

"I know that." Gabe was offended.

"Polaroid camera delivery system was a way to instantly print out pictures. It meant you didn't have to take your rolls of film into the drugstore to have them processed and turned into pictures, which usually took around a week. Later they came up with photo shops that could turn your film around in twenty-four hours. And then those went out when digital went in. But Polaroids were good because of privacy: no one would see your pictures unless you showed them around."

"Ah. So you could take like porno shots and not be worried about it."

"Yes, you could and yes, people did." Decker smiled. "You can always tell what new technology is going to take hold. If it has potential for pornography, it's a winner."

Gabe smiled. "I know I shouldn't have been listening, but if you want to find out about sex clubs, you should talk to Chris."

"It was over thirty years ago. Chris was around six."

"So you're saying that a kinky old man hasn't been to a sex club in thirty years?"

THE BEAST · 123

"He was almost ninety when he was murdered."

"So? He was rich, and there's Viagra. You should see some of the relics that my dad caters to." When Decker didn't answer, Gabe said, "Besides, my dad owes you."

"He doesn't owe me."

"He dumped me on you and Rina."

"You got a bullet in your ribs under my watch. I owe him."

"That's only because you were doing him a favor in the first place."

"Maybe at first, I was doing him a favor. Maybe now, he's doing me the favor." Decker gave him a gentle whack on the back of his head. "I appreciate your thoughts. They're good ones."

"I'm just sayin' . . ." The car was quiet. "Do you want to hear what Everett James had to say about Global Earth Sanctuary?"

A quick glance to the boy. "You're just full of information."

"With a father like Chris, you learn to listen a lot."

"You're just a little ole fly on the wall, aren't you?" Decker laughed. "What did you and Everett James talk about?"

"He does the accounting for the sanctuary pro bono. Ninety-nine percent of what we talked about was accounting. Basically, he told me how much money it takes to maintain the animals. When he heard about the old guy's death, Hobart Penny, right?"

"That is correct."

"Penny is an odd name for a gazillionaire."

"Irony abounds."

Gabe smiled again. "Everett did say that it was gonna be hard to keep the place going without Penny's checks. Even with Penny's donations, the place would get behind in their payments."

"Payments to whom?"

"He didn't specify, but he did say that the sanctuary got some of the food gratis: the meat in particular. You know, hamburger beyond the expiration date but probably still good to use. But even so, tigers and lions had big appetites. Also, many animals had very specific dietary needs. And then there were all the supplements and vet care. He asked me if I wanted to make a donation."

"That was inappropriate. I hope you didn't give him anything."

"I had twenty bucks in my wallet. I gave it to him."

"I'll pay you back."

"That's not the point. I happen to actually work an adult job. But he didn't know that. He did know I was seventeen. How many kids my age have enough pocket change to give away to charity? Sounds like the place is hard up."

Consistent with Vignette harping away on a will. "Did Everett mention anything about a mortgage on the property?"

"I don't remember him talking about that, but I kinda tuned him out when he talked numbers."

"What do you mean by numbers?"

"I dunno. How much they had to spend on food versus care versus this or that. It felt like one big math word problem. I nodded and smiled a lot."

"Did you pick up any hint that something funny might be going on, like the place was cooking the books?"

Gabe said, "What do you mean 'cooking the books'?"

Decker slowed down. "'Cooking the books' means impropriety in the accounting practices. Did he mention anything about embezzlement or fraud?"

"Nah, nothing like that." Gabe's face was one of concentration. "Everett said Penny's money was important. He said that Global Earth often had to take out short loans to buy food and medicine for the animals until miracle money came in. A specific type of loan . . . what did he call it?"

"A bridge loan?"

"Yeah, that's it. I'm impressed."

"What kind of miracle money is he talking about?"

"Money from unexpected donors."

"Did he mention names?"

"Well, Penny, of course. Sometimes it was a foundation or organization. Not PETA. He specifically told me that PETA didn't like that Global Earth kept the animals in enclosures. Sorry . . . I don't remember. Next time I'll take notes."

Again, Decker gently whacked him on the back of his head.

"Can I come back to the station house with you?"

"No."

"I'm bored."

"Then go back to New York." When Gabe turned sullen, Decker said, "If I get a phone call from an irate Persian mother, I'm not going to be happy."

"For Chrissakes, we're just friends okay? We went through a trauma together. We've got a bond that no one else understands. We're just gonna talk!"

"Do you also have a bridge to sell me?" Gabe crossed his arms across his chest and stared out the window. Decker said, "Guess I'm not so cool after all."

The boy fiddled with his iPhone and pretended not to hear.

Decker continued speaking. "Gabriel, listen to me. I know it's hard for you. I know you care for this girl.

I don't doubt your feelings. But Yasmine is a minor, and her parents don't want you around. You've got to respect their wishes until she's eighteen. That, my boy, is the long and the short of it."

The kid huffed.

Decker said, "You've got to call her up. You can tell her you love her, because you do. But you also need to tell her that it's not a good idea to get together until she's older. And then go back to New York and concentrate on your studies and let her concentrate on her studies."

"We're just going to talk. What's the crime in that?"

"Gabe—"

"Fine. Okay. You're right. I'll do everything you say, okay. Just let me do it in person."

"That's a mistake, son."

"She *asked* to see me, Peter. I can't tell her no. Yasmine was involved in that sadistic mess because of me. And she stood by me when she could have run away from those thugs. She put her own safety at risk. Yes, I love her, but I also prize loyalty and commitment: two things that neither of my parents understands. I know that the trial is over, but that doesn't mean that all the shit suddenly evaporates."

"I'm not making the rules, Gabe. I'm just telling you that it's going to be bad if you're caught. And I don't want to have to deal with it."

"Peter, we're just going to play catch-up. I swear that's it."

Decker sighed. "Where are you two lovebirds planning on meeting?"

"At the Beverly Hills library," he lied. "There's a little place right next door. We're just gonna get a cup of coffee. That's it."

"How long is this little tryst scheduled to last?"

"Around an hour . . . maybe a little bit more."

"When and what time?"

"Sunday around three."

"What excuse is she giving her parents?"

"That she's doing work in the library. They live real close. She does work there all the time." When Decker gave him a sour look, he said, "I swear I'll be back at the house by eight at the latest, and that's allowing for an hour travel time. Rina's taking me shopping on Tuesday morning, and then I'm leaving for New York on the red-eye. It'll end because of distance anyway, unless she comes to New York. There's certainly no reason for me to ever come back to L.A."

Decker was quiet for a moment. "I suppose that's true."

"I didn't mean it like that," Gabe said. "I mean I love you guys and all that stuff. But you two go back east all the time to see your real kids and I can always see you then."

"My real kids?"

"You know what I'm saying."

"I understand that Los Angeles isn't filled with happy memories for you. I'm not offended. But I want you to know that I wouldn't be wasting my breath—which at my age is a precious commodity—if I didn't consider you my real kid."

"I know you care. I'm sorry if I sound unappreciative."

"No apology necessary. Just saying that you always have a home with us."

"I know. And I'm really grateful."

"Good to hear. So you'll promise me one thing."

"What?"

"When you play the Music Center, you'll get us free tickets."

Gabe grinned. "I will be delighted to get you front row seats, even if I have to pay for them myself. I'll even arrange for backstage passes."

"You do that then we're square."

"That's gonna happen, you know . . . that I'm gonna play all the biggies like Music Center and Carnegie Hall and all the top venues in Europe and Asia. I've already chosen what conductors I want to work with, what sonatas and concertos I'm gonna play with each one and what I'm gonna do for encores."

Decker nodded and tried to stifle a smile.

"It's gonna happen."

"I don't doubt it, Gabe. You've got the talent."

"I've got the talent, I've got the drive, and I practice more than anyone else at my school. I'm *possessed.*" He patted Decker's back. "Like someone else when he's *working.*"

"Don't blame this on me. I refuse to take responsibility." A pause. "I do have a question for you. What are you going to wear to the Grammys?"

"One-button tux over a black tee and bright red lizard cowboy boots."

"Bright red lizard cowboy boots." He nodded.

"Real sick, huh?" A pause. "I think I'll wear my glasses instead of contacts, though. It's who I am."

"Indeed." Decker held back a smile. "Pretty sharp outfit."

"My dad's a first-class bastard, but a spiffy dresser. I guess it's just genetic."

Chapter Eleven

While flipping through the Polaroids, Decker said, "Interesting . . . and a bit voyeuristic . . ." He threw the pictures on the desk. "But the man was eighty-nine and a recluse. Maybe he hadn't given up his vices, but with his wealth and age, I doubt if he went out to find them."

"Escort services?" Oliver tried out.

"Yeah, sure, go ahead. Maybe he was shot by a call girl."

"It's happened before," Marge said. "She saw that she was dealing with an old man and decided to rob the place."

"First of all, he was not only shot but someone also bashed his head in. That's personal. Secondly, did you see anything of value there?"

Oliver said, "Maybe the assailant was looking for something specific. When he found it, he took it and left."

"Only problem with that, he—or she—had to get past the tiger first," Decker said.

"Tiki was dragging around chain," Marge said. "Stands to reason that she was chained up at one point. Maybe Penny was expecting a call girl."

Decker said, "If you like a call girl theory, find a call girl."

"Well, what theory do you like?"

"I'm still thinking about Vignette Garrison. She knew him, she's been at the place, and she had a rapport with the tiger. And she kept asking about the will until I told her that Penny was murdered."

"How'd she react?"

"Appropriately shocked. But in L.A., everyone's an actor."

Oliver said. "What did you learn about Global Earth?"

"They were running the place on a shoestring budget."

"Isn't that par for the course with nonprofits?" Marge said.

"Yep." Decker thought about his visit. "But I do have a few problems with Vignette Garrison being a murderer. For starts, she seemed sincere. Secondly, it wouldn't make sense to shoot the goose laying the golden eggs. Penny's money was the main reason that the organization stayed afloat."

"Now that he's gone, is the place going under?" Oliver asked.

"They have some support from other people and organizations, but Penny was the biggest donor."

"How do you know that?" Marge asked.

Decker smoothed his mustache. "From the accountant."

"You talked to Global Earth's accountant."

"It's secondhand information."

Oliver said, "Where'd you get the secondhand information?"

"I took Gabriel with me this morning," Decker said. "He was bored and asked to go. After the ordeal of the trial, I wanted to do something nice for him. He took a tour of the place while I was with Vignette. His tour guide was loquacious and told Gabe that he did the accounting for Global Earth gratis."

"So all this information is via Gabriel?" Marge asked.

Decker nodded. "He's credible. It seems to me that Hobart Penny was worth more to the organization alive than dead."

"Unless he left them a chunk of his estate in the will," Oliver said.

"If he did that, Darius Penny would know about it," Marge said.

"What do you think about him? Darius Penny?" Decker said.

"Seemed on the level. Do you doubt him?"

"No reason, but you know how it is. You want a lead, follow the money. He's coming out for the funeral on Monday, correct?"

"That's what he told me. We were planning to interview him in person then, unless you have an overriding reason to call him now. I'm working on setting up appointments with Darius and his sister after the funeral."

"We can wait until Monday, unless something comes up." Decker checked his watch. Four o'clock—seven back east. Darius was probably gone anyway. "How old are the kids?"

"Darius is fifty-five, Graciela is fifty-eight," Oliver said.

Decker said, "Still young enough where half a billion dollars would make a difference, even if they were wealthy in their own right."

Marge said, "Sabrina Talbot is coming in for the funeral as well."

"A family reunion," Decker said. "Ducky. And we have no reason to doubt Darius's veracity when it comes to his father?"

Marge simply shrugged. "You mean like a secret will? Isn't everything computerized nowadays?"

Decker said, "Yeah, if there's another will, some attorney has a copy of it." He began to sort through pink slips. "Find out anything at all from canvassing?"

Oliver said, "The body was a few days old before we got called in. It's hard enough to get people to remember what they did an hour ago let alone a couple of days."

"You're telling me a man was killed in his apartment, leaving behind an agitated tiger, and none of the neighbors saw or heard anything?"

Marge said, "We can go back and canvass again."

"Yeah, do that."

"It's okay with me. I wanted to check the video monitors in the area anyway. The old man's apartment didn't have any, but there are some neighboring structures and a few businesses. Maybe something was caught on camera."

"Good." Winter days were short. Sunlight was fading fast. Decker said, "You should go now if you're going to hunt around for cameras. Did you ever find something that matched the blunt force trauma on his forehead?"

Oliver said, "Nothing that I've bagged."

Decker said, "Take another look at the apartment. Hopefully it's no longer a health hazard. SID was there this morning. Go over and see what's left."

Oliver nodded. "Sure. But first I need a cup of coffee."

"I hear you on that one, bro," Marge said. "Artificial stimulants . . . don't you just love 'em."

No video cameras on either side of the apartment building, but across the street was a convenience market and a techie/computer shop, both with security cameras perched over the doors. The market was manned by a Korean couple in their sixties. It was a tiny alcove of a place stuffed with cans and boxes, most of them on shelves gathering layers of dust. There was a small produce section and a dairy case. The man and woman were eager to please. Marge felt bad and bought an apple. Oliver felt bad and bought a banana. The purchases made them cooperative. They offered up the security tapes, but neither was much of a conversationalist. When Oliver showed the couple a picture of Hobart Penny, they gesticulated ignorance.

The computer store was not much more than a storage closet crammed with shelving and overflowing with parts of broken laptops, tablets, and phones.

The guy behind the counter was in his thirties with a scrawny goatee and short-cropped hair. His glasses were thick, but the eyes behind them were sharp and bright blue. He wore a gray, long-sleeved T-shirt, jeans, and combat boots. He shook his head when he saw Penny, but that didn't mean he didn't have something to say. "That's the old guy with the tiger who was murdered? I mean the tiger wasn't murdered, but the old guy was, right?"

"That's who we're investigating." Oliver gave the man his card. "So the old guy never came here?"

"First of all, no one over forty comes in here. I mean you guys are probably over forty, but you're not here for anything to do with technology. I build computers, tablets, and smartphones. Most people just go into an Apple store and get ripped off. I could put something together that's Mac compatible and about a third the price."

"I've got a dial-up," Oliver said.

"See what I'm saying about people over forty."

"So you never saw the guy in the neighborhood?" Marge asked.

"Nope. But I was aware about the tiger . . . or the possibility of a tiger."

"Okay." Marge took out her notebook. "I didn't catch your name."

"I didn't give it to you." Marge waited. "Fred Blues. Fred as in Alfred; blues as in cerulean hues. I have customers from the apartment buildings around here. More than one of them told me they thought that someone was keeping a wild animal in the building."

Oliver said, "We never got any calls."

"Because no one saw anything and the noises weren't consistent. But I do know that a few of them complained to the manager—who obviously didn't do anything."

"George Paxton?"

"That's the guy."

Marge said, "Did any of them say who owned the animal?"

"Just that the noises were coming from the third floor. One of my customers said she knew it was the old man but couldn't prove it. She even went over to the place. When the old guy finally let her in, she couldn't find the animal but she could smell it."

Marge held up a finger. "She went inside his apartment?"

"Yep."

"And she didn't notice a tiger?"

"That's what she said."

"Did she check both the living room and the bedroom?"

"No idea," Blues told them. "I'm just saying what she told me."

"Could we have her name and number?"

"Uh . . . I have a privacy thing. How about if I call her up for you?"

"That's fine," Oliver said. "We'll wait."

"It might take me a while to find the invoice with her phone number."

"No problem," Marge said. "While you're looking for the number, could we grab the tape from your security camera. Maybe it caught something that might help us out."

"Sure. I got a ladder in the back."

"That would be great."

Blues came back, toting a step stool under his arm. "It's only a few risers, but you guys are tall enough."

Oliver thanked him and went outside with Marge. It only took a few minutes to retrieve the camera. When they came back, Blues was hanging up the phone.

"Her name is Masey Roberts." He wrote down a phone number and the apartment number. "She's more than happy to talk to you."

"Thank you. Do you mind if we take the tape with us?"

"Nah, go ahead. Just let me know if you find any-thing juicy on it. Maybe I can sell it to the tabloids. In this economy, everyone needs a few extra bucks."

The apartments were actually quite spacious when devoid of wild animals and blood and guts. Masey Roberts's place had the same open floor plan as Penny's with one bedroom and one bathroom. Shelving units lined the wall of her living space, which was deco-rated with fresh and dried flowers, silver framed pho-tographs, and lots of candles: the trifecta of girly stuff. She had a brown leather couch, a couple of comfy chairs, a dinette table for four opposite a flat-screen mounted on the wall.

The young woman was in her mid- to late twenties with curly shoulder-length hair that framed a long face. Pale complexion, round brown eyes, pixie features. She wore black running pants and a long-sleeved hoodie over a black T-shirt. Fuzzy slippers were on her feet. She was a wisp of a woman, but feisty.

She paced as she spoke. "I *knew* something was going on. I must have called the freakin' manager six times!"

"What did the manager say to you?" Marge asked.

"That I was imagining things and that he personally checked out the apartment twice. It was all in my head!

Paxton is a freakin' prick! We're all lucky that the tiger didn't escape and do real bad stuff."

"The guy across the street told us you actually visited Penny," Oliver said.

"Yeah, not that it did any good." Masey stopped pacing and sat down. "I knew something was going on. So did others, but no one had the balls to face the old man."

"Why's that?" Marge asked. "At eighty-nine, he would seem pretty harmless."

"It wasn't the old man, it was the strange noises," Masey said. "We didn't know what the hell we were dealing with. Only that it was spooky. When I finally summoned up my courage to knock on the door, the old man took forever to open up."

"Did he invite you in?"

"Yeah, he did." A pause. "I sat down on his couch. It was awkward. I finally just spit it out. I asked him if he had any exotic pets."

"And?" Marge asked.

"He said no. Then he asked me why would I think that?"

"And you said?"

"I said that I heard noises coming from his apartment. And I wasn't the only one. There were at least four or five people who heard stuff."

"And he said?"

"He said that was strange. Maybe it was the TV. Freakin' liar."

"I assume you looked around the place," Oliver said.

"He didn't invite me to take a tour, but it's a small place. Kind of hard to hide a tiger."

"Did you go inside the bathroom?" Marge asked.

"Yeah, I asked to use the bathroom. No tiger."

"What about the bedroom?"

"I didn't go inside, but the door was open," Masey said. "There was no animal in sight. But the place smelled like a zoo. Maybe the tiger was hidden in a closet or a trapdoor or something."

Marge nodded as she wrote. "How long did you talk to Mr. Penny?"

"About ten minutes."

"Ever have any dealing with him again?"

"Nope. I never saw him again. If the guy left the apartment, I never ran into him."

Marge said, "What about deliveries?"

"Yeah, I saw people come to his door."

"From where?" Oliver asked.

"Local markets mostly. FedEx came a couple of times. Once he got a delivery from the cleaners." She shrugged. "It's not like I was *spying* on him. It's just that when you hear weird stuff coming out the door, you get curious."

"Any visitors ever come in?" Marge asked.

"You mean the woman?"

"Yeah," Oliver said. "Tell me about her."

"I saw her two or three times. She had blond hair and wore stilettos." Masey smiled. "She looked like a classy hooker. But then again, Penny was really old. But you never know. I read in the papers that he was a gazillionaire. Wow, that's a shock. His apartment was like . . . nothing."

"What was in it?" Oliver asked.

"It was practically bare: an old couch and a chair in the living room. He came to the door with a walker, so maybe he needed floor space so he could get around."

Marge nodded but was puzzled. Neither one of them had seen a walker when they surveyed the crime scene. It was clear that they had missed some things, including where the old man could hide a tiger. "Is there anything else you'd like to add?"

Masey said, "When I stood up to leave, I asked him if he needed anything. He said thanks but no thanks. He said he was an old guy and that at this stage, he had everything he needed." She paused. "It was weird. The way he said it—like he was just waiting to clock out."

Chapter Twelve

A half mile away from Penny's apartment, Marge found a local coffee shop, one of the valiant few left standing, where she and Oliver ordered burgers and coffee. Not much chitchat before the food arrived. Afterward, refreshed with protein and grease, Marge felt her brain cells bloom. She glanced at the wall clock. It was already past eight. "Long day."

"Yeah, I'm ready to pack it in, but I'm betting that you want to go over the tapes at the station house."

"I was thinking that we'll view the tapes after we go over the crime scene." Marge leaned forward. "Masey Roberts was in Penny's apartment and didn't see the tiger. You just can't stow away a big cat like that. Plus, we didn't find a cage or a walker. There has to be a hidden closet or a trapdoor—"

"He was on the third floor, Marge."

"There must be a secret compartment somewhere."

"Probably."

"And this doesn't intrigue you?"

"Not after working for ten hours straight." But Oliver's mind was still reeling. "Even if there was a trapdoor or closet in the apartment, how do you get a tiger to refrain from roaring? Masey talked to Penny for a least a couple of minutes."

"Maybe the tiger was drugged. Didn't Masey say that it took a while for him to answer the door?"

"It takes more than a minute for a tranquilizer to kick in."

"That's what I'm saying, Scott. There's a hidden compartment and it's probably soundproof." Marge fiddled with a sugar package. "If I were him and wanted to hide a tiger, I'd rent one of the adjacent apartments and put a secret door between the two living spaces."

Oliver said, "Paxton never said anything about him renting two apartments."

"Maybe Paxton knew about the tiger and the second apartment, and Hobart was paying him off to keep his mouth shut. A second apartment would help explain a lot of things. And we were going to take a second look at the crime scene anyway."

"But I also remember saying that I'm not crossing the threshold unless the place has been cleaned up."

"If SID was there, I'm sure it's not as bad as when we first saw it." Marge finished her coffee and wiped her mouth on a napkin. "You don't have to go but—"

"I *hate* when you do that."

"Do what?"

"Say I don't *have* to go. If you're going, I *have* to go. Because if you find something important and I wasn't there, I'll look like a doofus."

"You know I always share the credit with you."

"I don't care about the credit," Oliver sulked.

"Then why mention it?"

"The truth is we still have a murderer on the loose. I wouldn't want to be alone in that apartment in this situation. I don't want you alone."

"And that's precisely why I always say you don't have to go with me to the crime scene, Oliver. It makes me feel self-righteous, but I know the truth. You're too good a cop to ever take me up on it."

George Paxton, the apartment manager, had gone AWOL. He was not answering his phone, so Oliver left names and numbers on the voice mail. Since they had legal access only to Penny's apartment, the two detectives had no choice but to revisit the grisly scenario. Yellow tape was still in place across the door. Marge peeled off the tape at one end, opened the door, and then replaced it back across the doorframe.

The fecal matter had been removed, but the stench lingered on. The furniture and appliances had been rerighted, and someone had cleaned up the decaying meat and food. There was more room to walk, but garbage still littered the floor. Fingerprint dust had darkened the walls slate gray. Neat little squares of bloodstained material had been taken from the couch and the chair. There was also fabric excised from the blood-soaked mattress in the bedroom. The electricity was still on, but who knew how long that would last?

Marge fished out her tablet from her oversize bag and pulled up a grid of ghastly pictures from the original crime scene. "Okay, the fridge was here when we came in . . ." She pointed to a spot. "And the table was here . . . the chairs were there."

Oliver looked over her shoulder. "Wow, what a mess! You know it still stinks in here. Like they forgot a pile somewhere."

"Yeah, it's pretty rank." She turned to him. "I'll take the living room, you can take the bedroom."

"Thanks. Maybe the bedroom will smell better." Oliver looked around. "Can I see the pictures from the original scene?"

"Yeah, sure." She showed them to him. "You can see here that Penny's head was on the pillow, canted to the left side."

"But he had a bullet wound in the back."

"Maybe it was a two-person attack—one basher, one shooter." Marge thought a moment. "Definitely a lot of force to take an old man out."

"Yeah, but it isn't overkill," Oliver said. "Just one shot and a bash to the head."

"I agree. It wasn't a rage killing."

"The bash came first. The guy was still moving, so someone shot him in the back."

"If you bash the front of the head first, the guy falls backward, which was how we found him. But then how do you pull off the shot in the back?" Marge shrugged. "I'd say it's two people going at it at the same time. Sounds like the motive was a robbery rather than someone wanting the old man out of the way." Marge looked around. "And for the umpteenth time, where was the tiger?"

Oliver said, "This isn't a corner unit. Our secret door could be in the bedroom or the living room connecting to a unit on either side. And it's possible that he rented the apartment under or over him. We could be looking for a trapdoor or something in the ceiling, although it would be hard for an old man to lead an animal up and down a ladder."

"Not hard for a tiger to climb, Oliver. They're cats. How many times as a patrol officer were you called down to get kitty out of a tree?"

"Those are house cats. Tigers are big guys."

"That's how big cats kill, Scotty. They sit in a tree and jump on your back and bite your neck until you bleed out."

"Lovely. Thanks for sharing."

"That's why I don't go biking in the Santa Monica Hills anymore. I once had a personal encounter with a mountain lion. He looked at me and I looked at him and we both decided to leave it for another day."

"You never told me that."

"It was traumatic. I put it in the back of my mind and forgot about it. Except obviously I didn't."

Oliver took out a face mask. "That must have been scary . . . meeting a mountain lion like that."

"That it was. Mountain lions love to chase bicycles, so as soon as I saw him, I stopped dead in my tracks and pulled out my gun. Then I quietly backed away, and as soon as he was out of sight, I took off as fast as I could. I've gone dead heat with many a bad guy, Oliver, but Mr. Puma by far had the biggest teeth . . . that is, until I met Tiki. I have nothing against wild cats. It's just that I like to have a considerable distance between us." She slipped on her face mask. "Ready to do this?"

Oliver rolled his eyes. "Let's."

At ten in the evening, Marge was surprised to see that Decker's office door was still open. She knocked on the frame. Decker looked up and motioned them in.

"Got a moment?" Oliver asked.

"Just finishing up my calls," Decker said. "What do you have?"

Marge said, "Some security camera tapes from businesses across the street from Penny's apartment. I doubt if they'll show something, but it wouldn't hurt to take a peek."

Decker checked his watch. "It's a little late to start watching hours of video."

"Yeah, it'll hold until morning."

Oliver whipped his head around. "Did I hear right?" He stuck his index finger in his ear and moved it around, as if something were blocked. "Did you actually say it'll hold until morning?"

Marge smiled. "I'll lock up the tapes and we'll view them tomorrow morning with fresh eyes."

"Sounds good," Decker said. "Anything else?"

"Yes, there is," Marge said. "Scott and I had a chance to interview a few people from the area." She sat down and gave him a brief recap. "It got us both to thinking. How do you hide a tiger in plain sight? The answer is you don't. So we started looking for hidden doors and compartments. We found a ceiling panel that leads to the apartment directly above Penny's place."

Oliver said, "We didn't go inside the space without authorization because we didn't know if all the apartments in the building were interconnected. There could have been someone living above Penny who might not take kindly to cops popping out their floorboards."

Marge said, "We tried calling the manager again to see if he'd let us inside or at least tell us that Penny didn't rent the apartment. Paxton is not answering his phone these days."

"Refresh my memory. Does Paxton live in the apartment complex?"

"No he does not. I'll find out where he lives tomorrow. What do you want us to do with that ceiling panel? We could knock it in and gain entry to the apartment above."

"Not without permission or a warrant," Decker said. "Did you find anything that would connect the two apartments—like a drop-down ladder or a rope ladder?"

"Nope," Oliver said.

"Could you see inside the above apartment once you took off the ceiling panel?"

"No," Marge said. "If Penny had a ladder to lead the tiger up and down, it might have come from above.

I did push on the panel, and it definitely wasn't nailed down. Still, I didn't want to displace it without an official okay."

"If we can't track down the manager and we're still not getting an answer by knocking on the door, we'll pull paper tomorrow and get inside."

"I think we're on to something," Marge said. "First of all, that would explain why people kept saying that the sounds jumped around. Maybe the tiger was living in more than one apartment. Secondly, the crime scene still smells. Both Scott and I felt that the odor was coming downward. Who knows what else was up there?"

"Or is still up there," Decker said. "Before we go opening panels, we should make sure that Penny wasn't also harboring other exotics."

"I'm with you on that one," Oliver said.

Decker said, "First, find out which apartments Penny was renting. If he was renting only his own, then we're back to square one. But if he was actually renting other apartments, then you're onto something. Then we'll have to call up Ryan Wilner and his crew. I want them to be with you before you open anything up."

Marge nodded solemnly. "For sure. I wouldn't like to open something up and have a Gaboon viper drop onto my face."

"You know that the stench could also be coming from something other than a wild animal," Oliver said.

"Another *body*?" Marge said.

"Why not?" Oliver said.

"The man was a recluse."

"Someone got to him, Margie," Decker said. "We all know that once you kill, it's a lot easier the second time around."

Chapter Thirteen

"First tape is from the security camera in front of the Korean market."

Oliver placed the cassette in the machine. He, Marge, and Decker stared at the TV monitor. Within seconds, a static and a grainy black-and-white scene appeared, the shot extending from the doorway of the grocery store to the curb. A sedan was parked in front—that much they could make out—but it was impossible to see the front or the back of any license plates. The cars also blocked the view into the street.

"What's this going to tell us?" Decker said. "You can't see the apartment building from the angle of the camera."

"Yeah, it's pretty useless." Oliver had taken off his suit jacket. His shirt was bright orange. It almost glowed in the dark.

Marge put on her glasses. Today she had dressed for comfort—wool slacks and a brown cashmere sweater that had begun to pill. "The start date is two days before we got the call about Penny, so we're in the right time frame."

The scene on the monitor appeared frozen. Decker said, "Why don't you advance it and see what pops?"

"No problem," Oliver said,

Marge said, "Once the car drives off, we should get a better view of the street."

Eventually they started seeing figures in the frames: a woman walking a dog passed by, two teenage boys going in and out of the store, three more people entering the market and coming back out. Pedestrians on the sidewalk. Two hours into the tape, a man in his thirties got into the sedan that was blocking the view of the street and drove away. The space was taken up immediately by a Volvo station wagon. A middle-aged woman came around the car and went inside the market. A moment later, she was out again, carrying a paper cup with a lid. She drove off.

More people in and out of the market, more cars in and out of the parking space.

Nightfall came. All was quiet. All was blurred. Without daylight, it was impossible to make out anything.

Day two at dawn: a day before the body was discovered.

The curb was devoid of cars, which allowed them to see vehicles passing by on the street. At 8:16, a Honda Accord parked in front of the camera.

More people.

More cars.

A whole lot of nothing.

At two-thirty in the afternoon, a red Ford Escort drove away from the spot, and thirty seconds later, the space was taken by a two-year-old light-colored Prius. Then a female figure appeared on the sidewalk in front of the market. She was garbed in a tight, dark sweater, skinny jeans, and fashion boots with stiletto heels. She was holding a duffel bag. She walked a few steps until she was out of the camera's range.

"Freeze," Decker said. "Did either of you notice a gym in the area?"

When both Marge and Oliver shook their heads, Decker said, "Is there a gym in any of the apartments nearby?"

Marge said, "Not in the complexes, no. They're pretty basic. It could be she has a treadmill in her apartment."

"Then why carry a duffel bag? C'mon, people. Does she look like she dressed for the gym?"

"I'll go backward and see if we can get a license plate off the Prius." Oliver reversed the tape frame by frame.

"Stop . . . right . . . there." Decker squinted, took his glasses off, put his glasses back on, then squinted again. "You can see the front of the car, and the frame for the license plate, but I can't make out the numbers."

Marge looked closely. "Five-*T-Y* . . . *R* or *A* . . . this could be enhanced if you think it's worth it. Or maybe the license will show better in the computer store's security tape."

"Just mark down the time and date of this frame so we can go back to it. Now forward it frame by frame. I want to get a good look at the girl."

Oliver complied. In slo-mo, the girl had light hair—assumedly blond—and was very curvy. Her age was impossible to tell—anywhere from twenties to fifties. "Masey Roberts remembers a blonde in stilettos of dubious intention going in and out of Penny's apartment. Don't you think the boots are a little S and M?"

"Definitely." Marge made a face. "But even if she is our service girl, she could be servicing anyone in the area."

Decker said, "See if you can get a copy of her face and take it to Masey Roberts. Maybe she can identify her as the blonde visiting Penny."

158 · FAYE KELLERMAN

"Will do." Marge chuckled. "Wow. Eighty-nine. I guess everything's possible with Viagra."

Decker said, "When you called me on the squawk box yesterday, Gabe could hear everything . . . which wasn't discreet, I admit. He told me his father's brothels patronized all sorts of men. Penny was definitely wealthy enough to afford home visits."

Marge said, "It could be nothing more than a sexy woman with a duffel bag, but if we can get a face ID on her, why not?"

Oliver said, "Maybe we can get a closer look at the license plate when she pulls the car away from the curb."

The tape kept rolling: more people in and out of the framework, but no one beyond the woman with the duffel caught Decker's attention. Two hours later, the blonde in the boots came back. Her hair was disheveled and she looked rushed and harried. She was dressed in exactly the same clothes, and she was carrying what looked like a foldable massage table, along with her purse. Oliver stopped the machine. "Where's the duffel?"

Marge said, "Where'd she get the massage table?"

"Very puzzling." Oliver inched the frames forward. They still couldn't get a decent read on her face, but they did get a partial on the plates.

THE BEAST · 159

Marge wrote the numbers down. "I'll check it out."

Additional viewing yielded nothing as interesting. Two hours later, the tape was up to the date and time of the police visit. Oliver ejected the cassette from the machine. He stood up and stretched, then checked his phone. "I called George Paxton at eight this morning. It's eleven, and he still hasn't called us back. It's beginning to piss me off."

"It feels like he's avoiding you," Decker said. "Call up a judge to see if you can't get a warrant to enter the apartment above Penny's unit. And then call back the manager and tell him you've requested a warrant. Maybe that'll light a fire under his butt."

Oliver rubbed his eyes. "Any judge in particular that you like?"

"Aaron Burger or Cassie Deluca."

Marge stood up. "Want some coffee before we continue with our movie night?"

"Sounds good. Let me check my messages and we'll meet back in a half hour."

Forty minutes later, they met back in the video room.

"Sorry I'm late," Oliver said. "Paxton finally called back. When I told him what I wanted, he began to hedge, claiming that Penny didn't rent the apartment above, but then he said that he really didn't know much about the tenants on the lease. Not that he'd tell me who was on the lease . . . privacy and all that jazz."

"He's right about that," Decker said.

"Yeah, unfortunately. When I asked him if he'd open up the apartment for me, just to make sure there are no leftover snakes or rats or anything, he flatly refused. He said if there's something stinky coming from the apartment, he'd open it up and get his only cleaning crew. I told him if he messed with the apartment and it turned out to be part of a crime scene, he'd be in shit's creek."

"What he'd say?" Marge said.

"We left it at that. The upshot: he won't go in, but he won't let me go in without a warrant. So I called up Judge Deluca. She wasn't keen on letting us in, either, since Hobart Penny isn't on the lease. But then I used the wild animal angle—public safety—and she relented. She agreed to let us enter the premises to check it out for beasts or any other public health hazards. If we don't find health issues, exotic animals, or a crime scene, we're not allowed to disturb the apartment."

"We can work with that."

"Yes, indeed we can. Deluca said to come by the courthouse at three and she'd have it ready for us."

"Good," Decker said. "Did you call animal control?"

"Yep. They'll meet us down there at four." He turned to Marge. "You're coming with me, right?"

Marge said, "I have to rearrange a couple of things, but I'll be there."

Decker said, "So let's finish up with the tape. I have a meeting in an hour."

"We can do this without you, Pete," Marge said.

"I've got a little time. Put in the security tape from the computer store. See if we can get a better angle on the duffel bag lady and her car."

Oliver said, "Why don't you give me the time of the lady's first appearance on the Korean market's security tape and I'll key up the same time on the computer store's tape." Once Marge gave him the information, Oliver clapped his hands together. "Okay, let's see what we got."

The computer store's tape showed only the hump of the Prius's hatchback: no license plate numbers. But they all spotted something else that was very interesting.

Another light-colored Prius.

The trio was suddenly perched at attention.

Decker said, "Which Prius belongs to Duffel Bag blonde in the boots?" It was a rhetorical question because all three were watching it for the first time. Nothing happened for five seconds, and then Duffel Bag came into view. Another ten seconds passed with Duffel Bag on the sidewalk in front of the two Priuses, tapping the toe of her boot. Then Duffel Bag was met by another babe: this one was a brunette. She wore a leather bomber jacket, skinny jeans, and stiletto dark boots. She carried another duffel bag as well as a massage table.

The two women did not embrace. They did not exchange words. They didn't even acknowledge each other.

But they did walk away together.

"Okay then," Oliver said. "Now we know where the massage table came from."

"Let's back it up," Marge said. "Maybe we can get the back license of one car or the front license of the other."

Oliver took the tape in reverse, and then advanced it frame by frame by frame. Massage Table Brunette had been the first one on the scene. The back of her car was not visible, which meant the license plate was out of the camera's range. But when Duffel Bag Blonde parked her car in front of the brunette's vehicle, the back license of the blonde's Prius was clearly visible. All three of them jotted down the number.

Decker said, "Speed it up. I want to see what's going on right before the cars pull away."

Oliver complied. Two hours later, according to the time on the tape, the blonde returned with the massage table and without the duffel bag. They watched the screen as Blonde put the massage table into the hatch. They could see Brunette's Prius from the front passenger door to the front bumper on the right side, but they couldn't make out any driver, even when the car left the curb and drove away, because Blonde's Prius was blocking the view. Blonde left about thirty seconds after Brunette.

Decker said, "That's frustrating."

"At least we got Blonde's license plate," Marge reminded him.

"Run it through and see what we're dealing with," Decker said. "There's something fishy about those two. Get back to me when you have information. Also, let me know when you have the warrant. I'm going to rearrange a couple of things. I want to be there when you guys open up the apartment."

"It's Friday," Marge pointed out. "We're bound to go past sundown."

Meaning the work would last into the start of Shabbos. On Fridays, Decker usually delegated evening work unless it was high profile. This was on the border. He said, "Thanks for being considerate. If it turns out to be nothing, I can probably make it home within ten minutes. If it turns out to be something, then you would have called me anyway." He stood up. "The way I see it: no harm, no foul."

Chapter Fourteen

A few clicks on the computer gave Marge what she needed. She pushed the print button and then went on to Google and Facebook, putting in the name she had received from the DMV. She printed those out as well. Her eyes swept across the squad room. Oliver was on the phone. She snapped her fingers until he looked up, then gave him the A-OK sign, and pointed to Decker's office.

The Loo was also on the phone. She gave him the computer printouts and sat across from his desk. He read the papers while carrying on a conversation. Finally, he hung up. "Casey's Massage and Escort?"

"According to the ads, they have professional masseurs and masseuses who work in the privacy of your home. The cars of choice are powder blue Priuses: the eco-friendly outcall service. Don't know if it's a legitimate operation or not. I'll run the name past vice. I've also called up Masey Roberts. We've arranged a meeting to see if this was the blonde that she saw going into Penny's apartment."

Decker nodded. "That would help. But we're still going to have to canvass the block and find out if Casey's gals were servicing anyone else. How many apartment units are in that single block?"

"A lot. But we'll do what we need to do," Marge answered.

Oliver walked into the office, and Marge brought him up-to-date. "Where is this establishment and why haven't I heard about it?"

Marge said, "It's on Saratoga Street, and I don't know why you aren't familiar with it. Seems like your kind of place. Want to rectify that misstep like right now?"

"Sure. Call them?"

"And ruin the element of surprise?" Marge made a mock gasp.

"Any thoughts on how we get them to divulge the names of their clients?"

"Tell them the truth," Decker said. "Say you're from homicide, not vice. That you have no interest in making their life difficult."

Marge said, "When we're done with Casey and friends, we can pick up the warrant for the apartment and meet Ryan Wilner at four at Penny's apartment."

"The two locations are in the opposite direction," Decker said. "I'll pick up the warrant. Let's all meet at four. Do you have Ryan Wilner's cell number?"

"I do." Marge wrote down the digits and gave the slip of paper to Decker. "We'll see you then, Rabbi."

"Casey's Massage and Escort." Oliver rubbed his hands together. "I think I'm gonna like this assignment."

"You might get frustrated, Oliver," Marge told him. "This could just be a case of look but don't touch."

The address placed Marge and Oliver in a two-story strip mall where over half the storefronts were vacant. Casey's Massage and Escort was on the bottom and sat between a chicken takeout on the right and an empty space on the left. No hours and days were posted anywhere. No blue Priuses sat in the parking lot. After the third knock with no response, Oliver jiggled the door handle of the offices of Casey's Massage and Escort and regarded the lock. "I could probably pop it with a credit card."

Marge said, "Could be the folk are out to lunch. Without an exigent cause, that would be breaking and entering."

"Looks pretty dark in there."

"How can you tell? The windows and door are completely covered."

Oliver said, "Are you sure you got the right address?"

Marge took out her BlackBerry. "Yes. This is the place. I suppose we have no choice but to call the number in the ad and ruin our surprise."

"Now that's a novel idea."

"Don't be smug." She read him the digits and Oliver punched them into his phone. A moment later, he cut the line. "Disconnected."

"It appears that the game is afoot." Marge ambled over to the chicken takeout next door. It smelled of salt, spice, and grease. The woman behind the counter was older, round, and Asian. With a furrowed brow, she regarded the detectives.

"Hello, ma'am. I'm Sergeant Dunn of the Los Angeles Police Department." She presented her badge, and the woman smiled. She stepped aside and pointed to the back room. "No, I'm not from the Health Department. Do you speak English?"

"Yes, yes. Up to code. Up to code. See."

"Do you know the people next door?" A blank look. "Casey's Massage . . . lots of ladies in boots."

"Ah . . . ladies." The woman nodded. "Eat breasts . . . baked, no fried. You want breast baked no fried? Real good."

Marge said, "Did they move out?" No response. "The ladies . . . gone?"

The woman shrugged.

Marge smiled. "Thank you very much."

"You want chicken?"

"Not right now, thanks." Marge smiled. "Maybe next time."

Oliver was on his cell. "I got a number of the leasing agent from the signs in the windows of the empty storefronts. Let's see where that leads." When the voice message kicked in, he left both their names and phone numbers. "Now what?"

"Well, we could sit and wait. Or we can pick up the warrant, since we seem to have some time. Save Decker a trip."

"I vote sit and wait."

"Why am I not surprised." Her cell rang and she checked the window. "Don't know the number." She punched the green button. "Sergeant Dunn." A pause. "Uh . . . yes . . . yes, we did call just a moment ago. Thank you for calling us back, Mr. Mahadi. We're currently in front of the building on Saratoga . . . yes, that's the address. We're investigating a tenant . . . or maybe a former tenant. Casey's Massage and Escort— No, sir, we are not from vice. We're from homicide . . . no, sir, we didn't find a body on your property.

Mr. Mahadi, do you have a phone number for the place
. . . yes, I have that one. We tried it and it's disconnected . . . you didn't know? We just tried it a few minutes ago . . . no, I have no idea. I was going to ask you
if you had any idea."

Oliver shrugged a "what's going on?" gesture.
Marge shrugged back.

"Mr. Mahadi, if you could come down to the address
on Saratoga and talk with us, it would be much simpler
to explain this in person than over the phone . . . a
half hour would be perfect. Do you have the keys to
Casey's— You do? If you could bring them . . . perfect.
I'll see you in a half hour. Thank you. Bye."

She turned to Oliver. "He's coming down in a half
hour with the keys."

"Want a cup of coffee? There's a Dunkin' Donuts
across the street."

"How about a chicken breast—baked not fried?"
She pointed to the takeout store. "I feel bad for the
lady. With the Casey clan gone, it seems she lost some
business."

"You get the chicken, I'll get some doughnuts and
coffee."

Oliver returned back fifteen minutes later with two
coffees and a box. "They had a special. I got a dozen."

"Trade you a cruller for a chicken leg."

"Deal." Oliver bit in. "Not so bad."

"No, actually, it's pretty good. And the place has an A rating." Marge relieved him of the box and picked out a glazed buttermilk. "Cops and doughnuts; we go together like Mom and apple pie. You know what this means."

"What?"

"I'll have to hit the gym doubly hard. I have no will-power anymore."

She finished off the doughnut and licked her fingers just as a black Mercedes pulled into the lot. The luxury car looked out of place: a yacht among rowboats. The driver was in his sixties, dressed in a black suit, white shirt, red tie, and patent leather oxford shoes. He had a full head of gray hair and sported a gray mustache. His eyebrows were silver and framed dark brown orbs. He was holding a key ring as he bounded toward them. "Anwar Mahadi. No one told me they move."

"Thanks for coming down on such short notice." Marge took out a notepad. "When was the last time they paid a rent check?"

"They were a month behind. Not too bad in this economy. I call up . . . say if you have a problem, call me and we make arrangements. If you don't call, I post notice. They tell me the check is coming."

"When was that?"

"Two weeks ago." He shook his head. "They never say something about moving."

"Maybe they didn't move," Marge said. "I haven't been inside the office yet."

"You say number is disconnected."

"They still could be doing business. Maybe they just got an unlisted number."

"One way to find out." Mahadi's eyes fell on Oliver. "What's in the box?"

"Doughnuts. Would you like one?"

"I don't eat lunch so why not I say." He took a sugar twist and granules dusted his hands. After a few bites, he threw it away and licked his fingers. "Good. Thank you." He knocked on the glass door, then pulled out the keys and opened the door.

It was dark inside, so Marge turned on the lights and Oliver opened the curtains.

The place hadn't been cleaned, but it was cleaned out. The space consisted of a waiting area and two offices. Not a speck of furniture anywhere, but there were cardboard boxes filled with garbage: lots of crumpled papers, solicitations, mailers, food wrappers, soda cans, and water bottles. The floor had gathered a thin layer of dust. "You say the last time you talked to someone was two weeks ago."

"About." Mahadi looked around. "I need to clean this up."

"Who did you talk to when you asked about the check?"

"Bruce Havert. Tall man in his fifties. Dyes his hair. I used to see him with black hair, then brown hair, then brown hair with gray roots. He has a very big chin. Wears sunglasses all the time. He and his wife or girl-friend . . . I never did know which one . . . they do the business with the ladies."

Oliver said, "The massage business."

"I tell them no funny business here. I'm a family man. They show me licenses . . . all the girls have licenses. Nothing bad. Just pretty ladies that give massage. Not even here they give massages. They go to houses. They pay their rent, no one complains, I'm happy."

Marge said, "How long have they been renting?"

"Almost one year. The lease was up for renewal. I was going to do them a favor and not raise rent. Hah. A lot good that would do."

Marge said, "And the lessee is named Bruce Havert?"

"Yes."

Oliver said, "What's his wife or girlfriend's name?"

"Randi with an *i.* She tells me that all the time. 'I'm Randi with an *i.*'"

"Her last name?"

"Never knew it. She wasn't on the lease. They all drive blue Prius. They take up parking spaces three, four, and five."

"What did Randi look like?" Oliver asked.

"Blond. Skinny, skinny. In her thirties. Stupid-looking lips—puffy but not sexy. She is nice girl, though. Always a smile. Maybe it is for my benefit, that I'd give her a break in the rent. I was already giving them bottom dollar."

"Did you ever see a brunette working for them?" Oliver asked.

"Lots of pretty girls. All skinny with lots of makeup."

Marge said, "Do you mind if we take a look at the lease?"

"I don't have it with me. I can get it for you."

"That would be helpful." She looked around. "Do you mind if we go through the boxes of garbage?"

"That's fine by me," Mahadi said. "You find something good, I want to keep it. All the rest, you throw in the Dumpster outside."

The man left, grumbling about having another space to rent.

Both of the detectives gloved up.

After going through the boxes of trash, the sum total of worthwhile paper was two very crumpled Visa receipts and one crumpled MasterCard receipt. Oliver was driving while Marge was looking up Bruce Havert on her BlackBerry.

"There are a ton of Bruce Haver without the *t* and an equal number of Bruce Havers with an *s*. I also pulled up Bruce Haverty. Nothing with Bruce Havert, although there is a surname Havert, just not one with Bruce in front of it."

"We'll run it through our computers. How about the names on the Visa and MasterCard receipts?"

Marge squinted as she tried to read the names hand-written in on the blank credit card slips. These trans-actions were obviously done over the phone. If Casey's Massage and Escort once had an electronic credit card machine, someone took it with them. "It's hard to read. This one looks like Jas . . . Jason. Rohls. It could be Jasper Rohls. I'm deciphering a lot of loops. The number is pretty clear, but I don't think the odds are high that Visa is going to give me the name without a warrant."

"Does it say where Jason/Jasper lives?"

"Nope."

"How about the others?"

"An address? No such luck. I think the names are Leon Bellard . . . Ballard. Leon Ballard. The MasterCard slip is written in another handwriting altogether. I can't read it at all." She put the receipts into an evidence bag, though she didn't have any idea if this was evidence or not. "I don't know if this massage parlor has anything to do with Hobart Penny's murder, but I am curious why it went under at the same time the guy was killed. Like Decker said, we need to interview all of the units around the area to find out which apartment the ladies serviced. Want to canvass with me after I show Masey Roberts the blonde on the security tape?"

"If Masey identifies the blonde on the security tape, why do we have to canvass the area?"

"One step at a time, Oliver. First, let's get something concrete to connect the dots."

"Fine. You connect away. In the meantime, I've got a weekend reservation in Santa Barbara."

"Do you now?"

"You're not the only one who enjoys paradise."

"Ms. Montenegro?"

"Not that it's any of your business, but yes, it's Carmen. And wipe the smirk off your face."

"You've been dating her for a while."

"Off and on . . . more on than off. Want to meet us for dinner on Saturday night?"

"That is so social of you. It must be her idea."

"Yes or no?"

"Will's coming to L.A. this weekend. If you wanted to be alone, you're safe."

Oliver smiled at her. "It's not that I don't love your company . . ."

"I'm not offended, Scott. We both need downtime without each other." Marge looked at her watch. It was almost four. "I should call Decker, make sure he got the warrant." A pause. "He'd probably call me if he didn't get it, right?"

"Right. You seem restless, Dunn. Everything okay?"

"Yeah, sure." She was restless. The future made her restless. "After the tiger extraction, things have been pretty quiet. Now it's all legwork, and so far, it's been another day of nothing."

Oliver said, "Wasn't a total loss, Margie. You made friends with the chicken lady, and I got a dozen doughnuts at half-price. The thing is that you don't need pastries to make friends. I, on the other hand, need all the help I can get."

Chapter Fifteen

Marge and Oliver arrived at Penny's apartment just as the sun sank: oranges and golds glittered in the west while rain clouds gathered in the east. Decker was at the curb, slapping papers in the palm of his hand. Marge parked nearby, and they all met up. A hundred feet away, a small, bald man with a goatee paced. He gave the trio a look and continued to tread the sidewalk.

"Who's the gnome?" Oliver asked.

"My first thought was a leprechaun." Decker turned up the collar on his coat. "It's probably the green sweater. That's George Paxton, the building manager. He's acting pissed, so I'm sure he's hiding something. When I asked him about the apartment above Penny's place, he was evasive when there's no reason to be evasive. The guy is tweaking my antenna."

"More like he's tweaking period." Marge rubbed her hands. As the sun went down, fog came in, the chill seeping into her bones. "We've got the warrant. It's a done deal."

"I told him we're going inside with or without his help, that it's a murder case and we're scrutinizing everyone. I guess he got nervous. That's when he told me that the apartment is leased to a corporation: The Last Hurrah—a perfect epithet for how Hobart Penny died."

"Did you look up the corporation?"

"I found this information out five minutes ago. I don't have Internet on my phone."

Marge took out her smartphone and entered the name. "Nothing jumps out."

Oliver said, "A dummy corporation."

Marge said, "If it's part of Hobart Penny's empire, why go through all this rigmarole to hide it?"

"Lawsuits maybe," Decker said. "If Penny was hiding exotic animals and one of them escaped and killed someone, he could use the corporation to protect his money."

"Doesn't he have personal money that could be attached to damages?"

"Don't know a thing about his finances other than he's wealthy. The whole thing is weird. Rich people are weird."

Oliver said, "You'd think that other tenants might have heard or smelled something if there were other animals."

"Snakes are silent," Marge said. "And they can go a while without eating." A pause. "Or maybe Penny used the place for other kinds of female wild animals."

"Did you follow up on the Saratoga address?" Decker asked.

"The address is there," Oliver said. "The tenants are not. Place was cleaned out."

"Okay . . ." In an effort to get warm, Decker folded his arms across his chest. "Find anything left behind?"

"Three handwritten credit card receipts," Marge said. "We'll check them out. Maybe they'll know something about Bruce Havert and Casey's Massage and Escort. So far we've got nothing to link the place to Hobart Penny."

"So what's the current plan?" Oliver asked. "Do we even have a plan?"

"We do," Decker said. "I'm waiting for Ryan Wilner to give me the go-ahead. He's at the apartment, scoping out the place. I think he's drilling a hole right now to peek inside. Once he's sure the place is devoid of critters, we'll enter. So far, no one has heard any roaring. If anything is in there, it's the strong and silent type . . . or dead."

Oliver cupped his hands over his mouth and blew out hot air. "It's getting a little damp outside. I noticed a 7-Eleven a block away. Anyone for coffee?"

Marge said, "I'll take a large."

"Ditto," Decker said. "I'm undecided about the caffeine. If it's all-night, I'll need it. If it's less than two hours of work, I'll want to be able to sleep tonight."

"You need to commit, Rabbi."

"Okay. Give me caffeine."

"Not feeling too positive."

"Undetermined. If I am lucky enough to go home, I'll just balance the caffeine with a couple of glasses of Kiddush wine."

Dressed in browns, Ryan Wilner came down thirty minutes later, shaking his head. Decker finished the last of his coffee. "You don't look happy."

"We need snake buckets. About forty of them."

"Good Lord!" Marge said. "Any of them loose?"

"From what I could see inside a peephole, they seem to be in cages, but I can't make out the entire apartment. Snakes hide in tight places. I don't know what kind of snakes he had or if they're venomous. We'll just have to wait until we get the buckets and the tongs and picks and boots and gloves. Should I be looking at any more apartments, or is that it?"

"I have no idea," Decker said. "There may be other apartments."

"It would be helpful if we could do this all at once."

"I realize that, but we could only manage a warrant for one because it had access to Penny's apartment. But now that you found snakes, I'm going to have a very serious talk with the apartment manager." Decker was livid. "We not only have a murder investigation, we've got an immediate safety issue!"

Wilner's cell rang and he took the call. "Someone's bringing over the buckets. Shouldn't be too long."

Oliver asked, "How much time will it take to extract all the snakes?"

"At least a couple of hours. We have to make sure the apartment is completely clear before anyone else can come inside."

Decker looked at his watch, then at his detectives. "Two hours should be enough time to vacate the floor. Start knocking on doors." He took a deep breath. Anger wasn't going to help the situation. "I'm going to talk to Leprechaun and it ain't gonna be about a pot of gold at the end of the rainbow."

He walked over to Paxton. "We need to talk."

"I'm not talking without a lawyer."

"I haven't arrested you yet, but I'll tell you right now, buddy, I certainly have a whole bunch of reasons to justify incarceration. Even in the best case scenario where no one gets hurt, do you have any idea how much this is costing us in manpower?"

The little man turned white. "I didn't know any-thing about a tiger!" A plea of desperation. "What do you *want* from me?"

Decker said, "One apartment with a tiger is enough to make my skin crawl. Now animal control is sending a crew with forty buckets to catch forty *snakes*! You rented that space to Penny knowing full well what his plans were—"

"I swear I didn't—"

"Are you out of your mind, Paxton? A venomous snake is a lethal weapon. It's the same as if you were storing a stash of guns."

Paxton blanched. "I . . . I want to talk to a lawyer."

"You want a lawyer, buddy, you get a lawyer." Decker moved into his space until they were nose to nose—which required some height adjustment. "But before you make a single, solitary phone call, you're going to tell me every single apartment that Penny or Last Harrah corporation or any *other* corporation rented, so we can clear the place of very dangerous menaces and ensure that no one gets hurt."

"I didn't know—"

"Because if you don't tell me right now and something goes terribly wrong—like a death—you're going down for murder—"

"I didn't know . . ." He waved his hands in the air. "I didn't know—"

"Paxton, right now I'm not interested if you knew or not. I'm not even interested if you got kickback or not, although I suspect you did. Right now, all I want to do is clear the apartment building of dangerous animals. *Get it?* Now how many apartments did Hobart Penny rent?"

The apartment manager was speechless.

"Okay, now I'm going to arrest you," Decker said.

"Wait, wait . . ." He started hyperventilating. "Please!"

Decker said, "Let's move this to somewhere private, okay." He thought about his own car, but there wasn't a protective grate separating the front from the back. Instead, he opted for a cruiser from one of the uniforms. Decker opened the back door.

"Inside." Paxton slid in and Decker sat next to him, crowding his space. He took out his notebook.

"Now how *many* apartments do I have to check out, George?"

His voice was small. "Four."

"Four?"

"I mean two . . . two not counting the one he lived in and the one above him. I swear I didn't know a thing about the tiger or the snakes!" He was white. "I thought he was using them as you know . . ."

"No, I don't know!"

"Love nests." A pause. "I thought he was using them for women."

"We'll get back to that in a moment." Decker finally caught his breath. "I need the keys to the other two apartments."

"I don't have them—"

"Where are they?"

"In my office."

"Where's your office?"

"About ten minutes from here."

"I will follow you to your office. We'll go in together to fetch the keys. But before we go, I need to know the other two apartments that he leased so I can inform animal control."

"Last Harrah also rents the apartments on either side of Penny." Paxton regained a tinge of color. "I don't know what's inside. I swear that's the truth!"

"This isn't about you, it's about public safety," Decker said. "You are referring to the two apartments on the same floor as Penny, on his left and right sides."

"Yes."

"What are the apartment numbers?" Paxton recited the numerals. Decker wrote them down. "What about the apartment below him?"

"It's vacant."

"You're positive that Penny never rented it?"

"He did rent it. It's currently vacant. I know because I cleaned it out two weeks ago."

"What was in there?"

"Nothing. By cleaning it out, I meant just painting it. It was spotless when he gave me back the keys." Paxton's bald head was sweating. "I remember thinking how empty it was. Usually tenants leave something. But that made sense. He wasn't really moving, just getting rid of one of his apartments."

"Wait here. I have to make some calls." Decker got out of the cruiser and took out his cell. When Marge answered, he said, "We've got two more apartments that need to be checked out."

"You are *kidding* me!"

"I wish." He gave her the numbers.

"What's inside?"

"Paxton swears he doesn't know."

"Do you believe him?"

"No, but that doesn't matter now. We're going to have to vacate the building. Take precautions. Penny has a bad track record."

"Right," Marge said. "I'll tell Wilner about the apartments."

"Good. I'm going with Paxton to pick up the keys."

"You know, Pete, when Oliver and I were there yesterday, we didn't smell anything coming from those apartments."

"Maybe we'll be lucky and they'll be vacant. At one time, Last Harrah had rented the apartment directly below Penny's place. That apartment is currently empty, but we need to check it out. Paxton's credibility isn't high right now."

"What's his role in all of this?"

"I'm sure he got kickbacks for not asking too many questions. He claims he thought Penny was keeping the places for women."

"That could be," Marge said. "Did you ask him why he thought Penny was keeping women?"

"Haven't gotten around to that yet."

"I was just wondering what could be in those apartments if we didn't smell anything."

"More reptiles? An aquarium filled with stone fish? Maybe a deadly insect collection?"

"Yeah, that could be," Marge said. "He definitely was an animal hoarder. A lethal version of crazy cat woman."

Wilner gave Decker a list of the live reptiles in the cages from the apartment above Penny's. Marge and Oliver read over his shoulder.

VENOMOUS

1. **Six western diamondback rattlesnakes**

2. **Six red diamond rattlesnakes**

3. **Five Mojave green rattlesnakes**

4. **Four sidewinders**

5. **Four Arizona coral snakes**

6. **Two king cobras**

7. **Two black mambas?**

8. **Two Australian brown snakes?**

NONVENOMOUS

1. **Four California kingsnakes**

2. **Two gopher snakes**

3. **Two mountain gartersnakes**

4. **Two large boa constrictors**

"At least that's what we think the reptiles are," Wilner said. "The rattlers I'm pretty sure of. The mamba . . . well, there are a lot of black snakes. There are also a lot of brown snakes. I'll have the herpetologist look them over to identify them. For the time being, we put them on the venomous snake side."

"There were two sides?" Oliver asked.

"Well not exactly two sides, but someone sorted them into venomous and nonvenomous. We also found a few dead ones. That's probably what stank."

Decker's eyes were still on the list. "So most of them were alive?"

"Yeah, most of them were okay and pretty well tended. I'd say it's been a week since the last cleaning, judging from the amount of feces."

"Are these common snakes?" Marge asked.

"Pretty much so. Some are easy to find in the wilds. All of them are easy to buy. How old was this guy?"

"Eighty-nine."

"Probably wasn't a snake hunter then, just a collector."

Oliver said, "Did you find any paraphernalia belonging to the tiger or other animals?"

"We weren't really looking for anything else but errant snakes. Now what is this about these two other apartments?"

Decker gave him the numbers and the keys. "The manager has given us written permission for you to check the contents inside and clear them of anything dangerous. I don't know what's in store for you. Maybe nothing."

"Whatever it is, we'll deal with it," Wilner said. "So far we've cleared the common hallway of any errant reptiles . . . gone over it at least twice. But I'd feel better if our agent was there with a bucket and a pair of tongs when people start coming back in."

"So you're going to stick around for a while?"

"You bet. Andrea will be with me. You met Andrea. She's our reptile person."

"Yes, I remember her, and the more help you can give us, the better. If the apartments on either side of Penny's are vacant, how long will it take before we can start letting people back inside? I'd like to tell the crowd something."

"I'd like another hour, even if the places are vacant. We've got to be sure."

"Of course." Decker turned to Marge and Oliver. "Is the building cleared?"

"Totally," Marge said. "We've got six uniforms with a perimeter around the place. No one's getting in."

"Good." Decker along with Oliver and Marge walked outside into a commotion of fog and chill and blinking lights. There was a swelling crowd of people. Undertone murmurs had transformed to overt grousing. "I'll address the residents. They have a right to know everything that I know . . . which isn't much."

Marge said, "What about Paxton?"

"I'll talk to him . . . find out why he thought Penny was keeping women." Decker rotated his shoulders. "You two go back to the station house. Start probing into Casey's Massage and Escort, Bruce Havert and his cohort, Randi with an *i*. I'll call you once the place has been cleared and we'll check out the apartments together. That may take a while."

"We're not going anywhere." Oliver grinned. "Hell, the party's just begun."

Chapter Sixteen

"High five." Decker slapped hands with Marge. "Poisonous insects *and* fish!"

"You're the man." Marge flicked her wrist to look at her watch. It was past midnight. She and Oliver had been called back to the apartment house about twenty minutes ago. In the early evening, it was chilly. In the dead of night, it was not only cold but also wet. Fog gave an eerie yellow glow to streetlamps as droplets glistened in the artificial light. Cars were top-coated in mist. She tightened the scarf around her neck. "What was lurking behind the walls?"

"In the insectarium—better known as the apartment to Penny's right—Wilner found tarantulas, scorpions, a whole lot of spiders, including the infamous brown recluse and black widow. There were also beetles, two Madagascar hissing cockroaches, and three ant farms with different types of harvester ants, which—according to Wilner—bite as well as sting. No bees. That's the good news."

"Bizarre, but at this point, not surprising," Marge said.

Decker said, "I'm still thinking about what Paxton said—that he used the apartments for women. Do you have anything on Bruce Havert and company?"

"Nothing new, but we haven't had much chance to investigate," Marge said.

"Right. Let's attend to the immediate problem. Wilner said the smartest thing to do would be to fumigate ASAP, since we don't know if something bad escaped and nested in the floors and walls."

"Charming," Oliver said. "I feel itchy already."

"What does he want to do?" Marge asked. "Like a total tenting?"

"Yes. Maybe tomorrow, maybe next week."

"So the apartment building is going to have to be emptied while it's being fumigated."

"At least thirty-six hours."

"Who's going to tell the masses?" Marge asked.

Decker regarded the group of tenants who had chosen to stay rather than hunker down somewhere else. There were about twenty of them. "I suppose that would be me. We need to make sure every single tenant is aware of the situation and all the pets and food are out of the building. Also, no one is allowed to sleep here tonight. Paxton's getting me a list with apartment numbers and phone numbers. We'll have to go through the contacts one by one by one until we can tick off all the boxes."

Oliver took out a notebook. "If the insects were in the apartment to Penny's right, what's in the left? The fish?"

"Actually the fish and the insects shared the same space," Decker said. "The apartment to the left was a food pantry for all the animals." He checked his notes. "One refrigerator and three big chest freezers."

"What about a tiger cage?"

"Wilner didn't say anything about that," Decker said. "He did a cursory glance at the freezers. There were lots of wrapped butcher paper packages plus plastic bags of frozen rats and mice. Food for the snakes."

"I thought snakes only eat live prey," Marge said.

"In general that's true," Decker said. "But Wilner told me if the prey is flash frozen—essentially fresh—you can thaw it out and warm it, jiggle the mouse on a line and make it look like it's alive. If the snake is hungry enough, it'll sometimes take it. If Penny had live rats, I don't know where he kept them."

"This is really more than I need to know," Oliver told him.

"There were also bags of fortified insect meal, fruit, and lettuce in the fridge. Cartons of frozen fish food . . . did I tell you about the fish?"

"Do I want to hear it?" Oliver said.

"There were tanks of stonefish, lionfish, scorpion fish, toadfish, puffers—"

"Don't know a thing about fish." Marge started jotting things down on her pad. "I take it they're all poisonous."

"Venomous. Although the toadfish is probably poisonous."

"Thank you for the correction," Marge said. "What's the difference?"

"Via Wilner, venom is injected into the prey; poisonous refers to plants and animals that can make you sick when ingested or touched. Although I don't know what would happen if you drank venom."

"Details not required," Oliver said.

Marge said, "Where do we go from here?"

"As soon as all the bugs and swimming creatures are removed, we can start escorting people to their apartments to pack up their belongings before the tenting. After the fumigation, they'll need to stay out until the place is cleared and aerated. They have to throw out the food inside except maybe what's in cans. The extermination company is printing out instructional handouts. It's going to be a logistical nightmare."

"Who's taking responsibility for the cost and the inconvenience?"

Decker said, "There are thirty-eight units. Penny had four units, and three units are vacant according to Paxton. That means we have to account for thirty-one tenants. Hopefully, they'll have family and friends who will put them up for a few days. If they don't, the city will provide for anyone who needs temporary housing. It ain't gonna be fancy, but they'll have a roof over their head. We can start with the few hearty souls that are still out. Be smart and be sensitive."

Marge asked, "Are we going to have a chance to look at Penny's apartments before we deal with the tenants?"

"Not the insectariums," Decker said. "There's too big a chance for a catastrophe if something escapes. We have to wait until after the tenting before we can go in there."

"What about the food pantry? Can we check that out?"

"Margie, why would you want to check out plastic bags of frozen rats and mice?" Oliver asked. "It sounds positively disgusting."

"I'm sure it is disgusting. This whole case has been one of the most itchy, yucky, ghastly, repellent crimes that I have ever worked on. I usually don't put my hands in tiger shit."

"So why make it worse?" Oliver said.

Marge shrugged. "I know you said no bodies, Pete. But you just never know what you're going to find in a deep freeze."

The division of labor was thus: Decker remained outside, answering questions, while Marge and Oliver checked out the pantry apartment. It wasn't a perfumery, but the smell wasn't as funky as they had feared. It was a mixture of butcher shop, pet store, and musty old basement. The heat had been turned off, but it wasn't as cold as it was outside, although it retained the dankness of a basement.

Marge gloved up. "Want to take a look in the bedroom and bathroom?"

Oliver frowned. "If I get bit, you'd better know CPR."

"No joke." Marge started opening the kitchen cabinets. She found dried fish and reptile food as well as dozens of bottles of animal supplements. There were also pet antibiotics, analgesics, and ten bottles of animal narcotics. Pet meds were much easier to buy than human meds. Often there was little difference.

Marge took out a camera and began to click photos. About twenty minutes later, Oliver called out from the bedroom, "C'mere. You'll want to see this."

When she walked inside the bedroom, she was surprised that it was devoid of furniture. There were some old blankets and tarps stacked on the floor along with piles of newspapers. Oliver was in the closet. It was empty.

"Steel reinforced." Oliver opened and closed the closet door. "Listen to the sound when I slam it shut." It made a distinct ping of metal. He pounded on the wall. "The whole thing is one big cage. Here's where he hid the tiger whenever he had company."

"This backs up onto Penny's closet, right?"

"Yep."

"So there should be a panel somewhere connecting the two spaces."

"I'm trying to find it, but the light is so poor. I'm looking for a seam. He wouldn't walk the tiger down the hallway from one apartment to another."

Marge agreed, "No, he wouldn't."

"Can I borrow the camera? I want to take some pictures."

"Sure."

"Find anything out there?"

"Just a lot of veterinarian products in the cupboards. I'm about to check the freezers."

"Have fun."

She came back inside and opened the refrigerator. As Decker said, it was stocked with rotting produce. It didn't smell horrible, but the shelves could definitely do with a good cleaning. She poked around the bins and shelves, and finding nothing hidden, she closed the door.

On to the freezers.

As predicted, the first freezer contained all things gross—plastic bags of frozen mice, rats, goldfish, grasshoppers, crickets, shrimp, algae green plankton, and other things unfit for human consumption. She sorted through them and, finding nothing, shut the lid down with a thump.

The second freezer was a mass of butcher-wrapped packages. Marge put on a face mask and started pulling out the white bundles and tearing off the paper. Inside were pounds upon pounds of cattle and hog by-products. The heaviest packages included leg bones chopped in half, but there were also dozens of hooves, ears with the fur still on, eyeballs, skulls, and ribs. When she had gone through all the packages, she tried to fit them back into the freezer. Since they were frozen solid, it took several attempts before she could shut the lid and get a tight fit with the rubber seal.

Oliver walked in. "I think I found a seam, but I can't figure out how to open it. Want to see it?"

"Can I take a look after I'm done with the freezers?"

"Sure. Find anything."

"Just a fucking house of horrors."

Oliver looked at his partner. She rarely swore. He put on a face mask. "I'll help you, Dunn."

"Nah, you don't want to."

"Come on, baby, we swore for better or worse."

"Don't say I didn't warn you." Marge opened the lid to the third freezer. "I've already found a lot of unsavory animal parts—eyeballs, ears, bones—"

"Did you find any balls and dicks?"

"No, I did not."

"Then I'm good to go." Oliver unwrapped the first package. It contained bones that still had some meat on them. The next two packages were identical to the first. "This isn't so bad."

"No, this freezer is better than the first two." She rewrapped a package of stew meat. After a few minutes, she said, "Bones and bones and more bones."

"Do you really think it's necessary to go through all of this?"

"We're almost done." Another package. "Chicken bones. We're into poultry now."

Oliver took out another three packages, all of them containing beef chunks. "You'd think someone would have labeled these. Not for taste preference. Just to know what you're feeding it."

Marge nodded. "Dealing with chicken legs are better than eyeballs, I can tell you that much. We've got a lot of chicken legs . . . legs, legs, and more legs."

Oliver started singing ZZ Top. "Someone could make a fine stock with the parts."

"This guy was rich beyond belief. He could have collected Renoirs. Instead he has a tiger and hoards venomous snakes and insects." Marge thought about that. "Probably that was the thrill. Cheating death."

"Who needs the shrink when you've got Marge Dunn? Do you know what I would collect if I had money?"

"Yes, I do know. Motorcycles. Don't you have a couple?"

"I've got one Harley and two Ducati racing bikes and a want list about a mile long. What about you, Margie? What's your secret passion?"

"I'm not much of a collector."

"C'mon. Everyone has a weakness. What's yours? Jewelry? Shoes? Romance novels?"

She grinned. "Oliver, you dog. You found my secret passion. But only those that have the covers with those shirtless, long-haired guys."

Oliver smiled. "You could always buy a wig for Will, and I'm sure we could find him a shirt with billowing sleeves, what do you think?" When he got no response, he looked up. Marge was white. "What's wrong?"

Marge cleared her throat, attempting to find her voice. She gave up and just showed the package to her partner.

"Oh God!" He looked away. "What the *hell!*" Oliver's breathing was shallow. "How many are there?"

"I don't know, Scott! They're all frozen together!"

"Put it down, Margie. We both need some air. Let's go outside, okay."

She placed the package aside, and the two of them stepped into the hallway. Marge bit her lip and raised her eyebrows. "You tell Decker and I'll call the coroner's office." A pause. "This is no longer our problem."

Oliver cleared his throat. "Well, it kinda is our problem."

"Not in the immediate." Marge exhaled. "Let's get a CI over here. It's time to let someone else experience the gross-out factor!"

Chapter Seventeen

A package of frozen fingers: probably female, judging by the size, but Decker wasn't sure of anything. With that discovery, the case had progressed from disgusting to grisly. Now SID had to go through each packet of meat with a critical eye, because who knew what could be mixed with the stew meat? Or what kind of meat had been cubed? The possibilities were endless and nauseating.

Decker's main concern was keeping the evidence intact. When protein defrosted, it leaked water, making the skin loose and soggy, so that any prints taken were distorted. It was imperative that the whorls remain as true as possible. Once the fingers were inked, there was no guarantee that the prints would be in the AFIS. But if they had been attached to prostitutes, there was a good chance someone was in the system.

It was one in the morning. The crowd of onlookers had thinned, and most of the people on the street were associated either with the LAPD, the lab, or with the coroner's office. Lights blinked and whirled in shades of reds and blues, casting a ghastly shadow on whatever was in the line of fire.

Marge walked up to Decker. "Go home, Rabbi. We'll keep you updated."

Oliver said, "When are you meeting with Paxton?"

"Tomorrow . . ." Decker blinked several times. "Actually, it's today . . . at eight. I put Donaldson on surveillance just in case, so he's not going anywhere."

"Then go home, Pete. You got six hours to sleep. We'll take care of whatever comes up."

"I'm okay." He turned to Marge. "Are you okay?"

"Depends on the definition of okayness." She rubbed her arms. "Did SID give you an idea on how many fingers were involved?"

"No. How many did it look like to you?"

"This is just a guess . . . maybe two dozen."

"And you?" He turned to Oliver.

"Same."

Decker said, "I don't want to be morbid, but at a glance"—*a very quick glance*—"it looked like all different kinds of fingers. I saw some pinkies, some middle fingers, some index fingers."

"I noticed that," Marge said.

Decker took a quick breath and let it out. "I'm hoping that maybe it's a few people who had all their digits cut off, rather than twenty-four different people each with one missing digit."

Oliver said, "So . . . what are we thinking. That Penny was a serial killer who fed body parts to his tiger?"

"I don't know and I don't feel like making a guess," Decker said. "You have the list of all the tenants?"

Marge patted her bag. "We'll deal with them in the sunlight."

"You should go home, Margie. You need some sleep."

"What I need is to forget that precise moment of opening the package." Marge swallowed. "It's not that dead people don't bother me. Of course, they do. But there is something particularly horrible about seeing human remains when you've been looking at chicken. It's just . . . ungodly."

She was shivering. Decker said, "We'll need to interview the neighbors again. Let's all go home and regroup in the morning."

"Won't argue with that," Oliver said. "I told the coroner's office to call me if someone finds more body parts. I live the closest."

"If you go in, I'll go in," Marge said. "Call me, okay?"

"Fine," Oliver said.

"Then let's pack it in." With that, Decker walked away, his stomach in a knot as his brain sparked horrific visuals. It was going to take awhile before he indulged in meat.

Rina was curled up on the couch, a blanket over her legs, reading a book. Gabe was in pajamas, lying over the love seat, his long legs dangling over the arm of the settee. They both looked up when Decker came through the door. "I can't believe you're both still up."

"Waiting for my own tiger." Rina put the book down and stood up. "Hungry?"

"I'll take a yogurt. Sit. I'll get it myself."

He disappeared into the kitchen. Gabe said, "Is he okay?"

"Probably not." Rina sighed. "He eats dairy whenever his stomach acts up. He must have found a body. I'll be right back."

"You know, it's after one. I think I'll go to bed." He stood and stretched. "Give you guys a little privacy.

Good luck and good night." Gabe went into his make-shift room and carefully closed the door.

When Decker returned, Rina said, "Gabe went to sleep. What happened?"

He shook his head. "I don't want to talk about it. But I'll be happy to talk to you. How was the evening?"

"Your grandsons asked for you. 'Where's papa?' "

Decker smiled. "How are they?"

"They are huge! They are not only off the charts for two-year olds, they're off the charts for *three*-year-olds. Cindy's starting to train them, not because she cares all that much but because they're starting to out-grow diapers. If she doesn't do it soon, she'll have to use Depends. They loved my food by the way."

"Who doesn't?"

"True enough. Sit down. I'll get some tea for both of us."

"I'm going to shower first."

"Fine. I'll bring it into the bedroom. You want another yogurt?"

"Sure."

As Rina had done so many times in the past, she prepared a tray for him. Usually she made toast, but being as it was Shabbat, she took two slices of home-made challah bread and slathered it with butter. Then she put the yogurt in a bowl and added fresh fruit. The tea was herbal, the hot water from a preheated urn. She brought the food in just as he slid into bed. The room was dark, the sole illumination coming from the open bathroom door.

"Here you go," Rina told him.

"Thank you. This is perfect." He ate a slice of bread in silence. "I have to go back at eight in the morning. I've got an interview that can't wait."

Rina checked the clock. "Then you should go to sleep."

"If I can sleep."

"I'll sing you a lullaby." She patted his knee. "Or I can talk and bore you to sleep."

"You never bore me." Decker dug into the yogurt and fruit. "So my grandsons are football players."

"Maybe basketball. Akiva is actually taller, but the kid has some heft. Aaron is all height."

"How's Cindy?"

"She's back in the field again. She likes being in the action."

Decker nodded. "As I recall, I was once like that."

"Don't sell yourself short, young man. You're still an adrenaline junkie."

"Not anymore." He started on the second piece of bread. "Seriously. I think about quitting LAPD all the time."

"That would be bad."

"Maybe bad for you, not for me."

"Peter, you can't *potchke* with your Porsche twenty-four/seven."

"I didn't say retire, I said I'm thinking about quitting LAPD. I'm tired of all the *ugliness*, Rina. And today was particularly ugly."

She placed her hand on his arm. "So if you aren't thinking about retiring, but you are thinking about quitting, do you have something in mind?"

"This and that." He finished up the bread and pushed the tray away. "I probably shouldn't be thinking of these things when I'm this exhausted."

"There's truth in your feelings, even if you are exhausted. But do get some sleep."

"I love you. Thanks for dinner." He paused. "What was dinner for the masses?"

"Chicken and corned beef."

"Any leftovers?"

"Of course. Do you want to try something?"

"Maybe tomorrow." He took a deep breath and let it out. "Certainly not today."

"Shall we call it a night?" Without waiting for an answer, she got up, removed the tray from the bed, and closed the bathroom door. She leaned over and kissed him.

He gave her one back. Then she gave him a kiss to his kiss. And then one thing led to another and hopefully a night of ugliness had turned into a night of beauty.

Peter was her best friend. Better than a best friend: the original FWB.

Paxton had a definite fixation with green sweaters. This time it was hunter green over jeans and sneakers. He wore glasses, but red eyes were peeking out behind the lenses. His head was bald on top: the remaining hair was brown mixed with gray.

Decker seated him in one of the interview rooms, his chair crowding Paxton against the wall. "Coffee? Water?"

Paxton thought about it, but then shook his head no.

Decker had already had two cups of caffeinated sludge. It was eight in the morning and he needed all the help he could get. He took out a notepad. Even though interviews were now videotaped, he always needed reminders of what he thought was important. "Thanks for coming in."

"Did I have a choice?" the apartment manager said.

"No one's coercing you to stay here, Mr. Paxton."

"If I don't talk to you, it looks bad for me." When Decker didn't answer, the apartment manager said, "I'm in a no-win position."

"How about if I ask you a few questions and then we take it from there?"

"I want you to know that I had no idea what Mr. Penny was doing—either with the tiger or anything else. Certainly not with something . . . like what you found."

"Were you ever in any of his apartments?"

"Just Mr. Penny's apartment. I never saw a tiger."

"Okay. How many times were you in the apartment?"

"Maybe three times. No tiger."

"What about the other apartments? Let's start with the snake apartment. Ever inside?"

"No."

"How about the insects and fish?"

"No."

"Never once?"

"Never. Why would I go inside? No one ever complained. The rent was always paid on time. There was no reason for me to barge in on someone's privacy."

"But you knew that Penny had rented those apartments."

"Okay." Paxton fiddled with his glasses. "I'll tell you what I did know and you can do whatever you want with the information." A pause. "Penny offered to pay me a surcharge over that amount if I would mind my own business . . . which I do anyway. I asked him why he felt the need to pay me a surcharge. He told me that he didn't want anyone—including myself—having keys to the apartments. I told him no. I told him I needed to get in and out of every apartment in the building in case of emergencies. He relented. He gave me a key . . . keys. All of them. And I made sure they worked. And you saw for yourself that the keys worked."

"Yes, they did." Decker waited.

Paxton exhaled. "I refused the surcharge. So I'm not the sleaze you think I am."

"You came in, you're answering my questions, you're being honest . . . don't see anything sleazy there."

Paxton squirmed, ill at ease with any kind of praise. "I didn't see Penny for quite a while after he initially rented the extra units. Then when it was Christmastime—this was about seven years ago—he gave me cash. When I asked him what for, he said he wanted to reward me for being cooperative. I told him it wasn't necessary, but he insisted. I probably should have given the money back. But it was the holiday season. I figured why couldn't I accept a Christmas gift from whoever wanted to give me one. At least half the apartments gives me a Christmas bonus."

"Okay." Decker paused. "How large of a bonus did Mr. Penny give you?"

"I don't think that's any of your business." A pause. Paxton threw up his hands. "Large."

Decker continued to wait.

Paxton coughed a few times. "Two grand . . . in cash. It's his money to do with what he wants. I was doing everything by the books. Never stole a dime from the owners. If Penny wants to tip me for service, that's his business." He coughed again.

"Would you like some water?"

"Yes."

Decker poured him water from a pitcher, and Paxton drank up greedily. "What brought you into his apartment on those three occasions?"

"Now that I'm thinking about it, it was more like five times."

"Tell me about them."

"Couple times I went to pick up the Christmas bonus." He picked up his water glass. It was empty, so Decker filled it. "Once he called me into his place to talk about renting the apartments on either side. Another time was to sign contracts. Once there was a complaint of noise." He held up an index finger. "One time!"

"Masey Roberts said she called you around six times after hearing noises and you told her it was all in her head."

The gnome bit his lip. "I don't remember."

"You don't remember."

"No, I don't remember!"

Decker kept his cool. "So what do you remember?"

"A neighbor complained about noises." The apartment manager turned red. "Loud growls and grunts. Being logical, I thought it was sex."

"He's eighty-nine."

"You never heard of Viagra?"

"What did you do about it?"

"I left a note in Penny's mailbox. I didn't tell him what I thought the noise was. Just that it was noisy enough for someone to hear, so please keep it down."

"Did he answer your note?"

"No . . . but I never got any more complaints."

"Which neighbor complained?"

"The one next door to the downstairs apartment."

"The apartment that's now vacant?"

"Yes."

"When did he vacate that apartment?"

"I told you. About a month ago."

"And he had cleaned it up before he gave you back the key?"

"It was perfect. I almost didn't bother to clean it. But I did for sanitary reasons."

"Would you mind if I had someone professional take a look at it?"

"Professional?"

"Someone from the Scientific Investigative Division."

"Is that like CSI?"

"Yes."

"You think something bad happened there?"

"I don't know. That's why I'd like to look it over. Do I have your permission to perform any test that we might want to do?"

"This sounds bad."

"It'll make a minimum of impact."

"Yes, yes. Go ahead."

"You thought that Mr. Penny was having sex in the apartment. Any reason for that thought other than the noise?"

"A couple of times . . . well, more than a couple of times over twenty years, I saw women with massage tables going in and out of his apartment—his and the one downstairs that he rented."

"Did the women look like call girls?"

"I don't know!" Paxton tried to look offended, and then he thought better of it. "Maybe."

"What did they look like?"

"It was a while ago—four, five months. I saw a woman leave his apartment. She had a massage table. At least that's what it looked like to me."

"What did the woman look like?"

"I don't remember the specifics."

"How about the generals?"

"Thin, young, long blond hair . . . big breasts."

"Do you recollect any of the other women who visited Mr. Penny's apartment?"

"They all looked the same."

"Thin, young, and blond?"

"Blond and brunette."

"Carrying massage tables?"

"I don't remember if *all* of them had massage tables."

"Did thin, young, big-breasted women go in and out of other apartments?"

"It's an apartment building, Lieutenant. People go in and out all the time. I only remember Mr. Penny because he was an old guy."

"How were they dressed?"

"Tight T-shirts, tight pants, and high heels. Didn't take Sherlock to make the deductive leap."

Decker pulled out a photo card of six faces including the two women on the videos. It was the same lineup that had been shown to Masey Roberts. She hadn't been able to identify any of them as women she had seen going in and out the apartment building.

He handed the card to Paxton. "Any of these ladies look familiar?"

"Maybe the blonde."

"Maybe?"

The gnome shrugged. "Couldn't swear to it."

Decker put the photo card away. "Did any of the women that you saw have logos on their shirts?"

"Logos?" He coughed and drank more water. "I have no idea."

"Did you happen to see the cars that the women drove?"

"Nah, I wouldn't know that."

"You don't recall seeing the same car model in the same color?"

"If you have information, tell me."

"Fair enough. There's a recently defunct massage company called Casey's Massage and Escort. I think it used to use powder blue Priuses."

Paxton thought a moment. "Nothing like that ticks any boxes." He regarded his watch. "How much longer?"

"Would you like to take a break?"

"No, I'd like to know how much longer. We've been at this for an hour. I've seen those shows. The cops keep going after the guy until they get a confession."

"What would you confess to?"

"Nothing."

"Then why would you think I was after a confession?"

"Because that's what you do. Can I go home?"

Decker said, "I'll need you to give me the name of the person who complained about the noises in Penny's apartment. I'll need to interview him or her."

"The Shoops—Ian and Delia. They still live there . . . next door to Penny's old apartment. They only complained once, but I know Delia was happy when I told her the apartment was vacant. I have a feeling it wasn't the only time they heard noise."

"I'll need their phone or cell numbers."

"Whatever numbers I have are on the list I gave you."

"I'm going to need to contact the owners about what we found. You know that."

Paxton shuffled his feet. "I've already told them."

"Good for you."

"But I don't see why they'd have to know about any Christmas gifts." When Decker was silent, the man said, "Is that a yes or a no?"

Decker shrugged. "Right now, I wouldn't see why that would be relevant. But I can't guarantee it won't come up in the future. Mr. Paxton, what do you think happened in those apartments?"

"*Me?*"

"You were closer to the situation than I was."

"I don't know if I should feel honored or if this is a trick?"

"I always ask that question. Sometimes I find that people like you are the ones who break the case." No one spoke, but Decker could see Paxton's shoulders relax.

"I really don't know." He swallowed hard. "From what I found out, the guy was obviously a nutcase with a death wish. I mean, keeping a tiger and all those poisonous snakes."

Venomous, Decker corrected silently. "A death wish for himself—or for others?"

"I can't believe . . . the guy was so *old!*" Paxton blew out air. "To look at him, you'd think he couldn't harm a flea."

"Maybe he couldn't," Decker said. "Maybe he relied on other things for protection—ergo, the tiger."

"A gun would be more practical—faster, smaller, and more deadly."

"Sure," Decker agreed. "But like you said, Penny was an old man. With a gun, you have to load it, lift it, aim it, and pull the trigger. There's kickback with a gun. There's also uncertainty. With a tiger, on the other hand, you just kinda sit back and let the animal do its thing."

Chapter Eighteen

Seeing Marge's eyes encased in deep circles, Decker asked, "Are you feeling all right?"

"Just not enough sleep. I've been thinking too much. Or maybe it's Saturday morning blues."

"I thought it was Monday morning blues."

"I've always been one to jump the gun." She wore her most comfortable clothes—black pants and a soft pink cotton sweater. She needed to be babied today. "What'd you find out from Paxton?"

Decker gave her a recap, then handed her a to-do list.

Get coroner's report on the meat packages.

Find out info on Casey's Massage and Escort: credit card slips, Bruce Havert, Randi with an i. If you hit a wall, hunt around for the powder blue Priuses. Probably leased.

Interview the Shoops.

Interview neighbors again to see what they noticed from the apartments.

Find out about exotic pet dealerships—may want to contact Vignette Garrison.

Check the apartment underneath Penny for possible forensics.

Talk to a shrink.

Marge said, "Is that last item for a profile for Penny or for you personally?"

"I haven't decided." Decker smiled. "I am curious about what made a man like Penny tick. If you need help interviewing, feel free to call up the reserves."

"I'll pull Wanda and Drew for that. They have good people skills. Lee Wang is already doing the computer search for Bruce Havert and Randi and Casey's. It does have blue Priuses. Oliver and I will check out the car dealerships. They should be open by now. Unless you want me to interview the Shoops first."

"I've already set up a time with them. They can't make it in until four tomorrow afternoon."

"So in that case, why don't you go home and try to salvage some of your Sabbath."

"I want to stop by the Crypt first."

"I'll go with you if you want," Marge told him.

"Nice of you, but it's not a two-man job. At eleven in the morning, why should we both smell death?"

With all his morgue visits over the years, Decker had gotten used to bodies. There were corpses laid out on the steel tables behind glass windows in the autopsy operating rooms. There were bodies wrapped up in plastic and stacked on shelves like carpets in the refrigeration room. Often, cadavers with toe tags were left in the hallway, waiting to be processed. There were not only bodies but also human remains floating in jars and sliced and diced on glass slides about to be examined under microscopes. But the one thing he couldn't get used to, no matter how often he visited the Crypt, was the smell: that distinct fecal blend of decay, rot, and sickening sweet formaldehyde. It always caused something uncomfortable to well up inside his throat.

By the time Decker had arrived, the frozen fingers should have been thawed out and ready to be printed. The fingernails needed to be clipped for trace evidence and studied for foreign DNA. Decker had acclimated to the underground life of a pathologist. His duties today put him inside one of the lab rooms rather than in the autopsy chambers, the closed door attenuating the stench ever so slightly. The examination space was long and narrow. If Decker held out his arms, he could span the width palm to palm with barely enough room to walk between the steel countertops covered by equipment and specimen jars.

The pathologist was a woman named Elsie Spar who by most accounts was around a hundred. Her shoulders were hunched, her hair was sparse and white, and when she talked, her dentures clacked. Decker had dealt with her before. The body may be stooped and bent, but the brain was thoroughly intact: vital and sharp with a keen intelligence and photographic recollection. She sat on a stool while Decker stood.

Elsie wasn't one who bothered with niceties. "You got all gray."

"Not *all* gray. If you squint, you can still see the orange streaks."

Elsie adjusted her Coke-bottle lenses. Her white lab coat swallowed up her small frame. "Nope. Just see gray. The mustache is still red. Do you dye it?"

"No."

"That's good to hear. More and more men are dyeing their hair—like little wusses afraid to get old. A man should look like a man, not a gender-neutralized manikin. I suppose you want to talk about the fingers."

"I do. Can I sit down?"

"Of course. You want something to drink?" Without waiting for an answer, she poured some water into a glass beaker and took a gulp. "Don't look so sick. It's Evian or Fiji—something overpriced. If someone had predicted that people would pay for water when I was a little girl, I would have figured him plum nuts. Would you like a glass?"

"I'll pass."

"Suit yourself. Anyway, the fingers. I sent over a dozen down to be printed. After we do that, we'll take some tissue samples for slides and DNA testing. But even without the microscopes, I'll tell you what I think, if you want to hear."

"That's why I'm sitting here."

"To me, most of the fingers look on the old side. A few may be fresher than that. Some look disarticulated postmortem."

"Okay." Decker was momentarily muddled. "By postmortem, do you mean corpses in cemeteries or people who were killed and then the fingers were taken off?"

"Can't say."

"Why do you think they're old?"

"Freezer burn." Elsie took a sip of water. "I'll get a better idea once I start with the microscopic examination."

"So why are you leaning in the direction of postmortem?"

"We defrosted the digits very slowly. You know what happens when things defrost, you get a collection of blood and water and cells and lots of other things.

I would have expected to see more blood in the fluid if the fingers had been immediately severed from the bodies and flash frozen."

"Got it. Did you see any presence of embalming solution?"

"Not in the fluid. When I check the tissue samples, I should be able to tell if the cells had been fixed. Couldn't smell any formaldehyde, which is what the mortuary might have used a while back. There are newer and better solutions these days. Until I check the microscope, I can't tell you anything more."

"Okay." His mind was still flipping through all the possibilities. "I suppose that it's a little more palatable to deal with fingers taken from corpses than fingers taken while the victim was alive. Maybe I should contact funeral homes for missing bodies."

"Whatever you think. That's your domain."

"Why would someone save a package of fingers from dead bodies?"

"No idea, Lieutenant. I don't work with living people. The working brain is much too complicated for me."

"I'm more or less talking to myself."

"I do that all the time. That way I get intelligent conversation."

Decker's mind was still whirling. "Did you get a chance to look at any of the meat packages?"

"Everything I checked under the scope was domestic beef or hog. If you're going to mix human flesh in with the beef, it's not going to look the same. And unless the guy is a professional, it wouldn't be butchered so cleanly. But . . ." She raised a finger. "But I haven't checked everything. It's going to take me a while to go through the packages."

"Understood. Anything else you want to tell me?"

"Not right now."

"When will the fingerprinting be done?"

"Within the hour. Stick around."

"Yes, I'll do that. Do you think someone might have a spare computer?"

"You want to work here or upstairs?"

"I'll work here if I have to, but upstairs is my preference."

Elsie smiled with plastic teeth. "Smell is a little strong if you're not used to it."

"How do you get used to it?"

"It's just something that I equate with work—neither good nor bad." Elsie shrugged. "As soon as I entered medical school, that first semester with my bone box, I knew I was going to be a pathologist. The science just fascinated me. The dead tell both of us their secrets."

"Yes, they do."

"Pathologists, like homicide detectives, have to be inquisitive people. We're both curious and nosy, Lieutenant, and dare I say it, just a little bit ghoulish."

Fingerprints in tow, Decker returned to the station house by two in the afternoon. Lee Wang, dressed in a crewneck red sweater and black jeans, was conferring with Marge and Oliver. Decker motioned the trio into his office and then shut the door.

"New developments." He recapped his morning with Dr. Spar and handed Wang the envelopes. "Put these through AFIS. If we get any hits, call up an expert to see if we can come up with a definitive identification."

Marge was taking notes. "Can I backtrack?"

"Sure."

"So the fingers came off postmortem."

"She thinks that some of them did."

"From dead bodies in cemeteries or recent murder victims?"

"Could be either. She did say that the fingers didn't contain a lot of blood in the residual fluid."

"So if it was a murder victim, the body could have bled out," Oliver said.

"Yep." Decker pulled out a stack of papers and passed them out. "While I was waiting for her to look at the tissue and for the fingers to be printed, I made a list of the local cemeteries. The biggest one is right in our own backyard. We've got about ten more in the L.A. area. I've included phone numbers and the head mortician. Just give them a call and find out if they've had problems with stolen bodies in the past. And we are talking about the past."

Lee Wang said, "I'll do it."

Decker said, "We know Penny's a freak. He may be a homicidal freak and these are trophies."

"That's as good an explanation as anything," Marge said.

Decker said, "Find out anything on the computer about Bruce Havert, Lee?"

"I found about a half dozen Bruce Haverts under forty. I've listed them all with phone numbers and I have pictures for four of them." He passed around his printouts. "I haven't made any calls so I don't know if any of these are *the* Bruce Havert."

Oliver said, "We can take these pictures over to Ki, the chicken lady, and to the landlord for ID."

"Yeah, Anwar Mahadi," Marge said. "Wish we would have had these when we checked out the dealerships. Maybe a face would have jogged a memory."

"Yeah, what happened with that?" Decker asked.

Oliver said, "None of the dealers remember Bruce Havert leasing Priuses. He could have been using a different name, though."

"What about the color? Powder blue is unusual, no?"

"Not for Priuses."

Marge said, "Even if Havert was using his own name, we can't get the dealers to divulge information about their customers without proper papers."

Oliver said, "We'll keep at them. Now that we have pictures, it'll help."

"If you don't get anywhere, check powder blue Priuses with DMV on Monday morning," Decker said. "It's one of the few leads we have. Plus, George Paxton says that he saw women with massage tables going in and out of Penny's apartment. Now we have women's fingers. The arrow is pointing in a direction that isn't looking good."

"Still, the murder may be orthogonal to the package of fingers," Marge said.

"I agree we can't get tunnel vision, but it adds to Penny's weird quotient." Decker leaned back in his desk chair and turned to Marge. "What's left on our checklist?"

"Wanda and Drew are interviewing the neighbors . . . not all of them are home because the building is scheduled for fumigation on Tuesday. You also wanted me to look up exotic pet dealerships. You're interviewing the Shoops tomorrow."

"Who are the Shoops?" Oliver asked.

"Neighbors of Hobart Penny who complained about noise coming from one of his apartments."

"What kind of noises?"

"Growls. I'm going to talk with them Sunday afternoon."

"When are Penny's two children coming to L.A.?"

"Monday night."

Wang took out a notebook. "What are their names?"

"Darius Penny and Graciela Johannesbourgh." Marge spelled it. "Sabrina Talbot is also coming in on Tuesday for the service."

Lee lifted the print cards. "I'll take these to an examiner. Then I'll start making cemetery calls."

Decker nodded, and Wang left the office. Marge stowed the Bruce Havert photocopies in her purse. "I'm off to see the chicken lady . . . maybe she can identify Bruce Havert. Even if she can't, I'm starved."

"I'll come with you," Oliver said. "I'm hungry, too. You need something, Rabbi?"

"No. I'm okay for now."

Alone and in silence, Decker heard his stomach growl. He was going to call up Vignette Garrison, but it was almost three and he hadn't eaten all day. Like any good engine, he needed fuel, and since his house was only fifteen minutes away, it made sense for him to eat at home.

Rina would have leftovers in the refrigerator.

He loved his wife. He wished he were a better husband. Not that he was a bad husband, but he wasn't around a lot. Rina never complained about his prolonged absences. She took care of herself. She liked to read and do puzzles. She liked to watch TV and listen to music. She exercised daily. She prayed daily. She learned Bible daily. She taught at the local Jewish high school. She kept in contact with all the kids, including Cindy. She called up her parents and often called up his parents. She spent time trying to help everyone else solve their problems. She had a very good capacity for solitude, but she was still very social. Even as he grumped, she dragged him to parties and affairs because it was "the right thing to do." He always wound up having a good time. She seemed to know when to push him and when to hold back.

She knew what was good for him—much better than he did.

Their marriage was a successful one. It only seemed fair that he gave credit where credit was due.

Chapter Nineteen

Shuffling through the photo array of the Bruce Haverts, Ki Park, better known to Marge and Oliver as the chicken lady, peered at each sheet with concentration and purpose. Neither detective rushed her, each one of them content to eat and wait.

"This one he-ah," Ki finally announced. "Next-door man . . . but older man now." She tapped the picture. "Not like this."

Marge finished chewing a french fry. "The man next door . . . how old was he?"

"Man next door?" Ki thought a moment. "Oh, forty, fifty."

Oliver looked at the photograph she had identified. "So this is the same man as next door, but in this picture, he's much younger."

"Ye-ah. Much younga."

"You're sure they are the same man?"

"Same man. He like drumsticks—fried and baked. Always with onion ring. He put five dollars in tip jar."

"Thank you very much, Ki. You've been really helpful. Could you pack the rest of my lunch to go?"

"Mine, too," Oliver said.

"Why you rush off?" Ki said. "Not good for stomach. You stay."

The woman was lonely. On weekends, the traffic in the strip mall was light and business was probably dead. The two detectives exchanged glances. Marge said, "You're right. We'll finish here."

Ki said, "I give you refill of soft drink."

"I'm fine," Marge told her.

"It free. You take it. You too skinny."

"Well, okay then." Marge held back a smile. "Your chicken is delicious. You know? I'm having company over. Could I get a whole rotisserie chicken to go?"

"Oh sure . . . right away." Ki gave a hint of a smile, and then covered her mouth. "You take fries, you take coleslaw and I give you biscuit for free. Deal?"

"Deal." Marge pushed aside her plate. "I'm going to get a little air. I'll be back in a minute to pick up my food." She left and Oliver followed.

He pulled out his cell. "Who're you having over?"

"No one. I'll split it with you, and we'll both have food in our refrigerators."

"Sounds good. The larder is pretty bare." Oliver punched in some numbers and waited. "Hey, Lee, we have an identification on one of the Bruce Haverts you pulled up . . . the one who was a dealer in Vegas . . . Great. Tell Decker and we'll be back in about ten minutes." He hung up. "Lee said he'll get right on it."

"I'll get the chicken."

Oliver pulled out a twenty. "My treat. Tell her to keep the change."

"Why, Scott. You old softie."

"Not really. I just appreciate anything done correctly, and the lady makes a damn good chicken."

Decker looked at the printout: Bruce Havert born in Albuquerque, New Mexico, with the year of his birth telling them he was forty-three. Not much in the way of biography. From the ages of twenty-six to forty-one, Havert worked as a blackjack dealer at Havana! in Las Vegas. During his sojourn in Vegas, the man had been arrested for two DUIs, one drunk and disorderly, one misdemeanor conviction of possession of marijuana. He had no current wants or warrants. For the last two years, he seemed to have walked off the face of the earth. "Not Mr. Joe Citizen, but for a Vegas dealer, it's pretty clean."

Marge said, "Yeah, he did hold down a job for fifteen years."

Decker said to Lee, "Did you call up Havana!"

"Yes, I did," Wang said. "Someone's supposed to get back to me, but as soon as I mentioned *cop*, I felt the brick wall come down. I'm not holding my breath for a callback."

"What'd you say that made them mute?" Decker asked.

"All I asked for was a verification of his employment."

Oliver said, "From our last job in Vegas, that's typical with the big casinos. The big guys are very private with their own policing and their own policies."

Marge said, "You know? We made contacts from the Adrianna Blanc/Garth Hammerling case. Rodney Major and Lonnie Silver. They work North Las Vegas, not the strip, but it's something. I'll give them a call."

Oliver said, "What brought Havert to L.A.?"

Decker said, "And until last week, he owned or managed a massage company. Maybe he was pimping women while he was in Vegas and decided on a change of scenery. Or maybe he was run out of town."

"Or the Vegas market was saturated," Marge said. "Less competition out here, or it's more spread out."

Decker said, "Where is he?"

"I've tried Facebook and LinkedIn, but struck out." Wang stood up. "There are other networking Web sites. And Casey's Massage and Escort did have its own Web site at one time. I'll backtrack . . . see if I can dig up some leads."

After Wang left, Decker took out a piece of paper and began to doodle. "Let's think this through. What *do* we know?"

Marge ticked off a list. "Penny had a single gunshot wound—a twenty-two—to the back, but more than one round was fired. We haven't found the gun. Penny was also clubbed in the head. No weapon found with that either. He was a recluse who collected wild, poisonous, and venomous animals. He had a tiger. The only one that seemed to know anything about the tiger is Vignette Garrison."

"Yes, she is definitely still in the picture," Decker said.

"She admits visiting him a few days before he died and giving the tiger the shots, so she's really in the picture. Plus, she's the only person we're aware of that could have done something to Penny and not have the tiger eat her alive."

"All true."

"But you don't like her as a suspect."

"I still think that Penny was worth more to Vignette alive than dead."

Marge wasn't so sure. "We also have a tape of two women with massage tables parked across the street from Penny's apartment. The women were driving blue Priuses. The license plate of one of those cars was registered to Casey's Escort and Massage—a business owned or managed by Havert."

Decker tried to keep a train of thought going. "And we like Casey's because Penny had a thing for weird sex and also because George Paxton said that he had seen sexy women going into Hobart Penny's apartment, some with massage tables."

Oliver said, "Plus Casey's was cleaned out right after Hobart Penny's murder and none of us are big ones for coincidences."

Marge said, "Which apartment did Penny use for his women? Obviously not the ones with the snakes and bugs."

"Who knows with that whack job?" Oliver said. "Did you talk to the shrink?"

"Still waiting for a callback." Decker checked over his notes. "Paxton said neighbors complained about noise from the apartment directly under him. It's being processed by SID, just to make sure nothing was butchered there."

Oliver said, "So if SID is in the building, what's going on with the fumigation?"

"That's been scheduled for Tuesday," Decker said. "Wanda and Drew had notified almost all the residents. They haven't come up with any new information. Most of them didn't even know the old man existed."

"So when are we talking to the neighbors who complained about the noise?"

"The Shoops. Tomorrow at four in the afternoon. Did you get a chance to call any of the mortuaries?"

"Two," Oliver said. "No one's around. It's a skeleton staff."

Marge laughed at the pun. "We should probably go down in person. We can do the close ones tomorrow, and the others we'll take care of on Monday." Her phone beeped and she regarded the text message. "That was Darius Penny's secretary. He'll be here Monday after four. He'll call when he gets in."

"What about the sister?" Decker asked. "The countess somethingberger. Is she coming in?"

"Graciela Johannesbourgh. I'll call up the foundation and get an ETA."

"Sounds good." Decker stretched. He had spent all of Shabbos working and had little to show for it. "It's getting late. We can call it a day."

Marge said, "Do you want me to stop by the apartment and check in on SID? It's on my way home."

"Yeah. Sure."

"I'll come with you," Oliver said. "What about you, Rabbi?"

"I'll leave in a few minutes. Finish up some paperwork." Decker waited until his office was quiet. But he didn't pick up his memos, nor did he deal with his pink phone slips. Instead he pulled out his cell and clicked on to his contact list, staring at a cell number, wondering if it was operable. Donatti had a predilection for changing phones.

Decker loathed the idea of asking him for help. Donatti was an ace in the hole: and Decker wasn't in the hole just yet.

It had been gloomy all weekend. Sunday morning's drizzle had turned into afternoon rain, droplets falling, speckling the asphalt of the parking lot. Even though it had been her suggestion, Gabe was convinced that she'd chicken out, especially once she saw the dump she had chosen.

The room was seedy, but not nearly as dirty as he expected. He knew it had been recently cleaned—the garbage cans with empty liners, a vacuumed carpet, and fresh sheets—but being there made him itchy.

He checked his watch for the fiftieth time. Then he drew back the curtains and peeked out the window. Repeating the same thing over and over and over until a pewter daylight started to give way to a dreary, wet night. He'd promised Rina he'd be home by eight. If things kept going this way, he'd be home way before his self-imposed curfew.

Finally, at 4:03, he saw a car enter the lot—a four-year-old, black Mercedes. It was all shadows outside, and bright headlights caught the dance of the rain as the Benz pulled into a parking spot. Gabe grabbed his coat and stood outside the motel room, waiting under the portico. The emerging figure was tiny, dressed in a yellow raincoat, jeans, and black boots. No umbrella. He ran to her and protectively slipped his coat over her head, and the two of them dashed inside the room. His heart was thumping in his chest and it wasn't because of the sprint.

He threw his coat on the chair and helped her off with her slicker. She was wearing a sweatshirt underneath. The hood was drawn over her head. He rubbed her arms. "Cold?"

"A little."

"I was getting worried." Yasmine was silent. "Second thoughts?"

"Maybe."

Yasmine was looking at him with those gorgeous black eyes. She was as beautiful as ever. Her pixie childlike features had matured into something breathtaking. He hadn't seen her in over a year, and he was as smitten as the day he first kissed her. For him, time and space suddenly compressed. There wasn't any world beyond the two of them. Gabe said, "We can leave. You know I'd do anything you want."

She broke away. "I don't know what I want." She stood in front of the drawn curtains. On a table was a bag from Subway and a bouquet of flowers.

Gabe said, "Those are both for you."

"And here I thought you were into decorating." A pause. "God knows the place could use it."

"We can go, Yasmine. Let's just sit in the car and eat dinner together."

She picked up the flowers—yellow roses with jasmine vines. He'd taken time out to personalize the bouquet. "They're beautiful, Gabe." Her eyes welled up with tears. "Thank you so much."

"You're welcome."

She brought the flowers to her nose and inhaled. "I listened to the third movement of the Moonlight Sonata."

"What'd you think?"

"Pretty dazzling." Another smile. "I can hear you playing it in my brain . . . your phrasing . . . see your fingers flying. It's weird because it's very vivid."

"How did I do?"

"You played magnificently, as always."

"Thanks. But all of it is rubbish compared to you." Gabe walked over to her and pulled her hood down. He drew his hands through her luxurious hair and released it from the jacket—a cascade of black waves that almost reached her waist. "Man, your hair got long."

Yasmine finally smiled; a thousand bright lights. "I have to make up for your lack." She touched his fuzzy head. "Mr. Movie Star."

"Coming to a theater near you."

She got excited. *"Really?"*

"No, not really," Gabe told her. "Even if it's ever released, which is a big if, it's destined for obscurity. So don't get your hopes up on walking the red carpet, okay."

"Dang!"

"That's me, always a disappointment."

Yasmine grew serious. "It hurts me when you talk that way. I worry about you."

"I'm fine!" He took her hand and kissed it. "I'm still the same arrogant guy you met two years ago." Then he kissed her fingers one by one. "Arrogant but heartsick. I missed you, cuckoo bird." He drew her into an embrace. "I missed you so much."

As tears fell down her cheeks, she hugged him tightly. "I missed you, too."

"You are simply sublime. God, I love you."

"I love you, too." Her fingers walked up his right arm and rested below his shoulder. "I want to see them again."

"My tats?" He laughed. "They're still there."

She yanked on his sweatshirt. "Take it off. I want to look at them."

He pulled it over his head, allowing her to check out the two armlets—her name surrounded by a jasmine vine in script and below that, music that had once bound them together. Yasmine touched the blue ink and then kissed the artwork. She rested her head on his bare chest. Midway down his right side was the shiny pink indent of a gunshot scar. The sight made her eyes water.

"What will I do when you leave?" she told him. "I'm hopeless."

"I'm yours, body and soul. Forever and ever."

She smiled as her fingers walked across his chest. His ribs protruded and his stomach was sunken—not a six-pack in sight. His arms were long and wiry with taut muscle from years of playing. His fingers were spidery appendages. In this age of buffed movie stars, he was beyond skinny. She loved every single nonmuscle on his body. She loved the fuzz on his scalp and the acne on his forehead that came whenever he was nervous. She loved the rosy blush on his cheeks that appeared whenever he was embarrassed or aroused. She loved his beautiful green eyes, which were dilated to almost black. She knew that he'd eventually fill out—that he'd regain the weight he'd lost from anxiety about the trial. And she knew that his hair would grow back and the zits would go away. And then he would be once again the most beautiful person in the entire world. But for right now, she loved his geekiness just as much as she loved his genius.

Even though the room was warm, his nipples were erect. Her fingers danced over them. His response was immediate. He kissed her softly, then passionately. He took off her sweatshirt. Underneath that was a sweater. He slipped his hand under the soft cashmere and ran his fingers over her bra that encased a full, soft chest. His eyes got blurry and his knees got weak. "We shouldn't stay here, Yasmine. You know something's gonna happen if we stay here."

"Do you want it to happen?"

"Of course I want it to *happen*." He kissed her again. Instant electricity—a direct blood rush from his head to his groin. He felt faint. "But only if you want it to happen. It's gotta be mutual wanting it to happen."

She threw her arms around his neck and mashed his lips. They kissed another minute. "Okay."

"Okay what?"

"Okay . . . it's mutual wanting it to happen. I mean the deed was done a long time ago."

He stopped kissing her. "Do you regret it?"

"Maybe right afterward, a little." She gave him a wide smile. "Now seeing you, I remember why I did it. Do you have you-know-what?"

"Yes I have you-know-what. I brought a whole box."

Yasmine laughed out loud. "A whole box? Talk about arrogant."

Gabe grinned. "A boy can dream."

"And a girl can make a boy's dreams come true."

Chapter Twenty

As Decker waited for his four o'clock interviews, he took out his index cards and tried to make sense of Penny's murder.

The man was a recluse. Still, someone out there got close enough to murder him.

Vignette Garrison had had direct contact with him. She had been to the apartment just a couple of days before he was murdered. She probably had access. She was overly interested in his will. She needed money for her sanctuary. But was Penny worth more to her alive than dead?

There were the girls from Casey's Massage and Escort. George Paxton had admitted that there were sexy ladies going in and out of Penny's apartment. There was no direct evidence that Casey's women had gone into the apartment, but there was circumstantial material, that is, the videos. And from canvassing, no one else owned up to using Casey's services. Maybe the ladies had seen something in Penny's apartment that was worth robbing.

Or maybe Penny had scared them and they felt endangered: a possibility, since his ex-wife had told stories of rough sex. But that had been years ago, before the man had turned old and feeble. Even so, he had a slew of lethal weapons at his disposal—a Bengal tiger, venomous snakes and bugs. If he had wanted to torture someone, he had many creepy ways to achieve that goal.

His intercom light started to blink: the Shoops had arrived.

The couple appeared to be in their thirties. Ian was short and slight. Delia was shorter and slighter. A good wind could have knocked both of them over. They both had brown hair and brown eyes with round faces. Ian was dressed in a slim-fitting polo shirt and jeans. Delia had opted for a knit dress that fell to the kneecap, and fashion boots hugged her legs. After Decker made them comfortable in his office, he thanked them and pulled out a notepad.

"I know that you're being inconvenienced because of the exterminators. We hope that will be taken care of very soon."

The two of them shook their heads in dismay. Delia said, "We knew the man was crazy, but it's truly frightening how crazy he was."

"Imagine if that animal would have escaped!" Ian brought his hand to his chest. "We have a two-year-old son." He flapped his hands. "I don't want to think about it."

"Don't think about it!" Delia said.

Decker nodded. "Did you ever talk to Penny about the noises you heard?"

"Of course!" Delia turned to Ian. "Like two or three times?"

"Three times," Ian confirmed.

"Can you tell me about those conversations?"

"Well, that's the problem," Delia said. "It wasn't a real conversation. It was like . . . Sir, I keep hearing strange noises from your apartment." She leaned across Decker's desk. "I had no idea he was renting the apartment upstairs. We thought the old kook only had the one apartment next to ours. And now to find out that he was collecting those vile creatures so close to our little boy—"

"Don't think about it, Delia!" Ian said.

Decker nodded. "What do you mean, it wasn't a real conversation?"

"It was two seconds," Delia said.

"Where did you talk to him? In the hallway? Did you knock on his door?"

Delia said, "Actually it was Ian who knocked on the door. But I was there. I think it was like the second time we saw him in person."

"He never left his place," Ian said. "We wondered how he survived."

"Did you ever see a delivery guy come to the door?"

"Nope. But maybe they came to the upstairs apartment . . . I never knew he was renting it."

Decker said, "He was renting quite a few apartments. But you two were the only ones who complained about noises to the manager. At least, that's what he told me. Could you tell me about your brief conversation with Mr. Penny? You knocked on his door and . . ."

"I knocked on the door and he opened it." Ian rolled his eyes. "He said it was the television."

Delia said, "A total lie."

"He said that he was hard of hearing and he must have turned up the volume too loud. Give me a break!"

"Total lies," Delia said. "That growling wasn't coming from a TV."

"I thought it was maybe a pit bull," Ian said. "I was terrified it was going to escape."

"We have a two-year-old son," Delia informed them for the second time.

"So you went to his apartment three times?" Decker asked.

"Actually, I went to the apartment about ten times," Ian said. "He only answered the door three times."

"And you never saw the inside of his apartment."

"Correct. He spoke to us while we stood outside in the hallway. But like Delia said, what we heard was no TV. And his tiger proved that we weren't crazy."

"Because in the back of your mind, you think 'am I a little crazy?'" Delia said.

Decker said, "Obviously you were spot-on. Did you ever hear any other sounds from the apartment?" When Ian and Delia exchanged glances, he said, "What?"

"You tell him," Delia said.

"We heard grunts," Ian said.

"Grunts?" There was no response. Decker said, "Like sexual sounds?"

"*Maybe*," Delia said. "Except the guy was so old!"

"Yeah, we used to joke about it," Ian said.

"Yeah, we used to joke that maybe we should call the ambulance proactively." The two of them smiled at each other, but then Delia grew serious. "Of course, now that he's dead in such an awful way, it doesn't seem so funny."

"You thought that maybe he was having sex when you heard the grunts?"

Delia waved her hand back and forth. "Possibly. Are men that age even capable of having sex? I'm not talking elderly. I'm talking old!"

"He was old," Decker told her. "So if you assumed it was sex, did you ever see anyone go in or out of the apartment?"

Ian said, "Twice we saw the same lady go in and out. She wore a short dress and black boots and was carrying a massage table. She was clearly of dubious intent. That's why we thought the grunts were those kinds of grunts."

"Tell me about the woman," Decker said. "What did she look like?"

"Big blond hair, big chest, and long legs."

"Artificial big chest," Delia corrected. "I'm not saying she was doing something illegal. Could be she was giving the old kook a massage. But it could have been something more, judging by her looks and her tawdry outfit."

"And you saw this woman twice?"

"Yes." Delia looked at Ian. "But we heard the grunting like . . . four, maybe five times?"

"Five times," Ian said. "Between the grunting and the growling, I'd finally had enough of being Mr. Nice Guy. I complained to the manager."

"We were at our wit's end," Ian said. "Paxton said he'd take care of it. And he did."

"After that, no more noises?"

"No more grunting, no more growling," Delia said. *"Finally!"*

"And when was the last time you heard the grunting or growling?"

"I don't remember exactly," Ian told him. "But within a month of our complaining, the old kook moved out, much to our delight."

"At least we *thought* he had moved out," Delia said. "We didn't realize he had so many apartments in the building."

"But at least he wasn't our problem anymore," Ian said.

"He still was, in a way. Now they're fumigating because of him."

"The man spread his malevolence everywhere!" Ian barked.

"At least we're finally rid of—" Delia stopped abruptly. "I'm sorry he was murdered, but he was a pain in the ass."

"That woman who you saw going in and out," Decker said. "Ever see any kind of logo or name on her shirt?"

"No," Delia said. "Do you advertise that kind of thing?"

"Some do, believe it or not."

"I never noticed anything." Delia turned to Ian, who shook his head no.

"We're asking this of everyone who had any contact with Mr. Penny," Decker said. "If you could give us an account of what you were doing last Sunday or Monday, it would help us with our paperwork."

"Sunday is easy," Delia said. "We had dinner with friends." She turned to Ian. "The Kotes and the Abelsons."

"That is correct," Ian said.

"Until what time?"

"About eleven."

"Then what did you do?"

"We left and went home to bed," Delia said. "I had to get up early to go to work and take the baby to day care."

"We can give you the phone numbers if you want," Ian said.

"Sure," Decker said. "What about Monday?"

The two of them thought for what seemed like a long time. Delia finally said, "I think we just came home from work, ate dinner, watched TV, and went to bed."

Ian raised a finger in the air. "It was lasagna. You made spinach and ricotta cheese lasagna with Bolognese sauce."

"What a memory!" Delia exclaimed. "I did indeed."

"You also must remember, Lieutenant, that at this time, we thought the old kook had moved out. We had no reason to even think that he was still in the building."

"We no longer heard the growls and the grunts," Delia confirmed.

"Okay. So Sunday night you were out with friends, Monday you were working, came home and made dinner, spent the night inside."

Delia nodded. "Yes. That is what we did."

Decker jotted it down. "Great. I do have one last question. What do you think happened to the old man?"

They were flattered by their inclusion. Ian said, "Maybe the massage lady tried to rob him."

"Or he refused to pay her and she got mad," Delia said. "I can see him making people mad."

"So you think he was murdered by the masseuse?"

"He never left his room," Delia said. "No one else visited him."

"You did," Decker said. "I'm not accusing you of anything, but if you went to his door to complain, maybe someone else did as well." Silence. "Anything you'd like to ask me?"

"Yes." Ian's manner was stiff. "When can we move back in?"

"You'll probably get an all-clear by Thursday morning."

The two of them sighed in harmony. Ian said, "The manager said that the city is making them fumigate."

"It is a city health and safety issue," Decker said.

"Damn inconvenient!" Ian said.

"I'm sure it is, but it's better than being bit by a recluse spider."

"That man was nuts!" Delia said. "I don't want to even think about that."

"No don't think about it." Ian took her hand. "Let's go out for a latte and a bagel."

Delia smiled widely at Decker. "He always knows what to say to calm me down."

There were voices outside, a key card being inserted into the lock.

The pounding started when the door was met with resistance from the security chain. Fully clothed, Gabe leaped up from the bed and stuffed a garbage liner bag with two used condoms deep into his knapsack and stowed the rest of the unused box under the bed. He rushed to the door, wearing socks but no shoes. "Hold on. Lemme get the chain off."

A quick glance at Yasmine: she was attempting to put on her boots. Her long black hair was wild and uncombed. Her wide dark eyes were in panic mode. He whispered don't worry. Being OCD, Gabe had remade the bed and covered it with towels before they had started eating, because everyone knew about motel bedspreads. Two half-eaten Subway sandwiches lay on paper plates along with an open bag of potato chips. It looked innocent enough, although the context was damning.

As soon as the chain was unhooked, the door flew open and Yasmine's mother stormed into the room: a Persian warrior on a mission. Sohala Nourmand was red faced and shaking but was decked out in designer duds. Her gust of an entrance was followed by two uniformed police officers.

Sohala grabbed her daughter's arm and yanked her to her feet. Then she pointed to Gabe. "You arrest him," she screamed at the cops.

"*Arrest* him?" Yasmine screamed back. "Mommy, are you *crazy?*"

"She is just a girl!" Sohala was trying to pull her daughter out of the room, but Yasmine resisted. "He takes terrible advantage of my daughter—"

"Calm down, ma'am, we'll take care of this." The police officer speaking was stocky and bald. His name was Ritter.

Sohala was still screaming. "You arrest him—"

"Calm down!" Ritter had raised his voice a notch.

"We were just eating!" Gabe pointed to the bedspread. "Look!"

"You eat in restaurant, not a motel room with curtains pulled down," Sohala yelled. She shook a finger in his face. "She is a minor. You arrest him!"

Yasmine was in tears. "Mommy, stop it!"

"I'm a minor!" Gabe countered.

"You're eighteen—"

"I am not! I swear, Mrs. Nourmand, we were just eating—"

"Maybe right now, you were eating. Before, who knows!"

"Quiet—" Ritter tried again.

"You are a sneaky one!" Sohala yelled. "I bet you give her *drugs* to take advantage of her."

Gabe was aghast. "I didn't give her *drugs*."

"You're *crazy*!" Yasmine shouted. "He saved my life, in case you've forgotten!"

Sohala paused but only for a moment. She glared at Gabe, regarding him with confusion. "Why are you bald? Now you're Nazi?"

"Mommy, *stop it now*!" Yasmine shouted.

"I shaved my head for a movie—"

"You are in a movie?" Sohala asked. "What movie?"

"A small, independent film—"

"I don't believe you—"

"It's true! Why else would I be bald?"

"Everyone *shut* up!" The second officer boomed. The man was five ten, broad, and blond. His name was Staggert. "Just shut up and don't talk, okay." He

ambled over to Gabe until they were nearly nose to
nose—a silly attempt at intimidation. First of all, Gabe
was taller. Second, compared to his father and the Loo,
this man was an ant.

Staggert barked out, "How old are you?"

"Seventeen."

He turned to Yasmine, who was wiping tears from
her eyes. "How old are you?"

"Sixteen."

Back to Gabe. "You're pretty big for seventeen. You
wouldn't be lying to me."

"I'm seventeen."

"When will you be eighteen?"

"June."

"That's four months away."

"That's why I'm still seventeen."

Staggert jutted out his chin. "You being a wise guy,
big shot?"

"No, sir. I'm a little startled. I'm sorry."

Staggert continued with the icy looks. "You got ID,
big shot?"

"In my knapsack." Gabe started toward it, but
Staggert told him to just stay put.

"That's your knapsack over there?" When Staggert
pointed to the corner, Gabe nodded. "So you won't
mind if I take a look at it?"

Gabe swallowed, knowing full well he had used condoms inside. "Go ahead."

Staggert carefully unzipped the top and did a quick search through the contents. He pulled out two vials filled with pills. "So you don't do drugs, huh?"

"They're prescription," Gabe said. "My doctor's name is on them. Call him up if you don't believe me."

Staggert read the labels. "Why does a kid your age need Paxil and Xanax?"

Gabe dropped his voice. "I have some anxiety issues."

"What does a kid your age have to be anxious about?"

Gabe opened and closed his mouth. It just wasn't worth getting into it with this moron. He chose the most expedient option and said nothing. Staggert continued on with the search and pulled out a file of sheet music. "You some kind of rock star?"

"I'm a classical pianist." Gabe crossed his arms. "I go to Juilliard."

"You go to school in New York?" Ritter piped in.

Gabe unfolded his arms and tried to appear calm. Just maybe this guy wasn't a cretin. "Yes, sir, I do."

Ritter, the older of the two cops, told Yasmine and Sohala to stay put. He came over to Gabe. "So what are you doing in L.A.?"

"Visiting." Gabe's eyes lifted to Yasmine. "I used to live here."

Ritter took the sheet music from Staggert's hand, clearly the senior officer of the duo. He said, "Go watch the ladies." Staggert tried to swagger over to the women, but being relieved of his post chipped off a bit of his bravado.

After skimming the music for several pages, Ritter put the sheaves back into the knapsack. "Where's your ID, son?"

"Can I reach inside my backpack to give it to you?"

Ritter nodded. Gabe retrieved his walled and pulled out a Nevada driver's license and gave it to the officer. He studied the card. The birthday put him at seventeen: green eyed, light brown hair, six one, one-forty. Except for his bald head, the description matched. His name was Gabriel Whitman. "You used to live in L.A.?"

"Yes."

"Why do you have a Nevada license?"

"That's where my father lives. I lived with him a couple of summers ago and took the test over there."

"But you don't live with him now?"

"No, thank God."

"What does he do?"

Gabe was too riled to think clearly so he told the truth. "He owns brothels."

Ritter's eyes jumped from the license to Gabe's face. "He owns *brothels*?"

"Yes, sir." He should have lied. The guy had a weird expression on his face.

"Brothels." He stared at Gabe, and then at Yasmine. "Just what were you going to do with her?" He lowered his voice. "Take a trip to Nevada, maybe?"

Gabe was confused. Then all the color drained from his face. "Oh God *no*!" He shook his head. "No, no, no, no, no! I have nothing to do with my father's occupation. I hate him . . . well, not hate. I dislike him immensely. I love her. I swear to God, I'd die before I'd let anything happen to her. I almost did . . . die. It's a long story. I'll stop talking now."

In the back of his mind, Ritter remembered the girl saying that the kid had saved her life. There was some history here. He continued to study him. "Where's your mother?"

"In India."

"Doing what?"

"She lives there with her new family. It didn't include me."

Ritter blinked several times. He looked back at the license. "So who did you live with in L.A.?"

At last! The opportunity to name names. "I lived in the Valley with Lieutenant Peter Decker and his wife, Rina. That's where I'm staying now." He now had Ritter's attention. "He works at Devonshire. He's the head of the detectives' division."

Though trying to keep a flat expression, Ritter's eyes jumped. "And if I was to call him now, he'd verify that?"

"Absolutely."

"So he knows you're here . . . in a motel with a sixteen-year-old girl." When Gabe didn't answer, Ritter said, "How'd you book a room?"

"It's under my father's name."

"The one in Nevada who you dislike immensely."

Gabe sighed. "Yes, sir."

"So *he* knows you're here?"

Gabe held up his hands. "I don't know if he does or doesn't. He wouldn't care. I asked his secretary to do it for me. Her name is Talia. You can call either one if you want. You can reach her, but he's hard to get hold of."

"What's your father's name?"

"Christopher Donatti."

"Where are your father's brothels?"

"Outside of Elko. Would you like Talia's phone number?"

Ritter didn't answer. Instead he took down the name and license number and handed it back to the kid. He recognized Decker's name. He'd give him a call. "Any other ID?"

Gabe gave him his Juilliard student card. Ritter gave it back and went on searching in the knapsack. It took a minute, but eventually the cop came to the garbage bag at the bottom. He glanced inside, wrinkled his nose, and immediately locked eyes with Gabe. The boy closed his eyes and whispered a desperate silent "please."

The seconds seemed interminable. Finally Ritter zipped up the backpack and turned to Sohala Nourmand. "Take your daughter home."

"Not 'til you arrest him!" Sohala insisted.

"If I arrest him, I'm going to arrest her, too," he shot back. "Both of them are underage. Officer Staggert, please accompany Mrs. Nourmand to her car."

"I have my car here," Yasmine said.

"Accompany both of the ladies to their cars." To Yasmine, he said, "Go home, young lady. If I ever catch you with this boy again, I will arrest him for statutory rape, do you understand?"

Sohala added her parting shot. "You *stay* away from my daughter!"

After the trio left, Ritter turned to Gabe. "I'm not kidding, buddy. If this would have happened four

months from now, I would have charged you with statutory rape."

"We're only a year apart—"

"Irrelevant."

"I'm just saying it's not perverted or anything."

"It's not perverted, no. But the point is, Gabriel, her
mother doesn't want you to see her. That's the long and
the short of it. You've got to respect that."

Gabe rolled his eyes.

"Don't do that in front of me," Ritter told him. "It
pisses me off."

"Sorry." A pause. "Really. I'm very sorry."

"It's over, buddy. Just pack up and go home."

"It's not over," Gabe muttered.

"Well, it's over until she's eighteen and a legal adult.
If you ever see her again on my watch, I'm going to
haul your ass into jail. I don't care who you know,
got it?"

"I understand," Gabe said.

Ritter stared at him. "You're a good-looking guy.
There aren't girls in New York?"

"I love her."

Ritter laughed softly. "You have the world in front
of you, kiddo. Don't be a jerk. Stay away from your
friend until she's of age."

He left, slamming the door behind him.

Gabe peeked out of the curtains. Sohala waited in her car until Yasmine had left in her four-year-old black Mercedes. Then Sohala started her new black Mercedes and drove away. It took another ten minutes of conversing before the cops left.

Afterward, Gabe was numb, abandoned in an empty hole of darkness. Whenever these moods started, he usually could temper them by banging on the piano.

Unfortunately, there wasn't a keyboard in sight.

He opened his backpack and dumped the garbage liner with the dirty condoms back in the can. He left the unused box under the bed. Without Yasmine, they served no purpose. He popped a Paxil. Even with the pill, he'd still be teetering on the ledge. But the abundance of serotonin would probably prevent him from falling into the abyss.

The wonders of modern medicine.

Chapter Twenty-One

It had been a long day, and it was about to be a longer night. The snicker in the cop's voice still lingered in Decker's brain.

Do you know a kid named Gabriel Whitman?

Two very screwed-up people had dumped their kid on him. Instead of playing golf and traveling the world, Decker was dealing with an adolescent. As he pulled into the driveway, he reminded himself to breathe and to think before he spoke, something he often had trouble doing with his own family.

He forced his face to relax as he opened the door, sweet smells tickling his nose. Rina was on the couch, reading a magazine. She put it down and stood up, a big smile on her face. "Hi, big boy. I waited for you, and now I'm officially starved." She gave him a peck on the lips. "Hungry?"

Decker smoothed his mustache. Obviously she didn't know what was going on. "Is Gabe home?"

"In his room." Her smile fell. "What's wrong?"

"I need to talk to him."

"About?"

Without preamble, Decker explained as much as he knew, all of the information given to him over a phone call from LAPD West L.A. division. He managed to keep his voice low, but he couldn't keep the anger out. "The kid lied to me." He felt his teeth clench. "I *hate* being lied to."

"I completely understand that," Rina said, gravely. "But he couldn't exactly tell you the truth."

"So now you're his advocate?"

"Don't get mad at me. I wasn't part of any of this."

"I expected him to have a friggin' cup of coffee with this girl and leave. That's what he told me he was going to do. Stupid jackass!" Decker stalked away and pounded on the door to his room. "Open up!" A couple of seconds passed and he pounded again. "Gabriel, open up the door. I need to talk to you now!"

The boy appeared at the threshold. Behind his glasses, his eyes were swollen but dry. He had red blotches on his forehead. He wore a green T-shirt, jeans, and was barefoot. "Jesus, I was looking for my glasses—"

"Come out of there and sit down!"

"Can you just calm down?"

"I am calm but I'm also angry. You can be calm and angry at the same time."

"Look, I'm sorry—"

"You lied to me, Gabriel. I trusted you, and you looked me straight in the eye and lied to me. You made a fool out of me."

"What did you expect me to tell you, Peter?"

"How about the truth for starters?"

"That she asked to meet me at a motel and I said yes? And what would you have said if I told you that?"

"I would have insisted that you call it off and none of this would have happened."

"*I* didn't want to talk about it. You *insisted.* So to get you off my back, I told you what you wanted to hear. And for the record, I didn't have to tell you anything. You're not my *father!*" He regretted the words as soon as they were out of his mouth. "You're not even my *stepfather.*" He was making things worse. "You're no relationship to me whatsoever! So why don't you just go back to your wife and real kids and leave me the hell *alone!*"

His diatribe was punctuated by an angry slam of the door.

Perfect!

Decker was seething. Part of his fury was directed at Gabe, but most of his ire was reserved for the kid's parents. Jaw clenched, he kept telling himself to breathe slowly as he walked away. Rina was waiting for him with a stifled smile on her face.

"Hungry now?" When Decker threw her a look, Rina took his hand and led him to the couch. "Why don't you sit down and I'll bring you something to drink?" An open smile. "Like a double scotch, maybe?"

"I'm glad you find this so darn funny."

"I don't find it funny, Peter, I'm just too old to take it to heart."

"Don't give me a line about being old. I'm twelve years your senior. Now that's old."

"So let a young chick take care of you." Both of them heard Gabe's bedroom door open. "Uh-oh! I think it's time to make my exit."

Decker grabbed her hand. "No way. We're in this together."

"I'm just getting a bottle of water. Why should I die of thirst while you two are having it out?" She broke away. "I *promise* I'll be back."

"Yeah, right," Decker muttered. "No wonder I spend so many hours at the office."

"I heard that," she said from the kitchen.

"You were supposed to hear that," he yelled back. He looked up and regarded the kid—a picture of dejection. "Yes?"

"I'm sorry."

"For what?" Decker stood up and began to pace. "For lying to me? Apology accepted. For speaking the truth? No need for apologies. You're right. I'm not your father or your stepfather or any real relationsh—"

"Peter—"

"As a matter of fact, what I should have done in the first place is call up Chris, your *real* father, and take myself out of the equation."

"Please don't call Chris—"

"It's not for revenge, Gabriel, but I have to tell him what happened. So if your ass winds up in jail, he'll know the backstory. Because I'm sure not going to bail you out."

"Don't call up my dad—"

Rina had walked in. "He's not calling up your father."

Decker said, "Why not? Knowing Chris, he wouldn't care a whit. He'd probably congratulate you and laugh at me for giving a solitary rat's ass."

"Peter, please!" Rina said.

"I'll do anything, okay?" Panic behind Gabe's eyeglasses. His voice rose in pitch. "Just *please* don't call Chris!"

"Why? I would think you'd be *happy* to get me out of your life!"

"What do you want from me, Peter? You want me to *beg*?"

"Peter, enough!" Rina told him.

Decker pulled back. He pointed to the couch, and the boy fell onto the seat cushion and threw his head back. Then he looked at Decker with pleading eyes. "I'd much rather deal with *your* anger than with *his* ridicule, which is exactly what's gonna happen if you call him up . . . 'God Gabe, you can't even fuck your girlfriend without screwing up.'" He looked at Rina. "Sorry about my language."

"Have some water." She gave him a bottle, but he didn't open it.

"Do I get one of those, or is it only for poor little adolescent boys?" Decker asked.

Rina rolled her eyes. "I'll be right back."

Decker was still pacing. "Did you use protection?"

"Yeah . . . I'm stupid but I'm not suicidal."

"You're not stupid."

"Yeah, I am. I totally screwed up. I'm sorry that you got involved. You don't deserve that. I'm not your problem."

"By facts on the ground, you *are* my problem."

"Sorry." A pause. Gabe said, "She didn't have to call the police on me."

Despite his anger, Decker felt himself smiling. He sat down next to the kid. "That was a little extreme."

"*I* would have gone out for coffee. The motel was *her* idea. And don't tell me I should have said no. No guy my age would have said no."

"You can't see her anymore."

"I know that."

"Tell me the truth, Gabe. How long have you been in contact with her? And don't tell me you haven't been in contact with her because I know you have been."

"I never said I haven't been in contact with her."

"Yes, you did." Rina handed Decker a bottle of water. "You told me that you haven't e-mailed her, texted her, called her, or talked to her on Facebook."

"That part is completely true." Gabe paused. "Snail mail. She has a POB."

"You *write* to each other?" Decker asked.

Rina smiled. "How quaint."

Decker said, "You can't contact her anymore, Gabe. Even by snail mail. No more contact!"

"I can't do that. You just don't understand—"

"I don't understand?" Decker shook his head. "Can you at least be a little more original than that?"

"No, you really *don't* understand." His eyes were on fire. "You weren't *there*!"

Decker was quiet.

Gabe was all passion. "That day, I laid it on the line for *her* . . . but she laid it on the line for *me*. And that's a lot more than I can say for my own freakin' mother, okay." He balled his hands into fists. "When she left me . . . the way she left me . . . you've never been abandoned so don't say you *know* how I feel."

"I don't know how you feel . . . exactly." Decker held up his hand. "And before you jump down my throat, I will explain. I was adopted. When I was an adult . . . after I married Rina . . . by chance I met my biological mother. It was traumatic. It was especially galling to me because she had five other children. In my childish mind, I felt it wasn't that she didn't want kids. It was she didn't want *me*. I knew at the time it was stupid, my biological mother was a pregnant and panicked teenager. I'm not saying it's the same thing as you, Gabriel, but I do have an idea of what it feels like to be given up."

The boy drummed his fingers against his leg. "So we've both experienced betrayal. So then you should know why I have to talk to Yasmine again. I don't want her to think that I'm breaking up with her."

"Gabriel . . ." Decker thought about his words. "Once she's a legal adult, you're off the hook. But until then, you're stuck. It's only a couple of years until she's eighteen."

"If her mother doesn't ship her out to Israel or something." Gabe shook his head. "I don't know why her mom hates me so much."

"She doesn't hate you—"

"Yes, she does, and I do know why. I'm the wrong ethnicity and the wrong religion. I can't change my origin of birth but I told Yasmine I'd convert to Judaism. Actually, I've already started to look into converting. I'd probably convert even if there was no Yasmine."

Rina sat down next to him. "Really?"

Decker said, "Boy, you really know how to get on my wife's good side, Mr. Charming."

"Stop it, Peter." She looked at Gabe. "Why would you want to convert, Gabriel?"

He thought about the question. "I dunno. I like you guys. I guess I'd do it to feel closer to my make-believe family."

"Gabriel, we are not make-believe." When he didn't answer, Rina said, "And you know you always have a home here."

"Thank you for saying that." He checked his watch. It was past nine. "I don't mean to sound pedestrian, but is there anything to eat? I'm starved."

"I'll go set up dinner." She went back inside the kitchen.

Gabe looked at Decker. "That was babyish . . . saying that you're not my father."

"It was juvenile, but you're still a kid. Forget it." Decker patted his knee. "You'll feel better once you're back in school."

"I'm not going back," Gabe said. "At least not for the next couple of months."

"Okay," Decker said. "Can I ask why?"

"I'm not in a good place right now. I think the trial affected me more than I thought."

"You need downtime," Decker said.

"Unfortunately, that's not going to happen. I have to go on tour in six weeks. I just got an e-mail from my agent. He's booked me in two more cities where I have to play a couple of pieces that I don't know all that well. I called up Nick. He said he can help me out, so that's the good news. I've e-mailed the school. The only thing I have left to do this semester is a couple of performance finals. I can pick that up anytime. If I'm too much for you guys, I can stay with my aunt. But I'd like to use the piano . . . in the garage . . . that you rented for me . . . when you still liked me."

"Stop it already." Decker smiled. "You're welcome to stay here anytime you want for as long as you want—with your make-believe family."

"Thank you."

"Okay, Gabe. You've played the sympathy card very skillfully. Even I feel bad. If you stop milking it now, you earn the victory."

"So I can stay here, as long as I don't see Yasmine."

"Yes. That is the condition. Sympathy or not, I'm not bailing you out of jail."

"I need to talk to her about it, Peter. You can understand that, right?" Silence. "Can you talk to her mom for me?"

"You've *got* to be kidding!"

"You're right. I'll talk to her mother myself."

"That's not going to happen." Decker tapped his foot. "Give me a couple of days. I need time to think about how to handle Stormin' Nourmand."

Gabe's smile was genuine. "God, I don't envy you."

Decker threw his arm around the boy. "I'll do what I can. That's all I'm saying. In the meantime, no contact with her. Got it?"

"Yeah, I got it." Gabe laid his head on the shoulder and didn't talk. It was nice to be protected by someone big and strong. It was also nice that someone cared.

Even if it was only make-believe.

Gaining a second wind over dinner, Gabe ranted about the injustices of the world. He turned to his best ally—Rina. "I'm so damn angry. How would you feel if Peter's mother tried to have you arrested?"

Decker said, "My mother is ninety-five. Pick another example."

Rina said, "Gabe, I really do get how you feel. But as a mother, I understand how Sohala feels. She doesn't know how wonderful you are."

"Can you tell her?"

Decker said, "I don't think either one of us have clout with her right now."

The doorbell rang. Rina got up and glanced through the peephole. She took off her apron. "Oh dear. It's Sohala."

"I'm outta here," Gabe said. "Does she look mad?"

"I can't tell. You live here. Just stay put." Rina opened the door. Sohala was dressed in party attire—a glittery black slinky sweater, black leggings, and boots. Her hair was up, and she had on a full face of makeup. As she gave Rina a kiss on the cheek, she sneaked a glance at Gabe and asked to come in.

"Of course you can come in," Rina said.

Another look at Gabe. He said, "I think I'm going to take a shower."

"Please, Gabriel, you stay here." Sohala's voice was soft. "May I sit?"

"Of course," Rina said.

Decker said, "Well, if I'm not needed, I think I'll clear the dishes."

Sohala dashed him of his hope of a fast getaway. "You stay here, too, please. Everyone stay. Please."

The teen sat on the couch between Decker and Rina. Sohala sat across from them. She gave the boy the full force of eye contact. "I want to tell you something. Gabriel. I am very sorry for my behavior this afternoon. There is a Persian bakery right near the motel. My friend told me about Yasmine's car in the parking lot. I got very scared. Yasmine doesn't answer her phone. I think maybe it is a kidnapper."

"Ah," Rina said. "That explains a lot. I'm sure you were shaken up."

"Yes, very much." The woman was happy to have found a sympathetic ear.

"I understand," Rina said. "Are you all right now, Sohala?"

"Not so good, but who cares about me? Certainly not my daughter."

"She loves you," Gabe muttered. "That's the problem."

"I don't care about her love, I care that she listens to me. She don't listen to me."

Gabe looked at her with soulful green eyes under his specs. "Why do you hate me so much?"

"Gabriel, I don't hate you. How could I hate a boy who saves my daughter's life? I'm sorry I tell the police to arrest you. I think you are a marvelous boy. But I want you to listen to me." She stared at his nearly bald head. "You really make a movie?"

"I was in a movie. I didn't make it."

"What kind of a movie?"

"Some stupid independent film."

"So why you bald?"

"Because I play a psychotic who has a breakdown. In the final scene, they put me in a straitjacket and shave my head. Until a month ago, I had long hair."

"You get paid for the movie?"

The boy was confused. "Yeah, I got paid."

"How much?"

The boy stared at her.

Sohala said, "Never mind. Doesn't matter. Gabriel, I know you love my daughter."

"I do, Mrs. Nourmand. I really, really do."

"If you do, you want what's best for her. That's why I ask you this. You have to tell her you don't see her anymore."

"I really don't have a choice, do I? If I get caught again, you'll have me arrested."

"No, I don't have you arrested anymore. But you still need to stop seeing Yasmine. You have to tell her that you want to break up."

"But I don't want to break up with her. That would be a total lie."

"So you lie."

"Why would I break both of our hearts for no reason?"

Sohala looked at him as if he were an errant child. "You are famous pianist who stars in a movie, no?"

"No, I am not famous. I'm just a heartsick guy who loves your daughter."

Sohala tried again. "Well some piano players are famous."

"Most are not."

"But it's what you want to do, yes?"

Gabe regarded her. "Yes, it's what I want to do. It's very satisfying."

"People pay money to hear you play so you have to be very good, right?"

He wondered where she was going. "Right."

"And to play for people, you must travel?"

"Of course."

"All over," she said. "Like to many countries."

"I hope so."

"You travel how much during the year?"

"About two months during the school year . . . more in the summer when there are a lot of music festivals."

"And after you graduate, you travel more, no? You can travel for very long time."

Gabe felt his stomach drop. "Not a long time." A fib. "A couple of months."

"Or maybe more, no?"

Gabe was quiet. This wasn't leading to a good place.

"Gabriel, Yasmine is sixteen. She is a child. Even when she turns eighteen and goes to college . . . even if she goes away to college . . . just what is she supposed to do when you're away so long? Sit in a room, waiting for you to come back only to go away again? And while you go after your dream, is it fair to ask her to miss out on her life? Is it fair to ask her to be lonely while everyone around her is out having fun?"

For the first time since this afternoon, he began to squirm. "I can do other things."

"Like what?"

"I can teach, you know." The words sounded empty even to his ears.

"And that is what you want? To be a piano teacher."

The room was silent.

"I don't ask Rina and the lieutenant for their opinions, but they know I'm right." She leaned forward. "Let her fly, Gabriel. Let her meet friends, let her go to parties, let her live a normal young life."

"I never told her she can't go to parties. I want her to have fun!"

"She won't do anything as long as you are around. You need to give her chance to develop. If you truly love her, you see that I am right."

Gabe felt his eyes watering up. "This isn't fair."

"And it's fair for you to have her wait for months until you come back to her?"

"She can do anything she wants," Gabe said. "I've always told her that."

"What she wants is to be with you all the time. To pack your bags and travel with you and be your little house pet. She is a brilliant girl. Give her a chance to truly sing."

Gabe didn't say anything and neither did Sohala. He turned to Rina. "This isn't fair." He looked pleadingly at Decker. "This is so *not* fair."

Neither one of them said anything.

Gabe said, "And you agree with her right?" His eyes darted between Decker and Rina. "Really. I want to hear what you think."

Decker went first, "I know you love her, Gabe. But Sohala is making a good point."

"So what do you want me to do?" The boy folded his arms across his chest. "Tell her I don't love her anymore? I'm not going to do that."

"No, I don't think you do that," Sohala said. "It wouldn't be true and it would be hurtful. Still, you must tell her to date other people. If it's meant to be, you two will go back together." She swallowed hard. "If she dates other boys and decides she still loves you, I promise I will accept you in my family if you convert."

Gabe stared at her. "You expect me to tell her to date other guys? Forget it!"

Sohala's eyes watered up. "Sometimes in life, you must do hard things. If she comes back to you after she tries others, I will support whatever she wants. Just give her a chance to grow up. You'll love her more as a woman instead of a little girl who idolizes you and can't see in front of her nose."

Again Gabe wiped his eyes. "I'll . . . *talk* to her, okay. But no guarantees."

"Good—"

"*And* with one condition." He looked at Sohala. "You got to get her to take singing lessons again. You *can't* stand in her way if she wants to perform."

Sohala narrowed her eyes. "I give her singing lessons again, hokay?"

"That's not what I said," Gabe told her. "If she wants to study opera, you have to help her do that."

The woman folded her arms across her chest. "That's not fair."

Rina interceded. "You can either both compromise or you can continue to battle." She stood up. "I'm going to clear the dishes."

"I'll help you," Decker said.

Gabe said, "If you agree to let her do whatever *she* wants, then I'll agree to what you ask."

"Hokay." Sohala wiped her eyes. "If you tell her good-bye, I agree."

First, calm Mom down. Gabe said, "And . . . for the record . . . I see your point. It's unfair to let her wait around for me." How the hell was he going to get around this? "I'll tell her to date other guys as long as you agree to encourage her as a singer. Do we have a deal?"

"You also have to tell her you date other girls."

"But I don't want to date other girls. What I do is my business."

"She won't agree to date other boys unless you date other girls. And you should date other girls. You tell her you go out with other girls and then I do every-thing with the singing, hokay?"

The ideas started to coalesce into a plan. He said, "Okay."

Sohala looked at him with suspicion. "I don't know if I trust you."

Good call, lady. Gabe said, "Mrs. Nourmand, I know we can't be together until you accept me. So we have a deal, right?"

"Hokay." Sohala was still not convinced, but what could she do. The boy was a snake in the grass. A very cute snake—she understood why Yasmine was blinded—but that wasn't the point. "Hokay, I bring her here so you can talk to her. She's waiting for me in the car."

"You mean I have to do this *now*?"

"Yes, now."

His heart started beating. "Can't you give me a day or two to think about it?"

"Gabriel, you change your mind if I give you chance to think. I know that. Set her free. It is the right thing to do."

He was antsy and edgy. He wanted to work out the details, but now there was no time. He had no choice but to hope for the best. "Okay. I'll talk to her now."

Sohala got up and tried to compose herself. "It is like our sages tell us, if not now, when?"

Gabe didn't answer.

Screw the sages.

Chapter Twenty-Two

Gabe thought she'd be despondent. Instead, Yasmine was furious. She sat opposite him, balled up in a navy blue hoodie, her arms folded across her chest. She glared at her mother and looked at him with suspicion. At that moment Decker walked in, turned around, and went back to the kitchen. To Rina, he said, "Want to go for a ride?"

"It's that bad?"

"Yasmine is now in the picture, and it looks like the shoot-out at the O.K. Corral. Ride? Yes or no?"

Rina put away the last of the dinner dishes. "Shouldn't one of us stay to make sure the house isn't burned down?"

"Good point," Decker conceded. "I'll be in the bedroom if anyone needs CPR."

"Maybe you should go out and act as a moderator to the parties involved."

"No, my dear, I'm done with domestics. If you need the police, call 911."

After he left, Rina steeled herself and ambled into the living room. Someone had to be the adult. She sat down on the couch.

Sohala began by directing the players. "You talk to her, Gabriel. You tell her what we talked about."

Gabe felt sick. He didn't dare look at Yasmine. "Your mother thinks we should break up . . . for a while."

Yasmine said, "I know what *she* thinks. Is that what *you* think?"

"Hear me out." Gabe felt a tic in his eyelids. "Just . . . *listen*." Yasmine was silent. "There is this girl that I know in New York—"

Yasmine had heard enough. She jumped up. "I hate you!" She glared at her mother. "I hate you, too. I hate all of you!" She picked up her purse and stormed out of the house.

Gabe leaped up and so did Sohala. He clenched his jaw and said, "Will you let me handle this?"

"I see how you handle it. You break her heart."

Rina really should have taken that ride. Instead, she said, "Gabe, take it easy."

The boy didn't heed her. "None of this would have happened if you hadn't interfered!"

"Of course, I interfere. You were in a motel with my daughter!"

"Fuck it!" Gabe ran after her, slamming the door behind him. She was already halfway down the block. "Yasmine!"

"Go away. I don't ever want to see you again."

"Yasmine, will you listen—"

"No."

He caught up with her and took her arm. It had stopped raining, but there was a fine mist. He had run out without his jacket and it was cold. "Yasmine—"

"Do you tell her you love her when you're with her like you do with me?" She yanked her arm away. "Do you tell her that, Gabe? *Do you?*" She hit him with her purse and marched off for a couple of steps. *"Avazi!"* Then she turned around and threw her purse at his head. "You . . . schmuck!"

He caught the purse with his left hand. "There is no other girl—"

"Liar!" She reversed directions, intercepting her mother. "Go away and leave me alone for once in my life!"

"Yasmini—"

"Can you just let us break up without spying on me? You go through my mail, you go through my phone, you go through my computer, you go through my diary. For God's sake, Mommy, can you give me a little privacy for *once* in my entire life?"

Sohala was wounded. "I give you privacy. You have your own room."

"Oh, please!" She shook her head. "Just forget it! Let's go home!"

"Can I please talk to you?" Gabe implored. He turned to Sohala. "Could you please leave us alone for a few minutes?"

Rina had come out. "This is my house, guys. Take it inside or everyone goes home."

No one moved.

Yasmine lowered her voice. "Give me a few minutes, Mommy. *Alone!*"

Rina took Sohala's arm. "We'll wait in the house. Keep it down or I'll call the police. Nobody wants Peter out here, right?"

Silence.

Sohala said, "Don't be long."

"Don't worry, I won't be long." She glared at Gabe. "I hate you!" She opened the door to her mother's Mercedes and sat in the passenger seat. "You know what? Go away! I'm done with you." She slammed the door and locked it.

Gabe knocked on the window, trying to keep his voice down. "Can you open the door? I'm cold."

"Freeze to death for all I care."

Gabe showed her the handbag. "I've still got your purse."

"Go away!"

"Fine." He began to walk toward the house. "Suit yourself."

She opened the car door. "Give me back my purse, you . . . !" When he kept walking, she said, "Gabriel, I'm serious!"

He heard the tears in her voice. He came back to the car and spoke through a closed window. "Can we talk now?"

"Give me my purse first."

Gabe clenched his jaw. "Fine."

She rolled down the passenger window. He thought about sticking his hand in the open window and trying to force open the lock, but in her frame of mind, she'd probably roll up the glass up on his fingers. He threw her handbag onto the driver's seat and waited.

A moment passed. Then she grabbed her purse, unlocked the door, and he went inside, hitting his knee on the steering wheel. "Ouch!" He pushed the seat back. "Your mother must be a dwarf or something."

"I hate you!"

His teeth were chattering. "Yasmine, there is no other girl."

"You told me your dad's a compulsive liar. You're a liar, too!"

"I've been faithful to you, body and soul. There is no other girl."

She turned to him. "Then why say such an awful, hurtful thing to me?"

"Yasmine, your mom sprung this breakup thing on me and I had to think of something. That's why I told you to hear me out. You didn't let me finish. Man, you have a temper!" He raised his eyebrows. "I like it!"

She hit him again with her purse.

"Stop it! There is no other girl!"

"Then why did you say that to me, *especially* after this afternoon." She started to cry. "Why did you *say* that?"

"Because I wanted to get your mom off my back. I was trying to convince her that I was breaking up with you. I could tell she was suspicious. I knew she'd be more likely to believe me if there was someone else waiting in the wings. She insists that both of us date other people. Not just you. Me, too."

"*Is* there someone else?"

"No! No one! When your mom popped this on me, I came up with an idea. It might not be the best idea, but considering I had about two minutes, it was the only thing I could think of."

"So the other girl is a total lie?"

"As a girlfriend, yes, it's a lie. I'll explain my idea if you'll listen." No response. Gabe blew out air. "Remember a girl named Anna Benton? You met her—"

"The blond, blue-eyed pianist with the long legs who swears like an HBO program. She must be about twenty, twenty-one by now."

"Twenty-one." Gabe was amazed. "Boy, you remembered everything. That was like two years ago."

"You don't forget someone that gorgeous who was giving me the stink-eye."

"She was not."

"Yes, she was." She squinted at Gabe. "You told me she's a lesbian."

"She is." When Yasmine gave him *that* look, he said, "Can I go on?"

"Not really." A pause. "*What?*"

"Look, Yasmine, Anna is a good friend of mine but she's crazy. She's on more psychotropic medicine than my entire class at Juilliard, and that's saying something because we're all on something. She's bipolar. For real. She's mostly manic. When she doesn't take her lithium, she's totally out of control. Even when she does take her medicine, sometimes instead of making her calm, she falls into a deep depression."

"Then why in the world are you *friends* with someone like that?" When Gabe tapped the steering wheel, she said, "Did you sleep with her?"

"You mean sex and the answer is a resounding no. Technically, I slept in the same bed with her, but we never came even close. Couldn't have done it if I *wanted* to."

"What happened?" This time Yasmine's voice was sincere.

"I will tell you." He let out a breath. It was frosty because of the cold. "When I first got to Juilliard, I was in a real bad funk. I thought I lost you forever. My mom was gone. The Deckers were three thousand miles away. My dad was God only knows where. I couldn't exactly burden Hannah or any of the other Decker siblings with my problems. I tried to cope, but I was sinking. Eventually I took a leave of absence. I got a doctor to say that I had mono, but really, what I had was a breakdown."

Yasmine's eyes watered up. "Why didn't you *tell* me?"

"I couldn't get hold of you, remember?"

Yasmine became furious. "I hate my mom."

"Don't hate your mom." He took her hand. "I'm serious. Don't hate her. I refuse to be that wedge between you and your parents. Moms are important . . . to boys, yes, but especially to girls. Even I don't hate your mom. I know she's just fighting for you. But I'm fighting for you, too. And we both know that I'm going to win, so let's have pity on the old lady."

She smiled as tears leaked onto her face. "I should have been there for you."

"I'm glad you weren't. I probably should have contacted my shrink, but I was trying to muscle it through without help. Terrible idea. I just . . . crumpled."

Silence. Yasmine said, "What happened?"

"I dunno, really. It came on so suddenly. I was having coffee with Anna. I bumped into her at one of those Sunday church concerts in Manhattan when I first got to New York. I was so low and she was this ball of energy. We started to meet for late night coffee after she finished work."

"What does she do?"

"Anna? She plays piano at a bar Sunday through Thursday in Brooklyn—some hipster place. On weekends, she waitresses at Hooters."

"*Hooters?*"

"It pays the bills."

"I'm not being a snob, I'm just surprised. She's a classical pianist."

"Yeah, welcome to the world of starving artists. Her apartment is a studio with barely enough room for a piano and a bed."

"Which you've slept in, but didn't have sex."

"Yasmine, stop it."

Her tone softened. "Go on, Gabe. Really. I want to know."

He said, "When we met up, we talked shop mostly . . . when she wasn't ranting about her love life. Anna rants a lot. That's the trouble with her playing. It's all passion and no finesse. Anyway, one night when she was walking me back to school—her apartment is a couple of blocks from Juilliard—I suddenly grabbed my chest and fell to my knees. I thought I was having a heart attack. I couldn't breathe."

Yasmine looked stricken. "Oh God!"

"I thought I was going to die. Anna called 911. Turns out it was a panic attack—the first of many. To make a boring long story short, I moved into Anna's apartment while on my leave of absence. She took care of me, Yasmine. She made me eat and made me practice at the expense of her own playing. She took long walks with me. She'd prattle on constantly while I was mute. After much cajoling, just to shut her up really, I finally agreed to see my shrink. He put me on meds, and I slowly started to function again."

Yasmine was crying. "That should have been *me*."

"No, no, no. You had your own issues. That's why I'm not mad at your mom. She took care of you. And as far as Anna is concerned, I've paid her back by helping her through her crises, which have way outnumbered mine. That girl survives on drama."

"She should have called me."

"How can I say this any clearer? I didn't *want* you to know. It's not only emasculating for me, I didn't want to scare you. It's over and done. I'm okay." She still looked worried. "Really, I'm fine. Before, I was in limbo. Now I know that even if it takes a while, we'll eventually be together."

He kissed her cheek.

"You should never doubt my love and fidelity. And I promise I will never let you down." He let out a whoosh of air. "What I was thinking when I brought up Anna is that she would be a perfect fake girlfriend for me. I could post pictures of us on Facebook like we're in a relationship because I know your mom will check up on me."

"Probably . . ." Yasmine tapped her toe. "Definitely."

"Anna would do it for me. Surely you know some boy in your community who could be a fake boyfriend . . . someone who needs a girl but doesn't want one."

"You mean someone gay?"

"Yeah. Someone who's still in the closet and doesn't want to come out yet but everyone knows he's gay."

"That would be my cousin. And that would be weird."

"Yeah, it sounds stupid, now that I say it out loud. Your mom wants me to stop seeing you. She's going to check up on us. I don't know how we can keep in contact. I sure don't want a repeat of what happened this afternoon. I'm open to any suggestions."

"So . . . you slept with Anna but didn't sleep with Anna."

"Yes. Exactly." A pause. "Yasmine, I love *you*. If we could be together for the rest of our lives, I'd be the happiest boy alive. All this drama saps my energy. It's good in fiction. It's lousy in real life."

"I want to be with you, too." Yasmine's voice broke.

Gabe licked his lips. "That being said . . . I am forced to think that just maybe your mom has a point." When she stared with watery eyes, he said, "You'll always be number one. But I can't fight who I am. I need my music. It's my fix. And I will be traveling a lot. Maybe your mom is right. You should go have fun in college. Go to parties and spring break and get drunk and have blackouts."

"Does that sound even *remotely* like me?" Yasmine rolled her eyes. "You know, even if I liked parties, who has time for them? Gabe, I'm *busy.* My parents weren't educated here. Neither of them knows what I go through, all this pressure to get into a good college. They don't even understand why I *want* to go to a good college. Community college is good enough for them. So I'm left by myself working my tail off, trying to convince them why I need an SAT tutor. Not all of us can waltz into Harvard and turn it down to go to Juilliard."

"I didn't waltz into anywhere when you've figured I've been banging away at the piano my entire life. It took over my entire childhood."

"C'mon, Gabe, you know what I mean. You're exceptional. And for the tiny percentage that's exceptional, everyone wants you."

"You're gifted, Yasmine. I made your mom promise to give you singing lessons again if I break up with you. If you want that, it'll happen."

"Gabriel, I don't have *time* for singing lessons." She got misty eyed. "I'm too busy learning stuff that I'll probably never use. My father tells me to be a doctor . . . like it's that easy. If I'm lucky enough to get into a good university, I'll have to work like a demon to get into medical school. And if I'm lucky enough to get into medical school, there's internship, then there's residency, then fellowship, then postfellowship, then a job, then partnership. And after all that, if I'm lucky enough for you to still want me, I'll probably give birth to our grandchildren, I'll be so old."

Gabe put his arm around her shoulders. "I know it's hard. I'm very proud of you."

Her lip trembled. She burst into tears. "I hate my life! I *suck* at everything!"

"No, you don't!"

"Yes, I do!" She was sobbing.

"Are you failing or something?"

"Of course not!" She was insulted.

Gabe rolled his eyes. Girls were so damn confusing. "Cuckoo bird, listen to me. And this time, really listen. This is what we're gonna do, okay?"

A pause. "What?"

"Your mom is . . . a little hotheaded." *Like mother, like daughter.* "I probably won't be in your life until you're eighteen. But once you're eighteen, we're home free. By then, I promise I will have converted. That's number one. I'm also determined to learn enough Farsi to understand your family . . . and your curses. What did you call me?"

"*Avazi.*"

"I know that's what you called me. What does it mean?"

"Asshole."

"Thank you very much."

"You don't have to learn Farsi. I'll teach you all the cuss words."

He laughed. "Look, if you do happen to find a gay guy to play along with the charade, I guarantee you that your mom will thank God that I'm heterosexual, okay?"

Yasmine smiled. "That's the wackiest thing I ever heard."

"Like I said, I'm open to suggestions." When she didn't answer, he said, "We'll figure something out. In the meantime, I'm not going back to school for six weeks. I've taken a leave of absence to practice for my upcoming engagements." He focused on her beautiful eyes. "Tell me, Yasmine. Where do you want to go to college?"

"I was thinking about Barnard. I want to be near you and in New York. If I don't get into Barnard, I'll go down the list of all-girl schools."

Gabe was quiet. "You're still afraid?"

"Duh, yeah." She looked down, tears spilling in her lap. "I'm being awful. Sorry."

"No apologies necessary." He kissed her fingers. "I'm sure you won't need this to get in, but it wouldn't hurt to make a CD of your singing. Your voice is really spectacular. Pick out a few arias. I'll rent some studio space and I'll put together a CD."

She wiped her eyes with her hands. "You'd do that for me?"

"I would do *anything* for you."

"What about my mom?"

"Just tell her the truth. I'm just helping you record a CD for college."

Yasmine said, "She'll never let me be alone with you."

"She can come to the sessions. I want to do this for you, Yasmine. I love you. And I'm sorry I did such a clumsy job. I was put on the spot."

"Gabriel, you must promise that if you are in a bad way, you'll call me. I mean I'm grateful to Anna, but *I'm* your girl. Promise?"

"I promise."

"Okay." Yasmine still wasn't convinced, but now was not the time. She looked at her watch. "We've been out here a half hour. I don't know how much more patient Mommy will be."

"So let's go in. But not before I get my kiss."

She threw her arms around his neck and kissed him with fire. It sent an immediate jolt below his belt. Yasmine bit her lip. "I'll talk to my cousin. It might be nice to help out some poor guy. Being gay in my culture isn't easy." She turned to him. "Can I really trust you with Anna?"

"Absolutely. Do you want Anna's cell number? You can call her anytime."

"Yes. And give her mine . . . just in case."

"Gotcha." He gave her Anna's number and stowed his phone back in his pocket. "All right, cuckoo bird. Let's go face the music." They both got out of the car. He took her hand, and the two of them slowly started toward the house. He started shivering. His heart sank. Time could be a killer. Distance was not a friend. Even with meds coursing through his system, the thought of losing her made him feel without purpose.

Like a dead man walking.

Chapter Twenty-Three

After the previous night's drama, Decker awoke at five-thirty in the morning to a quiet house. He read the Sunday paper, and when he was finished, he went out and got Monday's paper. When he heard Rina stir, he pushed the button on the coffee machine, and within minutes, it released the heavenly aroma associated with a new day of promise. He finished pouring just as she walked into the kitchen.

Rina picked up the mug and took a sip. "Aah, that's good." She joined Decker at the table. "Have you recovered from last night?"

"All that drama and he ain't even blood related."

As if on cue, Gabe walked into the kitchen, fully dressed, his eyes drooping behind his glasses. "Am I interrupting anything?"

It was five to seven. Decker said, "Where are you going so early in the morning?"

"Nowhere. I've been up all night, practicing." They stared at him, and he shrugged. "I couldn't sleep. I gave up around two. It actually was a good session. I'd feel energized if I wasn't so tired."

Rina said, "How about some breakfast for all of us? Sit down, Gabe, and entertain the lieutenant."

"I think he's had his quota of my entertainment." Gabe picked up the coffeepot. "This is caffeinated, right."

"Maximum strength," Decker said. "How are you doing, Romeo?"

"Okay." He set out forks, knives, and plates. "Are you still pissed at me?"

"I'm over it. Sit down, son. I've got a question for you, and it has nothing to do with last night."

"Bring it on."

"How well does Chris know Las Vegas?"

"I'm sure he has some contacts there. Want me to call him for you? I'd love to be useful instead of a pain in the butt."

"I'll call him if I need to. Do you have his current phone number?"

"I do."

He gave him the digits: a number that was different from the one Decker had in his contacts.

"What do you need him for?" Gabe said. "The hookers for your tiger guy?"

"You weren't supposed to hear that."

Gabe leaned back. "Vegas isn't his territory, but he's a major player in the industry. The one thing he knows is sex."

"The question is do I want help from your dad?"

"Yeah, there are always strings attached." They both drank coffee in silence. "Chris was okay when I lived with him, but he wasn't around much."

"Did he take side trips to Vegas?"

"All over the map. Talia would know his schedule."

Rina set down a plate of French toast and a bottle of genuine maple syrup. She took a seat at the table and rubbed her hands together. "All right then. This is very homey. What are your plans today, Gabe?"

Decker said, "Make sure they don't include getting arrested."

"I'm never going to live this down."

"It'll be a constant source of amusement for me in years to come."

"Great to be useful, if only to act the buffoon. I have a lesson with Nick at USC. I'll be done by noon. Want to meet for lunch, Rina?"

"One would work perfectly." She smiled at Decker. "You're welcome to join us."

"Thanks for the invite but I got plans—mortuaries and hookers. Can't get more primal than sex and death."

At three in the afternoon, Marge and Oliver interrupted Decker and his paperwork. They had been out in the field but looked none the worse for wear. Marge was dressed in her usual sweater and slacks; Oliver had on a blue blazer, slacks, and a white shirt with no tie. Decker pointed to the chairs, and they sat down.

Oliver said, "Darius Penny just called from the private airport. He'll be here at six."

"Sounds good," Decker said.

"The mortuaries we visited." Marge placed a list on his desk. "We went through six. No one admitted to any thefts of body parts."

"Why would they?" Oliver said. "That would imply incompetence." He got up. "Anyone for coffee?"

"Two Splendas and lots of milk," Marge said.

"Black," Decker said.

"Be right back," Oliver grumped.

Marge said, "We're not getting anywhere. I think we're on the wrong track."

"Speak to me."

"I called up Dr. Spar again to ask if she found any embalming solution in the frozen fingers. She hadn't."

"So you don't think the fingers came from mortuaries?"

"They weren't taken from embalmed bodies, but Dr. Spar is pretty convinced that the fingers were taken off postmortem. To me, that's says psycho souvenirs."

"Penny's a sadistic killer who removed the fingers of the women he murdered?"

"Well, both Paxton and the Shoops saw girls going into the apartment. Maybe some went in and but didn't come out."

Decker said, "I don't recall a spate of hooker killings. Besides, SID went over Penny's other apartment with luminol and all they found was animal blood."

"Animal blood contaminated with human blood."

"Okay, let's go with your theory," Decker said. "Suppose he did kill women? How would an old man get rid of the body?"

"He had a tiger, Pete."

"Now, there's an image. An eighty-nine-year-old sexual psychopath feeding his victims to his tiger. I don't buy it, Marge. It's not that old psychos don't exist. But I'm not loving the logistics of an old man chopping off fingers and feeding bodies to his wild animals. There would be a ton of blood all over the place."

Oliver came in and handed out the coffees. "We're back to Penny being a psycho?" He sat down. "Judging from his ex-wife's account, he was a psycho. But I'm thinking about him now: a very elderly man killing women and chopping off fingers and disposing of the bodies. It's a little hard to picture."

"The fingers were frozen for a long time," Marge said. "Maybe they were crimes of his youthful past."

"Interesting," Oliver said. "Why would Penny keep his souvenirs among his packages of tiger meat? Why not keep them in a place of honor?"

"Because a freezer is the only place you can keep body parts fresh," Marge said.

"Hold on a moment. Let me get my list." Decker rummaged through a file until he found what he wanted. "There were six index fingers—two right, four left—six big fingers—five right, one left—six ring fingers—three and three—and seven pinkies all from the right hand. No thumbs. We're definitely working with more than one woman."

"Unless she was Anne Boleyn." When Decker looked blank, Marge said, "The beheaded queen supposedly had six fingers on each hand. It was a bad joke."

Decker gave her the courtesy of a half smile. "Let's play this out. Penny was a psycho killer who took fingers for souvenirs. But the fingers were frozen together in one big lump, indicating that the digits were put into the package at the same time. I know that all it takes is a single bullet to kill someone, but do you really see Penny killing multiple women and disposing of multiple bodies in just a few sessions?"

Everyone agreed that it didn't make sense. Marge said, "Have you run any of the prints through AFIS?"

"We have a few decent prints, but it's an involved process to bring them back," Decker told her. "The ones we've run have come up empty."

"Too bad," Marge said.

"Let's try a different approach," Decker suggested. "Penny had a lot of exotic pets with different dietary needs. Some of the meat came from the grocery, but not all of it. What if Penny had sketchy people who delivered him meat at a discount, people less concerned with safety conditions. Maybe Penny didn't know what he had. We should still find out who supplied Penny's animals."

Oliver said, "You're referring to Vignette Garrison."

"Gabe told me that the accountant at Global Earth Sanctuary stated that most of the expense came from feeding the animals," Decker told them. "Maybe supplying food for Penny's animals was an easy way for Global Earth to make a few extra bucks."

Marge said, "I could understand one finger, Pete, but an entire package of digits?"

Decker conceded the point. "Still, the remains were mixed in with the animal meat. There's no harm in asking Vignette about her food sources. She's always hungry for money. I'm sure she supplied food for Penny's animal, taking a service charge for herself or the organization." He smiled at his detectives. "Pay her a visit bright and early tomorrow morning and ask her directly."

Decker was still debating whether or not to call Donatti when his desk phone beeped. He depressed the button. "This is Lieutenant Decker."

"Dr. Delaware is calling you back, sir."

"Oh yeah. Thanks." He pressed the blinking line. "This is Lieutenant Peter Decker."

"Dr. Alex Delaware returning your call."

"Thanks for calling back, Doctor Delaware. Do you have a moment?"

"I do."

"I need your services. Not personally, although it might be a good idea in the future. In this instance, it's a case."

"It must be involved if you're asking for my help."

"It is."

"Can you sum up the case for me in a couple of sentences?"

"Sure. It's a homicide case: an eighty-nine-year-old reclusive man suffered a gunshot wound to the back and blunt force trauma to the head. He was very rich, but he lived like a pauper. He was estranged from his family, but his foundation and his will and estate were still handled by his son's firm. His actual investments are handled by others. Besides the son, he also has a daughter. Both of them are wealthy on their own. His primary source of companionship seemed to be an adult female Bengal tiger that he had raised from a cub."

"The inventor, Hobart Penny. I read about him in the papers."

"Yes, Hobart Penny. Not only did he have a tiger in his apartment, but he also collected other venomous and poisonous animals, mostly snakes but also lethal fish and insects. When he was younger, his ex-wife said he had a predilection for wild sex and fetishes. She also told my detectives that he felt like a tiger trapped in a man's body. I don't know if that was still true as he aged. We also have reasons to think that he had prosti-tutes visiting him, even though he was eighty-nine and infirm. We're wondering if they had something to do with his death, too. He's just a very puzzling guy."

"I can see that. So how can I help you?"

"I'm not sure. I'm thinking if I could get a peek into his head, maybe that would help me with the case."

"All right. Let me do some research and I'll call you back."

"That would be great." A pause. "How much do you charge?"

"As long as we keep it to a couple of phone calls, don't worry about my fee. Just tell me what you want."

"Basically, I'd like to get a feel for what made him hum, and who would want to kill him."

"That's a two-part sentence, Lieutenant," Delaware said. "The first part I may be able to help you with. The second part is strictly your domain."

Chapter Twenty-Four

Originally Graciela Johannesbourgh was supposed to arrive Tuesday morning. Instead, on Monday evening, she walked into the station house with her younger brother, Darius Penny, at straight up six. Marge put them in an interview room outfitted with coffee, water, and doughnuts, although Marge was doubtful that Graciela had ever eaten a doughnut in her life. She was in her fifties and stick thin with a tight jawline and a made-up face that canted slightly to the right. It almost looked like a coquettish gesture had Marge not known her medical background. Graciela had blue eyes and coiffed blond hair that grazed her shoulders. Dressed in a black sweater and slacks and a bright orange blazer, she wore a gold chain around her neck and diamond studs in her ears.

Her brother, Darius Penny, was dressed in an upscale lawyer's uniform: charcoal gray suit, white shirt, and red tie. He was Marge's height, around five ten, with blue eyes. His hair, or what was left of it, was silver.

As the two siblings sat down, they talked softly. Graciela pulled a compact out of a pink leather bag and checked her lipstick. Marge noticed the Hermès label.

Marge said, "Is that a Birkin?"

Graciela looked up. "Yes, it is."

"It's beautiful." Part of her comment was to gain rapport. Part of it was genuine curiosity. "I've never seen one in the flesh."

"Take a look." Graciela handed Marge the handbag. "I have two of them. I bought this one ages ago to cheer me up. I know you called up the foundation and spoke to Holly. I have cervical dystonia. My head almost touched my shoulder, my neck was so twisted."

"I looked the condition up on the Internet. You'd never know anything was wrong today by your physical appearance."

"Kind of you to say. Thank God for Botox. I was terribly disfigured. I wouldn't have made it through except for a wonderful husband and a very supportive brother."

"I didn't do anything," Penny said.

"You visited me religiously, even when I told you to go away." She turned to Marge. "I was a shut-in." A throaty laugh. "In the last fifteen years, I've been making up for it."

Oliver and Decker came into the room. After all the introductions were made, everyone sat down. Marge held out the bag to Graciela. "That is truly a work of art."

"Take it," Graciela told her. When Marge smiled at the humor and tried to hand it back, Graciela said, "I'm serious. Spread the cheer, you know."

Marge was wide-eyed. "Uh, thank you, but I'm going to have to decline."

Graciela shrugged and threw the bag on the table. Penny took out a file folder and began sorting through pages. "I called the mortuary, which in turn called up the county morgue. The body will be released tomorrow. The funeral service will be at four-thirty tomorrow afternoon. Everything will be done at the grave. I suspect my sister and I will be the only ones in attendance, unless you want to show up. No pressure."

Graciela said, "Sabrina will come down."

"Oh yes. I forgot about her. So that makes three. A veritable crowd for Dad." Penny put on a pair of reading glasses and regarded his papers. "Did anyone ever get hold of a person from Global Sanctuary?"

"I did," Decker said.

"Is that place a con job?" Penny asked. "Dad was always ripe for a good con."

"No, it's legitimate. I was there."

"You were? How long ago?"

"Just five days ago, right after your dad passed."

"What is it? An animal sanctuary?"

"Exactly. It's where animal control took your father's tiger."

Marge asked Graciela, "Did you know about the tiger?"

"Not until Darius told me last week . . . although I wouldn't have done anything, even if I had known. Dad could take care of himself."

Marge raised an eyebrow, and Penny caught it. He said, "Dad was difficult."

"Difficult?" Graciela rolled her eyes. "That implies he was normal but cranky. I should be respectful of the dead. I should be a lot of things I'm not. My father was insane. Before insane, he was just plain mean. If he has any laudable attributes, I don't know of them."

"He was kind to the tiger," Marge said.

"Well, there you go. Learn something new every day."

Penny said, "Tell me about this place—Global Sanctuary."

Decker said, "Would you like to visit? We're going tomorrow. You're welcome to come."

"Will you be back in time for the funeral? Say by three-thirty or four?"

"We should be," Oliver said. "But I can't promise anything."

"I'll follow you there with a car service."

Graciela said, "We picked a casket over the phone. What's there to do other than putting him in the ground?" She turned to her brother. "Did you call a minister to handle the service?"

"The funeral home is providing one. Good enough."

"You're right. Because anything I'd say wouldn't be very nice."

Penny smiled. "Try to be forgiving."

"I'm here, right?"

"Yes, you are." Penny turned to Marge. "When are you going to this Global place?"

"Around ten."

"Do you have directions?"

Decker said, "I suggest you all go in one car, Mr. Penny. The place is in the mountains. It's hard to find. You should be back by two-thirty unless there's terrible traffic."

"Okay." Penny was still shuffling papers. "I'll be here, ready to go, at ten of."

Decker said, "May I ask your reason for wanting to visit the sanctuary?"

"Dad left them two million dollars. It's a small proportion of his estate, but it's not an insignificant amount of money."

"It's a lot of Birkin bags," Graciela said.

Penny smiled. "As the executor of the will, by law I am bound to follow Dad's instructions. But before any checks go out, I want to make sure this place had nothing to do with his demise." He put the papers down. "I suppose you can't guarantee that until you find out who did this. Where are you in the investigation?"

Decker regarded the lawyer. "You know, usually in murder cases, you get your suspects by following the money. I don't know if you're bound by confidentiality, but if you could tell us where your father's money is going, it might help."

"Confidentiality is arguable, since he's deceased." Penny picked up the papers. "But I suppose no one from the estate is going to sue me if I talk."

"Are there others besides Sabrina, you, and me?"

"I'm getting to that." He cleared his throat. "Let me go through this in an organized fashion. That's the only way I know how to be. Gracie, pay attention."

"I'm listening, dear."

Penny said, "Some of dad's holdings are in prime New York real estate. We can go several ways with that. If we choose to liquidate, that's going to take some time. My law firm will take care of that. The rest of his holdings are in stocks and bonds and other tradable commodities. We can liquidate all of those holdings with a few phone calls. This is where you come in, Lieutenant. You've been in his apartment. I have not."

"What do you want to know?"

"As far as I know, Dad had nothing of value in that place. Am I correct?"

"No Renoirs hidden in the closet," Oliver said.

"Any hidden cash?" Penny asked. "That would be like Dad."

"We didn't come across anything, but whoever murdered him could have taken a stash," Marge told him. "We'll turn the place inside out, but we have to wait until after the building has been fumigated."

"Why is the building being fumigated?"

Decker smoothed his mustache. "Well . . . your father owned more than just a tiger." He gave them a brief recap of the situation. Both of them were stunned by the magnitude but not surprised by the behavior.

Graciela said, "So actually Dad did own some collectibles."

Penny smiled. "I suppose it's safe to say that Dad's collectibles will not add any value to the estate."

"Too bad about the snakes," Graciela said. "All those shoes that won't be realized."

Penny smiled and continued with the will. "The instructions are that the bulk of his holdings should be split three ways: Gracie, myself, and Sabrina Talbot—his ex-wife."

"We've met Sabrina," Oliver said.

"Isn't she a hoot and a half," Graciela said.

"She seems like a nice lady," Oliver said. "She also appears to be very wealthy. I bring this up because she doesn't seem to need money."

"Put it this way," Graciela said. "If I needed a loan, I'd go to her before I'd go to the bank." She turned to her brother. "How much do we pocket from the old coot?"

Penny said, "Around eighty million each."

Oliver cleared his throat and looked away.

Decker had opened his notebook and was writing down information, at a momentary loss for words. "So you each get eighty million?"

"Before taxes," Penny reiterated. "Uncle Sam will take half."

"That's still a lot of Birkin bags," Graciela said. "Dad spent his money on what he wanted to do, and that was about the only honest thing he ever did do. He lied to my mother, he lied to Sabrina. He was vicious to me during the fifteen years I suffered from cervical dystonia, even suggesting that I was doing it to myself to soak money out of him. And I might add that I never asked him for a dime. Do you know what that horrible man did?"

"Gracie—"

"He tried to procure women for my husband while I was inflicted with my condition." She turned to her brother. "Don't scold me. Back me up on this."

"It's all true," Penny said. "He was a rotten dad."

Graciela said, "Am I mourning? Perhaps a piece of me, but a very small piece. For me, his inheritance is reparation. Some of it will go to my foundation. The rest will be put in my own trust for my children and grandchildren. I certainly don't need any of it to maintain my lifestyle, but I'm not going to refuse it. That would be plain dumb."

Decker looked at Penny. "You don't have to answer this, Mr. Penny, but what are you planning to do with the money?"

He took a sip of water. "Eighty million dollars is a lot of money to me. After taxes it'll be around forty million, which is still a lot of money to me. I don't need it to live on, but it does bump up my cash reserves."

He smiled. "Perhaps now's the time to get my wife her own Birkin."

"She already has one."

"She does? When?"

Graciela waved him off. "His right hand doesn't know what his left hand is doing."

Decker said, "As long as you're telling numbers, is there anyone else besides Global Sanctuary that stands to gain from your father's death?"

"Yes. I have some names. I haven't the slightest idea who these people are." Penny read off a sheet. "In alphabetical order we have Ginger Buck, Rocki with an *i* Feller, Vignette Garrison, Georgie Harris, Randi with an *i* Miller, and Amber Sweet. As you can see, they're all women—I'm assuming Georgie is a woman."

"They all sound like hookers," Gracie said.

"I won't argue with that," Penny answered. "Are you familiar with any of them?"

"Vignette Garrison is the head of Global Earth," Decker told him.

"So she's a legitimate person. What about the others?"

Oliver looked at Marge, then at Penny. "Randi Miller may have worked for a massage parlor that did outcall service. Your father may have been one of their clients."

"Big shock!" Graciela said.

Oliver said, "We didn't know Randi's last name, so this is helpful."

Marge said, "I'm wondering if Randi and Rocki are the same person . . . Feller and Miller?"

"How about Georgie and Ginger?" Oliver said.

"Could be," Marge answered. "Prostitutes alter their names to avoid having a record when the cops look them up. Let me go look them up, since we have last names."

"Perfect," Penny said. "I'm not cutting two checks if it's the same person."

Marge had her yellow pad in hand. "I'll be back in a bit."

Penny said, "It appears that Dad left Global Sanctuary some money and also left money to Vignette Garrison." To Decker, "Did he have something special going with this woman?"

"I think he liked her cause."

Graciela said, "How much did he leave these . . . women, Darius?"

"A million each."

"Not worth killing over."

Oliver made a face. "With all due respect, Ms. Johannesbourgh, I beg to differ."

Graciela didn't appear to hear him. "So Dad's estate was around two hundred and forty million?"

Penny said, "Yes. If we don't liquidate the real estate immediately, the buildings have a tremendous upside."

"Do we need to liquidate?"

"Not unless someone wants more cash."

"What's the proportion?" She turned to Decker. "You'd think we would have talked about this beforehand."

"You didn't know anything about your father's estate?" Oliver asked.

"No." She shrugged. "That's me. I'm so je ne sais quoi."

"Gracie, I'm going to have to put a gag on you."

"Make it a Ferragamo scarf and we have a deal." When Penny looked displeased, she said, "Okay. Back to business. What else does Dad own?"

"If we liquidate the stocks and bonds, it's about thirty million cash each before taxes. Although I wouldn't recommend liquidating anything. He's got a solid portfolio."

"What about estate taxes?"

"We have enough to pay taxes, but there won't be any leftover cash. But the good news is we won't have to liquidate anything to pay the taxes."

"So just split and transfer?"

"That's what I'd recommend."

"Your firm will manage the buildings?"

"We can put the entire holdings in trust for the three of us. Sabrina will have to agree to it."

"I'm fine with it. You can talk to Sabrina when she gets here tomorrow."

"I'll give her a call after we're done." He turned to Decker. "Are we done?"

"A couple of questions," Decker said. "It sounds like your dad could make enemies. But he was pretty reclusive for the last twenty-five years. Can you think of anyone who would have killed him now . . . as an old man?"

"I can't help you with that because I haven't been in my father's life for years," Graciela said.

Oliver said, "How did you feel about your father marrying Sabrina Talbot?"

Graciela said, "Dad was an incorrigible womanizer. I was surprised when he actually married again. Neither one of us went to the wedding."

"We weren't invited," Penny said.

"And wouldn't have gone had we been invited," Graciela said. "I had nothing to do with Sabrina until after they divorced. Dad gave her half of his holdings as part of her settlement. None of us were pleased with his generosity."

"Did you sue?" Decker asked.

"Gracious no. But even if we were inclined—and we weren't—it never came to that. Sabrina gifted two-thirds of the settlement to our children. It was an extremely gracious act. Sabrina deserves whatever happiness she gets."

"About your dad's enemies?" Decker turned to Penny. "Any thoughts?"

"No one comes immediately to mind."

Oliver said, "With the names in the will, you pointed us in a certain direction."

Marge came back into the room. The two siblings looked at her with expectation. "I pulled up a lot of information."

"Are they hookers?" Graciela said.

"A few have been arrested for prostitution."

Darius said, "Even so, they're entitled to the money, unless they had anything to do with Dad's murder. Being a hooker per se doesn't exclude you from being a beneficiary."

"You were always so straitlaced, bless your little heart." Graciela yawned. "How much longer?"

Decker said, "I'm sure I'll have some questions tomorrow, but I know it's been a long day for both of you." He gave them each his card. "If you think of anything that might help, please call, regardless of the hour."

Graciela nodded and stood up, holding her Birkin bag with two hands. Penny neatened his pile and slipped them into the folder. "Our car is waiting."

Decker said, "Thank you both for coming in. I'll see you both at the funeral."

Penny turned to Oliver. "I'll be here at nine-fifty."

Oliver was standing. They shook hands. "I'll see you then, Mr. Penny."

Graciela looked at the untouched treats provided. "Would you happen to have a lid for the coffee? I could use some caffeine. Also . . ." She made a face. "Maybe a paper bag? I just love doughnuts."

"Of course." Marge got up. Stick-thin Graciela was a good lesson about the errors of first impressions. "I'll find you something."

"If not, just a napkin or two is fine." She returned the smile. "I'll just wrap it up and put it in my hoity-toity Birkin bag."

Chapter Twenty-Five

After she handed the printouts to Decker and Oliver, Marge said, "This is what I pulled up for Randi with an *i* Miller aka Rocki with an *i* Feller. The gal wasn't much for originality."

"Darius Penny will be happy." Oliver's eyes swept over the printout. "One check instead of two means another million for the estate."

"A lot of Birkin bags," Marge said. "Our Randi should get her money, as long as she's cleared of Penny's death . . . which I'm not so sure about."

Decker was reading silently. Randi Miller was thirty-three years old, born in Montana. Her mug shots showed a thin woman with straggly blond hair, sunken eyes, and sallow skin. Her height said five foot five, her weight said 130. That was on a good day, judging from the bony arms and wrists.

Marge said, "I do see a resemblance between her and the woman in the store security video . . . the one carrying the massage table."

"I dunno." Oliver stared at the picture, then turned to Decker. "She looks a lot healthier in the video. What do you think?"

Decker studied the photograph. "I'd say yes, this is the girl in the video."

Her last known address was in Sylmar, California. Decker knew the area well because it was policed by Foothill Substation, where he had worked for fifteen years.

He wrote down pertinent information in his notebook.

Ginger Buck was also known as Georgie Harris, Georgina Harris, Lynette Harris, Lynette Amber Harris, Amber Sweet, Sweetie Pie, and Cherry Pie. She was thirty-six years old, homegrown in SoCal. When she was nineteen, she had worked the porn industry for five years under the name of Amber Sweet. Then she must have fallen on hard times. The next decade showed up charges for prostitution, drugs, petty theft, shoplifting, forgery, and several drunk and disorderlies. Her vitals put her at five foot seven, 140 pounds. Her mug shot showed a woman with prominent cheekbones and a big chin, features that were commonly altered in plastic surgery, and Decker wondered if some sugar daddy hadn't foot the bill for a new face. Brunette hair, her eyes were dark, and she had blemishes on her cheeks and forehead that might have indicated meth use.

Oliver said, "With a given name like Ginger Buck, she was destined for porn."

Marge said, "This was the other woman on the security tape."

Decker nodded. Ginger lived in the city of San Fernando, an unincorporated area that sat as a geographical island surrounded by the city of L.A. "Let's see if these addresses are still valid. If they are, bring the ladies in for questioning."

"Do you want us to visit the ladies now?" Marge asked. "It's past seven in the evening."

"If you're busy, Oliver can take one and I'll take the other."

She said, "This is my logic, Pete. Since the case is a week old, if they were going to run, they'd be long gone. If they didn't run, we should find out as much as we can before we move in. I'm thinking that we should get something on them, a positive ID that these are the girls coming in and out of Penny's apartment, and these are the girls that worked for Casey's Massage and Escort."

Oliver said, "How about if we take the mug shots to Ki Park, the chicken lady? The place should still be open."

"Exactly what I had in mind," Marge said. "And I'd also like to run them by Masey Roberts and George Paxton. I can do that tomorrow."

"The Shoops saw women come in and out," Decker said. "Show them the photos. Since Randi Miller lives within LAPD jurisdiction, I'm going to stake out the address for a bit. See if there's any action."

"Why don't you just go home?" Marge asked.

"Surveillance is more attractive than my home life right now." When they waited for an explanation, Decker told them about the previous evening. They reacted as he expected. They laughed. He said, "For a smart kid, he's so damn stupid!"

"What do you care, Deck? He's eighteen in four months. Then you're home free."

"You know it doesn't work that way," Marge told him. "How old are your children, Scott? Thirty plus? Do you ever stop worrying about them?"

"I never *worry* about them. I worry about myself. I'm the one with the gray hairs."

"You've still got a lot of dark hair."

"Courtesy of Grecian Formula."

Marge looked at him. "You dye your hair?"

"Don't you?"

"I'm a woman."

"So I'm vain. I know that age is gonna overtake me one day. But I'm not going down without a fight."

Randi Miller's address matched with a nondescript, beige-colored, two-story apartment complex a couple of miles north from Hobart Penny's apartment building. Casey's Escort and Massage was a mile to the east. It was eight-thirty, the evening cool with a fine layer of mist casting haloes around the streetlamps. He had the heat on high, the radio on low, tuned to the classical station instead of country. Gabe had influenced him more than he realized. With time on his hands, he called Rina for the second time in an hour.

"Anything?" she asked him.

"Nothing. I don't even know why I'm here."

"If you're sitting in your car to avoid domestic conflict, I will tell you that all is well. No mad Persians attacking kith and kin."

"How's the kid?"

"Practicing."

"How are my other children?"

"You mean the *real* children?" Rina asked.

Decker smiled, but a sad one. "Must be hard to feel so unwanted."

"He knows he's welcome here. We'd adopt him if we could. He'll figure it out. And in answer to your question about the other progeny, they're all doing very well. I talked to all of them and everyone was fine. I said a *Shehechianu.* Did you eat dinner?"

"I grabbed a soggy tuna sandwich."

"Yummy. What's your schedule for tomorrow?"

"So far I have a funeral at four-thirty. Want to go out tomorrow night for dinner? If all goes well, I'll be home at a reasonable hour and we can discuss the world over steak and a glass of red wine at La Gondola."

"Or I can buy steak and a bottle of cab and we can discuss the world while eating on table trays in the bedroom."

"What about the kid?"

"He's spending tomorrow night at his aunt's house."

"I like your idea way better than mine." His cell beeped. "I've got another call coming in."

"I'll talk to you later. I love you."

"I love you, too." Decker depressed the button.

Marge said, "Our chicken lady confirmed that Randi Miller and Ginger Buck used to work next door."

"By name?"

"No, not by name but by fast-food order. Randi liked grilled chicken breast, salad without dressing, and a Diet Coke. Ginger loved fried chicken wings, coleslaw, and an iced tea. Next step is to get the pictures identified by Anwar Mahadi, the landlord. I left a message on his cell. Where are you?"

"Two buildings away from Randi Miller's apartment."

"Oliver and I are five minutes away from Ginger Buck's. Shall we?"

"Let's."

After a minute of solid knocking, Decker left one of his business cards on the doorframe. The neighbor across from Randi's apartment opened the door and peeked out.

"Hello?" Decker asked. "Hi?"

Guardedly, she stepped outside. She seemed to be in her twenties with short dark hair and round brown eyes. She was wearing a terry cloth robe. "Did I hear you say you were the police?"

"Yes, ma'am." Decker gave her the business card. "I'm looking for Randi Miller."

The woman read the card and made a face. "I think you have the wrong apartment. No one named Randi Miller lives here."

"Okay," Decker said. "How about Rocki Feller?" A blank look. "Or anything close to those names maybe?"

"She told me her name was Ronni Muller."

"Ronni with an *i*," Decker said.

"I don't know how she spelled it." The woman looked worried. "So her name isn't Ronni Muller?"

"Do you know where she is?" Decker asked.

"She's not here anymore. The moving van came two weekends ago."

"You saw her moving out?"

"Yes, I did. She said she got a new job in Vegas."

"Any forwarding address?"

"Not to me." The woman studied the card. "You're a lieutenant?"

"Yes, ma'am. Does the building have a manager?"

"Whenever something breaks, I call Joseph. I don't know if he's the manager. I think he's like a handyman that works for the building."

"Do you have his phone number?"

"Somewhere. Is Ronnie like a fugitive or something?"

"Why do you ask?"

"Because why else would the police be here? I mean I've seen all the cop shows. The lieutenant always stays back and barks orders to everyone else."

"I can bark with the best of them." Decker asked again why she thought Randi or Ronni was a fugitive.

"Well, the different names for starters. Isn't that suspicious?"

"It's unusual," Decker said. "So you have that phone number for the handyman?"

"Yeah. Right. I'm Simone. Wanna come in so we don't have to talk in a hallway?"

"Thanks." Her apartment was small and spare. Neat, though. Someone with an organized mind. Simone disappeared and came back a moment later with the number. "Here you go."

"Can I ask you a couple of questions about Ronni?"

"Her real name is Ronni or Randi?"

"I think it's Randi Miller. Did she tell you anything about her new job in Vegas? Maybe she mentioned the name of a casino?"

"If she did, I don't remember it."

"So you don't know where she's going to work or . . ."

"Just that she got a new job in Vegas." Simone scrunched up her forehead. "You know, she could have said Reno or even Tahoe. It was somewhere in Nevada."

Instead of a city, Decker now had to consider the entire state. "Did you and Ronni ever socialize?"

"Like party together?" She shook her head no. "She didn't party. At least, she didn't party in her apartment."

That was a surprise. "Quiet person?"

"I never heard anything."

"Ever see the inside of her apartment?"

"Not really. We weren't friends. We weren't enemies. We were just neighbors. I'd wave. She'd wave. I'd say hello, she'd say hello. Couple of times I picked up a package for her. Once she picked up a package for me."

"Did you ever notice anyone going in or out of her apartment?"

Simone bit her lower lip. "Just a few times. I wasn't being nosy or anything, but you know how it is with apartments. It's important to know who's in your building."

"Tell me what you remember."

"A guy." She looked away, trying to recapture her memory. "Maybe six foot . . . slicked-back dark hair . . . a big chin." She regarded Decker. "He was wearing a black suit, no tie. He looked like a typical L.A. guy . . . an agent or a lawyer maybe."

Decker didn't have a picture of Havert on him. Stupid.

She continued on. "Once . . . no, maybe twice . . . I saw a woman. I wouldn't have noticed her except that she looked like a stripper. You know." She cupped her hands and placed them in front of her chest. "Big ones."

Decker took out the picture of Ginger Buck. "Would this be her?"

Simone's eyes widened. "Yeah, that's her. Oh wow! What did they do?"

"So far nothing. I'd just like to talk to them. If you see either one of them, could you call me?"

"Of course. But I don't think that Ronni's coming back. It wasn't just the moving van or the new job in Vegas or Reno or whatever. It was the look on her face, Lieutenant. It said as plain as day: 'good-bye and good riddance.'"

Chapter Twenty-Six

Over the cell, Decker said, "Randi Miller is no longer at her apartment. Neighbor said she packed out for Nevada." He explained the details. "Any luck on your end?"

"You got way more than we did," Marge said. "All we know is Ginger Buck isn't answering the door. We left our card. We called the manager and left a message."

Decker said, "What about Bruce Havert? Any address or a phone number?"

"All we have is the picture that Lee Wang pulled up on the computer."

"And nothing from the cops in North Las Vegas?"

"No. By the way, those guys are wondering if you have anything new on Garth Hammerling."

"They know as much as I do: that he was spotted in southern New Mexico about six months ago. I'm sure he's crossed the border into Mexico. If I had anything new on that monster, they'd know about it." Decker looked at his watch: almost ten. "Go home. That's what I'm doing."

"Are you coming with us to Global Sanctuary tomorrow?"

"No, I'll leave that up to you this time. I was thinking all last night about Vignette Garrison. Is Darius Penny going to tell her about the will?"

"Don't know. He might want to be careful, since she hasn't been cleared as a suspect."

"No, she has not been cleared," Decker said. *Not at all.* "Who supplied Penny with all those venomous snakes and fish and insects?"

"Pet stores sell some of them. Maybe mail order. Didn't Vignette tell you he got the tiger mail order?"

"She did. But even if Penny got them through the Net or mail order, someone had to set up the cages and tanks. Even if he did it all himself twenty years ago, once he got old, someone had to take care of the animals. You have to have your wits about you when you're feeding venomous animals. Penny was old and infirm."

Marge paused. "I think he had help and Vignette Garrison is a good candidate. But she wasn't around twenty years ago, Pete."

"She had a predecessor," Decker said. "I know it looks bad for the hookers, fleeing right after the murder, but I'm not ruling out Vignette. When you talk to her, ask her about the maintenance of Penny's menagerie, including the food supply. If she thinks that money is on the line, she might even tell us the truth."

"Or just the opposite." Marge said, "When money's involved, lying usually follows." A pause. "At least she didn't rabbit."

"As far as we know."

"If she didn't rabbit before she got money, she's not going to split with a carrot dangling in her face. What are you up to tomorrow?"

"Rina just asked me the same question. The only thing on the books is the funeral. I'll reinterview George Paxton and show him the pictures of Randi and Ginger/Georgie/Georgina Harris that we pulled off the computer. I want to let him know that we've still got an eye on him, especially since Penny gave Paxton hush money."

Marge said, "Paxton also had the keys to all of Hobart's apartments. And he was the only one who *knew* about Hobart's other apartments."

"Think he could get around a tiger?"

"He could if he knew Penny was alone in one apartment while the tiger was in another apartment."

"Motive?"

She thought a moment. "Didn't one of his children say something about his hoarding cash? When we saw the apartment, it was a mess. We could have missed a cache somewhere."

"Possibly. But don't you see Paxton more as an opportunistic thief than a murderer. I can see Paxton shooting him, but not bashing Penny's head in. Too up close and personal. Did we ever find a weapon for the blunt force trauma?"

"No, but I've been thinking about it, especially since hookers seem to be in the picture. The depression was almost round. The CI said it looked like a small baseball bat. What about a blackjack from a dominatrix?"

"When we find Randi and Ginger/Georgina, we can include that as one of our many questions . . . if we find them. Nevada has lots of hookers. Some are even legal."

"Lucky for you, Rabbi. You have a pet pimp."

Rina and Gabe were playing Scrabble. Gabe wore a T-shirt and sweatpants, and Rina was in pajamas and a robe. They both looked up when he came in.

Decker said, "Who's winning?"

"We're not scoring," Rina said. "It's speed Scrabble. We each have a minute to make a word. This is our . . . what, like our fifth game?"

"Something like that." Gabe was concentrating on his tile rack.

"I'll get your dinner." Rina dumped her letters in the bag and got up. "I had all vowels anyway." She went into the kitchen.

"I'm a little beat. Good night." When Decker didn't answer back, Gabe said, "Are you still mad at me?"

"What?" Decker's attention was elsewhere. "No, not at all. I'm thinking about your dad. I have to call him, and I'm not happy about it."

"You're going to tell Chris about last night?"

"You mean your encounter with Sohala?" Decker smiled. "Gabe, that's over and done with. I'm thinking about how to deal with Chris without looking like I need help . . . which I do. He's a night owl, right?"

"He's a night predator." Gabe looked at his watch. "He's up and running right now, that's for sure."

"Does he answer his phone?"

"I dunno. I never call him. I figure if he wants to talk, he'll contact me."

"Does he contact you?"

"He texts like once a week. *Are you alive?* I answer yes, and that's the end of it."

"Is he more likely to take a call from you or me?" Decker asked.

"You absolutely."

"Okay. Then I'll make the dreaded call." Decker regarded the kid, who looked forlorn. "Do you ever hear from your mother?"

"All the time. We Skype a lot. She wants me to come to India."

"And?"

"I've asked my agent for gigs in Bombay. You know, kill two birds with one stone."

"So you *want* to see her."

"More like I'm *willing* to see her." He paused. "If I get a gig, I'll go. Jacob offered to go with me. He's a good guy."

Rina came in with a plate of food and a glass of wine. "Who's a good guy?"

"Jacob," Decker said. "Your son."

"Our son. What'd he do?"

"Offered to go with me to India," Gabe said.

"You're going to India?"

"No, but if I go to India, he offered to go with me."

"Peachy," Rina said. "Yonkie is over thirty, but he has the impulse control of a seventeen-year-old."

"That's okay," Gabe said. "I'm seventeen with the impulse control of a thirty-year-old." A pause. "Except with Yasmine. I'm pretty hopeless when it comes to her."

Rina sat down and stroked Decker's hand. "Eat, my love." She turned to Gabe. "I'm glad you're back with your mom. You won't regret it."

He shrugged. "Well, I'd like to meet my sister." A pause. "She's pregnant again . . . my mother. She's not even married to the guy. She and Chris aren't legally divorced." Gabe threw up his hands. "It's her life. I'm over it. No sense pretending she doesn't exist."

Decker said, "If Jake goes with you to India, do I have to pay for his airfare?"

Rina said, "Stop pleading poverty all the time. The only thing we spend on is food. We haven't had a vacation in two years."

"Why not?" Gabe asked.

"Talk to the Loo," Rina said. "I go by his schedule."

"Don't do this to me, son," Decker said. "After last night, you owe me."

"I'm sure the lieutenant has his reasons," Gabe said.

Rina said, "The lieutenant works very hard." She kissed the top of his head. "But the lieutenant would do well with a couple of constructive weeks in Hawaii."

"I don't tan. I just turn red, burn, and peel."

"How about Yellowstone?" Rina said. "I've always wanted to see Old Faithful."

Decker gave her suggestion some thought. "I'd like that, too. It sounds like a good vacation, even for a stiff like me."

"Then it's settled. I'll make arrangements. But you can't flake out on me, Peter." She turned to the teen. "You can come, too, if you'd like, Gabriel."

"I think the lieutenant has had quite enough of me. But I thank you for the 'vite."

"The offer's open. And I'm glad you reconciled with your mother, Gabriel. You only have one mom."

"Seriously," he told her. "I only have one mom. But I also have a couple of guardian angels. How lucky can a dude get?"

The cell was under his pillow, vibrating at three in the morning. Decker grabbed it and said, "I'm here. Hold on." He slipped on a robe and went into the living room.

"I'm giving you ten minutes," Donatti said. "You have nine left."

"Could you please be civil once in a blue moon?"

"So make a civil call. You only call when you need me or to report bad news."

The man had a point, but damn if Decker would concede him anything. "You have pencil and a piece of paper?"

"What?"

"Randi Miller. Randi is spelled with an *i*. Also Ginger Buck." Decker listed all their aliases. "They're probably in Nevada."

"Don't narrow it down too much."

"Vegas, Reno, or Tahoe."

"That really helps."

"Do what you can, Chris."

"Murder suspects?"

"They are. I may be a lieutenant, but in my heart, I'm still a homicide cop."

"When did this happen?"

"A week and a half ago. After it happened, the girls moved out. Where can I fax you pictures?"

Donatti gave him a number. "Describe Ginger Buck aka Georgie Harris to me."

"In her thirties. She used to be a porn actress under her alias Amber Sweet. In her last mug shot, she was five foot seven, around a hundred forty pounds. She had short, shaggy hair, dark eyes, and acne. She could be a tweaker." A pause. "She sounds familiar to you, Chris?"

"When she worked for me, her name was Gigi Biggers. She had drug problems. They all do, but she couldn't keep it under control. I had to fire her. She has a Social Security number under that name. Want it?"

"Of course. How long ago did she work for you?"

"Five years maybe. Before I moved here full-time. Anything else?"

"Bruce Havert. He owned a business called Casey's Massage and Escort. It was closed and cleaned out after the murder. Havert employed the girls. Before moving to L.A., he worked as a dealer for eleven years at Havana!—the casino not the city."

"Tell me more about him."

"I'd like to except that's all I have. No phone number. No address for him in L.A. so I can't even get a forwarding address. I do have a picture. I can also e-mail you the link to the article where we found his picture."

"E-mail it to Talia. I don't do e-mail. I'm a Luddite. I don't do virtual life. Too busy doing the real thing. Send me his picture ASAP."

"Why are you so interested in Bruce Havert?"

"If he's pimping hookers in Nevada, he's moving into my territory."

"All of Nevada is your territory?"

"The entire world is my territory. Nevada is just my home base."

"Gotcha. You'll let me know what you find out."

"I will. If you can nail his ass for murder all the better. One less idiot to contend with. Speaking of idiots, how'd my son do at the trial?"

"Your son is definitely not an idiot, Chris."

"He's seventeen, all seventeen-year-olds are idiots, ergo he's an idiot. How is he?"

"Fine. You do know that the case was pled out, right?"

"Yeah, I know."

"And you also know that Gabe is still with us in L.A., right?"

A split second pause. "Why?"

"He's got some upcoming performances. He's getting help from his former teacher, Nick Mark. Gabe wants to stay with us for six weeks. Do you have a problem with that?"

"Not if you don't." Another pause. "Is he still seeing that little Persian girl?"

"I think so."

"Dummy. At his age, he shouldn't be hooked to a single girl. He should be screwing around."

"He's in love with her."

"He can love her and still fuck other girls. He's seventeen. What does he know?"

"I guess the kid has a moral compass, Chris."

"I know." Donatti sighed. "Where the fuck did I go wrong?"

Chapter Twenty-Seven

With Darius Penny in the backseat, Marge and Oliver were circumspect. They spoke to each other in low voices even though Penny was occupied with his own business call. Marge said, "I did a little online research this morning. You can buy almost anything by mail order if you claim it's for conservation. In some states, it's really easy to get licenses for private zoos. Ohio is notorious for people keeping big animals."

"What about snakes?"

"Most of the sites I checked out were pet shops, and most of the reptiles weren't venomous. But you can get venomous snakes if you want them. Exotics like king cobras and Gaboon vipers are ironically easier to find because they are exotic. Most of the people who keep

California rattlers are amateur snake hunters who had caught them. But sometimes they'll swap and sell."

"But someone would still have to set up the cages. He couldn't do that by himself."

"The thing is, Scott, if you take good care of them, snakes can live a long time—fifteen, twenty years—with the larger ones living even longer. So it is conceivable that the old guy bought them a while back and set up the cages a long time ago."

"What about insects?"

"Spiders live a lot longer than you'd think. Female tarantulas can live twenty years. Scorpions less so, but some have made it past a decade. Things like hissing cockroaches, shorter: one to five years. So those kinds of insects he probably bought when he was an old man."

Oliver spoke quietly. "Marge, he had to be paying someone to maintain the cages, especially if he was on a walker."

"I'm sure he did pay someone. But personally, I have my doubts about the walker thing. I think he carted out the wheelchair when he wanted the pity factor or he used it to distract or stall . . . like with complaining neighbors."

"Marge, even if he could walk on his own two feet, he was old."

"So he moved slowly."

The man folded his arms across his chest. "I didn't *pimp* for him!"

"I believe you. See. That was simple enough."

But Decker knew that wasn't the end of the story.

"What did you do for him? Besides ignoring his apartments, which contained deadly animals, for money?"

"It wasn't like that."

"It was like that. What else did he pay you for?"

"I opened the doors a couple of times for the ladies. Wasn't any big deal. Kinda like picking up a package." The man was red. "Can you leave me alone now?"

Decker focused on the bald man's face. "How many times were you actually inside Penny's apartments?"

Paxton's eyes darkened. "Why is that important?"

"Because the man was murdered."

"You can't think that I had something to do with it." Silence. "That's absurd."

"Tell me why it's absurd."

"Because I hadn't been in his apartment for weeks."

"Tell me why I should believe you."

"Because why the hell would I hurt him?" The gnome was pacing again. "He could only give me money if he was alive."

"So you kept him alive for the money?"

"No, you're twisting . . ." Paxton got furious. "I think you'd better leave."

"Okay." Decker made a point of looking at his watch. "I have a little extra time. Maybe I'll visit your boss now."

The man turned a deep shade of crimson. "You're blackmailing me."

"God forbid!"

"What do you *want* from me?"

"Just answer my simple questions. How often were you in Penny's apartments?"

"I told you I let the hookers in once or twice . . . at most a half dozen times."

"So we're up to six—"

"All I did is open the door for them at Mr. Penny's request."

Decker said, "Did you ever do repairs for Mr. Penny? Fix a clogged sink. Replace a lightbulb?"

The man seemed wary. "Yeah. Sure."

"Do it by yourself or did you call someone?"

"If it's just tightening a bolt or screwing in a light plate, I did it myself. If it was a major plumbing problem, I'd call someone."

"Okay," Decker said. "How often do you fix stuff for Mr. Penny? Once a month? Once a week?"

"Not even once a month. Three, maybe four times a year. And only for the two apartments that were on top of each other. The others . . . the units that were next to his apartment . . . I never went inside. And after what you found in there, I know why he never let me in."

"That's sort of why I wanted to talk to you this morning," Decker said. "Do you have any idea how he got hold of all those venomous snakes and fish and insects?"

"He got hold of a tiger. I would imagine fish and snakes are easier than that."

"Did you ever see any packages that were marked *livestock* or *live animals* or something like that?"

"No," Paxton said. "You're telling me that you can buy poisonous snakes and have them delivered in the mail in a box?"

"Mr. Penny had to get them from somewhere."

"Well I never saw anything marked *dangerous* or *poisonous snake*! Jesus, I would have called the police, okay?"

"Did Hobart Penny get *any* deliveries?"

"I know he got his groceries delivered. I know he had medicine delivered, but beyond that, I couldn't tell you."

Decker said, "His animals were well cared for. Who tended to all the cages and fish tanks?"

"Like I'd know? I didn't even know he had snakes and fish."

"You're the manager. You're supposed to know."

"Look, Lieutenant, I admitted that I bent the rules with Penny. But I wasn't his nursemaid. There are dozens of units in that building alone. I've got enough to do without spying on the guy."

"But you did notice the ladies. And you did open doors for them."

"He paid me a few bills to let them in."

"How much is a few bills?"

"Twenty dollars a pop. I did it around six times. One hundred and twenty dollars. It's not exactly a killing."

Interesting choice of words. Decker said, "You opened the door for these hookers around six times. But you're telling me that you didn't know anything about the tiger. Or his snakes and fish and spiders. Am I supposed to believe that?"

"Believe what you want, but it's true. If I knew about that shit, I would have called the police. A few skanks giving head to an old guy, I'm not gonna say anything. But a tiger or a rattlesnake? I mean, c'mon!"

His facial tics said he was clearly lying, but Decker moved on. "When the police went inside Mr. Penny's apartment, it was a sty because the tiger had made a mess. What was it like when he was alive? You were inside and I wasn't."

Paxton looked genuinely confused. "It was an apartment. It had a couch and a table and a bed."

"Neat? Sloppy?"

"I guess it was neat. There wasn't much in the way of furniture. Just the basics."

"Did he have a computer?"

"Not that I saw."

"A flat-screen on the wall? A DVR player?"

"He was eighty-nine and a recluse. I don't see him as the high-tech type."

"Lots of elderly people have TVs and they're ripe pickings for robbery. Did he appear to have anything of value?"

"If he did, he hid it under the mattress." Paxton pinkened. "I just meant that I didn't see anything valuable."

"Would you be willing to come into my office and answer these questions while hooked up to a polygraph?"

"Are you kidding me?" The gnome threw up his hands. "Yes. Sure. Next week? I've got a busy schedule this week."

"How about a week from today? Two in the afternoon?"

Paxton exhaled. "Fine. I'll come in. But the answers will be the same. The guy was eccentric but I guess most rich people are."

Decker paused. "One more thing, and this goes back to robbery as a motive for his murder. I know you said that Mr. Penny lived very simply. Did you ever see anything hanging on his walls?"

"Nope. The man lived like a monk."

"With hookers going in and out?"

"I didn't mean he was a monk. Just that his unit was pretty empty."

"No artwork of any kind?"

Paxton's laugh was unsettling. "Are you kidding me?" Another laugh. "Jesus, the man was weird with a capital W. You saw what he collected and it certainly wasn't art."

Chapter Twenty-Eight

As Marge pulled the car into a dirt lot, a thin figure wearing jeans, a jacket, and hiking boots came out of a trailer. She had straggly blond hair that stuck out from under a ski cap and wore gloves with the tips of the fingers cut off. Marge shut off the motor and got out. "Vignette Garrison?"

"Hi. Welcome."

"Sergeant Dunn of LAPD," Marge said. "This is Detective Oliver."

"Nice to meet you." She scrunched her forehead. "Do you want to do the tour first, or do you want to ask me questions? If you want to talk, we should go into the trailer. It's a little warmer there."

Slowly Darius Penny emerged from the backseat. He seemed to be most concerned about where he stepped, and for good reason. The lot was a muddy mess and his very shiny loafers did not appear to have rubber soles. First, he walked on his tiptoes. Then he gave up. He held out his hand to Vignette. "Darius Penny."

"Oh my God!" Vignette took his proffered hand and clasped it with her fingers. "Vignette Garrison. I am so sorry about your father. What a wonderful man he was!"

The lawyer winced as he extricated his hand. "Are we talking about the same man?"

Vignette's mouth opened and closed. "He was wonderful to Global Sanctuary." When she didn't get any response, she said, "He loved animals."

Penny eyed her up and down. "What exactly do you do here?"

"I'd be happy to give you a tour."

"It's smells a little ripe for eleven in the morning." His nose was wrinkled. "Or is that just me." He exhaled. "How about a summary of the place? I didn't bring my mukluks with me."

Marge smiled, but Vignette didn't catch the humor. She took in a breath and let it out. "We are the last stop for exotic animals that nobody wants or for people who can no longer care for the animals. We are a no-kill facility, unless of course the animal is a grave danger to itself or others. If it wasn't for places like this, a lot of these animals would have to be put to sleep."

"What kind of animals do you have here?"

"Everything really. I'd love to take you around."

"Do you charge admission?"

"Pardon?"

"Charge admission . . . like a zoo."

"This isn't a zoo." Vignette was confused. "Like we're kinda in the middle of nowhere."

"So I've noticed," Penny said.

"Mr. Penny, we're a nonprofit sanctuary. We depend on the kindness of people like your father to keep the place running."

"Is that the only way you secure money?" the lawyer asked. "From donations?"

"That, private grants, and some government funding. It's mostly donations. Your father was always so generous with us. He kept us afloat during hard times. And when you run a nonprofit, it's always hard times."

The lawyer looked upward at the mountains. Faint animal sounds wafted through the misty air. He sighed. "Well, this is the situation, Vignette." He made a face again. "In order to perform my executor duties, I have to see your operation."

"That would be my pleasure." Vignette's smile was wide.

Penny said, "Can we take the car through the pathways?"

"No, sir, it's way too narrow and steep for a car."

"What about that golf cart?"

"It's not working, unfortunately."

"How do you get the animals up and down?"

"We sedated them and take them on a gurney with wheels. Would you like to ride on the gurney?"

When Penny went silent, Vignette said, "If you need to use the bathroom, I suggest you do it now."

"Where?" Penny asked.

Vignette pointed to a porta potty.

Penny exhaled. "The pains of being a middle-aged man."

Marge said, "I'll use it after you." She watched him walk away and then turned to Vignette. "I need to ask you something and I expect you to be truthful. Did you know that Hobart Penny also kept venomous snakes and insects in his apartments?"

"Of course."

"*Of course?*" Oliver said.

"Yes, of course. Who do you think looked after everything? I went over every week to feed the animals and clean out the cages and fish tanks. I told Detective Decker that I was at the apartment just a few days before."

"But you never told the lieutenant about the snakes and the spiders when you spoke to him."

"He asked about the tiger. He never asked about the snakes."

Marge was barely controlling her anger. "We had to call animal control and remove everything and fumigate the building because we had no idea what was in there and if any of his creepy crawlies escaped. He had recluse spiders."

"They're legal to own," Vignette said.

"Are you hearing me at all, Ms. Garrison?" Marge said.

"Yeah, I probably should have said something. I was a little freaked-out about the old man dying and then that he was murdered." She shrugged. "I could have helped you with the removal. Where did you take the snakes? We have a herpetarium."

"I don't know, Vignette, you'll have to contact Agent Ryan Wilner."

"I could also take the insects. The tarantulas and scorpions I could just set free in the hills. I don't think we have enough electricity to take care of the fish tanks. I could call up some people I know who would take them . . . certainly the lionfish and the stonefish and the electric eels."

"Did Mr. Penny pay you to take care of his collection?"

"Of course."

"How much?"

"Not that it's any of your business, but a hundred dollars plus gas and lunch. It was an all-day affair. First I had to feed the snakes. Then after they had swallowed the prey and were content, I came back to clean the cages. Then I had to do the fish and insects. One hundred dollars was a bargain. But I did it because Mr. Penny had always been so generous with Global Sanctuary. I wouldn't have done it for anyone else."

"Did anyone else besides you know about Mr. Penny's snake collection?"

"The apartment manager would let me into the apartments when Mr. Penny wasn't available. I don't know if he knew what was in there or not."

Marge and Oliver exchanged glances. She saw Darius walking toward them. Even from afar it was impossible not to notice the disgusted look on his face. To Vignette she said, "Don't say anything to Mr. Penny about what we just talked about."

"Okay. But why?"

"He'll get creeped out and he's in charge of the will. Is that what you want?"

"No, of course not."

Marge exhaled and raised her eyebrows. "I'll be right back."

Vignette whispered to Oliver, "Is he really in charge of the will?"

"I don't know," he lied. "Ask him."

"That would be a little rude, don't you think?" A pause. "I think I should at least wait until the end of the tour. Show him what we do. I think he'll be really impressed."

What planet are you living on? Oliver said, "I'll be back in a minute."

"Where are you going?"

"To use the facilities after Sergeant Dunn."

"In the interest of time, you can just pee in the bushes," Vignette said.

As tempting as it was to pass over the Andy Gump, he knew it wasn't dignified for an officer of the law. "I'll wait."

"I should warn you. It's pretty rank in there."

Darius came back. "*Rank* is a mild word." He turned to Oliver. "How long can you hold your breath?"

"You should really just go outside," Vignette said. "All the guys do it outside."

Penny smiled. "Go, my man. No need for airs."

"Where?" Oliver asked.

She pointed to a spot. "It's completely overgrown. No one will see you."

Oliver started up the hill, the mud squishing under his rubber-soled oxfords. The air was cold and slightly decayed, but at least it was an open environment.

The advantages of outdoor plumbing.

The phone's screen was a number he didn't recognize. "Decker."

"It's Doctor Delaware."

"Hey, Doc, thanks for getting back to me so quickly."

"You know, I think we had another occasion to work together."

"Father Jupiter and the Order." Decker took a bite of his turkey sandwich. It was after one, and he was hungry. "You worked with some of the orphaned children."

"Some of them, yes. Do you know what happened to any of them?"

"I know what happened to Vega."

"I remember her. She was very bright. Is she doing well?"

"Very well. My sergeant, Marge Dunn, actually adopted her legally. She graduated from Cal Tech about a year ago."

"That's certainly a success story."

"Vega's lovely. A little hesitant socially. Could be because of her strange upbringing, but it also could be because she's so brilliant and thinks in another stratosphere. She has a boyfriend, though. Marge is thrilled."

"Very good news."

The conversation stopped. Delaware said, "If you could recap the case for me again, that would be helpful. I know I'll have questions."

"Sure. Like I told you, I'm dealing with an odd whodunit. Hobart Penny: an eighty-nine-year-old millionaire and recluse who died from blunt force trauma to the forehead. He also sustained a gunshot wound in the back from a twenty-two-caliber bullet."

"Did the tiger have anything to do with his death?"

"It doesn't appear that way. Strangely enough, it does seem that Hobart did have a good rapport with the cat."

"The animal didn't turn on him?"

"We don't think so—no bites, deep scratches, or anything to suggest a mauling. What we haven't leaked to the press was his collection of highly venomous animals—snakes, insects, and fish. All the animals appeared to be neatly confined to their cages or habitats. But we still had to fumigate the entire apartment building because some of the insects were very dangerous and we had no idea what might have escaped or what might have been hiding."

"So the reptiles and the insects coexisted with the tiger?"

"No, he had a separate apartment for the reptiles and another one just for poisonous insects and fish."

"The man was also a hoarder."

"Interesting way to look at it."

"What about Penny's past relationships? Anything to shed light on that?"

"He was married twice, each ended in divorce. His second wife and his adult children claim that he went off the deep end twenty-five years ago."

"When did he and the second wife divorce?"

"Twenty-five years ago."

"How did he go off the deep end?" Delaware asked.

"At that time, his ex, who is now in her fifties, claimed that Penny thought he was a tiger in a man's body. The final straw happened after he tried to rip off her face with his nails and attempted to bite her neck."

"Okay, I understand why the wife would think he was crazy," Delaware said. "Why do the children feel he went off the deep end?"

"For starters, he kept a tiger in a small apartment."

"Any other reasons?"

"He was a recluse, I suppose."

"I'm just wondering if they painted him as strange in order to deem him incompetent and take away his money."

"No lawsuits have ever been filed. No incompetency hearings that I know about. They seem wealthy in their own right. The son is the father's executor."

"What about the ex-wife?"

"Also wealthy. She had money to start with and then got a very generous divorce settlement from Hobart Penny. That caused friction between the ex-wife and the adult children. So the ex actually gave some of the settlement money back to Penny's grandchildren."

"That's unusual."

"It's a first for me," Decker said. "I didn't see the house, but my detectives told me that it looked like something out of Mansions R Us."

"Have you met the adult children?" Delaware asked.

"Yesterday. Brother and his sister seem to get along. Money doesn't seem to be an issue, although we all know it's always an issue. They're not primary suspects. That could change, but right now we have others who are higher up."

"Can I ask who?"

"Sure. A couple of massage therapists took off for Nevada after Penny turned up dead. The rumor is they did way more than massage. Penny seemed to have quite a large and unusual libido."

"The little blue pill."

"Doctor Delaware, what can you tell me about a guy who had millions but chose to live in a crappy one-bedroom apartment with a tiger. What can you tell me about a man who collected venomous snakes and dangerous spiders and poisonous fish?"

"What have you learned about him before he became a recluse?"

"Like was he always weird?"

"Something like that. What do you know of him as a young man?"

"Not much. His daughter hates him, and I use the present tense on purpose. She told me he was a mean man. No love lost with his son, either, although he is the executor of the estate. The ex-wife said he was always sexually aggressive, even before he started acting like a tiger. He used to cheat on her. Then he started going to sex clubs to indulge his fantasies."

"What about the first wife?"

"She's dead."

"I don't like armchair analysis," Delaware said. "But I'll say this. The man didn't suddenly turn weird. I suspect he was probably always a little odd. People who hoard—animal hoarders are just a subset—fill their homes with junk in order to shut out human contact. In the past, real relationships have been a challenge for them if they had existed at all.

"People like Penny tend to be socially awkward— not necessarily shy, the man doesn't sound shy—but maladroit with a limited range of emotional responses. They also have an underdeveloped sense of empathy."

"Like a psychopath?" Decker asked. "Or is it sociopath?"

"Psychopath, sociopath, anti-personality disorder, renaming things don't change the condition. I don't know if Penny was or was not a psychopath, but people like him tend not to read faces very well. And since they don't pick up on nonverbal social cues, they often respond in a maladaptive way . . . which pushes people even further away, and you get a vicious cycle."

"Okay," Decker said. "So he was always weird?"

"Probably."

"So what's with the tiger?"

"I'm speaking in generalities, okay. This may or may not fit your man."

"I hear you."

Delaware said, "Hobart Penny was wealthy and brilliant; he was an engineer/inventor, correct?"

"Correct."

"Unlike most inventors who tinker with very little outcome, he was highly successful. And like most successful people, he probably had a sizable ego. Men like Hobart Penny can afford to push people around—his children, his wives, his staff. But Penny sounds like a man who doesn't really relate to or care about people. So dominating them wouldn't be a big thrill."

"As opposed to dominating a tiger."

"Exactly. Dangerous animals and the notion of being able to control them would generate a feeling of omnipotence that, in my opinion, would be a very powerful aphrodisiac. When acting like a tiger failed to give him enough sexual pleasure, he went out and got himself the real thing. It feels like he decided to *own* his delusions. And since prostitutes were involved, I have this thought in the back of my mind."

"Lay it on me."

"I don't know if it fits your version of the murder, but here goes. Hobart Penny was still screwing hookers. But that wasn't enough for him or his delusions. I think he might have trotted out the tiger to scare his women to increase his sexual pleasure."

"He got off on fear?"

"Maybe."

Decker mulled it over. "Yeah . . . makes sense. The girl is doing a routine act and then all of a sudden, he trots out a Bengal tiger or a cobra to frighten them. Using his animals as lethal weapons."

"Think of it from the girls' perspective. Say the old man wants you to do something and you don't want to do it. He threatens you with a cobra if you don't cooperate."

"In a way, a cobra is worse than a weapon," Decker said. "A gun or a knife can be wrested away. A snake . . . well, you're kind of helpless. So before he can carry out his threat, the hooker bashes him in the head and runs away. It could be self-defense."

"That's your call, Lieutenant."

"The problem is that it wasn't just the threat of a tiger. The actual animal was with him when we found him. You can understand how the tiger coexists with the hookers when the guy was alive. He had control over her—the tiger was a she. But after he's dead, how does the girl or girls get past a tiger?"

"Was the animal chained up?"

"When we sedated her, she was dragging six feet of chain. So she could have been chained up. But the apartment was small. If she was chained in the bedroom, then the girls wouldn't have been able to get out of the door. If she was chained in the living room, she had a wide radius to work. Penny could have sedated the tiger such that it was nonthreatening. Of course, then the case isn't self-defense anymore. And where's the fun in dominating a sleeping tiger?"

"The thrill could be that at any moment the animal could wake up." Delaware paused. "Anyone on your short list of suspects other than the missing hookers?"

"We've got several people that we're looking at. One is a woman who works in an exotic animal sanctuary. My detectives are there now with Penny's son. The old man gave money to support her place. Plus she took care of the animal, so the tiger knows her. She's also mentioned in Penny's will. We always make a point to follow the money. But in this case, the guy was already giving her money. You'd think she'd just wait him out."

A pause.

"I may be working with more than one killer with more than one motivation," Decker said. "Got another question for you, Doc. Hobart Penny was renting several apartments to house his collection—his menagerie. One of the apartments was used as a pantry for the animal food. We were going through that apartment thoroughly, including a freezer that was filled with meat. One of the packages we opened was a bunch of fingers frozen together."

A long pause over the phone. "Human fingers?"

"Yes. Dismembered fingers, and not from the same person."

"How many digits?"

"Fourteen I think. The coroner thinks they were taken off of the bodies postmortem. We have no idea where they came from. We've taken prints but haven't gotten any hits yet."

Silence.

Decker said, "I know you work with Lieutenant Sturgis on stumpers. Did you two ever run into cases like that? It would be helpful to find a precedent."

"We found baby bones buried in a lockbox last year."

"Yeah, I remember that," Decker said. "But you got a solve on that."

"We did. I'll ask Milo to go through his case files."

"Thanks. I'll take any help I can get." A pause. "Any other ideas, Doc?"

"I'm probably having the same thoughts as you."

"Probably," Decker said. "The human fingers were taken as trophies by a serial killer. If that's the case, we might have a victim who is far less sympathetic than his killers."

Chapter Twenty-Nine

When talking about the animals, Vignette was transformed. Her spiel was informative with just the right amount of passion. Had she not been a suspect, Oliver might have even forked over a donation. Odd lady, but she knew her stuff. It was almost two by the time they returned to the parking lot. Penny blotted his face with a handkerchief. The walking, while not overly vigorous, had caused him to sweat. "Thank you for the tour."

"I hope I answered all your questions, sir," Vignette told him.

"I didn't ask any questions," he said.

"Well . . . do you have any questions?"

"I do." He took his phone from his pocket. "What is the best number to reach you?"

Vignette rattled off her cell phone digits. "Reception is poor up here. If you call, I'll get back to you as soon as I can: early in the morning or late at night."

"I'm in New York. Early to you is midmorning for me. And I'm almost always at my desk." He handed her a card. "If you have questions, give a ring."

Vignette rubbed the tip of her boot in the mud. "I'm assuming there's a reason that you've decided to visit our sanctuary."

"Indeed I did not come out for the air." Penny sniffed and made a face. "I will keep in touch and let you know when things are settled with my father's will. That's as much as I can tell you right now."

"Your father was always so generous."

"So it seems." Penny turned to Marge and Oliver. "I have what I need. We can leave whenever you're ready."

Marge said, "We have a couple of questions for Ms. Garrison right now."

Vignette said, "I'm running a little bit late with the animal checkups. Can we do this another time?"

"You just gave us a tour," Oliver said. "Everything looked fine."

She gave him a condescending smile. "It's more involved than that. Plus I have to start making the rounds in the city to collect food. We have a lot of animals, and that means a lot of meals."

"Just what we wanted to talk to you about." Marge smiled. "How lucky is that?"

Penny said, "I hope this won't take too long."

"That makes two of us," Vignette said.

Marge feigned a cheerful demeanor. "How about if Mr. Penny and I wait in the car to keep warm while Detective Oliver and you chat for a few minutes?"

Oliver said, "Where to, Ms. Garrison?"

"Vignette." She gave a sigh. "I suppose we can talk in my office. I won't say it's warm in there, but it isn't nearly as cold." She brought Oliver over to the biggest trailer. The furnishings included a metal file cabinet, several mismatched chairs, a scarred wood-top desk, and a floor heater that was giving off a few thermals. She plugged in an electric kettle. "Do you want some tea?"

"Hot water is fine."

Vignette gave him a forced smile. "Like I told you before, I'll be happy to help you with relocating Mr. Penny's reptiles."

"That's not my problem, right now."

"There's a problem?"

Oliver rubbed his hands together and placed them in front of the minimalist heater. "I know that you helped Mr. Penny with the care of his animals. I'm thinking that most of the critters had special dietary needs, right?"

"Of course."

"Did you supply the food for Mr. Penny's animals?"

"Sometimes, but not always. For Tiki, I know he ordered meat from the local grocers. But I ordered the stuff for the snakes and the fish and the insects."

"Did you supply him with any of the meat for the tiger?"

"Whenever I came, I brought meat with me. I could get it cheaper than Mr. Penny, and he liked to save money wherever he could."

"He did live frugally."

"He was generous with the important stuff . . . like the welfare of his pets."

"Is a tarantula really a pet, Vignette?"

"Yes, it is." She nodded. "They know their owners. They have personalities."

"A cobra? A scorpion? A stonefish? A recluse spider? These are pets?"

"Do you have a point?"

Oliver took out a notebook. "In one of Mr. Penny's apartments, we found a big freezer filled with meat. And that got us thinking. Who supplies the meat for *your* animals? Because you have a lot of animals, and it must be expensive to feed them all."

She poured hot water into two mugs. In hers, she also dropped a tea bag. She handed the cup to Oliver.

"Thanks."

"You're welcome." Vignette sat opposite him. "It is expensive. And in addition to food, the animals need supplements. Keeping wild animals healthy in captivity is a tremendous challenge."

"I can see you have a very well-run organization. Where do you get your food?"

"Sometimes the big chain markets will donate meat past its due date that's still good. That's where I'm going as soon as I'm done with you: from market to market, hoping to pick up items before they're tossed. It takes a while. I'd like to leave soon."

"As would I," Oliver said. "Where else do you get your meat? Surely past-due-date beef wouldn't suffice for all your animals."

"You're right about that. We also buy scraps from the local slaughterhouses—things like heads and hooves, which are usually turned into domestic pet food. We grind it up like hamburger, and it works well for additional feed. Even though it's not as expensive as regular meat, it adds up. Carnivorous animals eat a lot. We have to buy mice for the snakes. You can get live mice online almost anywhere, but that's also expensive. Sometimes we buy stuff from suppliers over the border."

"Mexico?"

"Mexico, Central America. It's a lot cheaper."

"I'm sure it is."

"We buy some produce from down south, although we have to be careful not to bring in insects and pests. It has to be cleared. We're extra careful who we buy from."

"Could I have a list of your suppliers?"

"Sure. Could I get it for you in a week? Like I said, I'm in a hurry."

"Well, this is the story, Vignette. When we went through Mr. Penny's apartments, we did a thorough job of examining all items in his residences. That meant we went through package after package of frozen animal food. In a murder case you go through everything."

She shrugged. "Okay."

Oliver studied her face as he spoke. "Among the normal frozen packages of meat, we found a package of frozen fingers."

The woman looked stupefied. "Fingers? Like . . . *human* fingers?"

"Yes. About fourteen of them, frozen together and wrapped in butcher paper."

She stuck her tongue out. "That's nauseating. Are you sure it wasn't a joke?"

"Like what kind of a joke?" Oliver asked.

"Like a practical joke. Maybe they weren't real."

"We did microscopic analysis. They were real."

"That's . . . repulsive!"

"In dealings with your suppliers have you ever come across any human remains?"

"No! Never! And if I did, I wouldn't ever use them again as suppliers." She made another face. Then she took a sip of tea. "That's dis*gusting!*"

"You seemed to know Mr. Penny better than anyone—"

"I don't know if that's true."

"You were at his apartments on a regular basis."

"I was with the animals, not him. A lot of the time, the manager let me in and I didn't even see Mr. Penny."

"But sometimes you saw Mr. Penny."

"Only in the context of caring for Tiki. My focus was on the animals, not on him."

"You didn't focus on a man that gave you a hundred thousand dollars a year?"

"Of course when I saw him, but it just wasn't all that often." She took another sip of tea. "I certainly don't know anything about human *fingers.*"

Oliver said, "Any idea where he got the human fingers?"

"No! Why would I know?"

"Because if you did know Mr. Penny at all, you'd know he had some odd proclivities."

"What do you mean?"

"Sexually kinky."

"Okay, Detective, now this is getting way out of my league."

"He never came on to you?"

"For sex?"

"Yes. For sex. Because if you two did have something going, now's the time to fess up. It's all going to come out."

She stared at him. "You do know that he was like eighty-nine."

"It didn't seem to stop him. He seemed to be . . . serviced on a regular basis."

"Serviced? Like with *whores*?" When Oliver shrugged, she said, "I am not a *whore*!"

"Of course not. I was just asking if you and he were . . . intimate?"

"*No! Never!*" Then she broke into laughter. "Although if I woulda known that he paid money for it, I might have been willing." She grinned. "I'm *kidding*, you know."

Oliver wondered if she was joking. The one consistency about Vignette was her money hungry appetite. But it did seem to be all about the animals with her. "So you don't know anything about the packet of fingers."

"The answer is still the same. I don't know a thing about human fingers." Vignette stared at him. "What does that mean . . . when you find human parts like that?"

"It could mean a lot of things." Oliver smiled and folded his notebook. "None of the outcomes points to something good."

Decker leaned back in his desk chair, feeling a monster headache coming on. It was a little after three. Forest Lawn was about a half hour away without traffic, but at this hour, he'd have to allow for more time. He looked at his detectives, specifically Oliver. "So you believe Vignette Garrison?"

"I believe her when she said she didn't have anything to do with the human remains. But I do think the fingers speak volumes about Hobart Penny."

"Serial killer," Decker said. "It's the most parsimonious explanation for the different fingers belonging to different people."

"I can understand keeping fingers as trophies," Marge said. "I'm just wondering how an old man like him would get rid of bodies."

"They could be from a long time ago," Decker said.

"So you don't think they're recent."

"Don't know. I mean how recent is recent? If they're very recent, he definitely had help."

"What about the apartment manager?" Oliver turned to Decker. "He was letting hookers in and out of the apartment. Maybe he also helped dispose of them."

Decker said, "I see Paxton more sneak thief than homicidal maniac."

"Maybe Paxton didn't actually kill them. Maybe he just got rid of them."

"We can ask him. He's agreed to come in for a polygraph," Decker said. "Give me a list of questions and I'll take it to the examiner."

Marge said, "What did you find out from the shrink?"

"That Penny was probably always odd and being rich or poor had nothing to do with it. He liked dominance, with humans at first, but then after a while it wasn't enough. So he bought wild, dangerous animals and took dominance to the next level. He probably got off sexually by scaring women using animals as lethal weapons. And he also thinks that the fingers point to a serial killer."

"A unanimous diagnosis," Oliver stated flatly.

"I still don't see Penny killing women in that apartment complex," Marge said. "Too small a space, the walls are too thin, too much activity. And he never left the place."

"What about the apartment below him?" Oliver asked.

"It was sprayed with luminol. Lots of animal blood but human not so much."

"Animal sacrifices?" Oliver asked.

"Could be," Decker said.

Marge said, "If we're assuming that the fingers were trophies of conquests of his past, it means he murdered the women when he was younger." She turned to Decker. "Do we have any match for the prints?"

"Not yet. This is the problem. Once the fingers were defrosted, the skin became loose and distorted: we lost some of those distinctive whorls and ridges. But we're still working on it." Decker thought a moment. "Let's look in our cold case files. Let's find out if we have some bodies in the data bank that are missing digits."

Marge said, "The guy, in his later years, was a shut-in. He obviously didn't go out and hunt victims. They came to him. How'd he get them?"

Oliver said, "Don't know the answers to your questions, but let's look at what we do have. We have two hookers who were scared enough to bolt overnight."

"They probably bolted because they killed Penny," Marge said.

Oliver said, "And they killed him because he probably threatened to kill them."

"Except now we have a very, very old man who was attempting to kill two younger women at the same time," Marge said. "I can see Penny as a serial killer. He had a package of frozen fingers. I'm just trying to figure out the logistics."

Decker said, "If he threatened the hookers from Casey's Massage and that's why they whacked him, maybe he had threatened other hookers in the past." He took two Advil dry mouthed and then stood up. He grabbed his jacket from the back of his chair. "Go out and talk to the ladies of the evening. I've got a funeral to catch."

Chapter Thirty

The service was done graveside at a cemetery five miles away from where Hobart Penny lived and died, in the green lawns and rolling foothills of the Santa Susana Mountains. The sun was bright and low on the horizon, tawny rays splashing the ground, providing some needed warmth. The temperature was cool, but not as frosty as the gathering. No one had been forced to come, but it was clear that the family's appearance was obligatory. Guests included Darius Penny, Graciela Johannesbourgh, and Sabrina Talbot, and a surprise appearance by Vignette Garrison. There was a rent-a-preacher who uttered a few utilitarian prayers. And then the family stared silently as the casket was lowered into the ground.

Nice casket, Decker noticed: polished wood and brass handles. Either Penny would have approved of the august status or he would have disapproved of the unnecessary expense.

Vignette Garrison sidled up to Decker. She wore a navy blazer over a blue blouse, dark wash denims, and sneakers. Her face was drawn in an appropriate somber expression. "Hi."

Decker said, "Nice of you to come."

"I could say the same for you. Do you always attend the funerals of your homicide victims?"

"I try."

"Do you like . . . look around to get clues and like to see who came and whatnot?"

"No, I come to funerals to pay my respects to those murdered under my watch." He stared straight ahead, watching the family. "And why are you here?"

"After all that Mr. Penny did for the sanctuary, I needed to be here."

"How'd you find out about the service?"

"Mr. Penny . . . the young Mr. Penny . . . well, he's not so young . . . I asked him where it was and he told me." Sun was streaming onto her face. She tented her eyes with her hand, as if giving Penny a final salute. "Who are the women?"

"The very tall one is Mr. Penny's second wife—an ex-wife—and the other one is Mr. Penny's daughter."

"Really? They look the same age."

"Sometimes it works that way, Vignette." Decker stared at the grave site. "My detectives told me that you didn't know anything about the fingers."

"God, no. Do we have to talk about this now?"

"When you found out about the fingers, did you suddenly see Mr. Penny in a different light?"

"What do you mean?"

"Collecting body parts . . . that's not a normal thing." When Vignette was quiet, Decker said, "Any idea where he got the fingers?"

"I already told your people that I don't have the faintest idea."

"Are you surprised that Mr. Penny may be part animal himself—and I don't mean that in a good way."

"I'm shocked. He was always so gentle with the animals. He never was weird with me, if that's what you're asking."

"Never came on to you?"

"No. I already told your other detectives that."

"Never offered you money for sex?"

"No. Why are you picking on poor Mr. Penny?"

"I'm not, Vignette. I'm just trying to find out who he really was." Silently, they both watched as workers began to shovel dirt on top of the casket. Then Decker said, "The fingers came from somewhere."

"I don't know anything about that."

"Vignette, would you be willing to come into the station and take a polygraph about your knowledge of Mr. Penny's murder?"

"Polygraph? That's like a lie detector test?"

"Yes."

"I told you I don't know a thing about Mr. Penny's murder."

"That's why I'm assuming you'd have no problem with taking a polygraph."

She licked her lips. "Do I have to do it to get the money?"

"You can't get any money until you're cleared as a suspect."

"Why should I be a suspect?"

"Are you willing to do it or not?"

Vignette made a point of sighing. "When?"

"I'll set something up. Would tomorrow work if I can swing it? The sooner you do it, the sooner I stop bothering you."

"Has to be next week. How about next Monday? But only if you do me a favor."

"The will?"

"We can really use the money."

"These things can't be rushed, Vignette, but I'll do what I can. Nice that you came, though. Really. I mean that." Decker wandered off and joined the family.

Graciela was dressed in a red suit and black boots. Darius had on a charcoal suit, white shirt, and blue tie. Sabrina wore a hunter green knit dress and a black shawl. The younger Penny said, "Any reason why she's here?"

Referring to Vignette, who was walking down the hill, back to her car. Decker said, "She came to pay her respects."

"Oh pish," Graciela said. "She just wants her money."

"I'm sure that's part of it," Decker said. "But maybe she deserves a little credit for civility."

"She's entitled to her money," Darius said.

Decker said, "How long before you distribute funds?"

Penny said, "I assume you have a reason for asking?"

"Vignette agreed to take a polygraph next Monday. I'd like to get that done before you give her anything."

"Don't worry about that. It'll be months before any checks are drawn. Everything has to be gone over with a fine-tooth comb. Do you suspect her of Dad's murder?"

"No, but I haven't cleared her, either. So far, she's been . . . cooperative."

"Do I hear hesitancy?" Sabrina asked.

"Not really. Lots of people are nervous when it comes to the police." He turned to Penny's second wife. She was statuesque and striking. "Are you doing anything specific after the service, Ms. Talbot?"

She gave him a half smile. "Why do you ask? Are you overwhelmed by my beauty and charm?"

Decker smiled. "I have some questions."

"I'm here right now. Shoot."

"It might be better to do it in private."

"Oh please," Graciela said. "We're all family."

"Private would be better," Decker reiterated.

Sabrina checked her watch. "It's a little after five. I could use a drink. How about seven o'clock in your ghastly interview room?"

"It is rather ghastly," Graciela said, "but they were very polite."

Decker smiled. "Seven is fine." He gave her his card. "For your driver."

"Thank you. I'll be there at seven—prompt and ready to answer your intrusive question. I may be a bit soused, but if anything, that should work to your benefit."

Porn, pills, pot, and prostitution: the *P* vices were by no means exclusive to the San Fernando Valley, but like every city, those that were inclined knew where to go for their fixes. It used to be that the streetwalkers didn't come out until after the sun went down, but a poor economy translated into selling the wares at all hours. The ladies had moved locations in the twenty-five years that Marge had been on the force. There were still some hot spots on motel row in Sepulveda, but most of the gals were now congregating around Lankershim between the 5 Freeway and San Fernando Road.

The sun was sinking, casting dirty amber light on the dingy areas. The chill was setting in, and the ladies in their miniskirts with their bare legs and high, clog sandals were probably feeling it. They moved like packs of feral canines, roaming for prey. As the patrol car cruised down the street, their soulless eyes followed the black-and-white like heat-seeking missiles. Marge was at the wheel while Oliver surveyed the sidewalks. Usually the girls had an easier time confiding in police-women, but even Marge had to admit that Scott had a good track record with them. He had an uncanny eye for picking out who would talk and always related to them with dignity.

Finally, he said, "Pull over."

Marge double-parked in front of a group of women, ages from around forty to seventy, faces that had suffered long and hard, women who had been discarded and brutalized, most of them addicted and some mentally compromised.

THE BEAST · 397

Oliver and Marge got out of the car. He flashed them the V sign. "Ladies, I come in peace."

A few errant smiles. One of the ladies stepped out of the circle. She stood around five feet six in heels and weighed around a hundred sixty, her belly protruding over the waistband of her too-tight jeans. She wore a rabbit jacket and something thin and sparkly underneath the fur. Backless sandals on her feet. Her complexion was pasty, her face was wrinkled. Black hair fell to her shoulders, and her lips were painted bright red. She chewed gum. When she smiled, a gold tooth winked at him. "You're not from vice."

"Homicide."

"I knew it. Never seen you before."

Marge said, "What's your name, hon?"

"Coco as in Chanel, not as in Chocolate. Who are you?"

"Detective Sergeant Marge Dunn. He's Detective Oliver." She showed the woman her ID.

"You speak Spanish?" Coco asked.

"I understand." Marge pointed to him. "He speaks pretty well."

Oliver said, "Your English sounds fine, babe."

"That's because I'm American. I just wanted to know if you wanted me to translate for the gals."

"Thank you for cooperating with your local law enforcement."

"I wouldn't go that far, but no need to be antagonistic."

Oliver said, "I can tell we're all going to get along."

"In your dreams, Slick."

"I have very good dreams."

Coco smiled. "Who died?"

"An old man around ninety around a week ago."

"The one with the tiger."

Marge smiled. A hooker who was up on current affairs. "Did you know him?"

"Just what I read in the papers. How many people around here keep tigers?" A pause. "He was murdered?"

"Yes."

Coco turned around and translated for the women. The women all shrugged ignorance. "No one here knows any old man with a tiger."

A woman in an ultramini spoke in Spanish. Coco interpreted. "She said eighty-nine is old for pussy."

"You never get old guys?" Oliver said.

"Not that old. You looking for something specific, Slick?"

Marge said, "Do you know anything about Casey's Massage and Escort?"

The woman thought a moment. "Sounds familiar." She translated into Spanish for the women. A car slowed down, then sped up when he realized the car that was double-parked was a cruiser. "You're hurting my income."

Oliver said, "What about Casey's Escort and Massage, Coco?"

"Sounds like a call-girl service."

"Your competition?"

"There's enough for everyone."

"I'm going to read some names," Marge said. "Stop me if anyone sounds familiar. Ginger Buck?"

Coco shook her head then translated for the women. "Strike one."

"How about Rocki Feller?" No recognition. "Georgie Harris? Amber Sweet?"

"Strike two," Coco said.

Oliver said, "Let me ask you this, ma'am—"

"Ma'am." Coco smiled. "I like it."

"I pride myself on courtesy," Oliver said. "I know this is an odd question, but do you know any ladies who're missing fingers?"

Coco's eyes went wide. "What . . . what did you say?"

"Maybe even missing any toes," Marge asked.

Coco was still stunned. Another car slowed and then sped up. "Uh . . . are you almost done?"

Oliver said, "We will be as soon as you ask your ladies about it."

Coco translated the question. Judging by the looks on their faces, Marge saw that they were equally horrified by the question. Coco answered a firm no about the missing fingers, not only for herself but also for the group she represented.

Marge thought of something. "Ask the girls if they know anyone who might wear gloves." The pause was enough of a tell, but Coco also raised her eyebrows, which meant that Marge definitely had hit a nerve. "Just get it out."

"She called herself Shady Lady." Another pause. "The gloves were kind of her . . . her like trademark. She doesn't work these parts anymore."

"Where does she work?"

"Beats me. Last time I saw her was like six, seven months ago."

"Describe her to me," Marge said.

"Thinner than me, younger than me, and smarter than me." A pause. "Maybe not smarter. Once I talked to her about doing outcall, getting off her feet and letting a professional handle her affairs. She told me she'd gone that route before. She looked at her hands and said, 'Never again.'"

Chapter Thirty-One

The session was taking longer than Gabe had anticipated. Yasmine's voice was beautiful but rusty. Her breath control wasn't there. He knew it, and even worse, she knew it. Although he hadn't uttered a word of criticism, after the umpteenth retake, she lost control of her emotions. With wet eyes, she took off the headphones. "I need air."

She ran out of the studio. Sohala put down the magazine and stood up, starting to go after her. Gabe held up a hand. "Can you give me a few minutes alone with her. Please."

Her mother was unconvinced.

"I just want to calm her down. Besides, what can I possibly do in a few minutes?"

"You're young. Who knows?" When Gabe stared at her, Sohala actually stifled a smile. "A few minutes, Gabriel. More than that, I take her home."

Gabe looked around the studio hallways. When he didn't see her immediately, he tried the most likely place where she'd run to. He turned the doorknob to the ladies' bathroom and found it locked. "Open up."

"I'll be out in a minute."

"Your mom only gave me a few minutes. Let me talk to you."

Yasmine opened the door while wiping her eyes. "I'm okay. Go back. I'll be fine."

"You sounded beautiful—"

"I did not sound beautiful. Don't lie."

"I'm not lying. I'm totally sincere. Could you use a few breathing lessons? Absolutely. But your voice is pure, and I can certainly edit out the little imperfections—"

"I don't trust you," Yasmine blurted out.

Gabe stopped talking. "What . . . what do you mean?"

"I don't trust you." Yasmine looked down. "Gabe, the last time we talked, you made everything seem so okay." She looked at his gorgeous eyes. "But it's not okay. I don't want you to see Anna ever again."

"Okay." Gabe shrugged. "I can do that. But we both know that's completely ridiculous."

"It's not ridiculous. I really don't know what went on between you two—"

"I *told* you what went on between us two. Nothing."

"You *slept* with her."

"It was more comfortable than sleeping on the floor. There wasn't even any room on the floor. I guess I could have retreated to the bathtub . . . oh wait, there's no bathtub in her apartment."

"I don't want you to see her again."

"Fine." Gabe sighed. "Let's go back before your mother starts hunting me down."

"You really won't see her again?"

"Yasmine, stop it. If you absolutely insist, I won't see her again. But Anna is the least of your worries. I care about her because of what she did for me, but it's not sexual. I have girls in my face like *all* the time. What are you going to do? Cut me off from fifty percent of the human race?"

Her eyes teared up, and she looked away.

"Look, you're not the only one with an active imagination," Gabe told her. "Your parents hate me—"

"They don't hate you."

"Yes, they really do. They're constantly trying to set you up with someone else. How do you think that makes me feel? My mother had an affair with a cardiologist and left me behind to go have another family, remember?"

"Your mother wouldn't have run away if your father wasn't such a shit."

"My father is a shit, but in my humble opinion my mother isn't too far behind." He threw up his hands. "What do you want from me? I'm a performer. I'm not saying I'm a rock star, but there is a certain percentage of the female population that is impressed with what I do. And FYI, most of my fans—male and female—are over sixty. So you have a distinct advantage."

"I'm jealous." Her lip trembled. "I hate being that way, but I can't help it."

Gabe tried to reach out to her, but she stepped away. He felt the flush of anger run through his face. "My bad! I shouldn't have told you."

Tears leaked down her cheek. "Now you won't tell me *anything!*"

"It'll be different when we're together. We'll both be calmer." He tried to soothe his already frazzled nerves, but he was moments away from losing it. "Let's just go."

"You hate me."

"No, I don't hate— . . . do you want to break up? Is that what this is all about? Are you purposely trying to push me away?"

"No!"

"Then stop acting stupid. And I'm not calling you stupid. But you are *acting* stupid." He checked his watch. "Forget it. We're going to need another session to finish up. Let's call it quits for today and I'll rent more studio time. Can you do Thursday?"

"This must cost a fortune."

Gabe smiled tightly. "Is Thursday okay?"

"Yeah."

"Okay." Another tight smile. "Let's go."

"I am acting stupid." She shook her head. "Of course you can see Anna. It's my problem, not yours." Sohala had come into the hallway where they were talking. Yasmine dried her eyes on her shirtsleeve. To Gabe, she said, "I'll see you Thursday."

"We're going home?" Sohala asked.

"Yes, we're leaving. Nothing is working well today."

"Yasmini, you sound beautiful."

"Thank you, Mommy. Let's go."

Gabe said, "Mrs. Nourmand, can I have another two minutes with her?" The woman's eyes narrowed. "Please don't make me beg. I'm too exhausted to beg."

"Hokay. You don't move from this spot. I go get Yasmine's purse."

"Thank you." When she left, Gabe said, "Do you have your phone?"

"No, it's in my purse. Why?"

Gabe took out his iPhone, punched in a number, and forced it in her hand. "Talk."

"What are you *doing*?" But before Yasmine could give the cell back, a female voice answered.

"Hi, Pookey."

Yasmine felt her heart beating as her face turned red with embarrassment and anger. "It's not Gabe. My name is Yasmine Nourmand. I'm—"

"I know who you are. Is Gabe okay?"

"Yeah, he's fine. I just wanted to introduce—"

"You're sure he's fine?"

"Yeah, he's fine—"

"Because he was a wreck when he left for the trial. He was scared shitless about you, that you were going to crack. I kept on telling him—from what he told me at least—that you don't sound like the kind of girl who'd crack. Then I told him, 'Gabe, if you want to help her, you need to calm down. Take some drugs, take booze, whack off, do something, but you can't let her see you like this.' The guy was a fucking basket case. I even offered to buy him a blow job. Did he tell you I offered to buy him a blow job?"

"No—"

"Course he said no. He's totally devoted to you. He's seventeen. He should be out chasing pussy. He doesn't even need to chase it. It comes to him. It's like, 'Hi, I'm Gabe' and whop, like a pussy appears. I keep telling him, 'You don't want it, I'll take it.' I guess it doesn't work that way. But I'll tell you one thing. I'd do any-thing for that guy. I wouldn't fuck him, though. I don't fuck guys. Did Gabe tell you I'm gay?"

"Yes—"

"Look, I know who I am. I'm crazy. Gabe's not crazy, but he's completely neurotic. If I had half his talent, I wouldn't be playing shitty dives in Brooklyn. Actually, where I work isn't a dive. But it isn't Avery Fisher Hall. If I had half his talent, I'd be a star. With my looks, I'd be a superstar. Is he giving you a hard time?"

"No—"

"He better not be. He can be a real pain in the ass."

She was talking so loud that Gabe could hear her, even though she wasn't on speakerphone. Yasmine looked at him with wide eyes. He mouthed, "I told you so."

"—really acerbic. Maybe he misses you and it drives him crackers. Or maybe he just needs sex. He watches a lot of porno. His dad gives it to him. He gives me the girl-on-girl stuff. You know his dad runs whorehouses, right?"

"Right—"

"His dad is hot. Have you ever met his dad?"

"No."

"I met him twice. He musta seen pictures because he thinks you're really cute. He told me that when Gabe wasn't there. Not that he wants to fuck you or anything. Or maybe he wants to fuck you. He didn't tell me one way or the other."

Gabe slapped his forehead.

"I never met his mom. Did you meet his mom?"

"No—"

"She sounds like a piece of work. They both sound like a piece of work. He likes his foster parents. You know the police guy and his wife. Have you met them?"

"Yes—"

"I've got to get back to work. Can you give him a message for me, Yasmine? I'm having a hard time with some fingering. I want you to write this down."

Gabe took the phone. "I'm here."

"Pookey, how *are* you? Are you finally getting sex?"

"What's the passage?" When she told him, he said, "Try a crossover with the index finger of your left hand. It'll free up your pinky for the C-sharp."

"That's still an octave plus three. We can't all have ape hands."

"Your hands are long enough. That's why you have to practice."

"Har-dee-har-har. Gotta go."

Yasmine took the phone. "Anna, wait."

"Hi, Pookey . . . or you can be Pookette. What's up, Pookette?"

"First of all, thank you for taking care of Gabriel."

"Man, that was the hardest thing I've ever done. I thought he was gonna die. He just dropped. And then he became a zombie for a month. I finally told him he had to get it together or I'd call you. It was a threat, but it worked."

Yasmine jumped into the conversation. "Anna, if he ever has any big problems, you *must* call me."

"Pookette, I *wanted* to call you. I knew I was in over my head mainly because I have no capacity to nurture. But he didn't kill himself, so I take that as a victory. Oh, shit, I'm late! My fans await. I also gotta watch my tip jar. We get lots of sketchy people. Bye, Pookette. Kiss Pookey for me." She hung up.

Wordlessly, Yasmine gave him back the phone. Gabe stowed it in his pocket.

Sohala came out. "I have your purse, Yasmine. Let's go."

Yasmine looked at Gabe. "Do we still have any studio time left?"

A glance at his watch. He said, "About a half hour. Why? Feeling better?"

"Yeah, I am." She looked at her mother. "Let's go back to the studio."

"You drive me crazy." The three of them walked back inside the sound room. "You stay, you go, you stay, you go—"

"Sit, Mommy," Yasmine interrupted. "I want you to hear something."

Gabe sat down on the piano bench and put on a set of headphones. But instead of going to her microphone, Yasmine sat next to him and put her hand on his knee. "Play the third movement of the Moonlight Sonata."

"Now?"

"Yes. I want my mom to hear you." A pause. "Do you not know it by heart?"

"Of course I know it by heart. I'm going to play it in a month. I'd better know it cold." Gabe shrugged. "Give me a minute. I need to get in the zone." He turned to her. "Sorry, but I need my space."

"Of course." Yasmine got up and sat by her mom.

"What are you doing?" Sohala asked her.

Yasmine said, "Just listen."

Gabe placed his fingers on the piano, closed his eyes, and began to play.

But of course Gabriel didn't just play. He transformed. The piano was not an instrument of the hands and fingers, it was a living organism interpreting the composition of the human brain. Words could describe other senses: the sound of rushing water, the smell of dewy pine, the taste of charred corn on the cob, the sight of a deep blue sky, the touch of a baby's soft cheek. But how could anyone describe something as sublime as Beethoven's piano sonatas with words? How could anyone describe the complexity of a sound so extraordinary? Yasmine could see Gabe's fingers fly over the keyboard; she could see the intensity of his face, the physicality of his posture playing a demanding piece. But there was no way to describe the product of what came out other than to hear it. Six minutes and forty-two seconds of pure, unadulterated awe.

When Gabe finished, he opened his eyes and nodded. "Pretty decent, no?"

Yasmine didn't answer. Instead, she turned to her mother. "Mommy . . . how can you possibly expect me to ever, ever give him up? How can I give up a boy who risked his own life to save mine? How can I give up a boy who makes music like that? And on top of that, he's gorgeous. I'd have to be *crazy!*"

Sohala was silent. Then she said, "He'll break your heart."

When Gabe started to speak, Yasmine held up her hand. "And if he does break my heart, Mommy, I will survive. Look at all the horrible stuff that happened to me. I'm still here. I'm still functioning. I can take heartbreak—even bad heartbreak—without evaporating, okay."

"You don't know," Sohala said.

"Then I'll learn. But I can't learn unless I experience it." Yasmine took her mother's hand. "I will never give him up. You have to *accept* that." No one spoke. "The relationship might die, but you can't kill it. At the very least you have to let us . . . *talk*! That's the only way we can figure things out."

The studio was silent.

"Hokay," Sohala finally said. "You can talk to him while he's here. It's hokay. No hanky-panky."

"No hanky-panky is fine," Yasmine said.

"It is?" Gabe said.

Yasmine smiled. "Stop it."

Sohala said, "Then after he leaves, you break up—"

"No, Mommy, you have to let *us* work this out. Not you—Gabe and me. If it's serious, he'll convert. If he doesn't covert, I'll break up with him. He knows that."

"That was never a problem," Gabe said. "I lived with the Deckers for two years. Believe me, I know the Jewish drill."

Sohala knew this was a battle she wasn't going to win at this moment. She stood up. "We go home now."

Yasmine said, "You go home, Mommy. Gabe will take me home." Her stare was fierce. "I'm going home with him. I'll see you in a couple of hours."

Sohala exhaled. "Yasmini, I love you, but you cause me all my gray hairs. If I die early, it's your fault."

"I will take the blame." Yasmine got up. "I'll walk you to the car and let Gabe finish up with the recording engineer."

She came back ten minutes later. Gabe said, "I made an appointment for Thursday."

"I'll practice more. I know I can do better."

"You sang beautifully. You did everything beautifully. You were masterly. Thank you for those wonderful things you said about me."

"I meant every word."

"Did I tell you I love you today?" Gabe took her in his arms and kissed her with passion. "This is probably hanky-panky, but you made the promise, not me."

They kissed. Then they walked out of the studio, hand in hand.

Gabe said, "You were . . . unbelievably terrific, Yasmini."

"I know." She smiled. "You're lucky to have me."

"I agree!" He kissed her hand. "Just please try to trust me, okay?"

She kissed his hand back. "I swear I will never doubt you again, Gabriel."

"Of course you'll doubt me again. And over the next fifty years, I know that there will be times when I doubt you. We love each other madly, but we're artistic: egotistical, hotheaded, perfectionistic, compulsive, and complete and unadulterated neurotics. But like your mom says, it's hokay. It's just the nature of the beast."

Chapter Thirty-Two

Her cheeks held a slight blush and her gait was a tad wobbly, but Sabrina Talbot walked tall and she was on time: a beautiful woman in a black dress with spiked heels and an open trench coat. Her blond hair framed a flawless face: the perfect nose, the sensual lips, the sky blue eyes. She held out a manicured hand, and Decker shook it, leading her into his office and offering her a seat. He closed the door. On the desktop was a pitcher of water and a glass. Decker sat down and picked up a mug.

"I'm drinking coffee," he said. "Can I get you a cup?"

"No, thank you."

"Water?"

"Nope." Her hands were folded in her lap. She looked around. "This couldn't be the ghastly interview room that Gracie was talking about."

"No, it's my ghastly office. They got the interview room because there were two of them and my office is small."

"And here I thought I was getting the star treatment."

"If the police station had a green room, you'd be the first occupant."

Her smile had wattage. "I'm assuming my presence here has less to do with my charm and more to do with pumping me for information." A pause. "I don't know what I could tell you that I haven't already told the handsome gentleman and the lady."

"Detective Oliver and Sergeant Dunn." Decker picked up a pen and opened his notebook. "We appreciate your cooperation and don't want to stress your good nature. I know you haven't had contact with Mr. Penny in quite a while."

"Years."

Decker took a sip of coffee. "I know you're close to his children, so I didn't want to ask questions in front of them—"

"You want to talk about our sex life—mine and Hobart's."

"I understand he became creepy and animalistic toward the end."

"He became crazy toward the end."

"People manifest craziness in all sorts of ways."

"He didn't get off on wearing a diaper and asking to be breast-fed. He went on the attack, and that was fitting with his personality. He was a very dominant man."

"He scratched you and claimed it was the tiger in him."

"I see you communicate with your detectives."

Decker jotted down a few notes. "That's how you run an investigation."

"The wounds went from my shoulder to my neck. The marriage was over. Actually, when I found the pictures and he admitted going to the clubs, I knew there was nothing left."

"Did you ever go with him to the clubs?"

"No. He traveled when he did those things, and he never asked me to join him."

"I'm sorry if this is personal, but I have to ask. Did he ever bring women into the house?"

Her sigh was from long ago and from being long-suffering. "Yes. Would you like to know the details? I do remember them."

"Humiliating?"

"Hobart enjoyed the humiliation. He enjoyed humiliating the world."

"How about pain? Was he into pain?"

"Biting and scratching hurt, Lieutenant. He never asked about my welfare."

"Did he ever slap or hit or whip you?"

Sabrina's expression was contemplative. "He scratched, he bit, he grabbed and held on tight. No hitting that I can recall."

"Did he ever threaten you with a weapon if you didn't do what he wanted?"

"No, I always did what he wanted."

"Did he ever try to choke you?"

"No. It might have progressed to that, but we split up."

Decker said, "What about the other women he brought home, Ms. Talbot? How did he treat them in your presence?"

"He fucked them in my presence."

"Did he bite them?"

"I'm sure he bit a few."

"Did he bite them hard enough to draw blood?"

She was thinking about it. "He drew blood, yes."

"Anything beyond the biting? Did you ever see Hobart hit or beat up a woman?"

"A few slaps on the butt." She bit her lower lip. "He didn't beat them up when I was around."

"Did you ever see him threaten a woman with a weapon?"

"Not that I remember."

"So, you never saw your ex-husband cutting a woman with a knife . . . even superficially?"

She didn't answer for a long time. Then she said, "I presume you have a reason for asking these questions beyond prurient interest." She leaned forward. "Did Hobart do something . . . bad?"

"That's why I wanted to speak with you alone. His children don't have to hear this . . . yet. In your ex-husband's apartment, we found body parts."

The woman went pale and covered her mouth. "Oh my God!" Her complexion had turned ashen. "Oh my God!"

"Do you need to use the bathroom?"

She shook her head no but poured herself a glass of water and bolted it down. "What kind of body parts?"

"Human fingers. More than one, and belonging to more than one person."

"Oh dear Lord!" Again she covered her mouth. "I don't know what to say."

"I have a reason for telling you this. I want to know if that awful image brings to mind anything in your past."

"Like what?"

"You tell me."

"I've never seen Hobart do anything that would end up with body parts."

"So you've never witnessed Hobart murdering someone."

"Good God no!" She leaped to her feet. "Absolutely not!" She started pacing. "He bit . . . he scratched . . . he liked doing the ass. That's not against the law though."

"That's not against the law unless it was forced."

"It wasn't forced. He paid the girls handsomely for it, which was amazing, because Hobart was a cheapskate."

"He paid for sex?"

"Of course he paid for sex. You talk about weapons? With Hobart, money was the ultimate weapon. How else would he get hot, young girls to come home with him?"

"Have a seat, Sabrina." Reluctantly she sat back down. Decker said, "You told my detectives that you were attracted to his magnetic personality. Maybe others were as well."

"No, they were attracted to his wallet, which was quite an aphrodisiac." She looked directly at Decker's face. "Hobart loved to spend money on *humiliation*. When I started enjoying it back door, he didn't like it anymore. So he sought other subjects to humiliate."

"Were they professionals? The girls he brought home?"

"They were pretty girls who'd do kinky things for money—which, I suppose, is the definition of a whore. The upshot is he brought home young girls and did stuff with them. He liked me to watch because it made me feel small. Sometimes he'd tie me up and make me watch. If I closed my eyes, he'd douse my face with water so I'd look." She sighed. "Are we done?"

"If we hadn't found body parts, Ms. Talbot, I wouldn't be asking you these questions." Decker said, "Were the girls ever alone with him or were you always there?"

Sabrina looked down. "Sometimes Hobart took the girls to a second room in the back of the house. I was *not* invited to join them. As you might have guessed, I was more than happy to be excluded and left alone."

"And the girls left the next morning alive?"

"Of course they were alive."

"So you *saw* the girls leave your house *alive*."

"I just assumed."

"Do you remember any of them leaving after a night with your husband?" When she didn't answer, Decker said, "So you didn't know what he did when he was alone with the women he picked up. Am I right about that?"

Her eyes formed tears. "I tried to blank it from my mind."

"You didn't know what he did and you really never knew what happened to them."

Her eyes watered. "He had a special room for them, and I was never invited inside the lair. After we divorced, I went into that room and I never saw anything bad."

"What did you see?"

"Actually, it was completely sterile. The walls had been freshly painted, and there was brand-new carpeting. I thought he was being nice. After all, he was so generous with the settlement. I thought . . . actually, I don't know what I thought. I was glad he was gone . . . out of my life."

Decker said, "So . . . the room had been repainted and there was new carpet."

Sabrina nodded while looking at her red fingernails. Her hands were unsteady as she wiped her eyes. "What does that mean, Lieutenant?"

Decker said, "It means, Ms. Talbot, that you probably dodged a bullet."

The paperwork was drowning him: reviewing what the other detectives had been working on, court cases, call assignments, and vacation times to figure out. Normally all this could have been easily done during working hours. But with Penny taking up so much of his time, Decker had fallen behind. He'd be lucky to get out by eleven.

Marge knocked on the open door, bringing in two cups of coffee. "You're still here?"

"Got another half hour of odds and ends to button up." He smiled at her. "Is one of those mugs for me?"

"Yes."

"Decaf?"

"It could be, but that would require another pot."

"Who cares about sleep?" Decker took the cup. "I'm much obliged, thank you."

She sat down. Oliver walked in a moment later and took a chair. "So, how is my Lady Sabrina?"

Decker took a long sip. "She called you handsome."

Oliver brightened. "That's nice. Did you tell her my middle name is Mellors?"

Marge was perplexed. "I don't get it."

"That was very esoteric, Scott," Decker said.

Oliver said, "Mellors was the groundkeeper in *Lady Chatterley's Lover.*"

"Oh . . . okay." She paused. "Wasn't Mellors supposed to be young and virile?"

He glared at her. "What did I do tonight to offend you?"

Marge laughed. "You're right. I'm sorry. And you are very handsome."

"Too little too late."

Decker said, "In answer to your original question, Sabrina Talbot was cooperative and forthcoming. This is the deal. Sabrina never went with Penny to his sex clubs. But she saw him bring women home. According to Sabrina, they weren't professional hookers, but they were young party girls whom he paid for sex. He was into humiliation. He liked to screw them in front of his wife. Sabrina never remembers seeing Penny threatening the girls. Apparently, he didn't hit or beat them. He just had sex with them. He liked it in the ass. That was about as kinky as it got."

Marge said, "Voyeurism, humiliation, and sodomy. On a kinky scale, I give it a six."

"Five," Oliver said.

"Whatever the rating, she doesn't remember any disarticulated digits. But there's more. Sometimes Penny was alone with the girls in a private room that was off-limits to his wife. During those times, Sabrina retreated to her bedroom and enjoyed the peace and quiet. So she has no idea what took place or what happened to the girls. When she woke up the next morning they were gone and Penny was at work doing whatever he did to make himself millions. After the two of them divorced, Sabrina went into the private room for the first time. It had been freshly painted and had new carpeting."

Oliver said, "The slaughterhouse was right under her nose. You think she might have heard or smelled something."

"The house is enormous," Marge said. "And how often do you think she went by the servants' wing unless he forced her?"

Decker said, "When you live with someone like that, it's easy to turn a blind eye. Back to business. I need you two to go back to Santa Barbara and take a look at Penny's fuck room with luminol. Set up a time and date tomorrow."

"That's not a problem, Lieutenant. I am happy to do that."

"Anything from the party girls on Lankershim?"

Marge recapped the night's conversation with Coco, including the gloved Shady Lady who didn't work call-girl service anymore. When she was done, Decker said, "Could be a promising lead. And if she is short a digit and knows who did it, we could have another suspect in Hobart's murder."

"A revenge murder from so long ago?" Marge asked.

"It's a dish best eaten cold," Decker said. "So find Shady Lady and talk to her."

"If we're going to Santa Barbara tomorrow, when do we fit that in?" Oliver asked.

Decker looked at his watch. "Girls should be coming out just about now. There's no time like the present."

Chapter Thirty-Three

It was almost eleven, but the lights were still on in the living room. Rina and Gabe at the dining room table, playing cards. They both looked up when Decker walked in. "Who's winning?"

"She's killing me," Gabe said.

"Must be gin rummy. She's ruthless."

Rina put her cards down, got up, and kissed her husband. "Paella is warming in the oven. Chicken and sausage."

"I love you."

"So take back what you said about me being ruthless."

"I'm referring to your card playing."

Rina handed him her cards. "Finish up for me."

Gabe put down the cards. "I'm done anyway. I know when I've been bested." He stood up. "I had a long afternoon in the recording studio with Yasmine."

"Yeah, right." Decker cleared his throat. "How'd that go?"

"We didn't finish. Her voice is a little raw. I told her to practice scales and we'll try again on Thursday."

"I meant how did it go with Mom?"

Gabe tried to stifle a smile but couldn't quite manage it. "I guess all the drama over the weekend turned out okay. Sohala has given us permission to talk to each other."

"Good for you." Decker smiled. "Anything specific that led to a change of heart?"

"I'd like to say I dazzled her with my piano playing—I probably did dazzle her—but it was Yasmine who made it happen. She just put her foot down, and her mother caved. I'm sure she'll monitor Yasmine's phone and computer and all that stuff, but at least I can call her without having to sneak around. I never wanted that."

"I know you didn't. Glad you worked something out. Now you have to go about the business of a relationship. That's the hard part. You know Sohala's right when she says you're both very young. You've got a lot of mistakes in your future. Try to make them small ones."

"I know all about mistakes. I'm the embodiment of my mother's misfortune, and I wouldn't make that mistake with Yasmine ever."

"Good to hear. Take the relationship back a couple of notches, Gabe. It'll be good for both of you. You won't be sorry."

Gabe's shrug was noncommittal. With sex, it was impossible to put the toothpaste back in the tube, but at least Decker had said it out loud.

The boy said, "I love her and she loves me. That's a real nice feeling."

"You're loved by many people, Gabe. Rina and me, your mother . . . even your father—as much as he can love anyone."

"Right-o." Gabe shrugged again. "I know my mom has sacrificed a lot for me. I know she loves me. But feelings are abstract."

Decker gave the boy a brief hug. "They are indeed."

Gabe smiled. "If I convert, will you adopt me?"

"You're almost eighteen, so that would be silly. But if you want, I'll call you son and you can call me Abba, like Hannah does. That way I won't compete with your biological dad, who would get angry if he thought I was trying to take his place."

"He wouldn't care."

"I will debate you on that one. The Chris Donatti I know never turns down an opportunity to be pissed off."

After stowing away his dish in the cabinet, Decker dried his hands and gave his wife a weak smile. He said, "You want some tea?"

"Sure. Thanks."

"Sit down. I want to talk to you."

"This sounds serious."

"Nothing's wrong. Just have a seat."

Rina pulled out a chair at the kitchen table. "What's going on?"

"How wedded are you to Los Angeles?" Rina looked up at him and stared. "I know you have your parents here. But if they weren't here, would you make L.A. your home?"

Rina continued to stare at her husband. "What's on your mind, Peter? Did something happen at work?"

"No, nothing like that." He took out two mugs. "I love my job, but I'm not sure that I love LAPD anymore: the bureaucracy, the red tape, the paramilitary structure. And I'm not sure that I love L.A. anymore . . . it's very . . . crowded."

Silence.

"Would you ever consider moving back east? You'd be physically closer to all the kids, including Gabriel."

"Sounds like you already have something in mind."

"I've been exploring some options in law enforcement. I wouldn't do anything unless you were a hundred percent behind me, but I figured it doesn't hurt to look."

"What kind of options?"

"I'd like to remain in some kind of detective's division. I've been looking at towns that are within three-hour driving distance to New York."

"Not NYPD."

"Not a chance. I'm way too old to start a career in the Big Apple, and that's not what I want anyway. I want a smaller town with less crime and grime. It's not that small towns don't have crime; they do—burglary, car theft, drugs, drunk and disorderlies, domestics, and even CAPS and murder. It's the proportion. I've been researching several college towns, places where there are Hillels or Chabads. I know you need Jewish life, but we don't have kids living at home. We don't need a Jewish day school or a peer group for them."

"So you're looking at college towns?"

"The one I like the best is Greenbury."

"The Five Colleges of Upstate."

"It's about a three-hour drive into Manhattan."

"Without traffic."

"Yes, without traffic. But at least you'd be within driving distance of the kids."

"What about Cindy?"

"Funny you should ask."

Rina stared at him. "She's *moving?*"

"Well, it seems that Koby has applied to medical school."

"*Medical school?*" Rina was shocked. "How long have you known about this?"

"Several months. Cindy didn't want to say anything in case he didn't get in. But then she figured she should prepare me for a possible move. Last week she told me he got in to a few places in New York and Philadelphia on an NIH nursing grant that would help pay his way to medical school and a Ph.D. program in nursing, as long as he commits to community service for five years after he's done. Cindy has been exploring NYPD or Philadelphia PD. She wants to live in a big city because the kids are biracial. New York or Philadelphia is good because they won't stick out."

"What about their house?" Rina said. "They *love* their house."

"Back east, they could probably swap across the board for a very nice and much bigger house in the burbs. Even if they scaled down to a tiny two-bedroom apartment in Manhattan, they'd save on car expenses and gas and could walk everywhere."

"But you don't want to live in New York City."

"No way. I'm not asking you to move right away. Just . . . think about it."

"I know it would kill you to be so far away from the twins."

"It's not only about me, it's also about you. When Rachel and Sammy have a kid, are you going to want to be so far away?"

"I have to consider my parents."

"I agree."

She thought about his words for a long time. "If I moved, I know my parents would move . . . probably to Florida." She shrugged. "We can visit all the parents at the same time. You know how well your mom and my mom get along."

"They've reached that understanding that revolves around old age and food."

Rina smiled. "As long as they're swapping recipes, all is well."

"Nothing is etched in stone, Rina. Just think about it."

She looked at her husband. "You've always lived in warm climates, Peter. How are you going to handle the winters?"

He shrugged. "The same way that millions of other people have handled cold climates: warm jacket, gloves, and a hat."

Oliver looked out the side window, staring at a barren landscape in blacks and grays. This particular street featured characterless apartment buildings illuminated by an occasional flood of urine-colored lighting. At first glance, everything seemed quiet, but since Marge was driving exceptionally slow, Oliver could ascertain movement in the shadows.

They've been riding around for several hours, racking up mileage on the cruiser, looking for girls in the trade, trying to get a bead on Shady Lady. They spoke to hookers in the West Valley, yakked with the ladies in the East Valley, gossiped with the gays in West Hollywood, and questioned the multitudes in Hollywood proper. They conversed with females dressed as males, males in drag, and even a few trans- genders whose sex was impossible to determine without seeing the goods. They stopped at sleazy motels and dark, booze-soaked bars. They spoke with proprietors, patrons, and employees. They crisscrossed through back alleys and made contacts with streetwalkers. The work took time, it took patience, and it took luck. By two A.M., the detectives had run out of all three.

As they mopped up the last of Hollywood, heading toward the 101, Marge saw a lone prostitute, sticking a wad of bills into the top of her fishnets—which fell way below her micromini. In the not-too-far distance, Marge spied two hooded men walking behind her. When the girl noticed them, she sped up.

So did the men.

When they were around ten yards away, the girl turned and started to run. Marge cranked up the siren. The men scattered, but the girl was still tearing down the sidewalk when Marge pulled over. "Slow down."

She kept running.

Marge kept pace in the car. "C'mon, honey. If I go away, you know your buddies will do a one-eighty and come back to get what they saw."

The girl slowed down, clearly out of breath. Finally she stopped and stuck her head between her legs. She was white and very thin, her right arm enveloped in a half-sleeved tattoo. There were other ink marks on her legs, ankles, and behind her neck. She was young with short hair dyed ice blond. There were pockmarks on her cheek, but she did have all her fingers. She was panting.

Marge said, "C'mon in. We'll give you a ride."

"I'm . . . okay."

"We're not arresting you." Oliver got out and opened the door to the backseat. "It's cold outside. Surely you don't want to be another nasty statistic."

Reluctantly, the girl got in the backseat, completely spent. At the moment, even jail was a better alternative to being gang-raped and beaten. Marge pulled away and did a U-turn until she was driving west of Hollywood Boulevard.

Oliver turned around and said, "Do you have ID?"

The girl's eyes darkened. She was still breathing hard. "I thought . . . you weren't arresting me."

"I'm checking your age." Then the girl handed Oliver her driver's license. Mindy Martin—age nineteen. "Current address?" She didn't answer. "Move around a lot?" Nothing. "Where does your pimp live?"

"No pimp . . ." Breath, breath.

Oliver said, "Where does your boyfriend live?"

"I'm supposed to meet him at . . . The Snake Pit."

"That's six miles west of here."

"I know." A pause. "You know, I wasn't doing anything."

"We're not from vice," Marge said. "We're from homicide."

"Ho-mi-cide?" Pronouncing each syllable as if she were learning it for the first time. "Like murder?"

"Exactly like murder. We're looking for a woman who calls herself Shady Lady. She's probably around thirty and she wears gloves. She might be missing a finger."

"Yuck!"

"You know anybody like that?"

"No," Mindy said. "I keep to myself. Both me and my boyfriend like it that way."

Marge said, "What's your boyfriend's name?"

"Nathaniel."

"Nathaniel what?"

"Nathaniel Horchow, if you must know."

"He doesn't mind you . . . doing what you're doing out here?" Oliver let the sentence hang in the air.

"Yeah, he minds. He didn't want me to do it, you know. But this is a very expensive city. I'm just doing it a little longer . . . until he breaks in." She pinched off a tiny bit of space between her thumb and forefinger. "He's sooooo close. Not everyone can get into The Snake Pit, you know. You need connections."

"Break in doing what?"

"Acting."

Marge looked in the rearview mirror. "Let me tell you your story, Mindy Martin. Are you listening?" No answer. "Okay, here goes. You're from the Midwest. Wisconsin, Iowa, or maybe Minnesota. You and Nathaniel grew up together, maybe even did a little acting in the high school play. Nathaniel's a good-looking guy in your little hometown. He's popular, athletic . . . a lady's man, so you were honored he chose you. Plus, he's got an artistic soul that only you understand. Certainly, his parents don't understand him. Nathaniel has dreams that don't include hanging around his hometown. First, he wanted to leave as soon as he hit sixteen and could drive away. But you . . . not so much. You told him at least to wait until you graduated. Then you both took off for Hollywood." A pause. "How am I doing so far?"

No answer.

Marge said, "It's been slow going for the career because Nathaniel's pretty face in Wisconsin—"

"Minnesota."

"My apologies," Marge said. "There are thousands of pretty boys out here in L.A. doing the same thing. Some of them are gay. As a matter of fact, I bet Nathaniel's been offered some gay porn, but you put your foot down at that. Still, you have no idea what he does when you're not around. And he's been hanging around some edgy-looking people. You two have been here about . . . two years maybe."

Silence.

"How far off am I?"

"How'd ya know we've been here for two years?"

"Because you're hooking in the field and you're not a hundred percent jaded. Another year or so, you'll go back home. Nathaniel will stay here. He'll survive by doing something. Maybe he'll get a legit job. More than likely he'll augment the income by selling some

438 · FAYE KELLERMAN

weed or meth, or giving BJs to rich men who are on the down-low. Eventually, he'll get arrested and do time. But unless he's hard-core, sitting in jail will give him time to think. Maybe he'll even come back to you. So if you want some advice, just pack up and go back home and wait a year or so. If he doesn't materialize, it's one of the three things: he never really wanted you, he's in jail, or he's dead."

"You don't know me." Her cheeks were red with tears. "He loves me."

"I'm sure he does," Marge said.

"Drop me off here," Mindy said. "I can walk."

"I'll take you all the way. The streets are deserted except for the goblins."

They rode in silence, the lights shimmering in the night fog. Finally she said, "Who got killed?"

"An old man," Oliver said. "We think he might have been involved with prostitutes. Ever work in the San Fernando Valley?"

"No. Don't have a car."

Marge said, "So Nathaniel drives you where you need to go?"

Again, she went mute. Ten minutes later they were five blocks away from The Snake Pit. Mindy's voice was quiet. "Let me off here. Don't want to show up at The Snake Pit in a cop car. Boo that."

Marge pulled over to the curb. Mindy immediately tried to open the back door but couldn't. Marge got out of the cruiser and opened Mindy's door, but blocked her access to freedom. "You hear anything about someone missing fingers, you call me, Mindy. I depend on people like you, okay?"

"Why? So you can insult them?"

"I'm just trying to point you in the right direction. Up to you if you want to walk that way or not. But do call if you hear anything. There's money in it for you if you give me a legit lead."

Her mood perked up. "Like I'm a confidence informer?"

Marge handed her a business card. "There's my number. Don't be afraid to use it."

"How much money?"

"You'll find out after you do me a service. If you found my lady with missing fingers and you told me about it . . . see, that would be a service. And that would mean money."

"Okay." A shrug. "I'll keep my ears open."

"Good. Because right now the score is one/zero in our favor because *we* pulled *you* out of a jam." Marge stepped out of the way so Mindy could pass. "Pay off your debt soon, girl. It's what keeps the economy humming."

Chapter Thirty-Four

Decker heard his cell vibrate under his pillow and glanced at the clock. Since it was two-thirty in the morning, it was either a drunk or him. When Decker depressed the green button, he whispered, "Hold on." Grabbing a robe, he tiptoed from the bedroom and into the living room. He turned on a table lamp.

"Hey, Chris," he croaked out and then cleared his throat.

"How's my son?"

"He had a good day. He and his girlfriend are now allowed to talk to each other."

"He's too young for a relationship. Lemme talk to him."

Decker smiled. "Chris, he's sleeping."

"So?"

"You've got his cell number. I'm not going to wake him up."

Donatti laughed. "Okay. Let the little bastard sleep. That is what most people do at two-thirty in the morning. Me? I've worked the night shift my entire life. Right now I'm stuck at the tables in Vegas, watching several of my high-roller clients, ensuring a good time is had by all."

"How's lady luck treating you?"

"I'm a bystander, but my clients are happy. That's good for me, because they're repeaters. Every businessman will tell you that return customers are his bread and butter."

"You are nothing if not savvy in the world of money."

"So you should appreciate this freebie."

"Freebie?" Decker was astonished. "More like payback for raising your son."

"What the fuck are you talking about? I send you money."

"I give it to your son."

"Well, then you're stupid, because I already give him more than he needs."

Decker felt blood rush to his brain as immediate anger welled up in his body. He forced himself to talk slowly. "I don't want your money, Donatti. I've never wanted your money. When I need help, I'm not shy to ask anyone. You have means that are unavailable to me and I know my limitations. But let's get one thing straight, buddy. You don't *ever* call me stupid. I treat you civilly. I demand the same treatment back."

Silence over the line. Decker expected it to disconnect at any moment. Instead Donatti's voice dropped a couple of notches. It was ice cold. "You know those pictures you e-mailed me."

Decker sat up. "You found the girls?"

"Not the girls, the guy . . . Bruce Havert. I'm looking at him as we speak."

"You're sure it's him?"

"Not positive. But I have a good eye for faces."

"That's right. You can draw."

"One of my many talents. He's dealing blackjack, standing about a hundred feet from where I am. His name tag says BYRON."

"Where are you?"

"At Havana! I've gotta go."

"Wait a moment." A pause. "Please, just give me a minute to think." Decker began to pace. Havert wasn't wanted, so police couldn't bring him in. There had to be another approach. "Chris, is there any way you can get his assumed last name without looking obvious?"

"I don't do obvious, Decker. You want personal info, ask the casino's HR department."

In other words, fuck off. Donatti was still seething at the rebuke. Decker said, "Yeah, you're probably right. Thanks for calling."

A beat passed. Then Donatti said, "I'm not doing anything. I could sit at his table and strike up a conversation . . . if I get a seat. It's a cheap table: twenty minimum."

"That would be helpful. Maybe you can hang around and act friendly."

"I don't do friendly, either. Besides he's not gonna talk unless I'm throwing around cash. Doing it the right way means sitting down at the table and playing cards. It'll be gambling with your money. If I win, you're free and clear. If I lose, I'll try to keep it under a thousand."

"I'd rather pay you to follow him home. You're pretty good with the stealth."

"No can do. I've only got an hour before I have to cart my clients back to Elko on prepaid jet. Are you in or out?"

Decker didn't even have to think. "Do it."

Marge knocked on Decker's open office door, holding a piece of paper. "This came in for you like at four in the morning. Who is Byron Hayes?"

Decker took the sheet. Next to his name was an address and phone number along with the line: *Cost for services rendered:* $0.00. Chris had a good night at the tables.

Marge's eyes widened in sudden recognition. "Is that Bruce Havert?"

"Hopefully."

"Where'd this come from?"

"Donatti was in Vegas yesterday. Once again Havert is at Havana! How's your schedule looking for a trip to Sin City?"

"I'll talk to Oliver. I'm sure we can swing it."

"Good. Call up your buddies in North Las Vegas. You want to drive, or should I book tickets out of Burbank?"

"I'd rather fly. Let me see if Scott is here." She stuck her head out the door. Oliver was at his desk and on the phone. She waved and he waved. A minute later, Oliver came into Decker's office. "I just got off the phone with Sabrina Talbot. She's expecting us at eleven."

"Change of plans," Marge said. "We're going to Vegas. We've located Bruce Havert aka Byron Hayes."

Oliver's face registered surprise. "Bruce Havert, huh? What about the girls?"

"That's what you're going to find out." Decker was staring at his computer monitor.

"If we're going to Vegas, who's going to Santa Barbara?"

"That would be me." Decker clicked the keyboard. "I can get you two a real cheap flight that leaves at ten-thirty. It's eight now, so you should have enough time to organize and get out of here. When do you want to come back?"

"Leave the return open, just in case we need to stay overnight," Marge said.

"Okay. So keep me updated. I'll handle your car rental. Do you need to go home and pack?"

"Nah, I've got enough for an overnight in my locker. What about you, Scott?"

"Same," Oliver said. "Is Havert a suspect or a witness?"

"You tell me, Detective," Decker said.

"Person of interest," Marge said. "I'll contact Lonnie Silver and get something going with him." She left to make her calls. Oliver stayed behind.

Decker faced Oliver. "You'll have a Ford Escort waiting at the airport. Tell me if you need overnight accommodations."

"Don't book a motel for me," Oliver said. "I'll probably fritter away the wee hours of the morning in the casinos. Say hello to the comely Ms. Talbot for me."

"I'll do more than that," Decker said. "I'll put in the good word for you."

"Don't bother. She's out of my league."

"I don't know, Scotty, she did say you were handsome."

Oliver beamed. "She's a woman of exquisite taste."

Breezing along the 101 North, Decker was thrilled by the lack of traffic. And the scenery sure was nice. He rode past miles of multi-million-dollar houses that stood on the edge of a deep blue sea. The air was cool but not cold. The sun was spreading warmth through the windshield of his car, rays bouncing off the ocean's surface, pinpoints of light flitting about like a swarm of glowworms. From the station house, it was a ninety-minute drive to Santa Barbara, and with the speed he was traveling, it turned out to be eighty-minutes plus. He turned off Olive Mill Road in Montecito and followed directions until he arrived at Sabrina Talbot's iron gates. He announced his name into a squawk box and was let in. He coursed through a sinuous drive lined with foliage until he stopped the car at the guardhouse. The guy who stepped out was black and big: shorter than Decker but heavier, and most of it was muscle.

The guard said, "You're not Detective Oliver."

"Change of plans. Detective Oliver had an emergency elsewhere, so you got his boss." Decker took out his badge. "Ms. Talbot and I had a lovely conversation yesterday. I do appreciate her letting LAPD barge in on her one last time."

"I need to make a few calls."

"Of course." Decker kept the window rolled down and breathed in the clean air. It was saline tinged because the property was close to the ocean. Five minutes later, a golf cart appeared. It led Decker to the entrance of Sabrina's estate—more like a stone castle—sitting on acres of forested greens and sprawling emerald lawns. Sabrina met him at the door. She wore a blue, sleeveless linen dress. She was tanned, blond, and gorgeous.

And she was tall. In her wedges, they were looking blue eyes to brown eyes. Hers were slightly glassy. She was holding something iced and frothy in her hand.

"Two days in a row," she said. "We have to stop meeting like this."

"Hopefully this will be the last time we'll interfere in your life."

"And just when we were getting to know each other." A wide, white smile. "More like you were getting to know me. I don't know a thing about you. Are you even married?"

"I am."

"*Alors.* You can come in anyway. Would you like something to drink? A soft drink perhaps?" She raised her glass. "Or something harder? Hard is always nice."

Decker said, "I'm fine, Ms. Talbot."

"So formal."

"Professional." Decker held up a briefcase. "I've got my SID kits and everything." A blank stare. "I was hoping that you'd let me run a few tests." Still a blank expression. "I thought Detective Oliver explained this to you."

This time, Sabrina's smile was forced. "Why don't we go inside?"

Immediately they were met by another large man, but Sabrina dismissed him with a wave. "I've got this one, Leo. Thank you very much."

"Are you sure, Ms. Talbot?"

"Positive." She glanced at Decker. "He's just here to run some wicked little tests."

"Maybe I should come with you," Leo said.

"Not necessary." She turned her back, and Decker followed. She didn't speak and he didn't ask any questions. She took him down a maze of hallways and foyers, crisscrossing through doorways and utility rooms.

Finally Decker said, "Are we still in the main house?"

"The storage and service wing."

"How big is the house?"

"Twenty-five thousand square feet." She wiped moisture off her forehead even though it wasn't hot.

Abruptly she stopped walking and leaned against the wall. Her complexion had turned pasty.

"Are you all right?" Decker asked.

"Fine." She took a sip of her drink. "I haven't been in these quarters for years. It's a flood of bad memories coming back in a rush." She was still sweating. "It makes me sick."

"Maybe I should get Leo." Decker looked around. "If I can find my way back."

"I'll be fine. Give me a minute." She took a deep breath and let it out. "Okay. Let's do it." She made some twists and some turns and a minute later she was standing in front of a closed door. She put her drink down and took out a key. "This is the room where Hobart kept his toys, his cameras, and his games played with human chess pieces. Would you like to see it?"

"You don't have to torture yourself, Ms. Talbot. I can do this without you."

"I'd prefer to be there." She unlocked the door and turned on the light.

The room was about fifteen feet square and windowless. Even after years of disuse, the place stank of stale, biological odors and humiliation. Sabrina looked around. Her face was pained, but there was nobility in her eyes. "I don't want you to think that this was the complete picture of Hobart. There was more to him than just unusual sexual proclivities."

"Of course." Decker put on a pair of gloves. His eyes traveled the empty, echoing space. "You cleaned this up."

"Of course. I scrubbed it myself with soap and Pine-Sol. It took me several days." She turned to him. "I was way too embarrassed to have the help do it. Then I had it painted. I locked it up and never went back. I'm seeing it for the first time in twenty-five years. It looks so harmless."

"It's only a space."

"True enough. The brain fills in the rest." Sabrina walked over to a closet and pulled out a key. She inserted it in the lock, but it didn't fit. She appeared perplexed. "Odd."

"How so?"

"This is where he kept all his . . . accessories. But now my key doesn't work."

"Maybe the lock rusted out."

"It's not budging. Would you care to try?"

Decker attempted to turn the key. No luck. "I can try to pick it. I brought my tools."

"Why did you bring tools?"

"I come prepared."

"I see." She turned to face him. "May I ask what kind of tests are you planning to do?"

Decker's eyes scanned the walls. "Should I pick the lock or do the tests first?"

"Whatever you want."

He retrieved his picks. It took him some time to align the tumblers, but eventually he heard them click into place. The closet was empty.

Sabrina shook her head. "I suppose he took his toys with him when he left." She turned and faced Decker. "The room hasn't been used in over twenty-five years. What do you hope to find?"

"I'm empirical, Ms. Talbot. One thing at a time. Right now I'd like to spray the room with luminol. It's nothing permanent and won't ruin anything. The spray binds to the iron in the hemoglobin. If there was blood that hadn't been scrubbed away, it'll show up as a blue glow, even after all these years. I'll have to turn off the lights. Luminol only shows up in the dark."

She turned off the light. With no windows, they were standing in pitch-black. Decker said, "I need to spray first."

"Sorry." She turned the light back on. Decker took out the chemical, added the catalyst, waited a few moments for the reaction to begin. He sprayed one wall with steady, even strokes. "Okay. Turn off the lights."

Small dots here and there, nothing to convince him that anything nefarious happened. But he circled the areas with a pencil before the glow disappeared. It took about a half hour of going back and forth between dark and light. Finally, he was done with the one wall.

Sabrina said, "This is going to take time."

"To do it right, yes. If you trust me, I can do it on my own. Or send Leo over here. No need for you to bother yourself."

"I'm not going anywhere." Her eyes focused on his. "Whatever you find out, I want to be here when you do."

"As long as you're not in a hurry." Decker went through the same procedure with the remaining walls and the floors. It took almost two hours. At the conclusion, he said, "I don't see anything here that gives me a bad feeling."

"That's because you weren't here and I was."

Decker looked at her. "I apologize if I seem all-business. I can appreciate the horror that this represents to you."

She stared at him. "You really have been at this for a long time. You say all the right things. I bet that handsome detective of yours wouldn't be nearly as sensitive."

"Detective Oliver has been at this about as long as me."

"Yet they call you, and not him, Lieutenant."

Decker smiled impassively. "I'd like to move on to the second room now: the space where you weren't invited to join Hobart and his girls."

Sabrina shrugged. "I suppose that's the next logical step."

They moved down the hallway. Sabrina stopped in front of another locked door, opened it, and turned on the light. The environment was also hermetic: white walls and white carpeting that were spotless. Decker squatted down and smelled the fibers. Nylon sprayed with something. He walked over to the corner of the room and picked at the carpet with a gloved hand. It wasn't coming up easily. "Can I pull this up?"

"Sure."

"Actually, Ms. Talbot. I'd like to pull up a sizable chunk of carpeting to expose the floor."

"Do whatever you want."

With gloved hands, he yanked at the carpet, heard the backing rip away from the nails. He dragged the carpet up and away. Then he repeated the procedure with another corner and flipped the carpet back on itself until he pulled up roughly half of the covering. Underneath was a pad. He lifted that up. On the subflooring was a big, black blob of damp moldy wood. Immediately, Decker sneezed several times. He wasn't generally allergic, but being this close to mold would drive anyone's nasal passages awry. "The wood's rotted."

"Yuck!" Sabrina said. "How'd that happen? The room hasn't been used in a quarter decade!"

"Fungus grows where it's damp. You might have a leak from a busted pipe."

"I should call a plumber. It's disgusting."

"You might need a professional mold remover. This could be toxic."

"Oh my God!" She recoiled in repulsion.

"Yeah, you probably shouldn't get too close. I'm going to spray this . . . just to make sure that the dampness is from water."

"What color will it glow if it's water?"

"It won't. You might not want to stick around."

"I've gone this far . . . I'm not leaving."

"Okay. It's your decision." Carefully, Decker sprayed luminol across the spot in a smooth line. "Can you shut the lights?"

"Yes, sir."

The room went dark.

But not completely.

The damp spot glowed an eerie, unnatural electric blue: a solid concentrated area in the rotted spot that feathered out into spatter and spray.

"Turn the lights on." When he got no response, he turned on a flashlight and flipped the lights back on. She was gray and limp. He took her hand and walked her out of the room. "Let's go back to the main house, okay?"

She nodded but didn't move.

"Sabrina, I need to make some phone calls and you need to sit down."

Finally she managed to find her feet, then move her feet, one in front of the other and very slow at that. It seemed like a long time, but eventually they were back in sun-lit hallways. They were met by Leo. His face reddened when his saw Sabrina's wan complexion.

"What the hell happened?" He was looking accusingly at Decker.

"She's not feeling well. Take her to a room and get her some water. I need to call Santa Barbara police."

"What happened!" The man grabbed Decker's arm. "Tell me what happened *right now.*"

Decker extricated Leo's hand from his arm. "Leo, I appreciate your loyalty. But the rule is you help her out *first,* and then you can come back and ask all your questions."

Chapter Thirty-Five

It had been over two years since Marge and Oliver had visited Las Vegas, a city of big resorts and last resorts, hunting for a serial killer named Garth Hammerling, who was still at large. Not that much changed in Sin City. It was early afternoon when they arrived, and since it was a hot day in the desert, the Strip was swarming with people in T-shirts, shorts, and flip-flops, hopping from one hotel to the next, all in the guise of having fun. The thoroughfare wasn't bad at night when darkness muted the monoliths and neon reigned supreme. But in the sunlight, the gargantuan buildings dwarfed anything life-size, completely incongruent with the flat terrain beyond the glitter. There was beauty in the desert, but Vegas wasn't part of it.

The rental car had come equipped with GPS, and the address given to Marge by Detective Lonnie Silver of North Las Vegas PD put them in a strip mall away from the action. A wind had picked up grit and tossed it into the air. Marge felt a layer of grime on her face and a few pebbles in her shoes. The Italian restaurant was a storefront, and lunch seemed to be top priority, since Bruce Havert/Byron Hayes wasn't suspected of anything. The tables were covered with checkered plastic and the seating was generic wooden chairs. No Chianti bottles, but there were posters of the hills of Tuscany hanging on beige walls.

Detective Lonnie Silver hadn't changed much: early fifties and eggshell bald with a round face, brown eyes, thick shoulders on a solid trunk. His companion was young with a full head of hair, short and on the slight side, with blue eyes behind a pair of black framed glasses. The two men stood as she and Oliver approached the table. Introductions were made; the little guy was named Jack Crone. Good handshake. His nails were clean and clipped. His demeanor spoke of someone who was fussy, which was a good thing for a detective.

Silver said, "You hungry?"

"I could eat," Oliver said.

"You should take the buffet. Five ninety-nine. The lasagna's good."

Oliver said, "*Five ninety-nine* for a buffet?"

"This is Vegas, baby."

"I can't even buy a box of noodles for five ninety-nine."

Crone signaled for two more plates. "Living expenses are cheap. Good place to live if you don't gamble. Unfortunately almost everyone who works in the gaming business does. So there's always desperation here."

The waitress was young, tattooed, and tired. She plunked the plates on the table. "Soft drinks are included but not wine. You want wine?"

"Not today," Marge said.

She left wordlessly. Lonnie doled out the plates. "Get yourself some lunch and then bring us up to speed."

The two of them took their plates to the buffet. While Oliver was done in just a few minutes, Marge took her time, perusing each item in the metal serving dish. When both were finished, they brought their food over to the table. Oliver had wolfed down the food in the time it took Marge to put a napkin on her lap, so he recapped the case while she nibbled.

Afterward Oliver said, "Has anyone contacted Havert?"

Crone said, "We waited until we heard the details. How do you want to handle this?"

Marge wiped her mouth. "It would be great if we could bring him in on some smaller charge. I'm sure Havert is pimping. Could we bring him in on that?"

"Just about every dealer, waiter, and bellman have side jobs as pimps. If we nailed him, we'd nail half the working force." Silver mopped up spaghetti sauce with garlic bread. "You want this guy for murder or what?"

Marge said, "He left L.A. right after Penny was murdered, but we don't know who pulled the trigger. If you bring him in, it won't stick."

Crone said, "How about if we ask him to come down for information on something irrelevant. If I don't mention L.A., maybe his mind won't go there."

"We do need information," Oliver said. "The guy who got plugged was no angel. It might have been self-defense."

"An eighty-nine-year-old guy is a threat?" Silver said.

"He had a twelve-hundred-pound Bengal tiger at his disposal," Marge said. "He also had venomous snakes, and spiders. And when all else fails, even an old man can pull the trigger."

By two in the afternoon, Havert had just awakened. Rather than wait for him to come to the police station, the cops offered to drop by the house. The neighborhood was a few miles away from the Strip, more Mojave than glamour. It was block upon block of small houses of white stucco with red tile roofs and two-car garages. Lawn was scarce. Most of the plantings were succulents and heat-tolerant foliage interspersed among beds of white rock. The group came up to the door and Silver knocked on the top of the screen. Havert shouted out, "It's open. Be out in a sec."

The cops went inside.

Furnishings included a brown cloth sofa, two tan chairs, a laminate coffee table and end table. There was a flat screen on a scarred dresser, wires and cables snaking all over the worn ivory carpet. An Xbox and a slew of games rested on the floor. Bacon was frying, and coffee was brewing. Havert came out, wearing a yellowed terry cloth robe. He stood six feet tall without shoes and could have used a shower. His darting eyes couldn't find a place to rest. He didn't ask for ID. "Sorry about the mess. Just got up . . ." He sniffed the smoky air and ran his fingers through greasy dark hair. "Lemme check on my food."

"Go ahead," Crone told him.

"You guys want some coffee?"

"We're fine," Silver said

Havert disappeared and came out a minute later with a paper plate of crisp bacon. He ate with his hands. He finally decided to sit down. "Yeah, so . . . like what's going on?"

Since Crone was from LVMPD, he made the introductions, and as soon as he mentioned LAPD homicide, Havert's face flinched.

Marge took out a tape recorder. "Do you mind if we record this?"

Havert's eyes grew even jumpier. "Why?"

"Because my memory isn't so great." She held up her notebook. "I use it as a backup against my own scrawls. Is it okay?"

"I guess so." He tried to act calm. "This is Vegas. What gives with LAPD?"

Marge gave him a reassuring smile. "You did live in L.A. up until about two weeks ago."

"A two-year stopover. Vegas is my home."

"Two years is a long stopover. Where'd you live while you were there?"

"I hopped around." His knee was bouncing; his robe was partially open at the chest. "Rotten city. That's why I moved back to Vegas. At least, here you know what you got."

Marge took out a notepad. "You left L.A. in a hurry."

"I just got fed up. Didn't have a lot, so I picked up and left."

"What got you fed up?"

"Everything. Like I said, it was a rotten city."

Silence. Silver said, "You know, Bruce, big casinos don't want any problems. The pit bosses don't like people with baggage."

"Everyone here has baggage."

"Not recent baggage. I'm sure you're good at what you do, but there's a waiting list for dealers about a mile long . . . lots of people itching to take your place."

"Why are you guys hassling me?"

Oliver said, "All Detective Silver is saying is that you've got a good job and I'm sure you want to keep it. Let me tell you why we're here. And then maybe you can help us out."

Marge said, "We're investigating the murder of an eighty-nine-year-old man named Hobart Penny. He lived and died in our district. He was an odd man—"

"No shit!"

Marge said, "So you knew him."

"Not personally." Bruce paused. "Am I gonna need a lawyer?"

Marge sized him up and took a chance. "Ordinarily I'd try to talk you out of calling your attorney, but since all we're looking for is information, go ahead and call him up. We'll wait. It's your money. I'm sure he isn't cheap."

Havert fidgeted. "No joke." A pause. "I didn't do anything to that man."

"I never said you did. All we're looking for is information."

Oliver said, "Tell me about Casey's Massage and Escort."

"It was legitimate. All the girls were licensed."

"Tell me about your business."

"Like what?"

"You can start with a list of your clients."

"That's private information."

"We're investigating a murder, sir," Oliver said. "Last time we checked, you weren't a doctor, a lawyer, or a person of the clergy."

"I'm not naming names."

"We appreciate your integrity. Just tell us if Penny was one of your clients. He's dead. He's not coming back to sue you."

Havert scratched his nose as he thought about it. Why deny the obvious. "He was a twice-a-week regular."

"What services did he get?"

"He booked massages. It was all legit. All of our girls were licensed."

"Yeah, you said that, and we believe you," Oliver said. "Bruce, we're not from vice. We don't care about an old man getting a rubdown in personal places. We're from homicide."

"Don't know anything about that."

Oliver said, "What'd you do with the cars?"

"Huh?" Havert said.

"The two powder blue Priuses that you leased."

"What about them?"

"You returned one of them when you still had six months to go and paid a penalty. You must have wanted out really quickly."

"I didn't pay a penalty. I sold the lease back to the dealer. Priuses are in demand. So you got your information wrong."

"My bad," Oliver said. "Did you sell both of them back?"

Havert's eyes kept flitting back and forth. "Why do you care about the cars?"

Oliver didn't answer the question, trying to keep him off balance. "Which girls did you send to Penny?"

"I don't remember."

"Sure you do," Marge said.

Crone said, "Lots of people on that waiting list for your job, Bruce."

Havert made a sour face. "I need coffee."

Silver stood up. "I'll get it."

"You'll get me coffee in my own house?"

"Just relax." Silver put a hand on his shoulder. "It's gonna turn out fine."

Marge said, "Detective Oliver was just asking you which girls you sent out for the massages. If Penny was a regular, he probably had preferences. The apartment manager saw the same girls going in and out."

"That little shit!" A forced laugh. "Don't believe a word the asshole says."

"Okay," Marge told him. "Why's that?"

"He was constantly pestering the girls . . . always trying to get a freebie."

Marge jotted down his words. "How many times did you talk to Mr. Paxton?"

Again the knee went up and down. "I never met him personally. But the ladies hated him. Called him a little cretin gnome with a little dick to match."

"How did the ladies know about his dick?" Oliver said.

Havert looked down. "I heard the girls talk about him. Like I said, I never met the asshole."

"Which ladies did meet the asshole?"

"You'd have to ask Randi. She did the assignments."

"That would be Randi Miller?" Oliver said.

Havert looked at him. "Yeah. Randi Miller."

"I'd love to talk to her." Marge smiled. "She isn't in L.A. anymore, either. Any idea where she might be?"

"Your guess is as good as mine. We split up for good after we arrived in Vegas."

"So she's here?"

"Don't know. I haven't had contact with her since we got here."

Oliver smiled. "That's bullshit."

"Check my phone." He got up and hunted around the apartment for his cell. He finally found it tucked behind a chair cushion. He handed it over to Marge and recited off ten digits. "That's Randi's number. Check to see if I've called it or not."

Marge checked the phone number and the texts: no calls between them for the past week.

The question was why. To Marge, it appeared as if they had both decided that they'd be better off alone, meaning that both he and Randi knew something about the murder.

Silver came in with a cup of coffee. He'd been gone for a long time. The detectives knew that he had taken the extra minutes to hunt for something—weed, pills, powder—something to use if Havert was uncooperative. He handed him the paper cup. "Here you go. This'll wake you up."

"I'm awake." Havert sipped in silence.

Silver said, "You want some more bacon? There's still some in the pan."

"Yeah, sure. Thanks."

"Your own police butler. How about that for service?"

Havert gave a weak smile and Silver left again.

Marge said, "Randi was your manager, your coworker. You two were together for a long time. Why did you suddenly stop communicating?"

"We had a . . . falling-out."

"What kind of a falling-out?"

No answer.

Oliver said, "Bruce, let me lay it open for you. We've got a murdered man and your girls were the last ones to see Penny alive."

"How do you know that?"

"We have security tapes. The timing matches up."

Havert went pale. "What . . . what kind of tapes?"

Marge stared at him.

Why was he afraid?

Because he was there.

It was probing time. Marge lied, "We know who went in and out of the apartment, Bruce."

Silence. Silver came back with the bacon. "Here you go." When Havert looked nauseated, Silver said, "I'll just put this here on the table."

Oliver said, "We need to talk to Randi Miller, Mr. Havert."

"I told you. I don't know where she is." When no one answered, he said, "She talked about going back home."

"Where is home? Montana?" When Havert didn't say anything, Marge said, "See we know all sorts of things. So just get it out so I know you're being righteous."

"Yeah, yeah. Missoula, Montana. She's thirty-three. She has been in L.A. since she was sixteen. She's had it up to her eyeballs."

"Is this number current?" Marge read off the digits.

"I wouldn't know. I told you I haven't called her since I left L.A."

"Call it."

Havert complied. The phone line registered as disconnected. He shrugged. "I swear I don't know where she is."

Marge said, "But you know she's from Missoula."

"That's what she told me."

"Do you have the name of her parents?"

"It's only her mother. I assume her name is Mrs. Miller."

"Do you have a first name?"

"No."

"What about the other girl? Ginger Buck?" Havert acted stunned. "Or was her name Georgie Harris?"

Havert stared at them. "You don't have any tapes, do you?"

Marge said, "We have a lot of tapes, which is how we found out about you and Randi and the Priuses. We tracked you down, using those security videos. That's why we're here."

"Where were the cameras?" He paused. "Did the freak have cameras hidden in his apartment?" Marge let her silence do the talking. Havert said, "If he did, then you should know exactly what happened."

More silence.

"If you do have tapes, then you definitely know that I had nothing to do with that freak's death."

Marge played along. "Absolute—"

"The man was a fiend . . . I mean c'mon . . . keeping a *tiger* in an apartment?"

"It's weird," Oliver said.

"He was a fucking monster!"

Marge lied, "We know you were there, Bruce. We know that, as clear as the tapes show your face. But sometimes the tapes and cameras don't tell the whole story. They just tell a story from one angle. And that angle might not be what really happened. So why don't you tell us what really happened?"

Oliver said, "Just get it out."

"I dunno what happened." Havert slumped and sank into the cushions. "If you have tapes, you have to know I wasn't there when it happened."

"Of course." Marge played along. Her mind was reeling. "But you did come afterward. We have you entering the apartment."

Havert's complexion turned pasty. "Randi called in a panic. She put me in a panic."

Marge said, "Bruce, the tapes we saw don't have audio. What did Randi tell you specifically?"

Havert swallowed hard. "She wasn't making much sense." Everyone waited for him to continue. He said, "I wasn't *there*. If you want to know what happened to him, you need to talk to Randi."

"It would help if we could find her. Help you out as well."

"All I know is that she's from Missoula and talked about going back home."

"What about Georgie Harris or Georgina Harris?" Oliver asked. "Any idea where she is?"

Havert sat back and regarded them with confusion. Marge's brain continued firing out all possibilities. He insisted he wasn't there when Penny was murdered. But Randi was, and she had called him in a panic.

If Randi shot Penny and no one else was involved, then Havert would have told her to leave the apartment immediately. Then they'd both pack up and skip town. He certainly wouldn't have gone to the apartment, placing himself at a murder scene, unless there was a good reason.

Like cleaning up a mess that could come back to haunt him.

Two girls went in carrying duffel bags. But Bruce mentioned only Randi coming out.

Marge whispered, "Bruce, we never saw Georgie leave the apartment. But we did see you lugging those duffel bags. And we could tell that it held more than just clothing by the way you were dragging it."

Silence. As four pairs of eyes went to Havert's face, the dealer looked down. Spots of water dripped down his cheeks. Marge touched his hand. He looked up, dazed but not confused.

"It's time to get it all out. Tell us how Georgina died."

Chapter Thirty-Six

Sitting on her white and blue French Regency sofa, Sabrina Talbot had gone through an entire tissue box in record time. "I don't know what happened!" she sobbed. "I was never part of what he did there!"

Her wailing was directed to Will Barnes from Santa Barbara PD. He was tall and large, and his once dark hair was giving way to silver. His relationship with Marge had been years in the making, and lately the two of them had been talking about rings. Since both of them were around the half-century mark, it wasn't a surprise that neither was in a hurry.

Hobart Penny's murder was in Decker's jurisdiction, but his potential murder victims were not. However, since Decker had a package of frozen fingers, he had more than just a passing interest in what had gone on behind the iron gates.

Leo Delacroix, Sabrina's hired henchman, was getting angry. "Is this really necessary?"

Will Barnes stared at him with incredulous eyes. Penny's private room had glowed like a radioactive igloo, as did the locked closet, where Penny had stored a variety of restraining devices. He and Decker figured that Penny had used the closet to stash his dead women, probably removing the fingers postmortem. But maybe not.

Barnes tried out his most patient voice. "I'm sorry to upset you but I have to ask questions. If we could get through them without so much emotion, it would go faster."

"How could I not . . . be emotional . . . ?" Sabrina's voice was in fits and starts. "I was . . . *married* to this man!" More sobs. "What does this say about . . . *me*?"

Decker stepped in. "Sabrina . . ." How could he say it without worsening the situation? "I'm going to be honest with you because I think you can handle it. This is the deal. Okay?"

She nodded and wiped her eyes.

"There is no doubt that something bad happened here."

"I didn't know *anything* about it!"

"I believe you. Just listen, okay?" Decker cleared his throat. "We found frozen body parts in Hobart Penny's apartment. If you can remember anything about the girls he had brought home—where they were from for instance—that might give us a start on where to look. I realize this was twenty-five to thirty-five years ago, but we have to begin somewhere."

"I'm going to be sick!" To prove the point, she got up and ran to the bathroom.

Decker rubbed his forehead. To Barnes, he said, "I know blood degrades, but I'm sure we can get some DNA and probably more than one profile."

"Agreed. Does she have any idea how many girls he picked up?"

"No. But even if it was once every six months . . . over ten years that could be a lot of girls."

"And she doesn't know where he picked them up from?"

"All she told me was that they didn't look like professionals . . . more like drunken party girls. Any idea about the club situation twenty-five to thirty years ago?"

"I just came here five years ago. They say this town caters to the newly wed and the newly dead, and it's been that way for a long time."

"There must be some clubs."

"Yeah, we have our nightlife. Lots of bars but mostly in restaurants. We have some dance clubs—a couple of salsa clubs, one hip-hop, a few C and W places in the Pass. We have singles bars, gay bars . . . probably anything you want. But it's scaled down to a city this size."

"Penny had been in his fifties when he lived here. If he went to hip places, then he'd probably stand out as an older guy."

"You throw around cash, you get the ladies." Barnes thought a moment. "What was popular in music thirty years ago? Was that psychedelic or disco or . . ."

"Disco would be more late 1970s." Decker pulled out a tablet that he often used to photograph crime scenes. "Okay. In 1985, Tina Turner won a Grammy for Record of the Year."

"She's pop."

"Yeah . . . oh, wow. *Thriller* came out in 1982." Decker looked up. "Wasn't that kind of a lead-in to the Goth movement?"

"That would seem about right."

"Here we go . . . 1980s in Canada . . . start of the Goth movement. . . . *Pornography* by the Cure. So you got *Thriller* and the Goth movement and probably an increase in satanic rituals. That would fit right in for a guy like Penny. He liked dressing up in costumes.

He was into sadomasochism." Decker looked up. "Any idea about the Goth scene here?"

"No."

Decker ruminated on his ideas. "You know if Penny was a regular at any club, he'd run out of girls pretty quickly. What the guy needed was a continual source of party girls. Aren't you about ten miles away from UCSB?"

"Yes, we are." Barnes gave him a thumbs-up. "A fresh stock of girls every single year—young and impressionable and away from Mommy and Daddy for the first time."

"Like you said, throw around enough cash and add drugs to the mix and a certain percentage could be talked into anything."

"Okay," Barnes said. "This is what I'll do. After I'm done with Ms. Talbot, I'll check the cold cases on file with the police. If nothing comes up, I'll find a contact at the university."

"Would the university involve Santa Barbara PD in Missing Person cases?"

"If the person wasn't found after a day or two, I'm sure UCSB police would make contact with all the local police stations. A missing girl would be well publicized."

Decker said, "Would you mind if I stuck around for a bit . . . nosed into your business?"

"It's both of our business." Barnes gave him a pat on the back. "I have the jurisdiction, but you have the body parts."

Havert wasn't as easy as they had hoped. With the mention of Georgie Harris's death, he began to idle. He took another cup of coffee, he asked for another glass of water, and then he asked to get dressed again. This time they let him put on clothes. The detectives strategized, and because it was murder, they elected to bring Havert down to the station house.

The dealer agreed to go with them, looking refreshed in a bowling shirt, jeans, and sandals. He had combed his black hair in a modern take on an Elvis ducktail. Four cops were too much for one interview room, so Crone and Silver decided to view the proceedings from the other side of the camera. It was about four in the afternoon.

The first hour consisted of building up rapport that Marge and Oliver had lost in travel from the house to the station house. But eventually they got him to the same mental space, edging him to move forward. Baby steps, but he had to start somewhere.

"You just don't understand what they were dealing with," he said.

Marge had the sympathetic ear. "I'm sure I don't. So tell me."

"The man was . . ." A hand through the hair. Lots of fidgeting. "I told Randi to be careful, that it was getting out of control. But the money . . . it's always about the money, right?" His eyes darted from Oliver to Marge, trying to get confirmation. "I mean he tossed around hundreds like toilet paper. Especially when it was both of them."

Marge took out a notebook. "Georgina Harris and Randi Miller together?"

"Yeah, the two of them could pull a couple of grand a session. Even with my cut, we all walked away happy."

Oliver kept the conversation going. "How long was a typical session?"

"Under an hour most of the time. A lot of money for a short period of time."

"How many times did he hire both girls?"

"Dozens."

Marge leaned in. "Bruce, I need your input. What went wrong this time?"

"Oh God, do you have all night?"

"As long as you want," Marge said. "Just take your time."

He checked his watch. "I'm gonna have to leave for work, you know."

Silence.

"I didn't have anything to do with his murder. I swear. He was crazy! You know about the tiger."

"Yes."

"He also had a whole bunch of other disgusting things in his possession: poisonous snakes and bugs and lizards."

"We found that out as well."

"He used to cart out the snakes just to scare the girls. He would offer them a hundred dollars per minute if they'd hold the snake. At first they were freaked, and he got off on that. But then Randi figured out pretty quickly when the snake had been recently fed and wasn't interested in biting. Most of the time, it just slept in her arms. She acted scared cause it turned him on. I thought that she was crazy. I mean, you can't predict what a snake is going to do, right?"

"Right," Oliver said. "Did the murder have anything to do with the snake or the tiger or . . ."

"I told you I wasn't there when it happened."

Marge said, "But you were there *after* it happened."

"Randi was hysterical. She didn't know what to do, and the tiger was starting to wake up."

"So the tiger was there when you arrived at the apartment?"

"Yeah, that was the problem. It began to move, and Randi was panicked. She couldn't just leave Georgie there . . . I mean, to the tiger, she would have been fresh *meat*." Havert made a face. "It's sickening to think about it."

"So when Randi called you, Georgina was already dead?"

"Of course she was already *dead*. Randi swore up and down that it was self-defense."

"Okay . . ." Marge looked up from her notebook. "Why don't you start with Randi's phone call to you? What did she tell you?"

"That Penny was dead and now the tiger was moving. What should she do?"

Oliver said, "What'd you tell her?"

"I told her to get the hell out. But then she told me about Georgie being dead. Should she leave her or what . . . God, I felt sick to my stomach!"

Marge nodded. "So what did you say to her after she told you Georgie was dead?"

"Told her I'd be down in ten minutes."

Oliver said, "Did she tell you any details over the phone?"

Havert scratched his ear. "Just that the old man pulled out a gun."

"Why?"

"I don't have a clue." Havert paused. "I still don't know why he did it. Randi said that Georgie tried to get the gun away while Randi hit him. Then the gun went off and Georgie was dead and then he was dead."

"Bruce, we have to break this down step by step, okay?" Marge said. "First Penny pointed the gun at the girls?"

"Right."

"Then what happened?"

"Uh . . . Randi told me that Georgie tried to get the gun away from him."

"So Georgie tries to get the gun. Then what happened?"

"There was a struggle. The gun went off and killed Georgie."

"So after Georgie was killed, what did Randi do?"

"She made a grab for the gun. Then it went off and killed the old man. It was self-defense."

Oliver and Marge exchanged glances. He said, "Randi shot the old man while the two of them were fighting over the gun?"

"Exactly."

"You mentioned something about Randi hitting the old man? What was that all about?"

"I think she was trying to get him off Georgie. I really don't know. I wasn't there."

"What did she hit the old man with?"

"Her fists, I think."

Oliver was dubious. He had seen the blunt force trauma inflicted on the old man's head. That wasn't done with a fist, even if the skull had been brittle. "I'm just a little . . . uneasy about something, Bruce. Both Georgie and Randi were street savvy and in their thirties. Penny was an old man. If I were betting on a fight, I would bet on the girls."

"The old guy was really strong!" Havert said. "At least, that's what Randi told me."

"So if he was really strong, when he pulled out the gun, why didn't the girls just run away? Surely they could outrun him."

"I guess they froze."

"They didn't freeze. You said they jumped him."

Havert was flustered. "I don't know. I told you I wasn't there."

Marge stepped in. "I'm confused, Bruce. You said something about Randi bashing the old guy over the head."

"I said Randi hit him, not bashed him over the head."

"Where did she hit him?" Oliver asked.

"She didn't tell me."

Marge said, "But you did see the body after everything happened."

"Yeah, for about a second. I wanted to get out of there as quickly as possible."

Marge nodded to keep him thinking she was on his side. "Could you be a *little* more specific about what the body looked like? It could be important later on."

"He looked *dead*, Sergeant. How much longer is this gonna take?"

"A while, Bruce. Unfortunately, we have a lot of questions," Marge said. "Where was the old guy shot?"

"In the head." He shuddered.

"Penny was shot in the head?"

"I think so. His head was a bloody mess. Can we move on?"

Marge said, "You know what would really help us out? The murder weapon."

"I don't have it."

"If Randi got the gun away from him, she'd have it, correct?"

"I don't know."

Oliver said, "Bruce, the gun wasn't left in the room. Either she has it or you have it."

"I don't have it," Havert insisted.

"So Randi has it."

"I don't know. Maybe."

"Did she toss it?"

"Maybe."

"Where?"

"I don't know that she tossed it. I don't know what happened to the gun. Swear to God!"

Marge digested Havert's story. Parts of his statements had the ring of truth; other parts were on the fly. Havert did say that Randi had whacked the old man, and that was backed up by forensic evidence. It was the shooting part that wasn't so clear. How did Penny, who was struggling to keep the gun, get shot in the *back*? "Could we go over this again?"

"I've got to go to work," Havert said.

Marge said, "You know you're not going anywhere. We'll let you call in sick to your boss. That shows we're not out to screw you."

"Am I under arrest?"

"We could charge you with a dozen things. The main thing is to hear the truth, and I believe that you're trying to be honest. Let's back it up again. Tell us from the beginning what happened?"

Havert was losing it. "How many times do I have to repeat myself?"

Oliver prodded him forward. "You picked up the phone and it was Randi in a panic. Go on."

"Like I already said, she was freaked. The old man had shot Georgie dead and in self-defense, she shot the old man. She asked me what she should do."

"And you said . . ."

"I told her to get the hell out of there. But then she told me that Georgie was dead. I couldn't leave her body there. I told Randi I'd be right down." A pause. "I wasn't thinking too clearly. I guess I shoulda called the police."

"It would have saved you some time and energy."

"I was scared. I run a legitimate business, but I don't know what the girls do on their own time. I didn't want to get them into trouble. I just reacted. I know it was dumb to remove the body, but we couldn't leave her behind. We couldn't let the damn tiger eat her, for God's sake!"

Oliver said, "What did you do with Georgina's body?"

"Buried it in Angeles Crest."

Marge nodded. That statement made total sense. That national forest was about twenty minutes from the crime scene: acres upon acres of unspoiled foliage that hid illegal activity, and it had always been a prime dumping spot.

Havert glanced away. "You're gonna want to know where, right?"

"Right."

"I don't remember exactly. We just drove and drove until we found a remote spot where the ground was soft so I could dig a hole, you know."

Marge said, "You dug a hole?"

"Yeah, of course. I wasn't just gonna dump her. Georgie deserved a burial."

A burial? Marge said, "You brought a shovel with you, Bruce?"

"Yeah," Havert admitted. "I mean, after Randi explained what had happened, I knew we were going to take the body. So I took a shovel with me."

"The body is buried in Angeles Crest," Oliver said.

"Yeah."

"And the gun, Bruce?"

"I don't know anything about a gun. Maybe Randi does, but I don't."

Marge leaned over and patted his knee. "This entire mess wasn't your fault, Bruce. You weren't even there. But the girls roped you into coming, so now you're involved—even though you didn't want to be involved."

He regarded her with suspicious eyes.

"This is your time to be honest with us," Marge said.

"I *am* being honest!"

"I know you are," Marge told him. "And that's why you know that Randi tossed the gun out the window while you were driving through Angeles Crest. You saw her do it, right?"

Havert rubbed his eyes. "No, Sergeant, I never saw her ditch a gun. Period. Case closed."

"Okay, Bruce, I believe you." Marge decided to move on. She'd readdress the gun later. "Let's fill in some more details, because there are lots of blanks between the time you got to the apartment and the time you took off for Vegas. I'm trying to get a timeline."

Oliver said, "Yeah, like returning the Priuses to the dealer."

"Why would I need two Priuses?"

Marge said, "What Detective Oliver is saying is that you had the presence of mind to take one of the cars back to the dealer before you took off for Las Vegas."

Oliver said, "And the presence of mind to clear out your office before you left town."

"There was hardly anything there: some folding chairs and tables and a couple of computers," Havert told him. "It took about an hour."

"What about the files?" Oliver asked.

"Everything was computerized except for a few receipts and stuff like that. I erased the computer hard drive. I tore up any paperwork and tossed them in a Dumpster on the way to Vegas. So I have nothing to show you."

That sounded like the truth. Marge said, "Let's back it up one more time—"

"Oh God."

"A little patience, Bruce."

"We've been going at it for . . ." He checked his watch. "God, I've been talking to you clowns for four hours."

"I just want to get things right. It's for your own good."

Oliver said, "You got a panic call from Randi. Then you went to Hobart Penny's apartment, right?"

"Right."

"In your car?"

"Yeah, of course in my car."

"So now you had *three* cars," Marge said. "Your car, Georgie's car, and Randi's car."

"Yeah, that sounds right."

"Okay." Marge thought a moment. "What did you do with the extra car?"

"You mean my car?"

"Yes, your car."

"I left it there until we could pick it up later."

"Okay." The logistics were getting complicated. Marge said, "Let me repeat this back to make sure I got it right. You and Randi left the apartment together. And you drove Georgie's Prius and Randi drove her Prius."

"Right."

"How long were you there . . . in the apartment?"

"Not too long."

"A minute, two minutes, a half hour?" Marge said. "I mean it probably took you some time to get the body out of there without anyone noticing."

"I don't remember how long. Not too long. The tiger was starting to move."

"And what did you do immediately after leaving the apartment? Bury the body? Clean up the office? Return the Prius to the dealer? What was the order of events?"

A long pause. "We went to clean out the office."

"So where was Georgie's body?" Oliver asked.

"In the back of my car." Havert looked ashen. "She was already dead. What difference does it make?"

"No one is challenging you, Bruce," Marge said. "Just trying to get everything down. What did you do after you cleaned out the office?"

"Returned Georgie's Prius to the dealer."

"And then?"

"We . . . Randi and I went back to pick up my car. And then we drove to Angeles Crest together. We didn't want her body dissect . . . descrated . . . desecrated." Moisture in his eyes. "That's why we took her body from the apartment. We didn't want to turn her into tiger shit."

"Also, the body would have connected you to the murder." Oliver shrugged casually. "Am I right about that?"

Havert didn't answer. Marge thought about Bruce's blow-by-blow account, which he had repeated over and over.

But there was still a missing step: transferring the body from the apartment to the back of his car without being noticed.

Marge took a sip of water while she thought some more.

She had told Havert that they had him "on tape" lugging the duffel bags out of the apartment. He never once denied it.

The duffel bags.

As in *plural.*

Something reverberated in her head, specifically Bruce Havert's job history. Marge said, "Let me back-track for a moment, Bruce."

"Oh God—"

"Just bear with me. Randi called you down to the apartment."

"Yes."

"She was panicked because Penny was dead, Georgina was dead, and the tiger was waking up."

"Right."

"So you told her you'd come down to the apartment to help remove Georgina's body. Because you didn't want her to be eaten by the tiger."

"Exactly."

"So you brought your shovel because you knew you were going to have to bury her."

"She deserved to be buried." Havert's tone was self-righteous.

"I understand. So you went to the apartment and picked up Georgie's body."

"I already admitted that. What's the point of repeating stuff over and over?"

"The point is you had to get her body out of the apartment without arousing suspicion. We have you on tape toting out the duffel bags that Georgie and Randi had brought with them."

Silence.

"Bruce, you were toting *two* duffel bags. Because . . . you know and I know . . . that Georgina wouldn't have fit in a single duffel bag. It was way too small for that."

Havert's face went green. Before he could speak, before he could ask for a lawyer, Marge said, "Along with the shovel, you brought a couple of butcher knives, right?"

Havert still didn't answer.

Marge said, "Bruce, she was already dead. She didn't know the difference."

Still no answer.

"You worked as a short-order cook," Marge said. "I'm sure you cut up a lot of chickens in your days."

More silence.

"You dismembered her, didn't you?" Marge's voice was even.

A nod.

"Could you answer the question with a yes or no? Did you dismember Georgina Harris?"

"Yes . . ." His voice was barely above a whisper. "I didn't kill anyone." Havert wiped his eyes. "How can I get you to believe me?"

Marge slid a blank, yellow legal pad and pen across the table. "It would help if you wrote down what happened in your own words. That way we can stop asking you all these questions."

Havert nodded. "I can do that."

"Good." Marge got up and so did Oliver.

They closed the door to the interview room and left him with his grotesque thoughts.

Chapter Thirty-Seven

B ruce Havert eventually wised up and got a lawyer, but there was more than enough to hold him, and that bought the detectives a little time. The arraignment was scheduled for tomorrow morning, and unless there were legal theatrics, the case would go back to L.A. It was unlikely that Havert would make the bond, but Detective Jack Crone had assigned surveillance duty just in case.

Shortly before ten in the evening, Marge and Oliver left the LVMPD to grab dinner. They found an Indian restaurant with an all-you-can-eat buffet for five ninety-nine, which would have been perfect except that the place was closing in five minutes. From behind a window, an Indian woman with a long gray braid and a lime green sari welcomed them in with a beckoning hand.

They came inside. It was warm and smelled of exotic spices. The buffet was still intact, but God only knew how long the food had been sitting there in tray warmers.

Lime Green Sari said, "I've got fresh batches in the kitchen. It's a little of this and a little of that. Let me make a plate up for you. I'll charge you the same as the buffet. I'm Domani, by the way."

"Thank you, Domani," Marge told her. "It all sounds good."

"Sounds great," Oliver said. "Are you sure we aren't hanging you up?"

"No, stay as long as you want. We're cleaning in the kitchen."

Marge thanked her. Both of them were exhausted. It had been a long day, and neither of them felt like talking. Domani returned a minute later carrying a tray of Indian specialties: tandoori chicken, tandoori lamb, fried shrimp, rice with vegetables and chicken, lentil dal, spinach with cheese, spicy eggplant, and a dish of mixed potatoes, carrots, and peas. There were three dipping sauces and a heaping mound of garlic naan. She gave them two empty plates and poured water. "Anything else?"

Marge was salivating. She didn't realize how hungry she was. "This is perfect."

"I'll bring out some chai. I've also got rice pudding when you're done. Bon appétit."

"Thanks." Oliver helped himself to the meat. "This looks good."

"Does it ever." Marge took some vegetables.

"Did you ever get hold of Decker?"

"I called, he called. He didn't leave a message and I didn't leave much of one myself. Havert's case wasn't something I could sum up after the beep. I did tell him that'd we're doing an overnight."

"Where are we staying?"

"Some suite-type motel. Looks clean enough and has several slots in the lobby."

"Great." Oliver took a big bite of lamb and dipped it in some spicy brown sauce. "Tasty. Or maybe I'm just starved." Another bite. "How much of Havert do you believe?"

"I was going to ask you the same question. I think he could murder someone—if you can dismember, you can murder—but I believe him when he said he wasn't there when the murder went down."

"Why?"

"Good question." She sipped water. "For one thing, I couldn't trip him up in a lie. He admitted getting the call, going down to the apartment, and bringing a shovel. Hell, he admitted dismembering the body and burying her. It's not like the usual: he prates on until he's caught with his foot in his mouth and has to back-track. What about you?"

"I'm still on the fence. Once we get him back to L.A., we'll ask him to take a polygraph on the promise that if he passes, we'll support a lower charge. I suppose the next step is finding Randi Miller and finding Georgina's body."

"If there is really a body. She may still have a beating heart. Maybe Georgina killed the old man and it wasn't self-defense. If we think she's dead, we won't be looking for her. She's free to start a new life from scratch."

Oliver said, "That's why we need the body."

Marge's cell was playing Mozart's *Turkish Rondo.* "It's Decker." She depressed the green button. "Hey, what's going on?"

"Where are you?" Decker asked.

"We're still in Vegas."

"How convenient," Decker said. "I'm in Vegas, too. We need to talk, and it's not something I want to do over a phone. Where are you, as in an address?"

"We're at a restaurant. Hold on." Marge got the address and gave it to him.

Decker consulted with the cabbie. "I'm two minutes away."

"It's Indian food. Are you hungry?"

"Starved."

"We'll save you some vegetables." Marge hung up.

Domani had been clearing away the buffet warming trays. "I can get you some more vegetables from the back."

"That would be great," Marge said. "Our boss is coming in."

"Your boss? At ten in the evening?"

"This is unusual even for him. It must be important."

"What do you do for a living?"

"Cops," Oliver said.

"You're cops?" The woman looked confused. "How come I've never seen you before?"

"We're from LAPD, not Las Vegas Metro," Marge said.

"Oh . . . that explains it. You're picking up a bum and taking him back to L.A.?"

"Something like that."

"Happens all the time. Las Vegas attracts lots of losers. I hope you mix your work with a little recreation."

"With the boss is coming, it's gonna be more work and less recreation," Oliver said.

Domani laughed. "Well, if you do have a chance to hit the Strip, good luck."

"Sure you don't mind us staying after hours?" Marge asked. "It sounds like he has lots to tell us."

"No problem." Marge gave her a fifty. Domani's eyes went wide. She said, "Are you kidding me? You can stay overnight as far as I'm concerned."

"A few hours tops. It's just our way of thanking you for cooperating with law enforcement." Marge smiled. "It's all yours as long as you keep that saag paneer and baingan bharta coming."

Wheeling a canvas overnight bag, Decker looked around then sat next to Marge and across from Oliver. He wore a polo shirt under a leather bomber jacket, a pair of jeans, and black leather cowboy boots. He sank back in the chair and looked at the ceiling. He smiled, but it was without energy. "Willy says hello."

"How's he doing?"

"He's a good guy, Marge. A good guy and a good detective." Decker opened his bag and pulled out a notebook and peered around. "Is this a good place to talk?"

The buffet trays had been cleared and the restaurant was empty. Clean-up noises were coming from the kitchen. Marge said, "The owner said we can stay as long as we want."

"Okay," Decker said. "Fill me in."

They did. As Marge and Oliver ran down the interview, Decker ate, nodded, and took notes. After answering all of Decker's questions, the recap took a half hour. When it was over, Decker had a monster headache. He popped another two Advil on top of the two that he had taken just two hours ago. He regarded his scribbles. "So . . . as far as the murder goes . . . we have a secondhand account of what happened and we don't even know if it's true or not." He rubbed his forehead. "Do you two believe him?"

"We were just talking about that," Oliver said. "Once we get him to L.A., we'll ask him to take a polygraph. If he passes, maybe we can get the DA to reduce some charges."

"You didn't book him for murder, right?"

"Right."

"So you have him on tampering with evidence, destroying evidence, mutilation of a corpse. That's serious stuff, but he didn't hurt anyone. Bail's not going to be set that high without a murder charge."

"He dismembered a body," Marge said. "We've got the yuck factor working for us."

"If he has any spare change, he'll make bond and be out in twenty-four hours," Decker said. "What about Randi Miller? Have we started looking for her?"

"She's not listed in the Missoula directory," Oliver said.

"She hasn't lived there in about fifteen years," Marge said. "Havert says she *might* be there."

"Is Randi Miller even her real name?" When Oliver shrugged, Decker said, "So we don't know that, either. What about parents?"

"We don't know her mom's name—first or last," Marge said. "If her mother's last name is Miller, it means calling up a lot of people. I say we wait until the county records open up tomorrow and look up Randi Miller's birth certificate. If one exists, we can find out her mother's name."

"Okay," Decker said. "If we find Mom, maybe we can find Randi. Havert pointed the finger at her. Let's give her a chance to point the finger at him."

Domani came out of the kitchen and looked Decker up and down. "So you're the boss?"

"In title only." Decker smiled. "Everything was great. Thank you."

"Ready for rice pudding?"

"I'm full," Marge said.

"For fifty bucks you get dessert."

When she left, Decker smiled. "You tipped her a fifty?"

"Including the food," Marge told him. "It's better than flushing it down the slots."

"I suppose that's true. You never answered my question. Do you think Havert's telling the truth?"

"Yes," Marge said.

"Mostly yes," Oliver said.

"I think his answers are plausible." Decker dry-washed his face. "We've got a real problem with the victim. I'm not saying anyone has a right to pop another person, but our victim is uniquely reprehensible. This case, no matter who's guilty of what, will never go to trial."

"You found blood in that Sabrina's house?" Marge asked.

"There was a room as well as a closet that glowed electric blue. Penny did bad things there and probably to multiple women. Will and I went over some cold cases, specifically missing person cases that went back thirty years ago: a twenty-two-year-old waitress and a twenty-year-old part-time student at a community college. Then, after that, we went to UCSB police and asked about missing coeds. It took a while, but they found two cold cases of missing girls—one was eighteen and the other was nineteen. I'm grateful that this mess belongs to Will and not me. But all of us realize that we might have matches for some of the frozen fingers. And that would explain the lack of blood in the tissue, sitting in the deep freeze for a very long time."

The table went quiet. Marge said, "Is Sabrina involved?"

"She knew that he took girls into that room but claims that she didn't know what went on."

"Do you believe her?" Oliver asked.

"I do. In my mind, she was more than happy to foist her monster husband onto someone else. I don't think she knew about the murders, but it was clear that she didn't ask any questions."

"In all fairness, no one expects her husband to be a serial killer," Marge said.

"Of course," Decker said. "She was distraught about it. But she didn't delve too deeply."

"So . . ." Oliver tapped the table. "Do you want us to soldier on with the current investigation? I mean, like you said, it's never going to go to trial. From what you just said about Penny, it buttresses Randi's claim that it was self-defense."

Decker said, "We've come this far, we're going to see it to the end."

Marge's cell rang. "Don't recognize the number." She connected the line. "This is Sergeant Dunn."

"Hi, it's Mindy."

It took about ten seconds for the name to register. "Oh, Mindy Martin from Sunset Strip. How are you doing, Mindy? Are you keeping out of trouble?"

"Never was in any trouble."

"Good to hear. What's going on?"

"I seen her." A pause. "The lady you were looking for with the glove."

"Fantastic, Mindy, good job." Marge pushed the button to be on speakerphone. "Thanks for calling and helping us out. Where did you see her?" There was a delay. "Hello?"

"Yeah, I'm still here. You promised to give me something for being helpful."

"That can be arranged, depending on how accurate the information," Marge said. "I'm not in town right now. How about if we meet tomorrow night somewhere—"

"I don't know if she'll be there tomorrow night or the next night or the next. But I can tell you where I seen her if you pay me something."

Marge said, "Let's set up a time to talk. How about if we meet in front of The Snake Pit?"

"I'm not meeting a cop in front of The Snake Pit."

"So tell me where." A long pause. Marge said, "Mindy, I'm going to have to meet you in person to hand over any money. Pick a place."

"Not The Snake Pit. How about where you picked me up?"

"That was around Sunset and Genesee, right?" Marge said. "What time?"

"How about nine? That's *when* I saw her. But I'm not telling you *where* until we have a deal. So bring the cash, okay."

"I get it, Mindy. I'll have cash. Sunset and Genesee around nine tomorrow evening, okay?" When the line disconnected, Marge shrugged. "Looks like I'll be going home tomorrow."

"The gloved woman is Shady Lady?" Decker asked.

"Hopefully," Marge said.

Decker said, "I'll book an afternoon flight for both of you back to L.A. If Bruce Havert needs to come back to L.A.—which I doubt, without a murder charge—I'll go with him. Let's pack it up for the evening. Tomorrow morning see if you can't get a bead on Randi Miller. Missoula's not a tiny place, but it's small enough for the police to know locals. If Randi did murder Penny, I want to hear about it from her, even if it was self-defense."

"Got it," Marge said. "So how much should I give Mindy Martin?"

"Twenty bucks maybe."

"That's lowball, Deck," Oliver said. "You can't even get a *hand job* for a twenty."

"You're not asking for a sex act, just for some information," Decker said. "Do what you think you can get away with."

"I'll do my best," Marge said. "Poor Willy. He's got a lot ahead of him."

"Thirty-five-year-old cold cases," Oliver said. "He'll be busy for a while."

"He's done his fair share of homicides," Decker said. "He should be used to it."

"Yeah, but he came to Santa Barbara to get away from big city crap."

"The life of a cop," Decker said. "You can run, but you cannot hide."

Chapter Thirty-Eight

After three hours of searching, Marge called it quits. It was one in the morning and Shady Lady remained elusive. With a long day behind her and an even longer day ahead of her, Marge could barely keep her eyes open. Driving on a stretch of monotonous freeway, she stayed awake on residual adrenaline. Then the Bluetooth kicked in with Decker's cell number on the screen of her console. She pushed the button to accept the call. "Thank you for waking me up."

"Sorry. Are you in bed already?"

"No, I wasn't being sarcastic, I'm grateful. I've been cruising Sunset Boulevard, fruitlessly looking for Shady Lady. Your voice is a shot of espresso. What's up?"

"Just checking in. So Mindy Martin's tip was bogus?"

"Maybe yes, maybe no. When Shady didn't show, I called Mindy and told her to call me the next time she sees her. She said she would and we left it at that."

"You believe her?"

"I remain hopelessly optimistic. Even if I'm disappointed, I refuse to live any other way. The bigger issue is why we're justifying Havert's self-defense story by gathering evidence that shows Penny as a knife-wielding psycho."

"Because Penny is a psycho. And if it was self-defense, I'm happy to set this unsavory cast of characters free—which we've essentially done with Havert."

"Meaning?"

"Bail was set on the high side because Havert left L.A. in a hurry. But when he agreed to wear an ankle bracelet, the judge reduced the amount significantly. He's back at work."

"When was he released?"

"About six hours ago."

"So you're back in L.A.?"

"No, I'm in Bozeman, Montana, freezing my butt off."

"Montana?" Marge sat up. "You found Randi Miller?"

"Yep. Your idea about locating her via county records was a good one. We located a birth certificate for Randela McMillan, who would be about thirty-two. We found the Social Security number, and once they matched, we made contact with the woman who was listed as Randela's mom, who still lives in Missoula. Randi Miller is seventy-five miles southwest of Bozeman, closer to Yellowstone on the Montana side."

"Here's your chance to slip in a little R and R," Marge said. "I, for one, have always wanted to see Old Faithful."

"You and Rina both. But probably not in these precipitously low temperatures. I remember a friend of mine saying that Yellowstone has three seasons: July, August, and winter. You might want to wait until there is ground covering other than white."

"When are you interviewing her?"

"I'm hitting the road at six to make it to her house at around eight. It's highway driving, but because of all the snow and ice, I'll allow a little more time."

"And she agreed to talk to you?"

"I'm not going away, and she realizes that. If it was self-defense, she might want to tell her side of the story."

"At least the air is good out there."

"The air is cold, Margie. Very, very cold. But the elk aren't complaining, so why should I?"

With sunrise still an hour away, it was dark and the air was bitter. It hurt to breathe, it hurt to move, it hurt to sip coffee, which went from hot to tepid in a couple of toe taps. Decker had left L.A. without good cold weather gear. He had on several layers, including his bomber jacket, but he was sans gloves and hat. Every inch of exposed skin felt the burn. When he got into the rental, he turned on the motor and headlights and cranked up the heat and fan to the max: a big mistake, since the vents poured out frigid air, but within a few minutes, Decker was able to warm his stiff fingers.

A half hour later, the sky started to lighten until it burst with a dazzling display of pinks and violets and oranges that surged over the mountaintops and sur-rounded him like a ring of fire. In the daylight, every-thing seemed more positive. The empty roads and a white landscape were no longer foreboding. Instead, the stark beauty allowed a man to think.

Was Havert's claim of self-defense valid and would forensics back it up?

Even if it wasn't self-defense, what kind of convic-tions were they going to get on Havert and Miller if Penny was a serial killer?

Then again, what kind of guy would dismember another human being?

If Georgina was sliced up in that apartment, her DNA had to be somewhere. But there had been so much mess and blood that it had been impossible to know what samples to take.

And where was Georgie's body?

Havert agreed to help officials look, but he wasn't sure where they had buried her. Was it all a ruse?

Also, why didn't any of the neighbors in the apartments surrounding Penny's apartment hear gunshots? They needed to be reinterviewed.

And where were the weapons? No gun was found. And there was no good candidate for the blunt force object. If Randi Miller didn't have the weapons, all sorts of possibilities opened up. If she did, and her story matched Havert's rendition, then self-defense it was, and the case was closed.

Maybe.

The boudoir pictures on the networking sites had showed a glamorous woman. Devoid of makeup and styled hair, and dressed in baggy jeans and a sweatshirt, Randi Miller looked plain with a hard-worn face. Blond hair was giving way to dark roots, her eyes were milky blue, and her pale lips had been stretched into a tight smile. Her sleeves were pushed up past her elbows, and her arms and wrists were straggly thin. She had tattoos on her neck and forearms. She offered him coffee. They both took it black. She cupped her hands around the mug for warmth. It wasn't cold inside, but it was far from toasty.

The house was prefab—a trailer without the wheels—with a living room holding a single couch, a bunk bed tucked into a corner, and a kitchenette. The bathroom was behind a door. There was a propane heater doing its best against the outside elements.

"I wasn't really running away." Her voice was nasal and harkened Scandinavia. "I just needed to decompress. I woulda contacted the police eventually."

Decker nodded.

She shook her head. "Asshole."

"Who's an asshole?" Decker asked.

"Penny. He was mean, but stupid mean. We woulda done anything he wanted, and he always had enough money to pay for whatever he wanted. It was like he *wanted* to shoot someone."

Decker put his coffee cup down and took out a notepad. "Why don't you start from the beginning?"

"I probably shouldn't talk to you without a lawyer."

"That's certainly your right."

"Am I under arrest?"

Decker sidestepped the question. "Bruce Havert told me some disturbing things, Randi. I'd like to hear what happened from your side before I do anything."

"I should get a lawyer."

"Up to you, Randi. It's your time and your money."

"Yeah . . . money. It's always about money. He just . . ." Her jaw was clenched. "He pulled a gun on her—on Georgie."

"Who did?"

"Penny. I don't want to talk about it."

"Okay," Decker said. "Let's put that on hold. Give me a little history? How many times had you gone to Penny's apartment before the incident?"

"Dozens of times."

"And about how many times had you and Georgie gone to Penny's apartment together?"

"Also dozens of times."

"What went wrong this time?"

"I dunno." She shook her head. "I didn't see it coming."

"Start from when you got to his apartment."

"Business as usual. He answered the door. We came in. We went to the bedroom. We always went to the bedroom because I wasn't gonna do it in front of a tiger."

"Was the tiger always there when you and Georgie came to the apartment?"

"Yes."

"And where was the tiger this time?"

"In the living room like always. She was sleeping . . . knocked out."

THE BEAST · 513

"Was the tiger chained up?"

"She had a chain on but she wasn't chained to any-thing. The asshole liked the thrill of danger. He liked having the tiger there even if she was knocked out. He liked controlling wild animals. And poisonous creepy things. He'd show us snakes and spiders and scorpions. Let them crawl over his arms and hands. At first, it freaked me out. Then you kinda get used to it."

"Did he show you snakes and spiders that day?"

Randi shook her head. "I think he could tell that we weren't afraid anymore, that the shock wore off." A pause. "Maybe that's why he decided to use the gun . . . to shock us." Tears in her eyes. "I guess it worked."

"So Georgie and you went into the bedroom."

"Yes."

"Okay." Decker nodded. "What happened next?"

She wrung her hands, kneading imaginary dough. "Georgie . . . she opens up the massage table . . . that's how it starts. We give him a massage." A pause. "That's how *usually* starts."

"Did you give him a massage?"

"No." She shook her head. "He just wanted to jump into it. No warm-up at all. That was okay with us. Sooner we do it, the sooner we're out of there."

"I understand."

"So we get into bed with him. Start doing what he likes . . . do you want details?"

"Maybe later. Right now I want to know what went wrong."

"I'm not sure. We're just doing him . . . orally. We were taking turns so we wouldn't get tired. With an old guy, it can take forever. This was one of those times. He just wasn't into it, Lieutenant. Maybe we weren't saying the right things or faking it good enough or . . ."

She brushed away tears.

"Maybe he just needed something more. Or maybe he just couldn't do it anymore and it made him mad. He took Georgie by the hair . . . brought her face near his. I thought he was gonna kiss her or something. Then I see he has a gun to her head. It was awful."

"Where did the gun come from?"

"I don't know. Maybe under a pillow." She licked her lips. "I thought it was a fake. I even joked about it. Big mistake. He pulled it away from her head and fired it. The bullet crashed through the wall. I jumped a zillion feet. That's when I got real scared."

"It would scare me," Decker said. "No one around heard a gunshot. That's weird."

"It was muffled. But then the wall exploded and I knew it was real. My fear musta turned him on. He got hard then . . . finally . . . after he fired the gun." She wiped her eyes. "I was down there and saw it spring to life." She bit her bottom lip. "Excuse me. I need more coffee."

"Sure."

She got up. "Wanna refill?"

"No, I'm fine, thank you."

She came back a few minutes later and sat back down. They chatted about extraneous things, but eventually, she got back on point. "After he shot the gun . . . everything started moving like at warp speed. I jumped up and Georgie grabbed his arm. And she and Penny started fighting over the gun. I'm screaming and she's screaming. Then I remember I have this blackjack . . . in my duffel. I'm trying to find it and that's when I heard the gun go off again." Her lower lip quivered. "He smiled when he shot her, this big grin . . . and the gun is pointing right at my face . . ."

She was actively crying.

"I was so scared . . . I . . ." She raised her hand. "I hit him." She brought her hand down. "Hard. His head cracked open. It was horrible. His blood started pouring out."

No one talked.

She swallowed. It seemed to get caught in her throat. "So much *blood*! I started shaking. I felt like I was gonna pass out. I was scared shitless."

Decker nodded. "I understand."

She said, "That's when I called Bruce . . . and he said he'd be right over."

"So Bruce wasn't there when it happened?"

"If Bruce was there, it wouldna happened. Bruce didn't want us to do him anymore. But the money . . . he gave us a lot of money: five hundred up to a couple of thousand for less than an hour's work. That's a lot of money for me."

Decker nodded again and said, "Tell me what happened after Bruce came over?"

"It was happening so fast. We had to get outta there 'cause the tiger started moving. I think she smelled all the blood."

"So what did you and Bruce do?"

"We left."

"You left?"

"Yeah."

"And what did you do with Georgie?"

"Georgie was dead . . . no doubt about that."

"Okay. But she wasn't left behind."

"No, she wasn't."

"So what happened?"

Randi averted her eyes. "We took her with us. We didn't want to leave her for tiger food."

"How'd you get her out of the apartment?"

"In a duffel bag."

"The ones you brought with you?"

She nodded but wouldn't make eye contact.

"One duffel bag was too small for her entire body to fit." When Randi didn't say anything, Decker said, "You've come this far. Get it all out. You'll feel better."

"She was dead, Lieutenant."

"Okay."

"She really was. She wasn't moving or breathing or anything. There was no pulse."

"You felt for a pulse?"

"I didn't have to. She was dead. And the tiger was starting to wake up."

"I understand. You had to make quick decisions."

"Exactly. And she was already dead. Penny shot her. I swear to God, it's the truth."

"I believe you."

"Do you really?"

"I do. And if you want everyone to believe you, take a polygraph—a lie detector test."

"I'll do that anytime you want."

"Good. That will really help your case."

"So when do we do it?"

"I'll set one up as soon as I can."

"Here?"

"It would be better for everyone if you came back to L.A. That would help your case as well."

"Is Bruce back in L.A.?"

"He's been in contact with us. He's also agreed to take a polygraph." Decker gave her a moment. "Tell me what happened to Georgina. You've been honest. Let's go the distance." Another pause. Decker said, "So Bruce Havert and you are in Penny's apartment—"

"We're both like . . . freaked."

"Of course. Penny is dead. Georgie is dead. The tiger is waking up. What happened next?"

She sighed as her eyes became wet. "I loved Georgie. I couldn't leave her for the tiger."

"I understand. So what did you do?"

"We tried to stuff her in the duffel but like you said, she was too big . . ."

No one spoke.

"We coulda thought of something better if we had time, but we were rushed."

"I get it."

She sighed. "Bruce broke her legs at the knees and tried to like . . . stuff her inside the duffel that way . . . she was still too long."

Silence.

"So . . ." Randi swallowed hard. "He got a knife from the kitchen." She cleared her throat. "After he did that, we wrapped her up."

"After Bruce did what?"

"He had to cut her legs off."

"Okay. Go on."

She cleared her throat again. "We put the different parts in a couple of garbage bags so she wouldn't leak when we left. We stuffed the legs in one duffel, and the rest of her in the other."

She blotted her wet face with her shirt.

"We put her back together when we buried her. We shoulda gone to the police, but I was scared that no one would believe me. Penny was rich and old. I knew the police would think we were trying to rob him."

"Were there things in his apartment worth robbing?" Decker asked.

"Not things, but he always had cash. Lots of cash. He always paid us in cash."

Yet when Oliver and Marge went over the apartment, there was nothing valuable anywhere. Decker said, "What happened to the cash, Randi? And be honest. Did you take it?"

"No." Randi was emphatic. "Everything was covered in blood. The bills were disgusting. All I wanted was to get out of there." She looked up at Decker. "I was scared for my life, Lieutenant. I honestly thought if I didn't attack him, I'd be next."

"So you hit him on the head."

"I hit him on the head, yes."

"And then you shot him."

She looked at him quizzically. "No, I didn't shoot him."

"You didn't shoot Hobart Penny."

"No!"

"Think hard before you answer."

"I don't have to think hard. I didn't shoot him. I woulda shot him if I had the gun, but it musta dropped or something. I never saw it after I hit him."

"After he killed Georgie and you hit him over the head, you didn't try to find the gun?"

"No. The place was a mess: all that blood and guts and brain. And then when we had to take the legs off. The stupid gun was the last thing on my mind. If I was to take something, it woulda been the money, but I didn't even take that. We left immediately after Georgie was packed up."

"So what happened to the gun?"

"I don't know." She looked at him. "You don't have it?" When Decker didn't answer, she said, "Like I keep saying, I never touched it."

"That's very interesting, Randi. You said you didn't shoot Penny—"

"I didn't."

"Okay. You didn't shoot Penny, but Penny was shot. What do you know about that?"

"Nothing!"

"Bruce Havert said you shot Penny."

"I never *touched* the gun. Ask me that question in your lie detector test and you'll see I'm telling you the truth!"

"Bruce said you shot Penny in self-defense."

"Bruce wasn't *there*. He got his facts wrong. I hit the old guy with my blackjack. I admit that. But I never *touched* the gun."

"Do you have the blackjack?"

"No, I left it with Georgie."

"Okay." Decker waited a few seconds. "When Bruce was inside the apartment, did you ever leave him alone in the bedroom with Penny?"

"I gotta think." A pause. "When Georgie wouldn't fit into the single duffel, Bruce went to get the knife." She licked her lips again. "And then when he started to cut, I went into the living room for about a minute, maybe? I came back right away because I was scared of the tiger."

"Did you hear anything when you were in the living room?"

"Like what?"

"Like a gun going off."

She shook her head. "No. I don't know what to tell you about the gun. If the old guy was shot, it happened after Bruce and me left. I didn't know he was shot until you told me."

"When he shot Georgie, how many gunshots did you hear?"

"One."

"Just one?"

"Yes . . . one besides the time he shot at the wall."

"You're sure."

"Positive."

And you don't know what happened to the gun."

"No."

Decker was puzzled. *If* she was telling the truth, there was a problem and a big one.

If she was telling the truth, it meant there was another person involved.

Chapter Thirty-Nine

Three days later, after Randi Miller and Bruce Havert had written down and reaffirmed their statements to the detectives, after the polygraphs were administered, and after the bisected body of Georgina Harris had been found in a shallow grave—the dead woman having sustained a gunshot wound through the heart—the death of Hobart Penny was officially ruled a justifiable homicide.

Blood evidence had come back: Georgina's blood, Penny's blood, even some of Randi's blood. Forensics also found a bullet in the wall. The evidence appeared to back up the stories. Randi Miller felt that the only possible way that she could disable Penny and save her friend was to hit the old man over the head. And after Marge interviewed Shady Lady—née Arlette

Jackson—who told her about Penny chopping off her finger, the judge was further convinced that his decision had been righteous.

There were charges: tampering with evidence, mutilation of a body, but because of the extenuating circumstances of the tiger, Randi Miller and Bruce Havert managed to get off with three years' probation. A light sentence, but expected, since the victim garnered no sympathy.

But not everything was neat and tidy. While the detectives did recover the blackjack, buried with Georgina, they didn't find the gun. Thorough searches of Havert's house and car, and Randi's car and trailer, failed to turn up any firearm at all let alone the offending weapon. And in her statement to the police, Randi had mentioned several times that Penny was in possession of a lot of money, even recalling blood-soaked bills. But when the detectives had searched the apartment, they never found a stash of cash. On the contrary, there was a dearth of valuables.

As a stickler for details, Decker was bothered. His desk had the original crime scene photos along with the autopsy report. He, along with Oliver and Marge, were leafing through the case files, trying to see if they could spot any money at all. Finally he plopped the file down on his desk and leaned back in his chair. "There were three gunshots fired that we know about." Marge and Oliver looked up. "One at the wall, one through Georgina's heart, and one in Penny's back." Decker held up his hands in a shrug. "And no one heard anything?"

"The gun had a silencer."

"Even so, there was a fierce scuffle."

"People were used to hearing weird noises coming from Penny's apartment," Marge said. "The guy was a serial killer. Maybe it wasn't the first time."

Decker conceded the point. He thought a moment. "When we first got the call, we had to evacuate the building because of the tiger. Everyone scattered for a few days. Now the residents are back and things have settled down. We only interviewed about a third of the building."

"I can get a team together to go back and canvass," Marge said. "You want to find whoever took the cash and the gun?"

"Exactly. If Penny wasn't shot by Randi or Havert, there has to be someone else involved."

Oliver said, "The autopsy says that Penny was killed by blunt force. I can see someone coming in and stealing the cash. But would anyone shoot the dead guy in the back?"

526 · FAYE KELLERMAN

"Blunt force might have *eventually* killed Penny," Decker said. "But the autopsy never specified *when* he died. Maybe he lingered on for a few hours before he died. It could just be that Penny moved or groaned or did something to show the intruder that he was still alive. So the guy panicked, picked up the gun, and shot Penny in the back, probably the final coup de grâce. Then he took the cash and the gun and got the hell out of Dodge."

Both Marge and Oliver agreed that the scenario was plausible.

Decker said, "The person may not be responsible for murder directly, but if that's what happened, it certainly wasn't a justifiable shooting. Moreover, the person was committing burglary." A pause. "Ideas?"

"George Paxton," Marge said. "Someone heard a noise and called up Paxton to investigate. He had the keys to the apartments. He could go in and out of the places anytime he wanted."

Oliver said, "I'd nominate Paxton as well."

"Then again, Randi and Havert told us that the tiger was beginning to stir," Marge said. "If the animal was up and about, Vignette Garrison was probably the only person other than Penny who could get past the tiger without getting mauled to death."

Decker nodded. "Ordinarily I'd go with Vignette. The tiger is a major deterrent against intruders. But *if* someone in the complex did hear the gunshots and call Paxton, and *if* Paxton went to investigate right away, the super might have had just enough time to shoot Penny, steal the cash, and get the hell out before kitty was fully awake and on the prowl."

"Hence the reason why you want to interview all the residents," Marge said. "I'll see if I can find someone who complained to Paxton."

"That'll take a while," Oliver said. "I say we bring both of them in for questioning. Since the case is basically wrapped up, they won't even realize why we're talking to them."

Marge said, "Call me crazy, but if I did something wrong, I'd be suspicious if I got a phone call from the police."

Decker said, "Agreed. So let's pay them a visit rather than bring them into the station house. It's less intimidating, but we'll still get an opportunity to feel them out."

Oliver said, "How do we bring up missing cash and gun so that they don't lawyer up?"

Decker thought a moment. "Both of them love money. Let's go out on the pretense of knowing something about Penny's will."

"Since when do the police talk about the will of a victim?" Oliver said.

"Every time Vignette sees me, she's asks about the will. She won't be a problem." Decker checked the clock. Ten after eleven in the morning. "I'll drive out to the sanctuary and talk to Vignette." He stood up. "I'll leave Mr. Paxton in your very able hands."

No highway accidents and an off-hour made the ride out to Global Earth Sanctuary a breeze. Even after he exited the freeway and drove the back roads, he made decent time because he knew where he was going. Behind the wheel, he thought about his future without LAPD. For the past week, he had listed the pros and cons of living in L.A. versus living back east.

After suffering through the cold of Montana, Decker had been having second thoughts about a true winter. He had always lived in sunshine. But the cold was not nearly enough to outweigh the practicality of living near his children. The more he thought about it, the more he couldn't picture himself being 2,500 miles away from his grandsons.

Of course, Rina was a consideration. Community was especially important to her. And being kosher and living in L.A., she had so many conveniences at her fingertips—bakeries, butcher shops, markets, and restaurants. Compared to what they had, they'd be going to a wasteland for anyone Orthodox. Rina told him she'd adapt, and that she'd be thrilled to be near the kids, but he wasn't sure if he believed her.

But a new and less intense job would mean fewer hours at work, so they'd have more time together. But he couldn't tell if she was just being nice . . . trying to support his decision.

Maybe she was excited about the move. She was already looking at real estate in the area.

Lots of land. You could have horses again.

What about you?

I'm always up for a new adventure.

He'd do anything for her . . . including the ultimate sacrifice.

If you're really worried about your parents, Rina, we can get a place with an in-law suite.

Wow, you must be really desperate to get out of town.

Rina had laughed when she said that. Thinking about it made him laugh. He was still smiling when he reached Global Sanctuary and pulled up next to Vignette's broken-down Honda. When he got out, the air was cool but not cold. The sky was clear, and it felt good to take in a deep breath.

He approached her trailer and knocked on the door.

No answer.

"Vignette?" he called out. "Vignette, it's Lieutenant Decker. Got some news for you."

Still no answer. She must be out tending the animals. He had two options—to look for her or to wait for her. The place was a maze of walkways and trails that shimmied past temporary enclosures of wild beasts. The animals were caged up, but not as secure as Decker would have liked. Global Sanctuary wasn't a zoo, and the animals weren't used to strangers.

Still, he hadn't come all this way to twiddle his thumbs. He started up the hill, calling her name as he walked. But whenever he opened his mouth, he was immediately drowned out by roars, snorts, grunts, and ululating. As he climbed deeper within the sanctuary, the paths narrowed, the brush grew denser, and it seemed to him that the animals grew more agitated.

"Vignette?" he called out.

No response.

Deeper and deeper into the mountains.

He finally saw her kneeling down in front of the grizzly bear cage, once again tending to the bear's injured paw. The bear was inside a makeshift enclosure while Vignette was on the outside, studying his paws. Decker didn't know the grizzly's specific state of mind, but he was sure making a lot of noises: growling and grunting loudly while Vignette was trying to quiet him in a calm voice.

The first time Decker called out, she didn't hear him. He was forced to raise his voice. "Vignette?"

She startled and jumped up, dropping his paw with a thud. The grizzly immediately sensed her fright and lashed out at the enclosure, buckling the wire fencing. Vignette's eyes went back and forth between the grizzly and Decker.

Another slap of the paws and the fence was completely down. The grizzly charged Decker, striking out, ripping his clothes down to his flesh. He managed to jump back, but the claws still scratched. His wounds hurt and were bleeding, not serious . . . yet.

"*Drop!*" Vignette screamed out to him. "Don't move, don't move, don't move!"

Decker learned, after years of working in military and paramilitary, that when one barked orders, it was best to follow them *immediately.*

He hit the ground.

Just as the bear was about to whack him a second time, Vignette was there between the paw and Decker's prone body. The claws sliced through her jacket and scored her shoulder with bloody parallel ruts. But she spoke with a firm voice despite the terror in her eyes. She pushed the beast in the chest. "Back, Cody! Back, back!"

The grizzly paused just long enough for her to shove him back again. He grunted out a sound that played a mournful melody.

Vignette was starting to shake. Her flesh was torn: blood was running down her shoulder. "Cody, back!" Another push. "Back, back, back!"

The bear retreated into the compromised enclosure. Somehow, she managed to walk him into his feeding pen, where she closed the gate and padlocked it with red fingers. The bear had followed while whimpering all the way.

Tears were running down Vignette's eyes. "Good boy, Cody. Good boy."

Her complexion grew pasty. To Decker she said, "Are you hurt?"

"No—"

"Stay where you are." She went over to her bucket of salmon and toted it with her uninjured shoulder to the bear. "Good boy, Cody. Good boy." She threw an entire fish into the cage. She watched as he gobbled up the fish and gave him another one. "Good boy."

Slowly she made her way back to Decker. "I think I might need help going down."

"I'll carry you." With all the adrenaline pumping into his body, he could probably carry a freight train. His heart was beating a mile a minute.

"No, that'll agitate him again," Vignette said. "I can walk. Just give me your arm."

"Lean against me."

"I'll get blood on your shirt."

Decker looked at his bare chest. Four neat red rakes across his torso. "What shirt?"

She actually laughed. They started down the trails. Halfway to the parking lot, she stumbled. Decker picked her up and said, "Don't argue."

When they finally did make it into the trailer, Decker set her into a chair and said, "Do you have a first aid kit?"

"Yes."

"I want to try to stop some of the bleeding before I take you to the hospital."

"I'm not going to any hospital."

"You're torn up. You need *stitches*."

"I'll be . . ." She swallowed hard. "First aid is in the drawer of the filing cabinet."

She was panting. Decker found the first aid kit and opened it up. It had everything he needed for the short run. He slipped on the latex gloves and immediately staunched the flow of blood. No arteries were spurting, but the gashes were very deep. Holding the wound with pressure from the fingers of one hand, he stretched out his other hand and managed to secure a water bottle from the top of her desk. "Drink."

"Thanks."

Decker pulled away one set of bloody gauze and unfurled the next roll, adding even more pressure with his fingers. He spotted a tube of Neosporin and a bottle of alcohol.

Vignette had drained the water bottle. She noticed him looking at the antiseptics and weighing his options. "Pour it on. I can take it."

"I'm just wondering if the best thing is to do nothing. I don't want to pour infection into the wound."

"I vote alcohol. If you don't do it, I will."

"Fine. Hold still. It's going to kill." Decker undid the cap and poured it directly on the gashes.

She let out a yell. "Wow that hurts!"

"Vignette, I'm taking you to the hospital."

"No!" She was adamant. "If the authorities find out that Cody hurt me, they'll put him down. We both know it wasn't his fault."

"It wasn't?" Decker did a second dosing of alcohol.

"Yeow!" she screamed. "No, it wasn't. You scared me, I jumped up, and he was being protective." Tears were streaming down her face. "If he wanted to kill both of us, he could have done it in a flash. Absolutely no hospital. No, no, no!"

He spoke softly. "Honey, you need *stitches*. You have no option."

"Yes, I do," she insisted. "I've sewn up animals when the vet can't make it out. I'm sure I can sew myself up."

"There is no way in *hell* you can do that."

"What choice do I have?" She looked at him. "Unless you want to sew me up. You seem okay with blood. You should take care of those scratches by the way. If you don't, they'll get infected."

"Forget about me. I'm fine." Decker blew out air. "Do you have a suture kit?"

"I have several suture kits. Do you know how to suture?"

"I've done it in the past . . . in the way past. But I did it a lot, so I think I'm okay."

"You were a doctor?"

"A medic in Vietnam."

"That is ancient history."

"Thank you very much." Decker removed the gauze. "Do you have any kind of anesthetic?"

"Mostly when I do animals, they're knocked out. But I do have some topical." She got up and swooned.

"I'll get it." Decker rewrapped the lacerations. "Don't move. Just tell me where everything is, all right?"

"In the lower file drawer . . . no, not that one . . . yeah, that one.

"Got it." He looked at several suture kits until he decided upon the needle and thread size he wanted to use. "I'd like to get the bleeding under control."

She was quiet. "Is it bad?"

"Yes, it's very bad."

"Do the best you can."

"I'm not happy doing this. You need a doctor."

"Go for it, Lieutenant."

After gently dabbing the swollen skin with topical, he opened the front flap of the kit and picked up the semicircular, prethreaded needle with a forceps.

The first stitch was the hardest. But some things were never forgotten. Decker said, "I'm sewing it loose because the wound is going to swell even more than it already is."

"You sound like you know what you're talking about."

"You need to see a doctor."

"Out of the question." She was a trouper. Barely moving even though he knew it was excruciatingly painful.

He said, "Thank you for saving my life."

"It was all just a big misunderstanding on Cody's part."

"Thank you, nonetheless," Decker said again.

"Why'd you come down here? I thought Mr. Penny's case was solved . . . that the hooker did it."

"That is the story."

"What does that mean?"

"It means that we have some loose ends that we're trying to tie up."

"Like what?"

"It's complicated."

"I'm not going anywhere," Vignette said. "Ouch!"

"Sorry." Decker's heart was still beating out of his chest. He was sweating, and it was cool inside the trailer. "Vignette, I'm going to tell you the truth because I owe you." He sewed another stitch. "There was another person who came into the apartment after the hooker left. I think he shot Penny in the back, although the old guy was a goner anyway. That person took a wad of his cash. We're looking for someone who had access to Penny's apartment and could get past the tiger."

In a soft voice, Vignette said, "It wasn't me. I didn't have a key to his apartment, just to the snake and insect apartments."

"A person could access Mr. Penny's main apartment through those apartments."

"First I've heard of it."

"When you're better, I need to ask you questions."

"I'm not doing anything. Ask away."

"It's not the time."

"Lieutenant, let's get this over with."

"Okay. When was the last time you saw Mr. Penny?"

"I told you that already. I saw him two or three days before he was killed. I fed and changed all the snakes and insect terrariums. And I cleaned all the aquariums. It was a full-day job. I saw Mr. Penny for about two minutes so he could pay me."

"I might not have believed you before. But I believe you now." She didn't answer. Decker's heart was still beating hard. He said, "Would you be willing to take a lie detector test?"

She looked up at him. "I already told you I'd do that. You never got back to me."

"We got distracted with the hooker. Would you take one now?"

"Absolutely. I had nothing to do with Mr. Penny's death and I'd never steal his money."

"I'll set something up . . . when you're feeling a little bit better."

"I'll be fine in a couple of hours. Got any codeine on you? Maybe you can swipe something from the evidence room." When Decker laughed, she said, "Actually I have animal painkillers. I'm not so sure on the human dosage, so I'll have to stick it out with Aleve."

"Aleve ain't gonna cut it. Aren't you nervous about Cody hurting you again?"

"Nah, he doesn't even know what he did. We'll be best friends tomorrow."

It took another fifteen minutes until Decker was finished up and was satisfied with his job. He cut the last stitch with scissors and dabbed the final result with alcohol and Neosporin. Then he wrapped up her shoulder, using all the gauze that was left in the first aid kit. "You need to get this checked out ASAP. If you won't go to a hospital, tell me a doctor I can take you to. You know you're going to need antibiotics."

"You, too."

"We're talking about you. Where should I take you?"

"I'll go to my vet. He'll understand my position. He's in Pomona thirty minutes from here."

"Give him a call. I'll drive you down."

"First I want to see how Cody is doing. I want to make sure he's not traumatized."

Decker was incredulous. "No, first you have to see a doctor."

"You're all take and no give, you know?"

Decker exhaled. "I've brought you bad news; I'll give you some good news."

Her eyes lit up. "You found out about the will."

"Nothing specific," Decker lied. "Only that you are in it."

Her grin was ear to ear. "That's great! When can I call Mr. Penny the lawyer?"

"Why don't you wait until he calls you? I'll see if I can hurry him along." Decker pointed to the phone. "Make the call to your vet."

"I don't have reception here."

"Then let's just go to Pomona and you can call from my cell." When she balked, he kept insisting. Finally he got her into his car. "As soon as I get reception, call your vet."

"This can't take too long. I've got other animals to feed."

"Vignette, if you don't take care of yourself, there will be no other animals."

She was quiet. Then she said, "You're right. I'm a little hungry."

"It's all that adrenaline depletion. I promise I'll buy you lunch after you've been seen."

She turned to him. "I'd rather you give money to the sanctuary."

"I'll do both if you remember that I'm a lowly cop. I live on a government salary."

"And you'll retire with a pretty sizable pension," she said. "But I don't begrudge you that. I wouldn't change places for anything. I could never ride around in a car all day."

"And I could never work with wild animals. Ain't it great that there're different strokes for different folks."

Chapter Forty

Paxton wasn't at his office at the apartment building. When Marge suggested that perhaps she should call him up so they wouldn't waste any more time, Oliver protested. "And ruin the element of surprise?"

"What element of surprise? We're not arresting him. The guy isn't going to admit to shooting Penny in the back."

"If he's guilty of something, Marge, he'll bolt as soon as we call him."

Marge got behind the wheel and shut the door. She waited to talk until Oliver took off his black jacket, hung it up on the hook, and slid into the passenger seat. "So what do you propose?"

"Let's drop by his house. It's about ten minutes away. If he's not home, no harm, no foul."

"Okay." Marge turned on the motor and opened the window. It was pleasant outside, and she was wearing a light sweater: too cool for the AC but too warm to drive without some air circulation. "We'll drop by his house. But if he isn't in, I'm going to call him and actually arrange something."

"Yeah, yeah," Oliver said. "Has Decker contacted you?"

"Not yet. Reception is bad out there."

"I'm gonna try anyway. Because if Vignette admitted to shooting the guy, we don't have to worry about Paxton."

"Sure."

Oliver punched in Decker's number. It went straight to voice mail. He stowed the phone back in his packet. "If Paxton's not home, wanna get some lunch. It's after one."

"After I make the phone call, sure. What's the address again?"

Oliver read off the digits. "It's about ten blocks away. Where do you want to go for lunch? Are you in the mood for Italian?"

"How about Greek?"

"Yeah, Greek's good. Let's do Yanni's."

"Great. If we have some leftover time, I'd like to go back to Ki Park, the chicken lady," Marge said. "Will's coming down. Her takeout is really good."

"Okay." Oliver smoothed his trousers. "You're not worried about it spoiling in the car?"

"How about we get the chicken after we talk to Paxton. I'll put it in the fridge at work. I'm sure Decker's going to want to compare notes." She looked at her watch again. "What time did he leave for the sanctuary?"

"A little after eleven."

"So he won't be back for a while." A car was parked in front of Paxton's address. Marge did a U-turn and pulled the car up to the curb directly across the street. "Okay. Here goes nothing."

"Like always." Oliver opened the passenger door.

"Do you want your suit jacket?"

"Sure . . . not that the creep deserves my sartorial splendor."

"Just for appearance's sake," Marge told him.

"Yeah, why not?" Oliver reached behind and put it on.

They got out of the car and crossed the street.

When they got halfway up the sidewalk, the shots rang out. A bullet whipped past Marge's head, a second grazed Oliver's arm. Marge grabbed him and they ran and ducked for cover behind the car parked in front of the house.

"What the fuck!" Oliver checked his arm. "Shit!"

THE BEAST · 545

"Are you hurt?"

"Just a graze! Motherfucker!"

Marge was already on the phone with 911. "This is Sergeant Marge Dunn, LAPD. Shots fired. I've got a wounded officer. I need immediate backups from all units. Do you have the address—" Another bullet exploded the driver's window of the parked car. *"Shit!"*

Dispatch from 911 said, "Units and ambulance are on their way."

"Hurry!" Marge drew her gun and peeked out from behind the parked car. The area around the house was devoid of pedestrians. A half a block down, a mother was walking her baby in a stroller. "Oh God! Look over there, Oliver. I've got to get her out of the area. Are you okay enough to cover me?"

"Yeah, I'm fine. Go!"

Blood was dripping onto his suit jacket. Marge wasn't so sure that it was just a graze, but Oliver wasn't letting on if it was something more. She darted out from behind the car and instantly another shot popped into the air. Oliver returned the fire and things turned quiet.

By the time Marge caught up with the woman walking her baby in the stroller, she heard the beautiful wail of police sirens. After the mother turned around and scurried in the opposite direction, Marge did a two-arm wave to the cruiser. When it pulled over, she showed her badge to the two uniforms and hopped inside the car. She realized she was out of breath. "We were on our way to a routine interview and the motherfucker began shooting at us. My partner's behind the red Ford Escort with a wounded arm."

The black-and-white tore down the street, arriving at the house, pulling up perpendicularly to the street to block oncoming traffic. There were already two other cruisers, which had come down the street from the opposite direction. The uniformed driver asked Marge, "Do you know who's shooting at you?"

"Haven't seen a face but the house belongs to a guy named George Paxton. Son of a *bitch*!"

Someone had relieved Oliver of his position behind the parked car. Marge spotted him several houses down the street, sitting on the sidewalk. He had taken off his jacket and rolled up his shirtsleeve. A cop had unrolled some gauze and was trying to mop up the bleeding from his arm. Marge showed her badge and moved in. "I'll do that. Check in to see if the ambulance is on its way."

"I did. It's coming."

"Then go back and help out your fellow officers. Be careful. The guy is crazy!"

"You're sure?"

"Yeah, positive. Go." After he left, Marge cleaned the area around the wound to inspect the damages. She groaned. "This isn't a graze, partner. You got shot."

"I did?"

"On the top below the deltoid. Can you move your arm?"

"Yeah." He demonstrated. "I can move it, but it hurts."

"Stop moving."

"You told me to move."

"Well, then stop moving now . . . bone doesn't appear to be broken . . . thank God!"

"What did God ever do for me that I should thank him?"

"You're in one piece, that's what." There were tears in her eyes. "You're gonna be fine."

"I could have told you that." A pause. "What caliber?"

"What?"

"The bullet wound. What caliber?"

"It looks like a twenty-two from the hole."

"The bullet ripped through my jacket, right?"

"Obviously."

"Fuck. That was an Armani I got on sale at the outlets."

"I'll buy you a new one."

"The department will buy me a new one. Sure it's a twenty-two?"

"No. When this is over, I'll see if I can find the bullet." She regarded the affected area. "It's pretty clean. How are you doing? Stupid question!"

"I'm okay, Margie, stop worrying." He shook his head. "What the fuck is that idiot doing?"

"I haven't the foggiest idea."

"Call Decker," Oliver said. "Let him know what's going on."

"As soon as you're taken care of."

"I'm fine." He yanked his arm away, peeled off the gauze, and looked at the bullet hole. "Yeah, it's probably a twenty-two."

"Can you let me finish whatever crappy job I'm doing?" Marge rolled out another section of fresh gauze. "Where's the fucking ambulance?"

"Stop getting so emotional. I'll be fine. I'll take a couple of weeks off and that's fine with me. Sometimes I fucking hate this job!"

The ambulance turned onto the street. Marge got up and waved. "Fin-a-lly!" The wagon pulled over and the paramedics got out. Oliver nodded to his partner. "Go find out what's happening."

"Let me call Decker first." The cell again went immediately into voice mail. "God, I hate this!"

"Go back and be useful, Margie," Oliver told her. "I'm in good hands. Better than yours. Go get the idiot before someone else gets hurt!" Under his breath, he muttered, "Motherfucking asshole!"

Marge walked back toward Paxton's house. From a distance, she saw a huddle of black uniforms on the front lawn of his home. She watched with curiosity, and as the pack parted, a little gnome of a man was hoisted up to his feet.

George Paxton was once again wearing green. His hands were cuffed behind his back, and he was being escorted by two officers to a cruiser. As one of the uniforms lowered Paxton's head to get into the car, the gnome's eyes found Marge's face. He glared at her and screamed out that he wanted a lawyer.

It was his right.

He was sure as hell going to need one.

Someone knocked on the doorjamb. When Decker raised his head from his paperwork, Marge gave him the thumbs-up. "We found a stash of recently washed bills. God bless the U.S. mint. Money is hard to clean thoroughly. Some of the bills had specks of blood on them. We took those for DNA analysis."

"Great."

"Most important, we found the gun. Ballistics says it's a match. Yay and double yay!"

"He actually kept the gun?"

"He did." Marge pulled up a chair opposite his desk and sat down. She was dressed all in black, as if in mourning, although Oliver was fine. He was already home, being doted on by his three sons, daughters-in-law, and his steady girlfriend, Carmen, whom he referred to as the Latina bombshell. In reality, she was a dedicated junior high school teacher in a high crime area.

"Any reason he didn't ditch it?"

"I really don't know," Marge told him. "Pride, carelessness, a lasting memory of his deed." She shrugged. "This is what I suspect happened, although I have no proof just yet."

"Tell me."

"Here goes. After one of the neighbors complained about shots coming from Penny's apartment, he went in to investigate. He saw that Penny was dead. But then rather than call the police, he began to stuff his pockets with the bloody cash left behind. Then Penny must have moved or groaned. Paxton panicked, picked up the nearby gun, and fired into his back. Then, realizing that the gun had his bloody fingerprints, he took the weapon with him along with all the cash. Maybe eventually he would have ditched it. Lucky for us, he was slow. Slow and stupid. Really stupid. Why would you open fire on the cops?"

"Some people panic and do moronic things. Some people, when faced with danger such as a charging grizzly bear, act cool, calm, and collected."

"How is Vignette?"

"With the money from Penny's will, she has already hired a full-time assistant."

"Good for her."

"They gave her extra you know . . . especially when I told them what she did for me."

"I take it you mean Penny's children?"

"Yep. Darius and Graciela . . . and Sabrina. It came out of their inheritance. I think they put around two million in a trust for the sanctuary. Vignette can't stop grinning."

"Too bad there are no enclosures for beasts like Penny," Marge said.

"It's called a prison," Decker said.

Marge gave him a forced smile. "Will said that they also set up a fund for Penny's victims once they find them. They're also funding cold-case detectives to reopen the file."

"They're good folk."

"Seems that way." Another forced smile. Marge tried to talk but couldn't get the words out. Decker regarded her face. "What's on your mind?"

"I got some news for you, Pete. Good news for a change."

Decker smiled. "Let's hear it."

"I'm engaged."

"You are?" He got up and hugged her. "I don't know why I'm so surprised. That's wonderful. When's the big day?"

"Somewhere in the future. But I'm getting a ring, so it's going to be official."

"Margie, I am happy for you. Anything Rina and I can do for you or for the wedding. Maybe give you a rehearsal dinner or—"

"Oh please. We're both so old. No bridesmaid, no groomsmen, nothing formal. Whenever it will be, it'll be a quiet affair and hopefully somewhere lovely. Santa Barbara is filled with beach and wineries and beautiful mountains. We just have to pick a time and a place. And yes, we will be sure not to make it on Saturday. We want you to be there. All of your family will be invited."

Decker hugged her again. "Did you tell Oliver?"

"I'm going to tell him tonight. But I wanted to talk to you first." She pointed to his chair. "Have a seat."

"Uh-oh!" Decker made a face and sat down. "Bad news?"

"Not really."

"Lay it on me, girl."

She licked her lips. "You know, Vega is now in Silicon Valley. She's doing great."

Decker felt his heartbeat quicken. "And your condo feels a little empty?"

"I'm putting it up for sale. Will and I . . . we're actually going to try and be a couple, Pete. Being a real couple means coming home after work to the same house or condo. At least, that's what it means to me."

"You're making a commitment."

"Yes. And because we're making a commitment to live together as a married couple, we just can't live that far apart. And that means either he comes down to L.A. or I go up to Santa Barbara. And we both know that SBPD is already full."

"Will wants a job here?"

"No, Will has a job that he likes just fine."

"Ah . . . I see. So where are you going?"

"Nowhere yet." Marge's eyes watered. "But in a year, I will have reached that benchmark of twenty-five years with LAPD. That's a long time and a good pension."

"You're retiring."

"Not exactly. I'm a little too young for that. I've been interviewing with Camarillo, Oxnard, and Ventura. They've got a couple of detectives retiring next year . . . there'll be space." She looked down at her lap. "Change is good . . . or so they say."

Decker bit his lower lip. "I should be furious, but I'm not. I'm actually very relieved."

Marge stared at him. *"Relieved?"*

"In six months, I will reach the benchmark of thirty years. That's also a long time and a good pension."

She stared at him. "So you're retiring."

"Not exactly," Decker said. "But I wouldn't mind something a little less hectic. I've been interviewing at a few places as well."

"Where?"

"Back east."

"Back *east?*"

"Koby got into medical school at Mount Sinai Medical School. He and Cindy and the boys are moving. That means all of our children, including Gabe, will be living near the Atlantic. I can take being away from the kids. They have their own lives. But I decided that I want to be a part of my grandchildren's lives. Rina wholeheartedly concurs. So I've been talking to a small eastern town in New York near the Five Colleges of Upstate. About three hours from all the kids."

"And?"

"And we're also putting our house up for sale."

Marge glared at him. "You're *leaving* me?"

"Excuse me?" Decker said. "You *left* me first."

"I'm not leaving yet. I'm giving you a year's notice. When are you leaving?"

"My plan is around six months."

"So you are *leaving* me."

"I suppose that's technically true."

"It's true in absolute terms." She stood up with her hands on her hips. "You bum!"

Decker stood and threw his arm around her. "I'll miss you, Marge Dunn. Truly we've been together a long time . . . longer than I've been with my wife."

"I'll miss you, too, Rabbi." She looked away. "But I've got you where I really need you."

"Where's that?"

Marge pointed to her brain and then to her heart. "Enough of this soppy stuff." She opened the door to his office. "Let's go out and celebrate my upcoming engagement. Dinner's on me."

"No, I'll pay."

"No, I'll pay." Marge grinned. "I'm the only one of the three of us who is currently uninjured. Let me clear my desk, get my purse, and we're out of here."

"That's fine. I have to make a few phone calls as well."

"Rina's invited, you know."

"Not this time, Sarge. It's just you and me." It took around ten minutes for Decker to finalize his paperwork. When he got to Marge's desk, she was staring at a pink leather bag. There was a cardboard box on the table and gift wrapping that had been torn into.

"New purse?" he asked.

"It's from Graciela," she said.

"Ah . . . the Berkoff bag."

Marge laughed. "Birkin."

"Nice. She was determined for you to have it."

Marge was shocked. "I can't keep this."

"Why not?" Decker asked. "She's a private citizen. The baroness can give you anything she wants."

"Pete, I can't. I mean I have no opportunity whatsoever to use this. If I put this on the arm of a chair at a restaurant, it'll be stolen. Well, maybe not at the restaurants Will and I go to. But anywhere fancy . . . I mean, this is a partial down payment on a condo."

"So sell it and buy a condo up north with your fiancé. Call it Casa de Graciela. And I, for one, can't think of a more fitting title. Because everything you've ever handled in these past twenty-five years has been done with aplomb and grace."

Her eyes watered up immediately.

Decker smiled. "Oh c'mon, Dunn, stop that."

Marge flapped her hands in front of her face. "I can't believe how weepy I feel. What the hell is wrong with me?"

"Admit it, Marge. You're just a sentimental old gal."

She hit him. "Not old." Marge stood up. "Let's get out of here."

Decker said, "How old are you again?"

"Figure it out yourself, old man." She slipped her fingers around the strap of the Birkin bag, regarding the pink leather handbag with loving eyes. Then she looked at Decker. "Besides, you should know better than to ask any woman—even one who loves you dearly—her age."